"Perhaps the two aspects o̲... ...rt of God are suffering and lov̲e... ...ollins crafts a masterful narrati̲v... ...ated by evil and the redemptive power of love. With sensitivity and imagination, he goes right to the heart of the human condition."
PENELOPE WILCOCK, author of *The Hawk and the Dove* series

"*House of Souls* is a gripping story that is simultaneously both enjoyable and spiritually profound. It is truly outstanding. In fact, it was so good it was hard to put it down."
DR. CLINTON E. ARNOLD, Former Dean, Talbot School of Theology, Biola University, USA.

"*House of Souls* is beautifully and imaginatively written and highlights the power of story in addressing the reality of suffering. Prepare to read a book that will be hard to put down."
SHARON DIRCKX, The Oxford Centre for Christian Apologetics and author of *Why? Looking at God, evil and personal suffering*

"*House of Souls* blew me away. It is a quite extraordinary piece of writing. The story grabs the reader with themes that go right to the heart of our human experience. Both Aidan and Evelyn are characters with whom we can identify, so their suffering teaches us with raw power. Their adventures cut right to the heart of what it means to be human. A magnificent achievement."
ANDREW PAGE, founder of The Mark Drama

"*House of Souls* is a novel both significant and profound. Significant in that it touches upon critical issues of the soul and mind, such as inner healing, interpersonal goodness, social evil, and lasting love. It is profound in that it approaches these topics with emotional sensitivity, spiritual insight, and sacrificial love. And there are times while reading to pause for personal reflection. This book will greatly impact you as you read."
ALLAN HEDBERG, PhD
author of *Jonathan Edwards: A Life Well Lived*

"*House of Souls* is compelling, beautiful, creative and clever. Collins is a wonderful storyteller, with a huge breadth of insight. It was stunning on a number of levels and didn't flinch from exploring human suffering in a way that was sensitive and insightful. It got under my skin, made me think and moved me deeply. A must-read."

LINDA ALLCOCK, author of *Head, Heart, Hands*
Women's Ministry Leader, The Globe Church, London, UK.

"*House of Souls* is one of the most compelling books I've read on the question of God and suffering. The main characters, Aidan and Evelyn, represent us all as they hurl their questions, anger and confusion at God. He claims to be good but often seems absent or impotent in the face of the world's pain. Is there an answer that satisfies? Maybe. You must decide. That's why this book works so well; it's a story which tugs at the heart and the soul, demanding a response. Highly recommended."

MELINDA HENDRY, Former ministry team leader,
All Souls Church, Langham Place, London, UK.

HOUSE OF SOULS

Richard Thor Collins

STARDUST BOOKS

Scriptures taken from the Holy Bible, New International Version®, NIV®. Copyright © 1973, 1978, 1984, 2011 by Biblica, Inc.™ Used by permission of Zondervan. All rights reserved worldwide. www.zondervan.com The "NIV" and "New International Version" are trademarks registered in the United States Patent and Trademark Office by Biblica, Inc.™

Scripture quotations taken from the (NASB®) New American Standard Bible®, Copyright © 1960, 1971, 1977, 1995, 2020 by The Lockman Foundation. Used by permission. All rights reserved. www.lockman.org

Scripture quotations from The Authorized (King James) Version. Rights in the Authorized Version in the United Kingdom are vested in the Crown. Reproduced by permission of the Crown's patentee, Cambridge University Press

Scripture taken from the New King James Version®. Copyright © 1982 by Thomas Nelson. Used by permission. All rights reserved.

Scripture quotations are taken from the Holy Bible, New Living Translation, copyright ©1996, 2004, 2015 by Tyndale House Foundation. Used by permission of Tyndale House Publishers, Carol Stream, Illinois 60188. All rights reserved.

Stardust Books

www.stardust-books.com

Copyright © 2022 by Richard Thor Collins
All rights reserved

Richard Thor Collins has asserted his right to be identified as the author of this Work in accordance with the Copyright, Designs and Patents Act 1988

No part of this publication may be reproduced, stored in a retrieval system or transmitted in any form or by any means, electronic, mechanical, photocopying, recording or otherwise, without the prior permission of the publisher or the Copyright Licensing Agency.

First published by Stardust Books in 2022

Cover design by Bruce Petersen (www.brucepetersen.net)

Printed and bound in Great Britain by Clays Ltd, Elcograf S.p.A.

ISBN 978-1-739166-50-2

1 3 5 7 10 8 6 4 2

Contents

1. Entertaining Strangers — 1
2. The Escapees — 7
3. Beach And Blood — 12
4. The Viatici House — 19
5. A Case Of Trafficking — 29
6. Life — 33
7. Miloš — 49
8. A Spot Of Bother — 59
9. Injury Time — 66
10. Lament — 79
11. Dragan — 85
12. Circles — 90
13. To My Love, Who Loves Better Than I — 97
14. Bad Karma — 105
15. Greater Goods — 111
16. Dorina — 129
17. Love Thy Neighbor — 138
18. Messing About In Boats — 144
19. A Fishing Expedition — 153
20. Srebrenica — 160
21. Sidney — 168
22. Freedom — 183
23. An Empress Among Babies — 203
24. The Truth Will Set You Free — 212
25. Worship — 217
26. Skeletons On TV — 226
27. Marketing — 234
28. The Problem Of Goodness — 242
29. A Little Cloak And Dagger — 256
30. Postman Nat — 267
31. Brief Encounter — 272
32. The Most Wretched Of Deaths — 277
33. From The Embers — 296

34.	Bratwurst And Corn Dogs	301
35.	The Big Story	306
36.	Tierra-7	323
37.	Grace	331
38.	Holding On	339
39.	Salvation	343
40.	The Gap	353
41.	The Bleeding	362
42.	Blue Jeans, Purple T-shirt	369
43.	A New Way Of Living	377
	Epilogue	382

For Bettina

Everywhere a greater joy is preceded by a greater suffering.
~ Saint Augustine

The unexamined life is not worth living.
~ Socrates

The meaning of earthly existence lies not, as we have grown used to thinking, in prospering but in the development of the soul.
~ Aleksandr Solzhenitsyn

As flies to wanton boys are we to th' gods.
They kill us for their sport.
~ William Shakespeare, *King Lear*

What in me is dark
Illumine, what is low raise and support;
That to the height of this great Argument
I may assert Eternal Providence,
And justify the ways of God to men.
~ John Milton, *Paradise Lost*

~ 1 ~

ENTERTAINING STRANGERS

Do not forget to entertain strangers.
~ Hebrews 13:2a

Tolpuddle, Dorset, England

November 1982

"It's a bit tight."
"Pick up the phone."
"I said it's a bit tight!"
"Phone? Electronic device. Should be right next to you."
"Listen, I don't need a phone to tell you it's too tight. This body is too tight. I can't breathe properly. I can't seem to move my legs. And my arms . . . Ow! They won't straighten." Asaph lay flat on his back on the bed. He tried to lift his head, managing to raise it a few inches before it fell back onto the pillow. He was breathing heavily with the effort.
"You know, Asaph, you need to pick up the phone!"
"I can't reach the phone. It's too far away. Hold on, hold on, my legs are moving . . . I think. Yes, I can feel the toes."
"Wiggle them. Go on. Wiggle them."
"Hey! I'm doing it. I can lift my arms. Wa-hey! I think I should be able to sit up now. Ooh yes, now I get it. I'm getting the hang of this." The lucidus pushed himself up, swung his legs over the side of the bed, and looked down at where he was sitting. The duvet cover was floral and the room smelled of potpourri. Then he remembered he was supposed to be visiting England. A thatched cottage in Dorset, to be exact.
"Pick up the phone," said the voice. "It should be in the bag next to you. We downsized it to fit in your bag. Apparently one day they'll

figure out how to make a phone weigh less than a medicine ball."

Asaph did as he was told. "Hello? Are you there?" He rubbed his eyes and held the phone to his ear.

"Yes, I am. Now we're going to do it this way from now on. No more talking to me direct, okay? Every time you want to talk, you just pick up the phone, press the green key, and start talking."

"Yeah, I got it now. It still feels a little tight."

"That's normal, remember? That's how a body feels when you first put it on. It's going to be quite a while before you're totally assimilated. So don't act like you're putting on a wetsuit. No bending backward and forward like you're desperately trying to push your arms through the sleeves. You'll just draw attention to yourself, which is unwise."

As he listened to further instructions, Asaph approached a pair of tiny, latticed windows and peered down at the road outside. A Vauxhall Cavalier was parked next to an Austin Allegro. He looked over toward a twelfth-century church tower that rose among the thatched roofs of the village cottages. It looked cold and damp outside.

"I'm in Tolpuddle then," he said.

"Yes, you are. No need to act like a martyr though."

He detected a smile coming across the airwaves. "Now remind me, I'm due to join the Post Office, right?"

"Yup. In Dorchester. But right now it's time to get a move on. No time for cream teas."

The lucidus started performing jumping jacks, working up a sweat. "You know, this body is feeling better all the time. It's starting to feel more like 'me.'"

"It's never going to be 'you,' Asaph. It's just something you put on. Like that shirt you're wearing. So don't get too attached to it. Listen, it's nearly 4 p.m. Your contact doesn't like waiting. What do they say there? Oh yeah. Toodle pip!"

Asaph left the cottage, and followed the directions he'd been given on the phone. *Just find the bus stop opposite the Martyrs Museum. It's not far.* Five minutes later he was sitting on a moist wooden bench, looking up and down the road. So this was England. A bit dreary, he thought, but then it was his first time. What did he know about England's climate in November? The air was cold and damp on his face—a new and not unwelcome sensation.

He glanced at his watch. Looking up, he caught sight of a figure marching purposefully toward him over the rise. He'd wondered if his partner would be easy to identify. Now he knew. He rose to his feet expectantly.

"Hello," said the lucidus, arriving with an outstretched hand and a broad smile on his face. He was wearing a green Barbour jacket, jeans, and Wellington boots, very much like the locals. "I'm Korazin. Pleasure to meet you. I don't think we've met, have we?"

"Asaph. First mission." They shook hands warmly.

"Okay, so I'm your lead today, my friend. Follow me and you'll do just fine. We've got a case of car trouble—let's see . . . Aidan and Naomi are their names—both twenty-one years of age. And then, as far as I know, we'll be off."

"But I was told I was working for the Post Office in Dorchester."

"Plans change. Sometimes with no notice at all. But don't worry, the wonders of the modern postal system await you on your next visit. In London, I believe. Mind you, today's rescue should be a good start, and the next time you strap on a body, it'll be a snap. This one a little tight at first?"

"How did you know?"

"Happens all the time. Sometimes I think we should just arrive here in a wetsuit. It'd be so much easier." He grinned.

"Was I—?"

"You were twisting so much, I thought you were Chubby Checker." Both lucidi started laughing, their voices wafting over the nearby fields. A herd of cattle stopped grazing; a dozen bovine heads turned in the direction of a sound the animals had never heard before. But then again, neither had most humans.

Asaph was warming to his companion quickly. "Is that a newspaper in your bag?"

Korazin handed over *The Guardian*. "Well," he said, "it's the obvious choice." They smiled at each other.

Asaph arched his back. Everything still felt a little constricted. He was feeling hungry and his head was aching. "So when do we get started?"

His fellow lucidus pressed a hand to his right ear, as though he was listening to an earpiece. "Right . . . okay, copy that." He adopted a look of mock severity. "Let's roll."

"And that was . . .?" Asaph was about to inquire further, but stopped himself. "Are you always like this?"

Korazin didn't reply. He just laughed and set off down the hill, followed by his new partner, who had to run to catch up. The road narrowed and they turned right at The Green, heading down Southover Lane. Entering a field on their left, they discovered a Land Rover parked up near the hedgerow. Asaph walked round the car, inspecting it. "Nice wheels," he said. They climbed in. Korazin found the key and drove out into the country lane.

"What do we do with this once we're finished?" asked Asaph.

"Izaak. England's his territory. He comes and clears up later." Korazin shifted gears. "I don't know what he does with the vehicle, but he takes care of everything. Kind of like a celestial cleaner."

"Sounds organized."

"It is." Round the next bend, they stopped behind a Morris Minor Traveller parked in a layby. Korazin went and knocked on the window. "Need help?"

A young man was sitting at the wheel with an attractive woman by his side. He rolled down the window. "Er, sure. That would be great. Do you know anything about classic cars?"

"Not exactly, but we can tow you."

Korazin retrieved a long, thick rope from the rear seat of the Land Rover. Once Asaph had maneuvered the car into position, he found a place to tie the rope. Soon the two cars were attached and ready.

"Right," he said, "I'm Kevin. My mate Alan is up there in the Land Rover. You are?"

"Oh, I'm Aidan and this is Naomi."

"Okay. Now, Aidan, let it take up the slack." He gave a thumbs up to Asaph. "And, yup . . . we're good to go."

"Got it."

"I'll travel with you, if that's all right. Just to make sure you're okay." Humans always accepted the word of the lucidi. Perhaps it was the authority in their voices or their bearing. Whatever it was, it worked a treat every time.

"Naomi, I suggest you ride with Alan."

Naomi did as she was asked and hopped into the Land Rover. Asaph pulled out and they made their way slowly past fields of cabbages, the vegetables spreading into the distance like a vast green ocean. The road gradually began to broaden, the hedgerows receded, and they reached the A35, where Asaph kept his speed at 40 miles an hour.

When Aidan was comfortable behind the wheel, his foot hovering over the brake, Korazin asked him about his family and his work. Aidan would normally have batted away probing questions from a stranger, but this time he found himself divulging personal details and wondering what he was doing.

"You're a lucky man," said the lucidus.

"Excuse me?"

"She's gorgeous. And I saw how she looks at you. You'll make a great couple."

The young man couldn't help blushing a little. "How do you—"

"Love, Aidan," interrupted Korazin, "is the most powerful thing in the entire universe. By far."

Aidan looked at him blankly, unable to respond. He gripped the wheel tightly. "It nourishes and revives a flagging spirit," continued the lucidus. "It heals and soothes a wounded heart, it transforms all it touches, and brings light into the darkest of places. Many waters cannot quench it; neither can rivers sweep it away. It demands all, and its returns are infinite. Love is patient and enduring, bold and brave. It's beautiful, Aidan." He paused, fixing the human with his penetrating green eyes. "And I know it when I see it."

Aidan didn't know how to reply. The hairs on the back of his neck were raised, his breathing interrupted. A cold sweat spotted his forehead. When he looked across at his passenger, he thought he saw the sides of his face glow slightly.

The creature by his side smiled at him. "It's just up here."

The cars drew up outside a garage on the outskirts of Wimborne Minster, and they all got out.

"You look like you've seen a ghost, Aidan," said Naomi.

"Not a ghost. Something else." His heart was pounding in his chest. The lucidi pushed the Morris Minor into the garage's workshop and disappeared inside. Sitting on a grassy bank, with the sound of drills and hydraulics in the background, Aidan and Naomi chatted about their plans for the evening.

When a man in brown overalls walked up to them later, they stood up. "Car's all repaired. That'll be thirty-five pounds."

"You serious?"

"Yup, just had to tweak a few things."

Naomi asked, "Where are the two guys who brought us here—Kevin and Alan?"

The garage owner looked confused. "Never heard of them."

Aidan got up and went to inspect the inside of the workshop. After checking the entire building, he returned with a shrug of the shoulders. "That's just bizarre," he said. "Where did they go?"

Time was short, so he paid the bill, jumped in the car, and drove off. Once they were motoring along, Aidan pulled a cassette out of the glove compartment, and pushed it into the slot.

"What happened back there?" Naomi asked.

"I have no idea," he said, turning up the volume. His resonant voice filled the car. "Come on Eileen!" His joy was infectious.

"Gotta love the dungarees in that video," screamed Naomi over the engine noise. With great gusto, they sang their hearts out to Dexys Midnight Runners, Ultravox, and Duran Duran.

By the time they arrived in London, they were hoarse.

~ 2 ~

THE ESCAPEES

*I cannot think of any need in childhood as strong as
the need for a father's protection.*
~ Sigmund Freud

Marston Hall Preparatory School for Boys, Devon, England

June 1971

Aidan lay staring at the ceiling of his dormitory. Pale moonlight washed the room in a stark, silver sheen, casting shadows across the dozen or so bunks that stood in regimental rows against the walls. All the beds were filled with boarders, each one far from home and comfort. Milligan, a large boy with legendary body odor, was already snoring. Bannerman, his neighbor, threw a slipper that struck him on the side of the head, but he simply turned over and rumbled on. Aidan also turned, pulling his legs up toward his stomach in an effort to douse the burning.

He remembered the elation at supper when he'd joined in the conversation. Some of the seniors were talking about football and he'd chipped in with something he'd seen in the newspaper at home. His parents didn't let him watch *Match of the Day*—it was on too late—but he was a fan of Liverpool, especially John Toshack. One of the seniors, Coke-Wallis it was, had said, "You're all right, Manning," and he had flushed with pleasure. He'd just turned ten, but the boys two years older had talked to him. They'd even listened to him.

But not long after, the discussion had shifted to pop music and he was lost. He should have kept his mouth shut. He should have known T. Rex had nothing to do with dinosaurs. And who the heck was Marc Bolan? His confusion had caused great amusement. He could still see their faces, jaws wide open, heads cocked back. The embarrassment paralyzed him, left him unable to think. None of the boys his age had come to his rescue. He felt like he'd been served up for the seniors to feast on. It was unbearable, sucking the air out of his lungs so that he'd found it hard to breathe. The whole table had found it hilarious. Questions had followed about Camel—nothing to do with the animal—and The Beatles. He knew Paul and John, but couldn't remember George at all. When the bell went, he'd never felt so relieved.

And so he lay with the rancor bubbling away inside. It was giving him a stomachache. The thought of what might happen next time made him feel sick. He looked across at the boy on his right. At least he had Piers. That was compensation of a sort.

His best friend grinned at him. "Hear that?" The distant clip of brogues on the wooden floor echoed dimly down the corridor. The deputy head was still about. When the sound had receded to a barely perceptible tapping, Piers slipped noiselessly out of bed.

Short for his age, he sported a shock of blond hair and was in the habit of flashing his impossibly long eyelashes at the matrons to get out of trouble. Aidan followed him toward the door. They poked their heads out and looked in the direction of Cruikshanks' retiring heels, no longer visible and now scarcely audible.

"That's his last circuit. Let's go." Aidan hesitated, unsure of himself. His friend unlatched the window and climbed out. "Come on! Before anyone else comes." Aidan stuffed his feet into his slippers, grabbed his bathrobe, and climbed out onto the roof. Piers went out regularly, but this was his first time. His heart rate surged as he worked his way down the ladder.

When they reached the next section of the roof, Aidan stopped and looked out over the grounds. The school was located half a mile from the small village of Princetown, home to Dartmoor's famous prison. In the distance, the moor stretched out before them, a vast open wasteland. Bleak and featureless, it undulated out in every direction. To the north, the colossal granite walls of the prison stood tall as sentinels. A full moon illuminated the surrounding landscape with an unworldly glow. We're not so different to the inmates, thought Aidan. Trapped and forced to wear ridiculous uniforms.

The Escapees

Once down, the pair darted across the terrace that divided the lawn from the playing fields. They reveled in the freedom and sense of mischief that went with escaping the clutches of the school building. When they reached the groundsman's hut, they went inside and started messing about with the equipment. Piers found a javelin and threw it at a tree nearby.

Aidan dragged some hurdles into line, setting himself for a race. "Come on, Piers, you prat. Race me!"

They took off down the track, but halfway down Piers clattered a hurdle and went flying. As he landed, he burst into fits of laughter and rolled around on the ground shouting, "Oh, oh! Please sir, I'm hurt. I think my toe's been crushed." Yesterday, Big Joe Bentley had cried out the same thing during football. Aidan started laughing so hard he crashed into the next hurdle and fell over. The two of them were making so much noise they didn't hear the creak of the double doors opening onto the back patio of the school. They did, however, see a light flashing out over the front lawn.

"Quick, hide! Stebbings is out!" They both jumped up, realizing they were totally exposed on the running track. As the beam of light advanced toward the playing fields, they sprinted for the gypsy caravan standing in the small copse to their left. When the teacher reached the track and saw the hurdles, he turned toward some sheds to the right of the caravan. The boys slowed their pace, stooping for no particular reason, except they remembered escaping soldiers doing the same thing in the few war films they'd seen.

"Why are we dipping our heads, you idiot?" hissed Aidan, once they'd found shelter behind one of the beech trees. "He doesn't have a gun." Piers tried to stifle his laughter but it was useless. The two of them shook helplessly, tears streaming down their faces, until the flashlight swept over in their direction, causing sufficient fear to calm them both down.

Leaves crackled underfoot as Stebbings approached the copse. Shetland ponies, who'd wriggled through the fence that day, had dumped their load in front of the clump of trees. The teacher's shoe squelched into something soft, causing him to curse. The escapees held their breaths, waiting while he bent down to wipe his footwear with some leaves. He was only a few yards away, but moments later, the light wavered and then flickered in a different direction. As they watched it retreat toward the staff cottages, they both breathed a huge sigh of relief.

They trotted along the edge of the lawn, trying hard to stay in the shadows. On reaching the swimming pool, they snaked round past a ladder attached to the side of the school building. Just as they were passing through the changing area, the iron gate leading to the front of the school creaked open. They froze. Carpenter-Isaacs, their gargantuan Latin teacher, came into view.

He was clad in a long silk robe.

Aidan couldn't believe his eyes. The enormous man, rolls of fat tumbling down his front and sides, shuffled toward them, removing his robe to reveal pink trunks with yellow flowers. They both pulled back behind some lockers. As they watched, entranced, Carpenter-Isaacs turned and pulled down the trunks, revealing his substantial backside. He waddled naked to the side of the pool and slid in.

The man was a hippo, clumsy and awkward on land, but transformed once afloat. Lying on his back, he sent spurts of water out of his mouth, like a whale emerging from the depths. They couldn't take their eyes off him. With majestic ease he rolled over, submerged, and started swimming underwater.

Piers sprang forward.

He grabbed the robe, scooped up the trunks, and ran full pelt toward the exit, Aidan following close behind. They both shot through the gate and disappeared, just as the teacher's head surfaced, his beady eyes squinting in their direction. "Come on, there's another way up." Piers grinned, shaking the trunks out and whispering, "Just look at the size of these! You could sail a ship with them."

Discarding the clothes behind a bush, they made their way round to the far side of the school, and climbed up some ivy stuck to the wall. As they padded across the roof toward the ladder below their dormitory window, they spotted a figure lumbering across the front lawn. Carpenter-Isaacs, without a stitch on, was tottering along as fast as his podgy feet would carry him. He was clasping his privates in his hands, looking around furtively, as though the headmaster might call out his name at any moment. The moon came out from behind a cloud and lit up his colossal white frame as it made its way toward the trees.

"Now that's a sight you won't forget in a hurry," whispered Piers, clambering through the window.

They both slipped into bed. Piers leaned across and punched Aidan on the arm, then lay back, arms crossed behind his head. "You did it," he said. "You did it!" Everyone else was asleep, but Aidan was wide awake, so he lay there staring at the ceiling for a while.

He was breathing heavily. From the excitement. From the fear. From the rush of adrenaline that coursed through his small body. He thought he would follow Piers to the ends of the earth. The boy had no fear. No fear at all. At least that was how it looked to Aidan, who shot his friend a grin. As his breathing slowed and he slipped toward sleep, Aidan drifted back to the agony of his humiliation earlier in the day. It seemed so distant, so unimportant now.

His soul fluttered inside him, then broke free.

From the pit of despair, he now felt like he was flying.

~ 3 ~

BEACH AND BLOOD

*Beauty of whatever kind . . . invariably excites
the sensitive soul to tears.*
~ Edgar Allan Poe

November 2004

Two figures walked down a gravel path toward a large house overlooking the ocean. The day was fine, the sun shining brightly, yet it wasn't too hot. The air was fresh and slightly damp from the breeze blowing in gently from the west. The long driveway was lined with hedges, topped every few yards by topiary sculptures. Spacious gardens fanning out from the house could be seen through the greenery.

Korazin hummed to himself as he strolled along. He enjoyed the reverberation in his throat and the sound pulsating through his eardrums. The bodies used by humanity were fascinating things. He'd been on several missions and was finally becoming accustomed to using one. His mental capacities remained unaffected, but his feelings were transformed. With a stomach that tightened, tears that flowed, and sides that ached after an extended period of laughing, emotions worked so much better. Besides, it was impossible for a lucidus to truly understand the human experience without putting on flesh, though he recoiled at the thought of being trapped in a body for an entire lifespan.

He stopped to take off his shoe. Tipping it up, he emptied out a pebble that had been rubbing against his heel. Bodies hurt, there was no getting away from that. Even loaned ones. It was a privilege to serve on a mission—he'd come to terms with the discomfort a long time ago—and, all things considered, a little sweat, thirst, and hunger were relatively small sacrifices.

On arrival, Korazin turned to his companion. "Voilà," he said.

Asaph gazed up.

The house was composed of a large central section with a wing on each end; it accommodated over twenty people comfortably. A hacienda in scale, the building stood three stories tall, was designed in a Mediterranean style, and boasted terracotta roofs and elegant arches shading the windows. The walls were daubed with light brown paint, and festooned every few yards with geraniums that poured out of flowerpots, giving the facade an air of exuberance and life. Leaning up against the wall on either side of the front door were two enormous ladders reaching to the roof.

Pushing open the massive oak front door, the lucidi caught their breaths. The hall was magnificent—the size of a tennis court. There was such a sense of grandeur and space. They looked around. A grandfather clock stood in one corner, its pendulum tolling the virtues of a slower pace of life. On the ceiling, Michelangelo's masterpiece spoke with silent beauty, while on the wall to their left *The Last Supper* was displayed. Down the far end stood the *Pietà*. The pair paused for a moment, silently worshipping, woken from their reverie soon after by a loud voice.

Through an open door to their left, a tall, regal-looking lucidus advanced toward them, offering his broad hands. "Ah, welcome, welcome, both of you!" His grip was firm and he smiled warmly at his visitors. "Korazin and Asaph, isn't it? I've been expecting you. Do come in. My name is Gamaliel. I'm one of the seraphs assigned to the Western Zone, as I'm sure you know." He surveyed his guests, turning to the shorter one. "Asaph, I believe Nathaniel is waiting for you at the other end of the house. So pleased you could make it today. It's just down the hallway to your right."

Asaph bowed and left.

Gamaliel faced Korazin. "Come, my friend," he said, his voice avuncular in tone. "Follow me." He led his guest through to a large room with a long table running down the middle. They sat down in two armchairs near some French doors that gave onto a patio. The view before them was spectacular. White horses were cresting on the ocean swell, the spume sparkling in the sun's rays.

Running down from the house was a path that zigzagged as far as a cliff edge, snaking its way through the undergrowth. It was bordered by wildflowers bending in the stiff breeze. The surf pounding the beach below blended with the calls of seabirds nesting on the cliff face.

"I don't know if you've been told," continued the lucidus, "but you are a late replacement for Baruch. He's been working on a reconciliation case in Japan. Two brothers who are taking their time. So, as it happens, you will be reacquainted with Aidan. Your earlier contact has turned out to be providential."

"I'm glad," said Korazin. "I warmed to him the first time, but that was over twenty years ago. Merely a blink for us, but a long time for humans."

"Indeed. You have some catching up to do. But today, my friend, you will be accompanying me in the mezcla."

"A visit to London?"

"Southern California." Korazin looked at him quizzically. "To pay a visit to a delightful little girl on a day out at the beach. The current plan is to improve Anglo-American relations." He smiled.

"Oh yes? Tell me more."

"Well, her name's Evelyn Machin. She's currently forty-three years old. Lives in Los Angeles. Venice Beach, to be exact. Mother to a daughter, Jasmine, aged 20, who lives in Torrance. Evelyn works at Harbor-UCLA Medical Center. I'll fill you in with more details later, but today we'll be cooling our toes in the ocean. Back in 1968, when she's seven."

Uncertainty settled on the tall lucidus. Korazin felt the mood shift. Gamaliel cleared his throat and continued. "Afterward, I'm afraid, we must visit the day of the trauma. Most lucidi, when they get their first view of horrific human depravity—either on a mission or in the mezcla—find the experience upsetting. It will be a struggle to watch, but you'll have to trust me. It is necessary; the Father demands it. If you cannot take the bleeding, then you are not fit to serve the Master who bled."

"Yes, sir. Understood."

Gamaliel got up and poured two glasses of water. He handed one to his guest. "Cheers!" he said.

Together they drank.

A moment later, they were sitting on a beach in Southern California. Surf broke on the shoreline, sending white water streaming up the sand toward two little girls who sat waiting. When the wave arrived, it washed up their legs and soaked them with pleasure. Some of it splashed onto their faces, causing howls of laughter. The younger one beamed at her sister in sheer delight, their shared joy rippling out and flowing up and down the beach. She made rude noises as she spat out the salt water, squealing gleefully. Her hair was already filled with pieces of seaweed and they'd only just arrived.

"On our fronts, Evie! On our fronts!" She rolled over and began kicking her legs up and down. However, she was too impatient to wait for the next wave, so she sat up and started throwing sand at her sister, who threw it back at her.

"Now, now, girls!" said a woman in her late thirties seated nearby. "Katie! I've told you before, sweetie. No tossing sand about, please!" Bonnie sat under a yellow umbrella, reading a book, occasionally looking up to keep an eye on her girls. A wicker basket lay next to her, overflowing with brightly colored plastic plates and spoons. A bottle of Sunny Delight was sitting in the shade, nestled in a bucket of melting ice cubes. Half-eaten sandwiches adorned the towels, along with empty chip packets.

The girls started building a sandcastle. In truth, Katie did little except flatten anything taller than six inches. "Stop it!" shouted Evelyn. "Listen, silly. I won't play if you keep doing that! Now you dig there." Her sister ran into the shallows, filled her bucket with water, and ran back to her mom to show her the mermaid she'd caught. Evelyn was making a start on a new castle. It needed a moat, so while Katie sprayed sand about, she began digging in a circle.

Further up the beach, the two lucidi sat, observing the girls' playful activity. Gamaliel smiled broadly. It seemed to him there was nothing more beautiful than the sight of children at play. Apart, perhaps, from children asleep. Their laughter was a tonic, filling him with gratitude and wonder in equal measure.

He sighed. "The joy of youthfulness is something we will never know."

"Yes, but to observe at close quarters what the Father has created, that is some compensation, don't you think?"

"Yes, indeed. And I'm grateful for this opportunity, although I think I should be wearing a hat! I fear I'm getting sunburned." He laughed. They sat in companionable silence watching Evelyn, who was now building a small city with roads and bridges. Katie decided to become a bulldozer and rendered her creation a pile of sand in less than five seconds.

"Come on, girls!" said Bonnie. "Time to get home." She packed up the lunch, while Katie ran around naked, having discarded her bathing suit. Evelyn wrapped a towel round her shoulders and picked up some bags. Together, the three of them labored back up the beach to the boardwalk. The two lucidi followed. One freeway and five surface streets later, they arrived back in Culver City. The lucidi followed the family into their house and stood in the corner of the living room.

After showering, the girls pulled out some fancy dress. Katie was a princess who swooned a lot while also fighting dragons. Evelyn was a doctor. As usual. She was lining up some plastic bottles on the coffee table when her sister let out a shriek, and dropped a kitchen knife onto the floor. In seconds, her mother had scooped her up and carried her to the couch, trailing drops of blood behind them. Evelyn ran over, a look of panic on her face.

"Katie!" she screamed, leaning over to get a better look.

Bonnie was calmness personified. "Be a good doctor, Evie, and go run a clean cloth under the hot water. Not too hot, mind. And bring the Band-Aids and Bactine." Evelyn did as she was told, walking back with the cloth held out proudly. Katie had cut herself on the leg, producing a shallow wound that had already stopped bleeding. "Ouch!" she said tearfully when her mom pressed the cloth to her skin. "It hurts."

Evelyn put her toy stethoscope in her ears and approached her sister. "I need to make sure she's okay. She might need some pills." Bonnie gave her some space to run her checks. Katie, it seemed, had a pulse in thirty different places on her body, including on her elbow and the top of her head.

"Well done, Evie. Good work." She leaned in close to Katie. "No knives, you hear? What were you thinking?"

Her youngest started crying again. She covered her face with her hands as her mother rubbed Bactine into the wound. "Ow . . . ow-eee," she wailed. "Evie's my doctor. She needs a paay-tient." Bonnie peeled off a Band-Aid and placed it over the cut.

"It's hurting, Mommy," sniveled Katie.

"Well, it will for a while. That's what happens when you cut yourself."

"Make it stop hurting, Mommy. It stings."

"I can't make it stop, honey. But I can do this." She planted a big kiss on the little girl's forehead. "Now, don't ever, *ever* do that again. Ya hear?" Evelyn lay on top of her sister, crushing her with enthusiasm, until Katie was giggling again. Seconds later, they were both running around the room, while Bonnie put all her knives on the top shelves of the kitchen cupboards.

The two lucidi walked out of the house.

"She's beautiful," said Korazin. "Truly beautiful in a way I can't even describe."

"That she is," murmured Gamaliel. He sighed and turned to his companion. "Korazin, my friend, there is no avoiding the next part. It is almost unbearable to watch, but it's also a requirement of the job. The Father tells us the mezcla has a purpose. It helps us create a bond with a suffering human being. It's not enough to hear about their pain. We must see it. The Son entered in thoroughly, far more thoroughly than we will ever do, so it's a small price to pay."

The mezcla shifted.

They entered a dimly lit room and it took a moment for their eyes to adjust. The abomination unfolded before them, and they were powerless to intervene. The scene was unspeakably terrible, tearing at their insides, and ripping from them their deepest emotions. Though Gamaliel had witnessed the event before, that didn't stop reddened tears from rolling down his cheeks. Korazin soon covered his eyes, weeping openly and without shame. He thought the heart in his body would stop functioning. He thought it would break. He pounded his fists into the top of an armchair, crying out to the universe to stop what was happening. He cried out to the Father, but the Father said nothing, did nothing. The universe was silent. The Father was silent.

It was over in three minutes.

~ 4 ~

THE VIATICI HOUSE

*There is one spectacle grander than the sea, that is the sky;
there is one spectacle grander than the sky,
that is the interior of the soul.*
~ Victor Hugo

January 29, 2005

Aidan woke up in a hole, moss pressed against the side of his head. The air was cool and damp, the earth beneath him curiously warm. He spat a leaf out of his mouth and sat bolt upright, bypassing his customary habit of wiping sleep from his eyes. He looked around calmly, fighting his fear. The hole was more like a shallow crater, and he was soon out of it, sitting on its edge. On three sides, he was surrounded by tall hedges; above, a sunrise was painting the sky shades of pink. A soft breeze rustled the branches. He looked down at himself. Jeans, dirty sneakers—which seemed to fit perfectly—and a cotton shirt of uncertain ownership felt comfortable beneath a well-worn leather jacket. But he felt . . . different.

Questions didn't take long to begin their assault. Where was he? How long had he been there? What the heck was going on?

He found it a little alarming to discover himself outside, when his last recollection was sipping a nightcap and then, well . . . a quick read before dozing off. Through the hedge he glimpsed the twinkling of dappled light off a large body of water. An ocean? His home was in West Kensington, a pleasant London suburb notable for its lack of oceans nearby. And generally, when you went to bed there, that's where you woke up.

His heart was pounding away in his chest, the thumps resonating in his ears making it hard to think. He stood up and ran his hand along a rough branch. It felt solid but there was something odd about the place. He couldn't put his finger on it. He blinked. Something was shining at the edges of his vision.

Then it hit him. Someone must have kidnapped him.

And left him in a hole? It didn't make any sense. Unless that someone was coming back. Time to get moving. Action first, answers later. It wasn't difficult to figure out he was in a maze. A substantial one. He stumbled around for a while, and tried to push his way through one of the hedges, but drew blood with his first attempt. He gave up. The branches were too tightly packed, and he had no tool to cut his way out. Better to keep moving. There had to be a means of escape.

He started to run.

Rounding a corner at speed, he crashed into a woman, sending her flying. He was met by a stream of abuse that shocked him temporarily, and although he attempted to help her up, his offer was firmly rebuffed. Well, at least he wasn't alone. She might be a little agitated but she clearly wasn't a kidnapper. And two people were definitely preferable to one. He bent over to catch his breath. As he straightened up, he spotted a part of the hedge further down that was less dense. Perhaps . . . He was just glancing back toward the woman when he received a swift kick to the midriff. His reactions were slow. She kneed him hard in the groin and took off.

Aidan was left in a heap, riding waves of pain known only to the male of the species. If this was a dream, it was turning into a nightmare. As ridiculous as it seemed, he pinched himself. Oh for goodness' sake, what was he doing? What a cliché! In any case, it all felt too real. The throbbing ache below his waist was definitely real, subsiding only after he'd lain on the ground moaning for what seemed like an age. He got up gingerly. In the distance, he could hear the woman's footsteps, accompanied by shrill invective aimed at her captors. He smiled, unable to resist a little schadenfreude. So she was still stuck in the maze. Well, serve her right.

From then on, Aidan decided to be methodical. He broke up some long branches and laid the pieces down at the entrance to sections of the maze that were dead ends. The technique gradually moved him toward the outside, though he was not aware of this until he

The Viatici House

suddenly discovered a patch of sunlight ahead. The instant he saw it, he picked up the pace, tearing headlong out of the maze, relief flooding his body.

Once out, he stopped in his tracks.

In spite of his predicament, the view caught his breath. He shaded his eyes, taking in a sight to enchant the senses. It was certainly worth a moment of contemplation. Above fields of gold, a vast blue expanse seemed to hover, adorned with shimmering flecks of white. The wheat in the foreground ebbed and flowed, much like the ocean in the distance. Far off, he could hear the soft rumble of the surf pounding the shoreline. Along a path to his right, wildflowers smiled up with myriad expressions of joy and delight. They swayed in the breeze like dancers at a ball. Behind him, the walls of the maze towered high and immobile.

Aidan looked around, trying to get his bearings. He wondered where the woman had gone. There was no movement or sound from inside the maze. He called out a couple of times, then gave up and began walking down a path that reminded him a little of the country lanes in Cornwall. After a mile or so, hedgerows rose on each side until he was flanked by thick vegetation left and right. The sun had risen in the cloudless sky and he was soon thirsty. He started to hurry. The hedges began to thin out and once again he was surrounded by wheat fields.

Arriving at crossroads, he spotted a signpost. It stood proudly signaling the way to The Viatici House. Was he in Italy? It was certainly warm enough. But if so, why not *Casa di Viatici*? He shrugged and was about to continue when he caught sight of a brown envelope flapping against the far side of the post. He pulled it off and peered inside. A piece of parchment was nestled at the bottom. He took it out and started reading.

There was once a king who ruled a kingdom of great beauty. The rivers and streams teemed with fish, and the countryside echoed to the lowing of its cattle. Beasts inhabited the forests; the hunting was plenteous. The people lived in peace for the king was wise. He charmed the surrounding monarchs at annual banquets and protected his borders. He was admired by all, but truly loved by only one.

His daughter. Her name was Faith.

Now the king lived in a large castle with many rooms. Each room was exquisitely decorated, but there was one he loved above all. It had high ceilings, yet it lacked both paintings and furniture. On two facing walls he had installed mirrors. Each was set at a very slight angle so that he was able to see his reflection disappearing far, far into the distance. The images seemed to go on forever. Though he knew not why, he delighted in this sight each and every day.

In the grounds of his castle there were two lakes, and on those lakes swam a dozen swans of unusual beauty. The king loved them and gave each one a name. One day, he fell into conversation with one of his courtiers, who told him he had seen a black swan in one of the villages. The king did not believe him.

"Swans are white and only white," he declared.

The courtier, not wishing to gainsay his majesty, bowed and left.

At dinner that night, the king broached the subject with his daughter. She told him she too had heard the same tale, and agreed to journey to the village to discover the truth. On her return, she informed her father that the story was indeed true. A black swan lived in his kingdom.

"I don't believe it!" he exclaimed. "Unless I see it with my own eyes, I refuse to believe there is such a thing as a black swan. I have only ever seen white swans!"

That night, a fire broke out in the castle. The king was trapped on the top floor with no way of escape. He stood on the windowsill, looking down, but all he could see was black, billowing smoke. All of a sudden, he heard a voice calling.

It was Faith. "Father! Jump!" she called. "The black swan has arrived to save you. If you jump, she will catch you."

"I can't see a black swan! I can't see anything!"

"Trust me, Father, the swan is there. She is ready to catch you. She caught me when I jumped and now she has come to catch you. Jump!"

The king hesitated. Looking down, he shouted, "There are NO black swans!"

The next moment, the fire consumed him and he perished.

Aidan took a closer look at the parchment, turning it over. It felt heavier than normal paper, more solid. He sniffed. It was emitting some kind of smell. Bringing it up to his face, he detected the faint aroma of his mother's perfume, unmistakably so. He started to feel drowsy and felt the need to sit down. Perched at the top of a grassy bank, he found he couldn't keep his eyes open and soon collapsed into the ditch behind.

On waking, it was impossible to know how long he'd been unconscious. He found himself swaying gently back and forth inside what looked like a carriage of some sort. It was comfortably furnished with red leather benches and sumptuous pillows. However, he discovered his hands were bound together with ropes. Unexpectedly, instead of discomfort, the bonds sent shoots of pleasure up his arms whenever he moved. Somehow, with the gentle rocking and the relaxation periodically flowing up his arms, he was not once tempted to try to escape. Instead, with a gentle breeze blowing in through the window, he began to snooze.

The sun was starting to go down as the carriage pulled into a courtyard in front of a large house. Aidan woke up and immediately noticed the ropes were gone. He stepped out cautiously. He didn't know what to expect, but surely a man holding out a tray of drinks wasn't high on his list of possibilities. His first thought was that his ideas about kidnappers needed adjustment. He shared the commonly held assumption that kidnappers were unlikely to serve hors d'oeuvres and aperitifs. And yet here he was, standing under a mackerel sky on a beautiful evening, a glass of sherry in one hand and a canapé in the other. He hadn't a clue where he was, or what was happening, but it seemed churlish to complain. After all, the service was marvelous.

As the man disappeared into the house, Aidan turned to look back at the carriage. Four unicorns stood playfully tossing their manes from side to side, shaking their bridles. Their horns stood out starkly against the hedges behind them. He blinked and was tempted to pinch himself again, when a tall, bearded gentleman with striking emerald eyes emerged through the front door. He wore a black frock coat, pin-striped trousers, winged collar, and cravat—the very embodiment of the word "dapper." His hair was long, straight, and silver-gray and hung down his back, but the most notable aspect of his appearance was his face. It emanated a soft white glow.

"Lovely, aren't they?" He smiled warmly. "Yet surprisingly willful. And impossible to break in, of course. But thankfully they enjoy working in teams." One of the creatures whinnied, as if on cue.

Aidan remained speechless. First unicorns, now a man with an incandescent face. Why try to understand when nothing made sense? Better to go with the flow. Besides, if they meant him harm, why serve sherry and hors d'oeuvres? The thought helped settle his nerves as he followed his host through a large oak door.

His reaction—a sharp intake of breath, widening eyes, and finally the upward tilt of the head—was apparently expected. His host smiled and left through a side door.

"*The Last Supper*," whispered Aidan, approaching the mural. It looked remarkably authentic. But then so did the *Pietà* and several other works of art in the hall. After examining each closely, he wandered toward the far end.

A man entered the room silently, walked past Aidan, and hung a small silver frame on the wall near some bifold doors that opened onto a balcony. He wore rough jeans, a dirty T-shirt, and had pruning shears poking from his back pocket. Once the man had left, Aidan stepped forward to read.

> *A breath, a burst of dust, the birth*
> *Of humankind, Love's overflow divine*
> *Stand tall and gaze upon the earth*
> *The sacred space, your home, your shrine.*
>
> *Snug fits your glorious cloak of flesh*
> *Hard-muscled, tendon, ligament, and bone*
> *Cocoon of mind and sense and home*
> *To that which moves the whole*
> *The will, the spirit, e'en the heart*
> *Encompassed all within the soul.*

Fusion for a time suspended
Our treasured guests whom we invite
To probe, inquire, the furious fight
And when the heart is jaded
Come sup on all that best delights the soul
Choose health and love and light
Be well
Be still
Be whole.

A light haze had settled on the horizon. The air wafting in through the doors was becoming cooler. Aidan turned round and was intrigued to notice the names of theologians and philosophers engraved on plaques above each doorway. Augustine. Luther. Hume. Kierkegaard. Only one door was open. *Descartes Room* was inscribed in gold lettering on the door itself. He entered tentatively to discover a spacious, well-decorated room with a long mahogany table running down the middle. Two sideboards stood against the walls. On one, various decanters, glasses, and beverage bottles were lined up; on the other, crystal glasses and silver cutlery were laid out neatly. Down the far end, French doors gave onto a patio overlooking the ocean. In the corner, his erstwhile fellow captive was seated in an oxblood leather wing chair. She appeared a lot calmer.

The woman looked up. "They truss you up like a pig too?" Her opening gambit wasn't quite what he was expecting.

"Erm, not exactly. I—"

"Listen, I'm sorry about what happened in the maze." Her tone was matter-of-fact. "Alone with a man in a confined space, I guess I panicked. I apologize." She paused. "I'm Evelyn. You?"

"Aidan." At first, he didn't know whether to engage in polite conversation or try to figure out what was going on. Evelyn picked up a glass from the occasional table by her side, draining what looked like a beer. He wandered over to the sideboard and picked up a Corona, downing it in seconds. The journey had left him parched. He poured himself a whisky, hoping to settle his nerves.

"Well, you hit the target," he said, "if that's any consolation." A smile crinkled the corners of her mouth. "Know where we are?"

"They pick you up in a stagecoach?"

"You could call it that. And let me guess . . . when you arrived, they were serving drinks."

"Yup. Couldn't resist the tequila."

"See the unicorns?"

"Now that's when I began doubting my sanity. You?"

Just then, a lucidus entered carrying a large tray of fruit and snacks. "The three Ds," he announced. "Are you—"

"Forget that," interrupted Evelyn. "You've got a lot of explaining to do. Where the hell are we?" She rose, jabbing her finger at her host.

"All in good time," came the reply. Korazin started laying out the refreshments on a sideboard. She was about to continue her tirade when a loud voice cut in.

"The three Ds!" Gamaliel entered the room, and started pouring drinks. "What a good place to start. Dreams, drugs, or death. You're guessing one of those. Am I right?"

The humans looked at each other and shrugged.

The conversation that followed was convivial and generally good-humored. Evelyn gradually calmed down, but in truth, she struggled, whereas Aidan's fascination grew by the second. Their discussion ranged over the who, what, and where, barely touching on the why.

"I know what you're thinking," said Korazin, offering Evelyn another beer. "Genetic engineering, right? Or horses with prosthetic horns." He stifled a grin.

"Hey, I say it like I see it."

"Unicorns."

"There are no unicorns." The lucidi smiled at each other. "Now hold on," she continued. "You think some cute story about a swan is supposed to impress me? You think—"

"No," interrupted Korazin. "We expect you to be consistent. You say it like you see it, and what you see is a unicorn. You're a doctor, right?" She nodded. "So you trust the scientific method."

"Well, as you said, genetic engineering. Or prosthetic horns."

"Okay, so let me get this straight. You went to bed last night, woke up in a maze, and met an Englishman near the coast of who knows where. You're now sitting with two people with unusual-looking faces who tell you that you've been migrated to a realm called the Espacio." He paused dramatically. "And the one thing you won't believe is that you've seen a unicorn?"

Evelyn glared at the lucidus. "Hell, I can't explain *any* of this. It's just . . . crazy."

"You're worried about men in white coats."

Silence spread out and filled the room. "With clipboards," said Aidan. Evelyn cracked a smile.

"Understandable," said Korazin. "And you're right to question the evidence, by the way. There's a little Spock in all of us."

A lucidus in a chef's hat entered bearing an oval serving dish piled with tender cuts of meat just off the grill. The table was promptly spread with fine bone china, dishes of tiny roast potatoes, and a variety of vegetables and relishes. Aidan suddenly felt very hungry. Evelyn resisted at first, not quite trusting her senses, but then succumbed. She reached for a soft seeded bun, split it, and made herself a hamburger dripping with relish, mustard, and onions. The food was a welcome respite from the mental confusion she was experiencing.

"So where are the wings?" said Aidan, wiping the corner of his mouth with a napkin. The lucidi both laughed.

"It's always about the wings, isn't it?" said Korazin. "Why the fascination?"

"I don't know. In the paintings, you guys always have wings."

Evelyn pushed back her seat. She turned to Korazin. "I don't want to be rude, but I think I've had my fill. Can you get me home?"

"Do follow me." Korazin accompanied her to the door.

Aidan watched them leave. He bent over and pulled down his sock, revealing the skin above his right ankle. So they weren't lying. His birthmark was missing.

Gamaliel's voice tore him from the mental maze through which he was stumbling. "More juice?"

Aidan pushed his glass forward. He sipped, paying attention to the liquid flowing down his esophagus. There was nothing dreamlike about any of it. And there was something about the place, something magical for which he couldn't find words. When he looked across at Gamaliel, the lucidus was holding out two pills. Aidan burst out laughing. "Oh, you have got to be kidding! Don't tell me I look like Keanu Reeves."

"This was Korazin's idea. Blue or red—I believe they do exactly the same thing." Gamaliel smiled as he watched his guest reach out and take both pills.

Aidan Manning, a British man in his forties, sitting in the Viatici House in the Espacio, looked down at the pills in his hand. He found he'd come to trust the person sitting next to him. The whole experience was completely wild. Unfathomable. Yet he felt safe. So when he looked at the pills, he felt no fear.

"Will I see Evelyn again?"

"Almost certainly."

"Is she going to be okay? She seemed—"

"Don't worry, Aidan. Please. She'll be just fine."

Aidan popped both pills into his mouth, took a sip from his glass, and closed his eyes.

"Rest, son. Rest well," said the lucidus, as Aidan returned to his bed in London, still fast asleep.

~ 5 ~

A CASE OF TRAFFICKING

Man is born free but is everywhere in chains.
~ Jean Jacques Rousseau

February 4, 2005

Aidan inspected his reflection in the mirror. He took off his wig and examined the underside, which was showing signs of wear. The door to the robing room swung open and a tall, manicured gentleman in his mid-fifties entered, catching him off guard.

"Morning, Manning," he said offhandedly.

Quentin Molsberry was a QC who couldn't hide his disdain for barristers in their forties who'd failed to make silk. He considered an appointment to the Queen's Bench a rite of passage, sweetened as it was by better pay, higher-profile cases, and a nice Chablis among friends at the end of a case.

"Morning," said Aidan, avoiding eye contact. He tweaked a few hairs on his wig and put it away in its box. Last time he'd come before Judge Heppenstall he'd been likened to a disheveled canine, which he hadn't appreciated. Nevertheless, he had to confess he rather liked the fancy dress. Archaic it might be, but Charles II would surely have approved. He thought he looked good in his wig and gown. At least, that was normally the case. Unfortunately, his precious horsehair accoutrement was looking the worse for wear. The previous weekend during Sunday lunch, a visitor's dog had slobbered all over it and treated it like a slipper. Strands of hair were now protruding at various unsightly angles. The gravitas the wig was designed to project was at risk of turning into amusement. Repairs were essential.

"By the way," said the QC. "I've got a big case starting next week. You may have read about it. *R v. Schillaci*."

Aidan didn't like Molsberry much; the man put on airs. However, he had no particular interest in demonizing opposing counsel. Most in his profession were perfectly able to get on outside the courtroom. He saw no reason to put on misleading appearances just for the entertainment of the public gallery. Even so, Molsberry tested his patience. He had a way of talking down to those on the other side, a habit Aidan found irksome.

"Jolly good," he said. "I'll alert the media, Quentin." The reply sailed over the QC's head. In his twenties, Aidan had been a highflier, tipped to take silk at the first opportunity. However, he also possessed a maverick streak that did him no favors among the ermine-cloaked hawks at the top of the profession. When his application for silk was rejected twice, he'd decided to withdraw from the process. Not that his failure had damaged his reputation. Indeed, he was more popular than ever. Criminals seemed to like him, so work flowed regularly.

"Good luck with the case." Aidan turned and left.

The weekend flew by. He spent Saturday afternoon with his son, Simon, driving go-karts round a track in North London. On Sunday night, he prepared a talk he was due to give at a sixth form college in Hounslow. He enjoyed lecturing sixth-formers; he was even allowed to run simulated court proceedings occasionally, which the students loved. Taking part in a moot himself just before the end of his last term at school had ignited his love of advocacy. Instead of pursuing a degree in English, he'd opted for the law, a decision he'd never regretted for a moment.

When Aidan arrived in chambers the next day, the first person he encountered was his clerk, bearing a tray laden with teacups. "Get you one once I've done the rounds, Mr. Manning," Tommy said quietly as he passed.

"You're a lifesaver," replied the barrister and headed for his office. Tommy was a genuine godsend. The young man's laconic manner disguised a calm efficiency below the surface. Aidan thought he was fantastic; Tommy had rescued him on numerous occasions, when he'd forgotten vital documents or discovered that the brief for Court One was staring up at him while he sat feet away from the judge in Court Two. Tommy never embarrassed him; he covered up for him without the flicker of a smile or smirk, and flushed with pride whenever Aidan's triumphs resulted in clinked glasses at the end of the day.

They were a good team.

A barristers' chambers was not like a traditional company with managers and employees. It was a group of lawyers who clubbed together to offer their services to solicitors' firms; as such, barristers were more like independent contractors than anything else. Because of this, they depended heavily on their senior clerk, whose job it was to assign the cases as they came in.

Harry, who'd held his post for years, boasted an East End pedigree to match any inside the Lincoln's Inn estate. He was flash, brash, and loyal as Lassie. The laugh was loud, the smile broad, and the jokes a light tinge of blue when the Head of Chambers, Mr. Blenkinsopp, was out of the office. Harry knew where the line was, which was why he only strayed over it occasionally. Clerks traditionally came from humble backgrounds. They acted as hustlers, horse-trading with solicitors' firms to ensure their barristers received regular work. Harry maintained good relations with most of the large firms in London, but to achieve this, he often had to cajole his troops. He was a master of the art of gentle persuasion, constantly massaging their egos, while also convincing them that a 9 a.m. shoplifting case in Blackfriars was an opportunity not to be missed. "Number 43 is a well-oiled machine, my friends," he liked to announce regularly to the open-plan office where the junior clerks worked. Any hint of cynicism from his underlings was met with a clip round the ear.

Aidan looked in his pigeonhole. *The Racing Post* lay discreetly beneath a pile of papers neatly tied up with pink ribbon. He thanked Tommy silently, took out the brief and walked to his desk. Sitting down, he undid a furl of papers.

R v. Bakic. Count 1. Trafficking Persons Into the United Kingdom for Sexual Exploitation, contrary to Section 57 of the Sexual Offences Act 2003. Count 2. False Imprisonment. Count 3. Controlling Prostitution for Gain. So he was a pimp who trafficked. He turned the page. Count 4. Rape. Goodness, the only charge missing was murder.

He leafed through the papers. The circumstances seemed odd. Police found the accused asleep in an empty house during a dawn raid. They retrieved a truckload of forensic evidence with Dragan Bakic's name all over the place. In addition, dozens of emails were discovered linking him with criminals abroad. It would require lengthy testimony to establish the authenticity of each one.

He turned the page. A pub landlord had singled out Bakic from a lineup as one of those present when money changed hands. Being identified at an exchange didn't look good. A couple of young girls who claimed they'd been trafficked were also due to give evidence against him. He closed the file.

This was going to take a Houdini-like effort to escape.

~ 6 ~

LIFE

The good life is one inspired by love and guided by knowledge.
~ Bertrand Russell

February 8, 2005

As Evelyn awoke, it was the smooth, white linen sheets that caught her attention first. They felt luxurious to the touch. She stretched, moving her back against the soft fabric. A glance at her wrist flooded her with the memory of her previous visit. Her watch was missing. Of course. She was in one of their rent-a-body getups. After climbing out of bed, she arched her back and touched her toes. Mmm, the body felt good.

Savoring the view from the balcony, she made a conscious effort to remember how the setup worked. The body was different, but what about the mind? She recalled the events of the past few days. They certainly felt familiar. She remembered that on Tuesday morning Vincent let his dog foul her yard again. And the lab was supposed to have dropped off those test results. Hmm, wasn't she due to pick up her mom's prescription tomorrow? The familiar pieces of her life back home fell into place. She looked in the mirror, noticing some blurring on the edges of her vision. That was supposed to go away, wasn't it?

Opposite the bed, clothes were lying on a Queen Anne chair. They apparently knew her colors, which improved her mood. She walked over and dressed herself. As she moved away, she ran her hand over the chairback, observing the beauty of its design. Stopping briefly, she blinked twice; her vision was returning to normal.

On arrival downstairs, she took a moment to look around the cavernous hall. It was quite something. The art on the walls could have occupied her entire morning. She moved from a Vermeer to a

Velázquez, stopping finally in front of the *Pietà*, peering at it up close. It looked real. But it couldn't be. Surely.

"It's real." A voice broke her train of thought.

"Yeah, right." She turned round to see Gamaliel standing in a doorway.

"No, seriously. It's real. All the art here is the real thing. Physical objects have the capacity to 'present' in more than three dimensions. The *Pietà* is sitting in St. Peter's Basilica right now, but it's also here. On that plinth, right in front of you." She had only just arrived and already her head was spinning. "Trust me, Evelyn. It can do both at the same time. All it takes is a little imagination."

The tall lucidus came forward, smiling. "Welcome back," he said. "It really is very good to see you again. The Espacio takes some getting used to but I have every confidence in you."

"I'm not surprised you prefer it up here," she replied. "And I'm not surprised you're all into Greek philosophy with its disdain for the body. You should come down and see what a real body feels like one day, instead of floating around up here."

"Good morning, Evelyn!" Korazin's deep voice startled her. "How right you are." He came and stood next to her, gazing up at the *Pietà*. He said nothing, allowing the quiet to relax her. When he spoke, he did so softly. "We're well aware that the Espacio might create the wrong impression. We haven't all turned into Platonists, I can assure you. We have an extremely high regard for the physical. That's why you're in a body. It may not be yours, but it's essential you wear one, just like us. As you can see, we do very little . . . floating." He paused, breathing deeply. "Now, what do you say to a little breakfast? I'm famished." He led the way into the Descartes Room.

Evelyn surveyed a full spread laid out on the table—toast, eggs, bacon, sausage, muffins, fruit, and a tray of croissants. She poured herself a glass of juice and started filling her plate.

Aidan, who was sitting in an armchair near the patio doors, looked up. He sipped from his cup. "You should try the coffee."

"Aidan, right?" He nodded. "Listen. About last time. I was a little, er . . . upset. A bit thrown by," she waved her hand around, "all this."

She sat down. "So Mr. British Man, what do you do when you're not here yakking with strange men in fancy suits?"

"I'm a barrister." He walked over and joined her at the table. "Nothing to do with coffee."

"That's an attorney, right?"

"Yup. At least, I present the cases in court. They're prepared by solicitors, people whose work does *not* involve knocking on doors. Just in case you were wondering. I'm what's called a member of the Bar, and no, I do not serve cocktails."

Evelyn tucked into her breakfast, feeling more relaxed. "You know, I think our attorneys also have a bar. It's where they drink people's blood." She paused. "Come on, I'm kidding," she said, laughing. "Wasn't it Winston who said we're two nations divided—"

Aidan cut in. "By a common language. Actually, that's Bernard Shaw and Oscar Wilde."

"The Importance of Screwing the Lower Classes, right?"

"You like Oscar Wilde?"

"Not especially, but I read."

"Fiction?"

"Philosophy and religion."

"You're kidding."

"Gotcha." She burst out laughing. "You'll get used to me, Aidan. Lucky for you I've been reading some English writers recently. Right now, I'm into P. D. James and Robert Harris." She wiped her mouth and sat back.

"An Anglophile then. No wonder they put us together. I just finished *Fatherland* myself. Now that's a great read."

They were about to dive into a discussion when Gamaliel came and stood at the end of the table. "Do accompany me outside," he said. "It's such a lovely day. Bring your food." They walked through the double doors and sat down around a large wrought iron table. An awning stretched out over the patio, providing shade. Korazin handed them both sunglasses, which enabled them to look out over the ocean without squinting. The view was glorious.

"So where shall we begin?" said Gamaliel.

"Begin what?" Aidan looked confused.

Evelyn sat forward. "Well, we're not here to discuss Derek Jeter's batting average, are we?" Aidan looked at her quizzically. "Sorry. Baseball's probably not your thing, is it?"

"Life!" interrupted Korazin. "Why don't we start there? We've always found that a good place to start."

They both turned to look at the lucidus, who sat calmly, waiting for them to respond. "Oh, I bet life *is* good for you, isn't it?" said Evelyn. "Living up here in the clouds downing mango juice and munching muffins all day." Both lucidi smiled at her but didn't respond. "No, hold on. This is a test, right? We're not here to debate why poppies look red to us or whether we all see red the same way, are we? No, no, I saw the plaques above the doors. This has got to be the big kahuna. Epicurus, Hume, and dozens of others. Am I right?"

"Epicurus said a lot of things, but I presume you're referring to his original statement of the problem of evil."

"Yup. Is God willing to prevent evil, but not able? Then he is impotent. Is he able, but not willing? Then he is malevolent. Is he both able and willing?"

"Whence then is evil?" finished Gamaliel. "Quite right. Oil and water. So, where better to start than by talking about life? Has it no value?"

"Of course it has value," retorted Evelyn, "but that's hardly the point. Just because we enjoy certain aspects of life, that can't possibly compensate for the horrendous conditions that make life a living nightmare for the majority of people."

"Good one." Aidan turned to Korazin. "You're in check, I believe. And the game's only just started." He looked over at Evelyn, who was staring at her opponent, waiting for a reply.

"Are you familiar with Robert Nozick?" asked Korazin.

Evelyn hesitated, a little confused. "Enlighten me."

"Philosopher from the 1970s. He presented an interesting challenge. Suppose, he said, you had the choice to hook yourself up to a machine that realized your every dream, gave you every pleasure you desired, allowed you to achieve all the goals you chose. Think of it as *The Matrix*, but without the downsides, like Agent Smith.

You'd enjoy constant pleasure and fulfillment, but none of it would be real. It would just be a mental simulation generated by a software program. Would you make that choice?" He fixed Evelyn with his emerald eyes.

She found herself wrong-footed, not quite sure what to say. "Well, let me think." She paused. "No pain, just pleasure, right?"

"Yup."

"Well, offer that to the serfs of nineteenth-century Russia and trust me, you'd run out of machines."

The lucidus turned toward his other guest. "And you, Aidan? Would you make use of the machine?"

"I'd have to think, but . . . er," he hesitated, "probably not. Seems like a cop-out. The problem is, you would begin with the full knowledge that you were cheating. I don't think many people would do that."

Evelyn stared at him, stone-faced.

"Interesting," said Gamaliel, re-entering the discussion. "You see, Nozick surmised that most people would choose *not* to use the machine. Any ideas why?"

"No, stop," said Evelyn, wagging her finger. "I know where this is going. Reality trumps fantasy, right? But that *completely* misses the point. This is about why a creator appears unwilling . . . or unable . . . to reduce the amount of suffering in the world."

Gamaliel held up his hands. "Touché. You're absolutely right, Evelyn. Our point is simply that humans have an inbuilt intuition about suffering. Most people understand that you can't simply eliminate it without altering something very profound about what it means to be human. A software program, however realistic it might be, just cannot deliver a human life. That's why the majority of people accept that at least *some* suffering is inevitable." He got up and went to the railing, where he looked out over the ocean.

"What it means to be human?" she said scornfully. "I'll give you human. You want a list? Labor camps. Cancer. Torture. War. Slavery. Prostitution. See, I prefer Thomas Hobbes. The life of man, solitary, poor, nasty, brutish, and short. The question is this: why is a creator, all-powerful and all-loving, unable to achieve a better world? If this is the best he could come up with, then what kind of conclusions do you think we should draw? Seriously." She sat back and folded her arms.

Aidan started nodding. "I feel I have to agree with Evelyn on this. Child abuse, disease, violence. If you survey the whole breadth of human history, the suffering is staggering; it's endless—and for what?"

Aidan's question weighed heavily on the group.

Evelyn, however, wasn't finished. "Have you ever witnessed human depravity in its vilest forms? *Have you?* Maybe if you saw first-hand the disgusting things humans are capable of, you wouldn't give us this nonsense about how wonderful life is. You just glide around—"

"We can arrange that," said Korazin.

His words stopped her in her tracks. "Excuse me?"

"I said we can arrange that."

"You lost me."

Korazin spread his hands on the table in front of him. "It's called the mezcla. A versatile means of wandering through time." There was often a pregnant pause after a lucidus introduced the mezcla. The concept for most humans was hard to digest, even though they sat in the Espacio. Korazin divulged as much as they needed, but less than they desired, answering their questions with good humor and a fair dose of patience. Aidan thought his head was going to explode. Evelyn looked like someone had explained quantum mechanics to her in two simple equations. A unicorn was one thing, but this was quite another.

Gamaliel placed four glasses on the table and started pouring. "Water is the universal conduit," he said. "A truth unaccountably discovered by filmmakers, although I suspect an errant lucidus myself!" He winked at Korazin. "Now, if you would each pick up a glass."

Aidan hesitated. The prospect of visiting an event from the past, though intriguing, was suddenly a little unnerving. He wondered if something might go wrong. "This is safe, right?"

"Perfectly."

Aidan looked at Evelyn, who shrugged and picked up a glass. He followed suit. "Cheers!" said Gamaliel, and they all clinked their glasses together and drank.

Seconds later, they were lying prostrate on the ground. Evelyn picked up a handful of rich, red earth. She looked around. The room had vanished. The house had vanished. Her three companions began sitting up, brushing dirt off their clothes. She looked down at herself. Her clothing was different: khaki shorts, a pale linen blouse, and walking boots. Over her shoulder was a travel bag. She spat a piece of savannah grass out of her mouth and looked across at Aidan. He was decked out in knee-length shorts and a light brown shirt.

"Hey, this wasn't my idea," said Aidan. They both looked at the lucidi, who were straightening their rather fine safari suits.

"Rwanda. 1994," said Gamaliel. "One of you has been reading a newspaper article on the genocide."

"So this is *my* plan?" Evelyn was incredulous.

"You wanted to show us an instance of horrendous evil," said Korazin.

"Now listen. Just wait a minute. I don't necessarily want to go around watching people kill and maim each other. I didn't sign up for that. In fact, I didn't sign up for any of this. This is you guys. You're the ones who yanked me out of my body and started this whole thing."

"Calm down," said the lucidus. "Everything is going to be just fine. All we're going to do is find a church where an atrocity took place." He regretted his words instantly, but it was too late.

"*All* we're going to do? Just a run-of-the-mill atrocity? Are you nuts? I don't need this. *I don't need any of you!*" She marched off down a rutted road. Korazin looked at Gamaliel.

Aidan ran after her. "Evelyn, we should stick together. Please."

She stopped walking and turned to face him. "Stick together? Listen. As far as I'm concerned, this is just one huge nightmare. I'm just playing along because what else am I supposed to do? But when I find myself somewhere in Africa, apparently about to witness an atrocity, they've gone too far!"

He watched her stomp off down the road.

"Now I've done it," said Korazin.

"Patience, my friend," said Gamaliel.

Evelyn kept walking for a couple of miles until the heat tired her out. She sat down on the side of the road and looked back. The others were nowhere to be seen. Up ahead, there was a clearing and a gentle slope running down to a river. The Kagera. She remembered the name now, from the article. She also recalled the conversation earlier during which the lucidi had assured her she couldn't be seen in the mezcla. That, at least, provided a little comfort.

Approaching the river slowly, she reached the bank and stopped, gasping, convinced her eyes were playing tricks on her. The river was brown and moving swiftly. It was rich in silt and carried elephant grass and other debris gathered on its onward rush toward Lake Victoria. But that wasn't all it carried. She watched as clusters of bodies drifted past. Many were bloated. Almost all had hideous gashes. Some were decapitated. The water looked reddish in places. When a pair of dead babies floated by, she shrieked and wheeled away. Stumbling up the bank, she peered down the road, looking for the others.

"Aidan! Korazin!" she cried, reaching into her bag and pulling out a water bottle. Her hands were trembling as she drank. It took a few minutes before her nerves were under control. Taking a deep breath, she stowed the bottle and continued down the road.

Nearing what seemed like midday, the sun high in the sky, she reached the village of Rusumo, the word scrawled on a battered sign lying face up by the road. She didn't recognize the name. Men with machetes and spears were scattered in groups along the roadside, laughing and joking. Many were drinking; bottles were strewn about, ending up in piles and in ditches. Further on, small houses started appearing, rough-hewn and coarsely built. When she'd walked the length of what seemed to be the main street, Evelyn heard a commotion up to her right. She followed the noise. A sizable group of men, perhaps twenty or thirty, were gathered outside a small house.

She peered at the name on the wall. Bourgmestre Gacumbitsi. This name she remembered. A couple of men with rifles slung over their shoulders were guarding the door. She knew they couldn't see her, so she walked in. It was dark inside, but when her eyes adjusted to the dim surroundings, she was able to make out a large heavyset man sitting behind a desk. He was sweating profusely. Two men stood in front of him clasping their hands together, their heads bobbing up and down. The language was beyond her, but it was impossible to mistake what was happening. They were pleading. Desperately. It was coming back to her now.

So this was the house of the local strong man, Gacumbitsi. He was a Hutu who exercised a powerful influence over the local gangs. They'd been whipped up into a state of frenzy by Radio Mille Collines' broadcasts and other propaganda, describing the Tutsis as inyenzi—cockroaches. Yet this wasn't just tribal warfare. It was genocide, prepared years in advance by a clique close to President Habyarimana. Lists had been drawn up, index cards carefully filled out, so that the killers could identify the right people. It was all meticulously planned. The Interahamwe, the killing squads, were skillfully manipulated when the right opportunity arose, which it did with the death of President Habyarimana in a plane crash on April 6, 1994. How ironic that the leader of the Interahamwe was Robert Kajuga, a Tutsi whose father had changed his family identity to Hutu. Or so she'd read.

If anyone could stop what was happening in this part of the country, it was Gacumbitsi. But he wouldn't, would he? He would ignore the men standing in front of him, pleading for their lives. And there was nothing she could do to stop it. She watched, stunned, as the large man behind the desk spat out his response.

"Tell them to shelter in the church at Nyarubuye," he said suddenly in English. The two men bowed and started thanking him.

Nyarubuye. That's where it happened.

She remembered now, and shuddered. Gacumbitsi barked an order at one of the guards and marched out through a back door. Evelyn ran outside. She passed a gaggle of children playing in the dirt as she left the Rusumo commune and followed the men, who were making their way toward Nyarubuye.

The road had deep ruts, with trash littering the shallow ditches on each side—discarded car parts, empty bottles, and tin cans. Evelyn covered her head with a headscarf she found in her bag. The walk was exhausting, and she was relieved when at last she came upon signs of human habitation. As she approached, something moved on the edge of her vision. They had warned her that might happen when the mezcla shifted. She wasn't sure how it worked, but it didn't matter. The scene in front of her captured all her attention.

As she stood staring, Aidan arrived, his face drained of color. Evelyn barely noticed him as she stumbled toward the center of the village. Around the various small shacks lay hundreds and hundreds of dead bodies. Many were buzzing with flies. Some were blown apart by grenades, but most had died from machete wounds of various kinds. Dozens were missing their heads. They picked their way around the site, looking in through open doors. Inside a classroom, a teacher lay surrounded by four children. There was still chalk on her fingers from the last lesson. Their faces expressed every kind of horror imaginable. Shock, terror, surprise, anguish.

Evelyn was struggling to hold back the tears when she remembered Korazin's mention of the church. A large wooden building with a cross mounted proudly on the roof stood barely a hundred yards away. She walked over and stuck her head inside the door. The butchery was appalling, causing her to pull back. Bodies lay everywhere. A woman lay on her side in front of the altar, her hands still held together in supplication. She'd been decapitated.

Evelyn felt her legs weaken; she stumbled back into Aidan's arms, thankful he was there to catch her. When she'd recovered, they walked over to the two lucidi, who were standing under an acacia tree. The four sat down at the base of the tree.

For a while, they were each lost in their own thoughts.

Eventually, Korazin said quietly, "The villagers had gathered in the church to pray. Some of the younger men had tried to defend themselves with homemade weapons—bows and arrows—but it was useless. There was no way out of Nyarubuye. The Interahamwe were all over the area, so they just sheltered in the church, hoping and praying."

"So you admit it then," said Evelyn. "These people were praying and no help came."

Korazin nodded. "No help at all."

"Just over there." Gamaliel pointed to his left. "That's where Gacumbitsi arrived in his car. He got out and started handing out machetes to the local police. At first, they used guns. Then they finished people off with machetes. They chased them through the fields and into the classrooms. Even in the church there was no escape."

Silence enveloped the group.

"What is there to say in the face of such horror?" whispered Evelyn. There was no reply. No one uttered a word.

Gamaliel handed them each a water bottle.

Re-entry was quick, a couple of seconds. The adjustment took longer. Aidan had a headache—he thought it might be from the shift in air pressure—while Evelyn arrived trembling and drained, her face drawn and pale. As they all took their seats around the table, Gamaliel poured her a glass of juice. "If you wish to go and rest, Evelyn, you are more than welcome. As you said earlier, you did not sign up for this. If you wish to leave us and not return, just give the word." He smiled at her.

"I can just go home?"

She got up and walked out onto the patio, breathing in deeply and enjoying the smell of the ocean carried on the breeze. When she looked back at Aidan, she could see him sitting patiently, his hands folded in his lap. He'd started to grow on her. She surveyed the room; the table was still arrayed with fruit and other tempting foods, while the lucidi sat erect, faces gently glowing. Korazin and Gamaliel. Such unusual names. There was nothing in her earthly life that came anywhere close. She hesitated, but not for long.

Opening the French doors wide, she strode back to her seat. "Dostoyevsky!" she exclaimed.

Aidan perked up immediately; he leaned forward and addressed the room. "I must say, he was on my mind too. I presume you're thinking of Ivan's speech in *The Brothers Karamazov*." They both turned to look at Gamaliel, who sat unperturbed at the end of the table.

"Yes, Ivan does have a point," said the lucidus, "and of course Dostoyevsky writes so well, it's hard not to see the force of Ivan's argument. Perhaps you'd like to summarize it."

The quote jumped into Aidan's mind. The Espacio stimulated his memory, supplying the words so that the quotation arrived complete. "Imagine that you are creating a fabric of human destiny with the object of making men happy in the end but that it was essential and inevitable to torture to death only one tiny creature and to found that edifice on its unavenged tears, would you consent to be the architect on those conditions? Tell me, and tell the truth."

Korazin took over. "No, I wouldn't consent, said Alyosha softly." He paused. "There are few who make such a persuasive argument."

"Well?" said Evelyn. "What's the answer? Is the suffering of children justified as long as one day we are given eyes to see the worth of such misery?" Neither lucidus responded or moved for a while.

When Gamaliel finally spoke, his voice was thick with emotion. "The suffering of children is probably the single most enduring mystery at the heart of the universe. It is certainly the most heartbreaking."

There was silence around the table.

The tall lucidus rose from the table and faced his guests. "It has been my privilege to hear your arguments today, Evelyn. You have made a powerful case. I can also see it's been a tiring day. While your earthly bodies rest, you should do the same here. We will resume our conversation tomorrow morning."

"Join us on the patio?" Korazin opened the French doors, letting in a waft of honeysuckle. Evelyn and Aidan walked out to find the wrought iron table laid for breakfast, all four plates laden with delicacies. They poured coffee, laid linen napkins on their laps, and began to eat.

"How did you both sleep?" Gamaliel joined them at the table.

"Like a log," said Evelyn, finishing off a piece of toast.

"Do you have any more of this jam?" said Aidan, holding up an empty jar.

Their conversation contained none of the adversarial engagement of the previous day. Instead, they probed the lucidi with questions about the Espacio, wondering who had built the Viatici House and whether the sun was the same one they could see from Earth. Aidan was just enquiring about the life expectancy of a lucidus when Korazin jumped in. "What about some mountain biking?"

Evelyn turned to Aidan. "Do you bike?"

"You never forget, right?" A grin lit up his face.

They found the bikes leaning against the front of the house with helmets dangling from the handlebars. After fastening their chinstraps, they adjusted the seats and were about to take off when Korazin emerged from the house. Sporting a replica *maillot jaune*, he looked like he'd just arrived from the Tour de France. Aidan couldn't help smiling.

"You may laugh, earthlings, but do you have the legs? *Do you?*" Mounting his bike, he tipped his head back, and roared with laughter. Then he careered up the front drive at a frightening pace; it was all the humans could do to keep up. When they'd slowed down a little, Evelyn headed off through some of the rockier sections, leaving Aidan to navigate the main path as they made their way up into the hills behind the house.

On reaching the summit, the three of them sat down beneath an olive tree. They drank deeply from their water bottles, gazing down at the sight below. In one direction, vineyards rippled across the hills. Row upon row of vines, their grapes ripe for harvest, sprouted from rich brown soil. Aidan spotted various workers with baskets on their backs, making their way up and down the rows. In the other direction, snowy peaks jutted out against an azure sky.

"Who harvests the grapes?" he asked.

"Lucidi," said Korazin. "The Espacio is a good training ground for us before a first visit to Earth. It accustoms us to a physical environment."

Aidan was about to speak when, from out of nowhere, Gamaliel appeared, standing just a few feet away. "Ready to start again?" He sat down on a boulder.

"Whoa," said Evelyn. "You scared the life out of me. Where did you come from?"

"The powers of a seraph." He laughed. "The best is yet to come!"

She looked at the two lucidi and marveled at what she saw. They seemed so . . . normal, and yet at the same time so extraordinary. How frustrating that she couldn't remember them after waking up.

Korazin interrupted her thoughts. "Well, yesterday was brutal, wasn't it? The scale of human suffering can be overwhelming. It would be easy to remain there, to skew our evaluation of life by focusing exclusively on suffering to the exclusion of life's joys. And before you jump in, Evelyn, we don't wish to offer an argument aimed at balancing joy and sorrow. This is not about balance or compensation. Instead, we're here to encourage perspective. Suffering can destroy that. It can also ingrain in you a deep ingratitude that turns you inward. So this morning, let's just focus on joy."

"*L'chaim!* To life!" announced Gamaliel. "The Jews celebrate the gift of life with a toast and we rejoice with them. Hmm, so why don't we list some of the good things in life? People, activities, the treasures of the earth that humans enjoy each day. And remember, every single one is a gift. You have done not one thing to deserve any of this. The Father owes you nothing. He gives lavishly and in abundance."

"I'll start," said Korazin, his face glowing. "Rocky Road ice cream. Any time I visit, I look for that flavor."

Evelyn didn't look convinced so she turned to Aidan. "Okay. You go next."

He hesitated, looking straight at her. "Beauty," he said.

"Hey, wise guy. This isn't my body you're looking at!"

"But it's close, right?" he laughed. "Okay," he continued. "Women. Smiling. Sailing. Liverpool FC. Fish and chips."

Evelyn addressed Korazin. "So that's what we do? List our favorite things, like Julie Andrews in *The Sound of Music*?" He nodded. She sighed. "Okay, you got me . . . Mountain biking. Surfing. Music. Beethoven and Mozart, obviously. Einaudi. James Newton Howard.

Movies. Friends. Volleyball. Sunsets."

They listed joy after joy—from kids popping bubbles, to the smell of pine trees, to road trips with the top down. It turned out Aidan was particularly fond of food. "Spaghetti," he said. "Seafood. Asparagus. Eggs. Cheese. Lots of cheese. And a really juicy steak. Medium rare. Plus, lemon chicken, beef with cashews, and number 46. Can't remember what that is, but it's *really* good."

Evelyn couldn't control her giggling, almost choking on her words. "You've only mentioned your son once, but mango chutney's on your list . . . what . . . *three* times, I think! What's the deal with that?"

"Well, Simon's a great guy, but does he add a tangy zest to my cheese sandwich? I think not." His deadpan lasted for a second before disintegrating, sending them both into fits of laughter. When she'd calmed down, Evelyn turned to Korazin. "I think we're done here. My friend is apparently too distracted to continue."

They all lay back on the grass and gazed up at the sky. The sun had risen behind the hills, its rays painting the undersides of the clouds a delicate pale pink. The grass was still slightly damp from the morning dew, but the moisture was not uncomfortable. When they sat up and looked down the coast, they could see fishing boats coming round the headland.

Korazin said, "Do humans respond to suffering primarily with the heart or the mind? Ah, now there's a question. As one who has always enjoyed the presence of the Father, I like to remind myself of his wisdom, which is far above my own. 'For my thoughts are not your thoughts, neither are your ways my ways, declares the Lord.'" He paused. "The ability to appreciate the gift of human life is itself a gift. It is received by open hearts in the mysterious interplay between his action and your will. So, by way of invitation, let me finish with some thoughts of my own."

He stood up and looked out over the ocean.

All life's a gift of the Master Builder
Bird and beast, the old and the childer
So when you give, His own you return
And when you withhold, His mercy you spurn.

Matter in motion, love's forms entrusted
Each breath an act of grace imparted
Though stain of sin, your hearts misguided
Your ears stone deaf, your eyes blindfolded.

The wind in the trees, the promise of morning
A pallet of pinks in the sunrise now dawning
Creator of all, birthing souls, setting free
Made fearfully, wonderf'lly, imago Dei.

Beauty divine hid from all in plain sight
A shadow in darkness, a mist in the night
The universe bursting with glory, ablaze
On His radiant splendor, our sure fixèd gaze.

Evelyn looked up at the lucidus, who stood serene, a look of contentment on his face. She thought back to the first time she'd visited the Espacio. Waking that next morning, she'd recalled almost nothing, just a few vague images. It was so infuriating. Surely there had to be a way to remember more. She glanced across at Aidan. He was becoming more likable. Pity about that kick on the first day. That must have hurt.

Gamaliel's voice broke the silence. "Race you back?"

"But you haven't got a bike," said Aidan, sitting up.

"Wings, remember?"

"But I thought you said you didn't have wings."

"I said that?"

Aidan hesitated.

"Retractable!" The lucidus turned round.

"Okay, then. Show us."

The back of his jacket rose a little. Then fell back.

He laughed and started running down the hill.

"Catch me!" he shouted.

~ 7 ~

MILOŠ

To die, to sleep;
To sleep: perchance to dream: ay, there's the rub.
   ~ William Shakespeare, Hamlet

February 9, 2005

Evelyn rose early, threw on a pair of running shorts and a T-shirt, and went to the kitchen. She switched on the TV. SigAlert on the 10. Thank goodness it wasn't on the 405. She poured herself a glass of orange juice and called out, "Søren!" A scruffy West Highland terrier pushed his way through the dog flap and trotted over. He nuzzled her legs.

She put a leash on her dog, grabbed her keys, and left the house. Turning onto Washington Boulevard, she zigzagged her way down the busy sidewalk until she reached the boardwalk, where she began to run, Søren trotting along by her side. They were soon passing the rows of beachfront stores that made Venice Beach famous. There were more sunglasses and tattoo artists than in the rest of Southern California combined, Evelyn was sure of it. She ran past a couple of vendors selling medical marijuana, and arrived at Muscle Beach. Men with oversized pecs were attempting to increase the extent to which they were oversized. Arnold Schwarzenegger's faded photograph adorned a wall; it showed him working out at the famous outdoor gym during his glory days, surrounded by onlookers clearly impressed by his efforts.

She turned off Mildred into Dell Avenue, passing a house that looked like it was designed for Hansel and Gretel, all higgledy-piggledy, with Gaudí-esque tiling and soft lines. Across the canal was a house seemingly constructed of nothing but stainless steel. In the Golden State, you were free to paint your home any color you liked, and choose whichever persona you wanted. A couple of mornings ago, she had passed a man on the boardwalk wearing a tutu and dressed as the Statue of Liberty; he was advertising his row of watercolors by rollerblading up and down in front of them. Most people didn't even glance in his direction. Evelyn loved Venice Beach. There was no one to tell her how to live. Not her mother. Not her sister. No one. And that's how she liked it.

Back home, she showered and put on some navy blue scrubs. After making a smoothie, she slid onto a stool in the kitchen and picked up the paper. *Local attorney accused of kidnapping son from wife's home. Christopher Manning, from Tustin, CA, was arrested yesterday after emergency services discovered a small boy hidden in his two-bedroom apartment . . .* She sipped her drink, turned the page, and stopped. Christopher Manning. She racked her brain. Manning. Hmm. The name rang a bell. Had she seen a patient with that name? Quite possibly. She'd seen hundreds of people during her career. Had someone named Manning sued her? No, she would definitely remember that.

She looked up at the clock. 7:45 a.m. She was late.

Knocking back the rest of the smoothie, she grabbed her bag and ran out the door.

Walking into the ER was like walking into the TV show. Except the people who worked there weren't as good-looking. Or even half as wealthy as its illustrious cast list. Harbor-UCLA's trauma department pulsated with activity, the freeway system regularly offering up drivers to its operating rooms—random victims of the careless and reckless.

"MVA. Coming through!" shouted a paramedic pushing a gurney down the passage. "Severe head injury and probable arm fracture." Evelyn liked Patrick, the paramedic who was often on duty when she was. "Into Trauma Room 1!" she said. "What have we got?"

"Patient is a Caucasian male in his late twenties with head injuries, lacerations to both arms, and a possible humerus fracture. Smells of ethanol and is obtunded. Discovered down on 3rd Street in San Pedro. Witness says he stumbled out of a door into the road.

Hit by a delivery truck, hence the head wounds. But we've also got slashes to the wrists."

"What are his vitals?" she said.

"110 over 60, with a pulse of 90. Respirations 30," Candy, the charge nurse, called over her shoulder. Evelyn began her clinical examination, checking the airways, breathing, and circulation. She inspected the cuts to the wrists that were still bleeding briskly, and reapplied the pressure dressings while she continued with her assessment.

"Do we have a name?"

"Miloš Radović."

"Miloš? Hello? Can you hear me? My name is Dr. Machin." She bent over the patient and opened his eyes. "Do you speak English, Miloš? You've been in a traffic accident. We're gonna take care of you." The young man was unresponsive, his eyelids giving no hint of movement.

Immediately the alarm on the monitor sounded.

"BP down to 80 systolic!" shouted Candy.

"Okay, people," said Evelyn. "Start two bags NS wide open. We need to send blood for CBC, CHEM-7 and electrolytes. Let's also get an EKG and send off a tox screen."

She was momentarily confused. What was the connection between an MVA and slashed wrists? This was about much more than a fight with a delivery truck. Chen, the other attending physician, managed to get instant access with a wide bore cannula and started some colloid solution to help the blood pressure. "Can someone get me some blood?" said Evelyn. "Get some O negative in here!"

One of the nurses hooked up a bag, while the rest of the team began assessing the head wounds and the arm fracture.

"We're not stabilizing him . . . what's going on?" Miloš's blood pressure was falling rapidly, in spite of the pressure to his wrists and the blood transfusion. "Come on. What's going on?"

She concluded that the bleeding from the wrists and the cuts to the head were not severe enough to cause the fall in pressure. He had to be bleeding internally. "Someone get radiology here now! We need chest and abdomen films now. And let's get an ultrasound of his abdomen and a CT scan of his head."

The radiologists hurried in, pushing equipment. The ultrasound suggested some fluid around the spleen, although the volume was small.

"He needs the OR!" shouted one of the attendings.

"Not so fast," said Evelyn. "Something doesn't add up. Is the tox screen back yet?"

"Not yet," said the attending, "but given the fluid, he needs a laparotomy."

"Whoa, let's slow down. We need to know more first. Patrick, is he on any meds?" The paramedic shrugged his shoulders.

She leaned in close to Miloš. His face was pallid, his breathing light and irregular. Although she was losing him, she wanted to try one more time. "Miloš, listen to me," she said. "You need to help us here. Your blood pressure is dropping and we're doing everything we can. Come on, please open your eyes. Please." His eyes fluttered, opening slightly. "Miloš, you slit your wrists, didn't you?"

"I want die." The young man's voice was feeble, barely audible.

Evelyn could feel his life ebbing away, as though he was retreating through a door and closing it slowly behind him. "Did you take any medication, Miloš?" No response. She tried again. "Listen, I don't know what's going on in your life, but let me tell you, it's not worth throwing it away. It really isn't."

As the team continued to work, Evelyn and her patient were in their own bubble. She blocked out the world to focus all her attention on the young man. "You slit your wrists, didn't you, Miloš? But later you had second thoughts. And that's a fantastic sign. It means you want to live. You do, Miloš. Trust me. That's why you ended up outside your apartment, looking for help. Am I right?" He looked away. He was regaining consciousness but was very weak. "Miloš, stay with me. Please. See all the people here? We're here to help you." She leaned in a little closer, almost whispering. "Come on, don't give up. Tell us what you did *before* you cut your wrists. Did you take any medication?"

Miloš screwed up his eyes; tears trickled from the corners.

That was enough.

"It's an overdose," she announced, looking up at her team.

"Are you sure?" said Chen.

"Trust me. I'm sure. Let's get a nasogastric tube in and start lavage. Let's also give Narcan in case opiates have been taken. That may explain the pinpoint unresponsive pupils."

Candy placed a wide bore NG tube and started a charcoal preparation routinely used in suspected overdoses. The Narcan took instant effect and Miloš suddenly became more alert. His blood pressure shot up; he sat upright and started talking aggressively in his mother tongue, before falling back and closing his eyes.

Evelyn tore open a dressing pack. "Miloš, I'm going to take a look at the cuts on your wrists. I need to clean them up and then I'll sew you right up like a cushion. You okay with that?"

He nodded. "Like cushion," he said, smiling weakly.

She injected local anesthetic into his left wrist and slowly took the dressings off. The cuts weren't quite as bad as she feared they might be. After irrigation, cautery, and some of her finest suturing, the wounds were closed and re-covered with fresh dressings. It didn't take long to repeat the trick on the other wrist.

"We'll put your arm in a splint until the swelling goes down a bit. Then we'll put it in a cast later," she said. "These guys will take care of you. They're a little rough, but they mean well." She smiled at her team. "And we will need to admit you for observation, Miloš. The psychologist may want to see you too." His face fell. Why couldn't he visit the cute female doctor who'd just saved his life instead?

"I'll see you for follow-up."

Evelyn walked to the reception area. Doctors and nurses buzzed around looking busy. She went and wrote on the huge whiteboard where they tracked each patient. Things had calmed down a little, which relieved some of the tension caused by her overflowing inbox.

"Hey Patty, good weekend?" she asked. Patty was African American, large, good-humored, and ate a couple of doctors for breakfast. She also smothered them with hugs and planted purple lipstick on their cheeks at regular intervals throughout the day. She was big in every sense of the word. A smile flashed across her face.

"Chris Rock couldn't have had a better one!" she replied,

emphasizing the word "rock." Evelyn backed up and turned round.

"You're kidding. He didn't."

"He did!" She held up her left hand and displayed a diamond big enough to choke on.

"Well, congratulations! Finally, a man prepared to put his money where his mouth is. I'm very happy for you."

"Thank you. Just gotta nail down a date."

Evelyn gave a look of mock disapproval. She wagged her finger at the woman whose smile could probably signal ships off the coast. "Uh-uh, Patty. No stone should come without a date. Give it back, honey. Give it back!"

"Are you kidding? He bails and I still make a couple of grand!"

"Now you're talkin'." Evelyn headed off down the hallway with a chart containing data from the path lab. Miloš was showing near-normal hemoglobin, which was a great relief; there was no more bleeding. The ER was rammed that day and it was a couple of hours before she was able to check back with her patient. She stuck her head round the curtain.

"Well, good afternoon, sir. How are you feeling?"

"They gave me bad food."

She looked at his chart. "Miloš Radović, right? Am I pronouncing that correctly?" He nodded and took a bite out of his bread roll. "Well, Miloš. All I can say is, 'Don't do that again.' You hear?"

Her smile made him blush a little.

Evelyn had dealt with hundreds of patients over the years. From gunshots to gangrene, she deemed herself unshockable. She'd also treated her fair share of suicide attempts. Sadly, Los Angeles served them up on a regular basis. But there was something about Miloš. He didn't seem like any of the other cases she'd dealt with. Not that there was such a thing as a typical case. People who attempted suicide spanned the entire demographic spectrum, and came from Palos Verdes as often as Compton. She looked at him, wondering how he'd ended up in the ER. He was over six feet, had thick dark hair, and, from the looks of it, he went to the gym. On a better day, he might even have picked up some modeling work. But then there were the eyes—sunken with dark rings.

"Miloš," she said. "You're not in trouble." She made some notes on the chart. "As I said when you were about to check out completely back there, life is worth something. Don't always know what that is, but trust me, it is. Have you got a girlfriend?"

He smiled. "In America, you ask many personal questions."

"Well, have you?"

"Girl I like, she is very pretty."

Evelyn said, "You're a good-looking dude, Miloš. You got a lot going for you." His face darkened. "Where did you grow up?"

"Bosnia. I'm living here seven years now."

"I'm going to refer you to a psychologist." He looked away. "Well, we can talk about that later." She turned to go. "Just don't make me sew you up again. We're practically out of thread."

She pulled back the curtain and left.

The roads in Torrance were sometimes eight lanes across but there was still congestion. Evelyn drove west on Sepulveda, passing the Sears on the corner of Hawthorne Boulevard. In a world filling up with superstores like Target and Costco, surely its days were numbered. Early evening yellows flickered across her windshield as she turned left onto Anza Avenue. When she arrived at Patterson Senior Living care home, it was almost 7 p.m.

The décor was designed by people with the aesthetic sensibilities of a chimpanzee. Evelyn had little patience with those who cut costs in care homes by rounding up goods from *Big Lots*. Well, maybe they adorned their own homes with pastel shades and faded flower prints. Perhaps they liked fake plants gathering dust. After all, it took all sorts. Several residents sat around reading magazines, while others looked like the chair was slowly consuming them, and getting up would be a problem. She hurried down the passageway.

Her mom was exactly where she'd left her at the end of her last visit: seated in front of the TV, knitting something purple. Evelyn walked over and kissed her on the head. After pouring herself a glass of orange juice, she perched on the edge of the couch.

Bonnie put down her knitting and pressed mute on the remote. "You're looking lovely today, honey," she said, looking up. She was only seventy-six, but was frail, with various chronic ailments. A visit from her daughter, however, always produced a sparkle in her eyes. They discussed her treatment, her neighbor with a TV permanently set at top volume, and the broken window latch. Evelyn would have happily spent the evening giving her opinions on angina or the latest prices at Home Depot but, inevitably, her mother zeroed in on her private life. "What happened to Bobby?" asked Bonnie. "I liked him. I thought he looked nice."

"Mom, Bob's dating Cheryl, remember? Plus, he's old enough to be my father."

"Reggie, then? You talk about him a lot." She picked up her knitting and began counting stitches.

"I play volleyball with him on Fridays."

"I like the bald man. He's very polite."

"Not when he's serving at me," said Evelyn under her breath.

Her mom sighed. "So how's Jasmine? She hasn't visited much recently."

"Mom, do we really have to go there?"

Bonnie resumed her knitting. "I thought you two had made up."

"She's in Torrance. With her boyfriend, the one we don't like."

"Kevin, wasn't it?"

"No. Kevin we like, remember? No, she's with Floyd."

"When did you last talk to her?"

"You're at the end of the row, Mom. You gotta pay attention."

"Still not talking?" Evelyn looked away. "What would your grandma say? She'd give you a good hiding, and quite right. She'd start telling you her pa's rescuer would have expected more; you know how she was. You'd think she actually met the man."

Evelyn went to the kitchen and returned with another glass of orange juice. Her mom said, "I heard from Katie yesterday. That was nice, although I worry about her. Told me she got into a fight with her boyfriend." She paused, thinking. "Now, what was his name again?"

Katie lived in DC and was doing something important with politicians. Evelyn didn't have much time for Katie's superiors but she was very proud of her sister. After starting out in the office of Jim Hahn, LA's city attorney, she'd followed him to city hall when he became mayor in 2001. Her time among the LA city elites didn't go unnoticed when she decided to apply for jobs in the nation's capital. Evelyn still remembered the day the call had come through. A week later, her sister was two and a half thousand miles away.

Evelyn missed her terribly, bending her ear for hours on the phone after Jasmine took off. Their childhood bond, forged by living with a volatile father, was strong and enduring. Some nights, she thought she might have sabotaged the prospects for an important bill in the House; Katie was far too kind to tell her to shut up.

Out of the blue, she blurted out, "Why didn't you leave Dad?"

Her mom didn't reply, but Evelyn knew she'd heard. Bonnie stopped her knitting and began perusing the pattern she'd torn from a magazine. "Please hand me that ball of wool," she said quietly.

"Sorry, Mom. I just don't know how you—"

"It could have been a lot worse."

"Mom!"

"Enough!" Bonnie took a deep breath. "It was a different world back then." The residue of pain seeping from the old lady's heart seemed to permeate the room. A sad smile crossed her face as she leaned across to pick up her daughter's hand. "Listen, honey. I know you don't . . . you know . . . believe any more, but you gotta hold on to hope. Because without hope, well, there's nothing, is there?" Evelyn pulled a loose thread on the couch. "I pray for you, honey. Every night I pray the Lord would do something in your life. You put on a brave face but I know you. You're like George Foreman in those grill commercials. He may be tough on the outside, but he's soft on the inside. And it's the inside that counts, my love. It's the inside where we live."

Evelyn rose from her seat and went to the kitchen. She put the carton of orange juice back in the fridge. "Listen, I gotta go. Now remember," she said, "make sure they give you the right quantities on the next prescription, so I don't have to keep coming down and tearing them off a strip down at Kaiser. I've had it with those idiots."

"Whatever you say, honey. Whatever you say."

Evelyn placed a ball of wool gently in her mother's lap, kissed her on the forehead, and left.

A short time later, she was sitting in her car next to the curb, punching a speed dial number. No answer. She tried again. No joy. She tried texting. *Happy Birthday*, she wrote. *Go away*, came the reply. Her phone buzzed. She picked it up.

"Jasmine? Is that you? Did you have a good birth—"

"Mom! Go. Away!"

"I just wanted to wish you a happy birthday." Silence.

"Where are you?"

"Oh, just down in Hermosa with friends."

"Liar. You're at the end of the street. I can see you. Now, why don't you put the car in drive and go home?"

"Jas—!" The phone went dead. She drove down the street and stopped outside an apartment block. As she watched, someone came to the window and pulled down the blinds. So much for inconspicuous surveillance.

She threw the phone onto the passenger seat and drove off.

Back home, Evelyn collapsed onto the couch and put her head in her hands. No tears came. Just a dull ache—the same one she usually felt after contact with her daughter.

She took a couple of pills, and went to bed.

~ 8 ~

A SPOT OF BOTHER

Whenever I hear anyone arguing for slavery, I feel a strong impulse to see it tried on him personally.
~ Abraham Lincoln

February 9, 2005

Aidan arrived in chambers a little late, tossed his coat onto a hook, and walked over to his pigeonhole. When he turned round, he almost bumped into Harry. "Mr. Fenwick waiting for you in the interview room, sir. I've given the PCMH on the Gorski case to your junior, Ms. Dunbar."

"Thanks, Harry," he called out as he hurried off toward his office.

The senior clerk followed him in. "Did you hear Mourinho last night at the press conference?"

"Can't say I did." Aidan dumped a huge brief onto his desk.

"Ref, he need glasses," said Harry in a mock Portuguese accent that sounded closer to Indian than anything else. "Even I see offside and I sit on other side of moon." He guffawed and marched out of the room, calling out behind him, "Priceless! Worth every penny!" The man was clearly in a good mood. So much the better. Far less stress for everyone.

Tommy entered with a blind.

"That going up today?" Aidan patted the windowsill behind him.

"When I have a spare minute, sir."

"Fantastic. You're a star."

"Mr. Fenwick's here for your con, sir."

"Been waiting long?"

"Quarter of an hour."

Aidan grabbed a sheaf of papers and walked into the interview room. A bespectacled man in a dark suit rose to greet him. "So sorry

I'm late, Bill. You get coffee or tea?" He looked at the table where a china teacup sat, recently emptied, next to a half-eaten cookie. "I see the clerks are doing their job. Very good."

He sat down and undid the brief.

"Sorry for dumping this one on you, Aidan. We had Perkins over at McIntyre's, but he pulled out. Case starts in a couple of weeks, which isn't ideal, I'm afraid. Mind you, it might grab some headlines."

Aidan shuffled some papers about. He would normally have had a month or two to prepare a big case, but not this time. It would mean a few late nights but that was better than turning down the work. He hated doing that. "No worries, Bill. Let's get stuck in. Can't say I like our chances much, though." He picked up his pen and opened his pad. "Okay, hit me."

Fenwick turned his attention to the papers open in front of him. "Dorina Ibanescu. Romanian woman, aged twenty-four, claims Bakic was in the pub during the exchange. She's now in a shelter in Hampstead. Tatiana Kopkalic, Serbian, aged twenty-five, is the one with most of the ammunition. Trafficking, rape, the works. I'm expecting them to peg the trafficking charge first; then, having established the reliability of the main witnesses, our man will look so bad, the jury will suspect he planned the Beslan massacre. I'm afraid we're going to have to go heavy on the prostitutes. That's our only hope."

"So what do we know about Dorina?" Aidan flicked through some papers and started reading. "From Pitești, apparently. Claims her boyfriend, Razvan Moceanu, invited her to come to the UK for a job. Waitressing. Arrived last July. She claims she was met by the boyfriend at the airport and taken to a pub. Money exchanged hands. Do we know any more about him?" He looked up at Fenwick.

The solicitor shook his head. "So far nothing on him. We've got an artist's drawing, that's it."

"Okay, so Dorina spends the first few months in a brothel in King's Cross. She's forced to hand over her passport. She's lost, confused, distraught that her so-called boyfriend has just sold her, and she's terrified, of course. Apparently she was raped repeatedly by Dragan's brothers, Goran and Jakov. Anything on them?"

"Nope. Disappeared."

"So she's there from August until November . . . o-kay." He turned a page, hesitating. "But in November she's driven to a different brothel in Camden Town. A place run by our man, Dragan, apparently. What do we know about her time in Camden Town? Does she make any friends? Can she identify other key players?"

"Whoa, whoa, one at a time. Right. Apparently she never left the building." Fenwick rifled through some papers. "Passport stolen, bars on the windows, and she was trapped. Let's see. Friends? Apparently, she did try, but as soon as it looked like she was making progress, the "friend" disappeared. Plus, she spent an awful lot of time locked in her room. It was a miserable existence."

Aidan pushed a button on the intercom. "Tommy? Could you bring in some more tea? Thanks." He turned back to Fenwick. "By the way, what do we know about the boyfriend?"

"Not much. A name. Razvan Moceanu. That's about it. Records show he entered the country about a year ago. After that, nothing. Maybe he slipped across the Channel. False passport. No way of knowing."

"So . . . ," Aidan glanced down at the paper in his hand, "Dorina's forced to work as a prostitute for several months. What happened to the money she earned?"

"Well, that's often why they keep going. She states that they promised to let her go, once she'd paid her dues. Apparently, some of the girls managed to pay their way out. At least, that's what she was told. It's all lies, of course, but desperate people end up grasping at straws. It's all in there. Actually, she talks mostly about Goran and Jakov. Funny that. Dragan doesn't feature as much, which gives us a whiff of a defense. I think we want to pin most of this on those characters, if possible. It's Tatiana who's the problem. She's claiming rape. Why go for a Section 18 or 20, when you're accusing a man of rape?"

Tommy backed into the room holding a tray with tea paraphernalia. He unloaded tea and biscuits, and left.

"Milk?" said Aidan.

"Milk and two sugars, thanks."

"So what's our boy have to say?"

"Zilch. Called for an interpreter but told him squat. I believe that's your department, Aidan. You're good with thugs." The barrister smirked. Fenwick went on, "Thing is, he probably has a bunch of aliases. The name we have, Dragan Bakic, may not even be his real name. It probably isn't."

Later, alone in his office, Aidan picked up the photo of his client. He looked into his eyes. The expression was blank, as though the man was staring right through the camera. No, hold on. There was an emotion lurking in there. It wasn't completely blank. He had seen it many times and it hid a multitude of secrets. Dragan would need careful handling.

The phone rang; he picked it up.

"Mr. Manning, it's your dad on line one."

"Okay, thanks." The line clicked. "Dad? Hi . . . yes, I did . . . I know, what a goal, that was something, wasn't it? So can you make Simon's game on Saturday? Oh . . . you can't? I thought you had it in your diary. Okay, that's fine . . . yup, yup, big case. I'll let you know how it goes." As he put the phone down, he murmured, "Or perhaps you can just read about it in the paper."

When he arrived home that night, Aidan poured himself a glass of wine. He lived in a comfortable flat in West Kensington. Almost all the four-story Edwardian terraced houses in that portion of West London had been converted into apartments during the post-war period. He was lucky to buy in before the prices rose to eyewatering levels. It boasted three bedrooms, one for sleeping, one full of bookcases, and a box room for dumping piles of paper and clothes.

He walked into the kitchen, pulled a Tupperware container out of the fridge, and peered at its contents. Then he exercised some faith. It definitely looked like fish, but the vintage was harder to discern. He'd cooked on Tuesday, so it was surely within the three-day limit. The pale pink substance he was holding might not look good, but microwaves were modern-day miracle workers; they could turn almost anything into food.

He spooned his dinner onto a plate, and pushed it into the

microwave. Two minutes later, it dinged. Ding for done. Ding for "Couldn't you be bothered to cook properly tonight?" Well, no, he couldn't. It had been a long day and cooking was a twice-weekly activity, generating leftovers to be consumed on the remaining evenings. He thought he was doing reasonably well just by including some semblance of green on his plate now and then. The ding should be replaced with a soothing voice saying, "Well done, sir, you've worked hard today. Enjoy your meal and have a nice day." On second thoughts, perhaps not. Too American.

He was sitting in the living room with a tray on his lap when he heard the door latch click. His son, Simon, let himself in, and marched into the kitchen. The young man was soon pouring himself a glass of Chardonnay. "Your wine supplies are running low!" he said loudly.

"Then bring a crate next time you come," Aidan replied, setting his tray aside and joining his son in the kitchen. Simon plonked himself down on a chair, his shoulders slumped. He looked across at his father. "I'm in a bit of trouble."

"Oh yes?" said Aidan sitting down opposite.

"Two days ago, I was at a party."

"With Beth?"

"No. Unfortunately. Otherwise none of this would have happened." He took a deep breath. "Anyway, I was with Jerry Maddox from Two Para, just back from Iraq, and we went out for a few drinks. I've known the guy since uni. Nice chap. So we're out with a bunch of his army mates and you know how it is—heavy drinking, sexist jokes, a slew of racist epithets. Not exactly my scene and, you know, maybe I shouldn't have been there, but I was. I couldn't leave. So anyway, I got home a bit late, a little unsteady on my feet, which Beth just hates, and she just blew up."

"So you had a row, what's so—"

"It gets worse. Someone had put a thong in my pocket as a joke. It fell out as I was taking my jacket off."

Aidan whistled through his teeth. "Okay, now I get it."

"So what am I supposed to do? Now she won't talk to me at all. Nada for two days. It's just so ridiculous, I can't stand it."

Aidan looked at the man sitting in front of him with his head in his hands. He was twenty-two, broad, and his normal slightly cocky demeanor was nowhere in sight. He hardly recognized him. It was true, Simon could be a little arrogant, not to mention sanctimonious at times, but all in all he was proud of him. After university, he'd worked his contacts book and found work as an associate producer at the BBC. Quite prestigious. So he'd rowed with his wife. Who didn't?

But what had happened to his religion? Getting drunk with squaddies was hardly the behavior of a regular churchgoer. Aidan used to take him to church when he was young, and even though he himself had wandered off, something must have stuck, because Simon still attended. "She'll come round. Just give her time. Marriage is built on trust and— "

"I didn't do anything wrong!"

"It's called reasonable doubt, Simon. And you just placed some in her mind."

"But she should know me by now, that I'd never—"

"Doesn't make any difference if the action creates doubt. Listen. Marriage is built on trust, which takes time; and so far, you've been married just under a year. Now stop fretting, get yourself a towel, and crash in the spare room. No harm done. Let me talk to her."

Simon got up and trundled upstairs to bed.

Aidan opened a cupboard and pulled out a small plastic bottle. A rhythmic throb was pounding away behind his temples. After knocking back three aspirin, he collapsed into an armchair, picked up the remote and jabbed it at the TV. He ingested the news until *Newsnight* came on. Jeremy Paxman's sneering tone intensified his headache, so he turned it off and headed for bed. After his nightly ablutions, he dragged on some boxer shorts, and slid between the sheets. But instead of falling straight to sleep, he reached over and picked up two small photographs.

A woman's face smiled up at him. She was sitting on top of a bus in Ecuador. He remembered the day just over twenty years ago when they'd taken the trolleybus, an *autoferro*, from Cuenca to Chunchi. The roof was piled high with huge sacks. They'd climbed up on top and spent the journey screaming out Bruce Springsteen songs as the vehicle jerked from side to side, barely clinging to the track on its way round the mountain. The snapshot captured her laughter, her beauty. Her long brown hair streamed out behind her and she was threatening to throw a banana at the camera. The day had been intoxicating. They'd sat on the roof because life tasted better up there. In fact, it tasted so good, he thought he would never experience joy like it ever again.

And he never had.

He looked at the other photograph. A man's face was covered with goggles, but it wasn't hard to see his expression. He was beaming from ear to ear as he plunged toward the earth. His brother, Bruce, had enjoyed fear as much as gorgeous women and risks on the stock market. Aidan remembered watching him fall, remembered him jumping up and down after he'd landed, his jubilation ringing out around the airfield. The joy from long ago wrapped itself around his heart, and blended with his sadness.

Ten years felt like a day.

~ 9 ~

INJURY TIME

Every nerve that can thrill with pleasure, can also agonize with pain.
~ Horace Mann

February 10, 2005

Aidan put down his knife and fork; he wiped the corner of his mouth with a napkin, and sipped his coffee. Korazin poured himself a glass of juice and sat down next to his guest. Gamaliel entered through a side door, carrying yet more food. He put it down and took his seat at the head of the table.

"You know, I could get used to this," said the Englishman. "I'm starting to enjoy the food, the weather's a lot better than London, and as far as I can tell, I'm not yet going insane . . . unless what I've just said means I'm officially certifiable!" He laughed.

Evelyn entered the room. She was wearing blue shorts and a sports bra; her auburn hair was tied back in a ponytail. Aidan thought she looked gorgeous. Korazin watched his gaze and smiled.

"Good afternoon, Evelyn," said the lucidus. "I believe we've caught you napping again this evening. Aidan's currently in a deep sleep, while you are dozing in front of Letterman. Are you hungry?"

"Not really. I feel a bit disoriented, to be honest. Got a lot on my plate. By the way, do you see everything that's happening to me back home?" She poured herself a glass of water and sat down. "Don't worry, I'm not getting much sex right now anyway. Be my guest, watch me on the john, if you want. I don't really care." Korazin's face reddened. "Well, look at you!" she said. "Never thought I'd make you guys blush. Thought you'd have seen it all by now."

The lucidus cleared his throat. "Well, mostly. I—"

Evelyn suddenly stood up. "Listen. Could we could cut the religious talk today and go biking instead? Any chance of that?"

Korazin breathed a sigh of relief. The comment about the john had left him a little flustered. He glanced at his companion, who nodded. "Sure," he said, rising from his seat. "Front of the house. Fifteen minutes. I'll bring the bikes round."

When they met later, both lucidi were decked out in cycling gear. This time it was Gamaliel who was wearing the *maillot jaune*. Aidan caught Evelyn stifling a grin. Korazin tossed him a snack. He was about to tear off the wrapper when he noticed writing down one side. *Manna Bar*. Manna Bar?

"You've got to be kidding. Manna? What is it?"

"That's what the Israelites said."

Aidan read out the slogan. "The food of the lucidi."

"Indeed. Made from various grains, lucidus sugar—the natural kind—and secret ingredients." He winked.

Aidan took a bite. "A bit chewy." He gave some to Evelyn.

"Mmm, a little sweet for me, but not bad."

"Wait, it has a sell-by date," said Aidan. "Is that a joke?"

Korazin smiled. "Asaph's idea. You'll see it has today's date. Make a batch, eat a batch, that's how we roll. They're like Cinderella at the ball. They turn into pumpkins at midnight." He laughed, took a huge bite, and licked his lips. "Mmm. ¡Cilantro y azúcar! El sabor del cielo. ¡Vámonos!"

They headed off up the front drive, Aidan making sure he didn't drop too far behind. For some reason, he felt full. "Sure you didn't give us lembas bread?" he called out.

"Do I look like an elf to you, Aidan?" Korazin looked back and bellowed with laughter. Standing on his pedals, he powered up the track at a pace that had the rest of them gasping to keep up. Aidan thought he was fitter at home. He soon found himself at the back. The sky was cloudless and a light wind stroked their faces as they pedaled up into the hills. Before long, they had turned off the stony track and were cycling along a narrow path. They made their way gradually up toward the head of a hiking trail, passing through a forest heavy with the scent of pine needles. When they'd been cycling for about an hour, they stopped for a rest. They found a rock to sit on and pulled out water bottles to slake their thirst.

Aidan put his hands on his hips and arched his back. "Ooh, my lower back. What kind of body did you give me this time? It hurts."

"Same as last time, Aidan," said Korazin. "That's what bodies do, I'm afraid. They hurt. They're supposed to."

"But why so much? You know, that's a good question. Why do bodies have to hurt so much? Think how much pain you could eliminate just by redesigning the body."

Evelyn's response was unexpected. "Well, actually, your body is remarkably well put together." She looked across at Korazin, who raised his eyebrows.

"You said it, not me." The lucidus stood up and walked over. "Aidan," he said, "let's talk nerve endings. The body is full of them, but they aren't distributed evenly. They seem to be located exactly where they're needed. You have a lot in your skin, for example. Lots in your fingers. And your face has got them all over the place. The eye is a thousand times more sensitive than the sole of your foot, and for good reason. It needs a lot of protection. Your skin is specially designed to protect you from the external world, but once you get past it, your internal organs are relatively free of nerve endings. You can burn the stomach, slice through the brain or stick needles into your major organs, and you won't feel much of anything. Why? Because you're already protected from the outside. Mind you, that doesn't mean you can't feel pain internally. Catch!" He threw Aidan a bicycle pump. "The intestines are acutely sensitive to inflation. When you have colic, that's your body telling you something's gone badly wrong. And if you haven't passed a kidney stone, you know nothing about pain. It's excruciating."

"Okay, okay," said Aidan. "I get all that, but I still don't understand why it has to hurt so much. For goodness' sake, once I know I'm in pain, I make adjustments. I pull my hand out of the fire. Why does it have to keep hurting so much?"

"You want to get rid of pain?" Gamaliel enjoyed this particular challenge. "Let me tell you about a Croatian family I know. They have a very unusual condition; they're missing a single gene: SCN9A. It's the gene that codes for pain perception. It regulates the pain signals transmitting the sensation of pain to the brain. When it's faulty, it affects a person's ability to feel pain. So one of the family, Dimitar I think it is, he doesn't respond to cold water. He goes swimming in the dead of winter when the water's just above freezing. Swims for hours and emerges hypothermic. He's been told to stop, but he just keeps doing it. And then there's Raisa, who has a similar problem. She doesn't detect temperature either. In her case, she eats piping hot food as though it's lukewarm. She often gets blisters on her tongue. And as for Bepo, he's the worst. Probably because he's a boy. He went to the doctor a few weeks ago, complaining he couldn't bend his arm. Turns out he'd fallen off his bike months earlier and broken it."

"Fine, fine," said Aidan impatiently. "But you still haven't really explained why it can't be made . . . I don't know . . . less painful. Why can't we have some kind of mechanism that tells us we're in trouble, like a flash of light behind the eyes or something, so that we'd act to prevent further damage occurring?"

"Good question. Which is why you won't be surprised to hear it's been tried. A team of doctors once designed a pain system to do exactly that. Alert the subject to a complication. First, they installed a hearing aid that buzzed when the sensors detected pain signals. Problem was, most people kept overriding the warning. They just ignored the buzz, as long as they didn't feel pain."

"So why didn't they try electric shocks or something?"

"They did. But again the subject would just turn off the system whenever they wanted to do something that might produce pain. Even highly intelligent people would do it."

"So put it out of their reach."

"You finally got there, Aidan. The system has to be beyond your ability to tamper with it. And you've already got that. It's designed to protect you, to alert you to danger, and turning it off can end in disaster. Plus, you've got to ask yourself what you want. Electric shocks every few seconds, or a nuanced pain system that protects you from danger?"

"Come on, let's get moving," said Evelyn, eager to reach the summit. The trail took them high above 8,000 feet. Soon they were above the tree line, surrounded by rocky outcrops. The sky was a dark, rich blue. It became harder to find their way, but the lucidi pressed on. They were fit and pushed the pace. By the time they reached the top, the humans were gasping for breath.

"Wow," said Aidan, bending over to catch his breath.

"Feels good, huh?" Korazin handed him a water bottle.

He stood up and arched his back. "Okay, I give up. I need some pain to feel alive. Is that your point?"

Korazin grinned at him. They all looked down into the valley, drinking in the beauty before their eyes. Aidan turned to the tall lucidus by his side. "Well, sir. To get down, I could use some of those wings you hide on your back."

"Wings?" said Gamaliel.

"Yes, wings."

"I don't use wings."

"Yes, you do. We saw them last time."

"No, you didn't."

"I saw your jacket move."

"Aidan, Aidan. Just listen to you. You're a skeptical lawyer, who presents evidence to the court. From someone who makes reasoned arguments, I'm a little disappointed with 'I saw your jacket move!' Oh, I'm afraid you're going to have to do a lot better than that. And who would have thought it? You used to love singing 'Hark the Herald,' and now look at you! You're accusing a lucidus, nay, a seraph, of being deceptive. What has happened to you?" He laughed loudly.

"Come on. Show us those wings!"

"Here!" said Gamaliel, throwing his water bottle to the Englishman. He mounted his bike and started careering down the mountain, followed shortly after by Korazin.

"Nice work, guys," said Evelyn a little sarcastically. "Abandoning us on the top of a mountain." She untied her hair and shook it out.

"I have a hunch they know what they're doing." Aidan watched as her thick auburn hair tumbled down onto her tanned shoulders. He couldn't help wondering what she looked like back home. Her eyes, in particular, were striking. They found a nearby boulder and sat quietly for a while, taking in the view. Down in the valley, the densely packed forest thinned, giving way to heathland and, far in the distance, a patchwork of farmers' fields, quilted to the horizon.

The sinking sun was being lowered down the dome of the sky, the air cooling as it descended. Their unspoken curiosity hung between them until Aidan glanced at Evelyn.

"You okay?" he asked.

She hesitated. "I dunno, it's like they know everything about me. It's all a bit intrusive, if you ask me. And I could do without all the religious mumbo jumbo." She paused. "'Course, it's beautiful up here. Almost *too* beautiful. Just waiting for them to hand us the bill." She smiled. "So what about you? You ever into religion?" Aidan looked down and picked up a pebble, which he tossed over the edge. "Come on. Spill the beans. What happened?"

"Nothing."

"No, no, don't think you can just sit there, mister. Out with it. What happened?"

Aidan didn't reply.

He could still see his face, hear his voice, the memory triggering anger at its recall. Jack Stonehouse was the curate of the Anglican Church where he worshipped in his early twenties. Aidan knew him socially, though he always sensed his connection with Jack's crowd was tenuous at best. Nevertheless, he joined in heartily with the banter that swirled around the pub after Sunday services. In fact, he felt sufficiently secure not to seek clarification when a weekend in the country was mentioned as they all left one evening. He was sure he'd caught the date, the rendezvous, and the recommended clothing for hiking and clay pigeon shooting. There was a cheery goodbye; he thought his social life was looking up.

The following Friday evening saw him striding confidently toward the group assembled on the pavement outside the church. To be included with some of the more fashionable people from church was a step up. It felt good to be included at last. Such was his chirpy mood, he didn't register what he was seeing as he approached.

One by one, three people squeezed themselves into the back seats of the Volvo station wagon. He could hear their laughter as they closed the back doors. Another one, an attractive girl named Melanie, opened the passenger door and got in. The rear of the car faced him and it was easy to see the trunk was completely packed with luggage. Although it was plain as day that only one seat remained—for the driver—it didn't once cross his mind that the car was now full. If he'd observed more closely, he might have had time to turn back and avoid embarrassment. As it was, he walked right up to Jack, who was applying the finishing touches to the roof rack.

"What are *you* doing here?" said the curate, turning to look at the man in front of him with a mixture of curiosity and irritation. The look on Jack's face became imprinted indelibly on Aidan's memory. There was a sneering quality to it; the brows furrowed and the head held back as though he was peering down at an unwelcome canine. The question itself was laden with contempt.

As he sat looking down into the valley, he remembered his first, visceral response. He recalled the dryness of his mouth and the cold sweat spreading across his forehead. A splitting headache followed shortly afterward. He was humiliated and in shock, a swirl of emotions that initially rendered him speechless. He wanted to ask why there wasn't a seat for him, but realized that would just embarrass him further. So he simply retreated, mumbling, "Er, I'm sorry, I must have made a mistake. Sorry." Aidan remembered the burning sensation in his chest and stomach as he turned and headed back toward the Tube station. He hurried along, eager to escape the terrific pain welling up in his heart. Of course, it made no difference how fast he walked. He carried the wound inside, throbbing behind his forehead and pounding in his chest.

As soon as he'd turned the corner, he sank down onto the steps of a fine Georgian terraced house, one of the many for which Kensington was known. He sat absorbing his enormous social faux pas, beginning with embarrassment, before moving on to anger at himself for not turning back sooner. The anger quickly dissipated, however, to be replaced by humiliation, and from that flowed a different kind of anger, projected not at himself but at Jack.

The following Sunday, he slipped into church late, hoping to avoid attention. The ploy failed. After the service, the curate moved through the pews and soon found him at the back. He said in a jokey voice, "Did you think you were coming to Somerset last Friday? After you left, I saw you had a bag." Aidan remembered looking up at him nonplussed, as though the man had arrived from Mars. Then the penny dropped. The man wasn't intentionally trying to humiliate him. He simply didn't care; he was bereft of compassion.

Jack's deficit in this area was well known to the congregation, though it was quietly tolerated, since the curate possessed charisma. His jokes from the pulpit about his poor listening skills and lack of empathy generated polite sniggers of recognition. However, to Aidan, Jack's apparent awareness of this deficiency merely added to his guilt. If he knew he lacked compassion, then he shouldn't be a curate. In some denominations, leaders were called pastors, weren't they? Shepherds who cared for their flocks. What a sick joke that was.

The following Sunday, as he left church, he told the "friends" who'd sat in the back of the Volvo that he intended to find a congregation closer to home. But that never happened. And he never saw the "friends" again either.

He stared at the ground, reflecting on how far he'd come since that Friday evening many years ago. The whole experience should have washed over him, leaving him free to pursue his life goals uninhibited. That would have happened to any normal, sane person. So they hadn't invited him. So what? A simple enough misunderstanding. He had made plenty of other friends in the intervening years. In fact, his social life had blossomed after taking up full-time employment as a barrister a year later. And in many ways, the pain had receded . . . but not entirely. Evelyn's question about church still touched a nerve. The incident on the pavement next to a full car still rankled deep inside, like a wound refusing to heal, one that remained perpetually raw and sensitive to the touch.

Evelyn waited. The man by her side was lost in his thoughts. "A penny for something in there? Anything at all?"

"I avoid religion." He stared out over the valley, avoiding Evelyn's gaze, which seemed to pierce his soul. "Enough about me," he said. "What about you?"

Evelyn scuffed her feet against the dirt. "Well, I'm from LA. Dad used to work on the oil derricks, Mom at home with all the talent."

"Happy families?"

"Could have been worse. Dad got into fights. Patched him up more times than I can count. My mom, though, she could have done anything, but back then women didn't get to combine career and family."

"You got siblings?"

"A sister. Katie. Lives in DC. She's dating a guy in musicals. He's in *Cats* right now, I think. Last year it was *Phantom*."

"Nice."

"Yeah. Nice work if you can get it, right? And if you don't run off with the leading lady. Had Katie on the phone just the other day, all riled up about some party they'd been to."

Aidan leaned back, enjoying the breeze on his face. "So . . . you married?"

"Are you always so direct?"

"I'm a barrister. Can't help it."

"No, I'm not married."

"Kids?"

She hesitated. "A daughter. Jasmine. Raised her and put myself through medical school at the same time. Not sure what I'm prouder of, that she's still alive or the degree on my wall."

"Kids'll drive you nuts, though, right?"

Evelyn looked away. "You got that right."

A kestrel flew up, hovered for a moment, then dropped toward the valley floor. They both followed its dive, briefly lost in their thoughts.

"Has your family always lived in LA?" he said, changing the subject.

Evelyn's face brightened. "Well, I don't know much about my dad's family. My mother's, on the other hand, I can trace back six generations. My grandma in particular was one incredible lady. Florence Doyle. Magnificent woman, gray hair tied up in a bun, black lace, big skirts, used a broom like a weapon. She was four feet ten and strong as an ox." She paused. "*Her* mom, my great-grandma, lived in San Antonio, Texas, and by all accounts was a first-class bitch. Her name was Dorothy. When my grandma had my mom in 1939, just before the war, that was it. Out of wedlock, out of the house. Strict Catholics, of course. What do you expect? So, my grandma came cross-country to California."

"She sounds memorable."

Evelyn sighed and began recounting events from over thirty years ago as though they'd taken place last week. They seemed so vivid, so real, so firmly imprinted on her memory, she could have described every detail of the room.

The ritual took place every Thanksgiving, late in the evening, once the sun had retreated and the shutters were closed for the night. Grandma Florence turned off all the lights and gathered the family around the table. All except for Wayne, Evelyn's dad, who knew when his presence wasn't required. She lit candles and placed them around the room. Evelyn remembered the atmosphere of reverence that was created for the story to come. When they were all seated around the small kitchen table, Florence would go to the mantel and take down two items that lay there throughout the year.

A locket and a whistle.

"It's the night of April 14, 1912." She injected a conspiratorial tone into her voice to heighten the drama. Her eyes widened. "My father, named Fearghas for his forebears, is on the deck of the *Titanic*, looking out to sea. The stars are shining brightly and the ocean is calm. Up ahead lies his destiny, though he doesn't know it." While she sipped slowly from her coffee cup, the girls squirmed in their seats. She continued. "Well, just before midnight . . . CRASH! They strike an iceberg and the great ship begins to sink. You can imagine, can't you, how terrifying it must have been for my father. He never had a chance of reaching a lifeboat. He traveled in steerage, my dears, where they put the poor folks and, of course, he was Irish." Evelyn and Katie couldn't take their eyes off their grandma. They knew what was coming but sat enthralled.

"So he does what he can, helping the women and children into the lifeboats until the ship is reaching its final . . . catastrophic . . . end. He tries to keep dry as long as he can, but eventually . . . time's up! He can't swim, but he climbs up on a railing, looks around, and bids farewell to this world. And in he jumps. *Sploosh!*"

The girls yelped with surprise and started giggling. Their grandma didn't miss a beat. "So there he is, flailing about, sinking into the murky depths. He's about to meet his doom." She paused, enjoying the moment. "When suddenly, out of nowhere, a man dives in, swims down and down, and with a mighty arm pulls him up to safety."

"Hurray!" shouted the girls, jumping up and down on their seats.

"Settle down now," said Bonnie.

Florence lowered her voice. "So there they are, lying on a piece of wood. And when your great-grandfather finally opens his eyes, he sees the kindest face you ever did see. An Englishman. Saint George. And a dead dragon lying next to him, his tongue hanging out and smoke billowing out of his mouth!" Florence let out a howl of laughter. The girls descended into fits of giggles that continued for quite a while until their mom could restore order.

Their grandma became serious. "Anyway," continued Florence, squaring her shoulders. "So they're lying on the raft and the man hands over two things. A locket." She paused. "And a whistle. He offers no explanation. It's all very mysterious. Open the locket, my dear." Evelyn carefully undid the clasp and opened the little door. Inside was a faded sepia photograph of a woman wearing a long dress meticulously embroidered along the seams. Her grandma always asked the same question. "Whose photograph do you put in a locket, girls?"

"Someone you love."

"That's right," said Florence. "Someone you love. Whoever that lady is, it's someone he loved. Probably his wife, I'm guessing. So he kept her picture close to his heart."

"Aren't lockets for girls?" Katie squeaked.

"Not always. They're used by people to keep a secret. Even boys like to keep secrets sometimes."

"Oh," said the little girl. "Can I see?" They each took turns admiring the photograph, then handed the locket back to their grandma, who set it aside and picked up the whistle.

"One toot, and one toot only, mind." She handed them a genuine brass whistle from the *Titanic*. The ship's name was engraved on the side. Evelyn ran her finger over the lettering, enjoying the weight of the whistle in her hand. It felt heavy. Both girls were allowed to blow it once, while their mother and grandma put their hands over their ears and grimaced. When they'd finished, they put the whistle back on the table and sat quietly, ready for what came next. It was always the same, and it always made their mother cry. Evelyn, who was holding her mother's hand, could often feel her squeeze more tightly as she listened to her own mother's voice.

Florence continued, almost whispering. "And if the story stopped there, it would be a tragedy, nothing more. But it doesn't. That dear man, who thrust the locket and whistle into my father's hands, well, we discovered he'd done something quite extraordinary. He'd left us with a picture of the dear Lord Jesus. Because just like the Lord Jesus, who loved us so much that he plunged into our world to save us, he too had done the same for my father. Sweethearts, if there's some savin' to be done, the Lord he'll come to the rescue, of that you can be sure."

"What happened to the man?" Evelyn always asked the same question. She knew the answer, but for some reason, although it pained her heart, she wanted to hear her grandma's reply.

"He passed away, God rest his soul."

"That's not fair," she said.

Instead of responding, her grandma continued, "Let's bow our heads, shall we? On this day of Thanksgiving, we give thanks for your servant, who gave his life so that another man could live. As the descendants of the man who was saved, grant that each day, we might become people . . .

Who give rather than take,
Who listen rather than speak,
Who love rather than hate.

We give you thanks, gracious Lord, for life and health and breath. And we thank you for the one true sacrifice of the Lord Jesus Christ, who gave up his life to save us. Amen."

Evelyn couldn't remember all of the prayer, but she remembered enough. Toward the end, her voice contained a cynical edge that surprised Aidan. He felt a gap opening up between them. The quiet that followed was unsettling. Suddenly, she spat out, "'Course, all that 'coming to the rescue' is just a crock." Her bitterness spewed up from below. Though he'd sensed a change in her mood, the comment still caught him off guard.

Aidan didn't know what to say, so he sat in silence. The remnants of joy left over from her story slowly dissolved, leaving him feeling depleted. Her anger weighed heavily on him, even as the evening wind soothed his face, his soul.

~ 10 ~

LAMENT

Therefore I will not keep silent;
I will speak out in the anguish of my spirit,
I will complain in the bitterness of my soul.
~ Job

February 12, 2005

Evelyn found herself sitting on a chair in the hall. Her heart sank. She wasn't in the mood. She rose from her seat and looked out toward the ocean. Well, at least they vary the weather. The leaden sky was a mottled collection of grays and creams, the clouds scudding along furiously at a couple of hundred feet. A strong wind was bending the branches of the eucalyptus trees growing on the edges of the property. It felt as though it was late afternoon, but since she'd just arrived, it was hard to tell exactly.

She walked into the Descartes Room.

Gamaliel rose to his feet as she entered. "Ah, Evelyn. Such a pleasure to see you again. Please. Come and take a seat."

She glanced at the lucidus standing at the other end of the room, barely registering his presence. Unable to look Gamaliel in the eye, she ran her finger distractedly along a picture frame hanging on the wall to her right. The house was fascinating—she'd just noticed *Las Meninas* by Velázquez in the hall—and one day, if they ever invited her back, she was determined to explore it. But not today. She often went through a low in February and this year was no exception.

"You want me to take a seat?" she said. Her tone was aggressive and offhand. She looked up at the ceiling. "What? More bonding? Is that supposed to make me feel better? Is that it?" She felt a little guilty for speaking to the lucidus rudely, but it was too late. He could handle it, surely. "Listen," she continued. "You think you know me?

Sounded last time like you thought you knew me. Well, you don't. You can't possibly know what I've been through." She paused. "One other thing. If this place is supposed to give me some answers, then perhaps you could direct me to the person who's really in charge."

"The Father."

"Who?"

"The Father. He's the one in charge."

"O-kay. So if he's the one in charge, why aren't I talking to him then?" Her hostility seemed to increase her self-confidence. "He's never shown his face around here, has he? Is he scared? Scared we might go too far?"

Gamaliel watched his guest impassively. He neither smiled nor frowned. He simply waited until she had finished speaking. "You're right, I don't know what you've been through. But I would like to extend to you my deepest sympathies. If you would like to speak to the Father, he's always available. He—"

Evelyn interrupted. "Enough! I can already guess what he'd say. In any case, hasn't he got a universe to run? You know, you should have left me in my bed tonight." She walked past the lucidus, opened the French doors, and went out onto the patio. A layer of mist was hovering above the ocean. It was starting to drizzle. The wind had dropped.

Time stalled; she looked behind her. The lucidus had disappeared. Yet she didn't feel alone. Quite the opposite. After sitting down on one of the loungers, she leaned her head back against a cushion, eyes closed. Her limbs felt heavy, and though she tried to resist it, the sense of other rested in the back of her mind. It was inescapable; she could neither avoid nor control it. After a while, she leaned forward and wiped the water off her skirt. It splashed onto the patio. Rising from her seat, she looked about. There was no one else nearby and no one in the Descartes Room. She walked over to the railing. Well, it couldn't hurt, could it?

"You listening?" she whispered. Unexpectedly, talking to thin air felt completely natural. The presence of a person surrounded her, wrapped her up. It was invisible yet tangible, impossible to describe. She wasn't talking to thin air at all and she knew it. "You're out there, aren't you?" she said. "Or maybe you're in here. How do I know? But you're definitely somewhere."

She stared out at the ocean.

The night of the trauma came crashing into her consciousness, unbidden. It sat there, demanding a response.

"You just watched, didn't you? The way you're watching me right now." She looked up at the clouds and felt the soft rain falling on her upturned face. Sadness draped itself over her, smothering her heart and mind. It mixed with the grief gnawing away at her insides. The loss of her innocence, which could never be regained, was a constant ache in her heart. Back home, it simmered away in the background, dulled by time and the cares of the world. In the Espacio, however, there was nothing to deaden her awareness of what lay hidden. The "presence" acted like a pot of boiling water full of dirty linen; it brought the impurities to the surface. Evelyn recalled the events of February 12, 1971 as though they'd taken place that day. She'd been over them in therapy dozens of times, but they were still there.

She felt foolish, incapacitated by memories wandering the halls of her mind, callously indifferent to the pain they were causing. Gripping the wooden handrail to steady herself, she was unaware of a splinter that had buried itself in her palm.

"You have no idea, do you, what it feels like to be so scared you can't even move? Paralyzed. Sitting there like a dumbass duck on a shooting range. I felt so . . . helpless. I couldn't even cry out. What was wrong with me? I should have been able to do something. But I just couldn't. I couldn't." Tears started to well up in her eyes. She brushed them away roughly. "The whistle, remember? That was a sick joke, that was. Oh, if you blow it, Mom said, help will come. Help, my ass. It didn't even work. Do you know how that felt? Do you? To call for help and realize you've been duped. No one's coming. No one really cares. Your sister can't help . . . and you? Nothing. *You did **** all!* Because you could have, right? You could have stepped in when you saw what was happening, but you didn't. You didn't. Why? *Why?*"

The release of emotion felt good, like a soothing balm, but it was temporary. The pain soon returned—throbbing, aching. Warm rain drubbed thickly on her skin, generating a fiery heat that started to rise within her. She looked down toward the clifftop. Ever since that day, she had wrestled with her sense of identity. She was a confident, professional woman, she knew that—but deep down, a nagging doubt persisted. That she wasn't worth saving. That when it came down to it, she was worthless. Hours of mental exercises had helped her cope but that's all they did. Help her cope.

She didn't want to cope. She wanted to heal.

"You know what I've figured out over the years? Might not seem like much but here it is. It's the loneliness. Pleasure brings people together, it brings us closer to those we love. But pain? It sends us off into our own private hells. We're all alone. I was all alone. I've always been alone! No one can join us in our pain, it's reserved for each of us alone. We should be able to share it, but we can't. No one understands it. No one can feel it. No one. It's not fair. *It's not right!*"

The rain was falling in sheets now, bouncing off the railing. It was making her clothing feel clammy. She pushed back her hair and re-tied it. Down the far end of the patio, a wooden stairway led to a herb garden. She walked down it and onto a path leading out toward the cliffs. When she arrived at the cliff edge, she peered over. Waves were pummeling the rocks at the base, sending plumes of spray into the air. She sat down on a boulder a few feet back, holding her head in her hands.

Her soft voice broke the silence. "Did you hear us when we prayed? Mom prayed every night, asking for all kinds of stuff. She even asked for groceries, didn't she?" Her body relaxed as the memories pulsed through her head. "My mom trusted you . . . she still does . . . Makes me remember that time when Katie got lost in the mall." A small smile unexpectedly crossed her face. "We looked everywhere, talked to every store owner, the security guards; nothing. She was gone. So Mom and I sat on a bench and prayed. We prayed to you that day. We remembered . . . you. We needed . . . you. And it felt right. And good. Especially when Katie came out from behind the counter in that candy store."

She paused, picked up a stone, and threw it out toward the ocean. Time sagged for what seemed like an age before an echoing clatter sounded from the rocks below. "I wanted to believe, I really did.

Sometimes I still do. At night when Mom prayed, I tried. You know all this. *I tried!* But who listens to a little girl who's in pieces?" Her voice trailed away.

From deep down, the emotion she'd been battling under the surface broke over her. As though her momentary softening had left her exposed to its assault.

Shame.

The fire was kindled, rapacious in its efforts to engulf her. It roasted her from the inside out.

"Do you know how much soap I used?" she whispered. "I used to save up my pocket money to buy soap. The other kids were trading baseball cards and buying Oh Henry!s and I was down the laundry aisle, trying to work out which soap had the strongest odor. Not the sweetest. The strongest. But I never could get clean, could I? Of course I couldn't. Because shame doesn't rub off! You know that, don't you? It never, ever, rubs off. It just sticks to you, gets under your nails, and in your ears and up your nose. It goes down your throat and buries itself so deep, no amount of soap is ever, ever going to wash it away. It never, *ever,* goes away. You know that, don't you?"

She took a deep breath.

"Love," she continued. "I know people who think you're love. You make us, you stick us on a rock, and then you abandon us. And that's supposed to be love? I'm sorry, but I'm right back in that old movie, the one with Paul Newman. What we have here is *a failure to communicate*! Are you getting that? Coz love is about connection and compassion and giving and . . . and healing. Last time I looked it didn't involve standing silently to the side while a violent crime is taking place. So you know what I think?" She threw another stone over the edge of the cliff. Anger began rising in her gut. She'd been holding back as long as she could, but could do so no longer.

She stood up and bellowed at the sky. "I'm not the guilty one! *You are!*" The volume of her voice emboldened her. "And I'm not the one who should feel shameful. You should! How dare you call me up here to lecture me on the whys and wherefores of life and its meaning. What gives you the right to toy with us like playthings? You're nothing but a disgusting voyeur. It's you who should feel shameful. Because it's shameful what you've done. Shameful. Shame on you! SHAME ON YOU!" She was spitting with fury by the end, her rage flying into the wind.

When she was finished, she looked back up at the house. Gamaliel and Korazin were standing on a balcony, watching. She turned her back on them and began again, her voice rising with intensity. "Gotta tell you, though, the night sky is something else. Wow. It's quite the eye-opener. I bet you think that's supposed to impress us. Get us all quaking. Bet that massages your massive ego. Well, you're not the only one who can do something flashy. Two can play at that game. So just one more thing. Don't you ever, ever bring me here again. You hear? I'm done with you. *Now leave me alone!*"

Evelyn walked to the edge of the cliff and peered down, before glancing back up at the house. The lucidi stood stock still; she was too far away to see the pain etched on their shimmering faces. Nor could she see the blood trickling from the corners of their eyes.

She looked out over the ocean one last time.

Then she closed her eyes.

And jumped out into the void.

~ 11 ~

DRAGAN

There are two freedoms—the false, where a man is free to do what he likes; the true, where he is free to do what he ought.
~ Charles Kingsley

February 14, 2005

Aidan stood looking up at the main entrance of Brixton Prison. It was drizzling. A notice in red lettering was posted on the wall: Beware—CCTV in Operation. Another by its side informed the public that visitors were "liable to be searched." The prison, dating back to the early nineteenth century, was an ugly brick building surrounded by thirty-foot-high perimeter walls topped with razor wire. It was home to almost eight hundred men. Some were serving life sentences, while others like Dragan, who'd been denied bail, were there on remand. All of them were held in tiny cells they shared with either one or two others. Daily ablutions had to be completed in front of their cellmates. Fights were not uncommon.

The barrister walked into the reception and completed the formalities, signing his name in a large book. Fenwick arrived late, a little out of breath. "So sorry, Aidan. Nightmare on the Northern Line." He shook his head, rainwater falling onto the floor in front of a warder who stared at him with as much sympathy as he reserved for a lifer in for sexual assault.

"This way," said the prison guard flatly as he began walking down the corridor. Everything clinked in the prison, as though the entire place was made of metal. When they arrived at the interview room, the warder pulled out a huge bunch of keys. Aidan wondered if there was any door in the prison without a lock on it. Perhaps even the visitors' toilets had locks on them. Getting stuck inside one of those didn't bear thinking about.

"Know who we're up against?" he said.

Fenwick leafed through some papers. "A . . . Quentin Molsberry, I think."

"Great. That's all we need. Daily condescension from the prosecution."

The interview room was stark and poorly lit. Fenwick took a seat at a rectangular metal table and dumped his papers on it with a loud thwack. The guard walked out, returning shortly after with a large man who shuffled in and sat down opposite his lawyers. He wore a light gray jacket and blue jeans. Remand prisoners were allowed to wear their own clothing.

"He says he doesn't need an interpreter," mumbled the warder as he left.

"Fine by me," said Aidan, trying to catch Dragan's eye. It was impossible; the prisoner sat staring fixedly at the table's glinting surface. He was bulky with massive shoulders, pushing forty, and wore a blank expression on his face. His head was shaved, a stud punctured one earlobe, and tattoos ran up the left-hand side of his neck.

"Mr. Bakic," said Aidan. "May I call you Dragan?"

The big man shrugged his shoulders and said nothing.

"Dragan, my name is Aidan Manning. I'm going to represent you in court. Beside me is Bill Fenwick. He's your solicitor. He helps me prepare your defense. Do you have any questions for us before I begin?" The Serbian shook his head. Aidan opened his pad. "So, tell me what happened."

"I paint houses. I have receipts."

"You paint houses. You have receipts. Well, that's a start."

"I not know what happened. They wake me very early."

"The police raid, you mean."

"Наравно полиција, мамлазе! Of course police, you moron!" Dragan spat the words out.

This wasn't going to be easy. "Well, why don't you tell me about the business you ran. It was your business, right?"

"Of course not! Goran and Jakov, they run whorehouse, not me! I have painting receipts!"

Dragan

Aidan sat back and looked at his colleague, who was thumbing furiously through some papers. "Ask him about the documents they picked up," said the solicitor without looking up.

Aidan turned back to face the Serbian, who was drumming his fingers on the table. "Dragan, why don't we start again? First of all, Mr. Fenwick and I, we're on your side. We're here to help you. If you say you just lived there, then fine. We do, however, have a problem with various items found in the house. For example, a mobile phone, an email account that shows you were in contact with a man who brings in girls from Eastern Europe. They're questioning him right now, so we have time on that one. But there are also the girls. A number of them claim you beat them. One says you raped her. Tatiana Kopkalic. Perhaps you'd like to tell us about her."

What followed was a diatribe during which the prisoner claimed he'd never done anything violent in his entire life. His outburst was accompanied by repeated blows on the tabletop, which rang around the room. When he'd finished, no one spoke for a few seconds.

Undaunted, Aidan leaned forward. "Good. I'm glad you're certain of your innocence, Dragan. Proving it in court, however, is not going to work if you blow up like that. Do I make myself clear?" The table leg received a hefty kick, sending paper flying into the air. "So how did you end up in London?"

The big man refused to answer.

"I can't help you unless you help me, Dragan."

It was clear the interview was over. They wouldn't be getting anything else out of Dragan Bakic that day. After bidding Fenwick farewell, Aidan headed for Brixton Tube station. As he walked, he hit a speed dial number on his phone.

"Billy? A grand on Sparky. Cheltenham, 3:30 p.m. Got it?" He waited for his bookie to confirm. "What? It's in the post, mate . . . Yeah, seriously . . . What, boxing? Who's fighting? Klitschko? Which one? . . . If it's Wladimir, but not the other guy . . . Okay, fine. Put a couple of hundred on Wladimir to win by KO. Gotta run. Bye."

When he alighted at Hammersmith, his phone vibrated. It was his daughter-in-law.

"Aidan, I—"

"Beth," he interrupted, "how very good to hear your voice. I've been meaning to call you about that scallywag you married. Terrible. You should throw him out. I know I would." He waited for a reply but none came. He pressed on. "What a disgrace he is. He should be locked up—" There was a sense of mischief in his voice that she completely missed. The tirade she was about to launch was halted before it began. Her anger seeped away like a deflating balloon.

"He's not that bad, Aidan. Stop it."

"Sorry," he said. "You're right. He's not that bad. In fact, he deserves a second chance."

Beth, who'd called to rail against her husband, found herself completely wrong-footed. "Okay. You got me. Good one. I'll reverse some psychology on you when I see you next, you—"

He started laughing. "Listen, Beth. He loves you. You know that better than anything."

There was silence on the end of the phone.

"I've gotta go." She hung up.

Later that evening, Aidan sank into the sofa with a cup of tea in one hand and the paper in the other. He looked up from his article on the war in Iraq and noticed a Bible staring at him from the bookcase opposite; the light was playing on the gold lettering running down the spine. It was a while since he'd dipped into it but, with Beth and Simon on his mind, he recalled a section about peacemakers. They could do with some help. He seemed to remember the passage used the word "blessing" a lot, whatever that meant. He smiled, wondering where all these religious ideas were coming from. It had been a long time since he'd even considered his past beliefs.

Nowadays he had no time, no need.

He picked up a photo sitting on the side table next to him. He'd forgotten just how beautiful Naomi had looked on her wedding day— the happiest day of his life. The vicar standing next to them wore a huge embroidered cross on his vestments. Just behind and to the left of the man's head, a lectern was clearly discernible. It was fashioned from two large brass angels, each one with a wing spread wide open.

He took a second look.

He'd never spotted those before. He peered at the photo more closely. He didn't know why, but they felt significant in some way. There was something about them. He stopped for a moment, thinking. No, he couldn't work it out. As far as he was concerned, angels were fairies wrapped up in religious language. There was nothing about them that was real, so what possible meaning could they have?

He put the photograph back on the table and headed for bed. Simon could do with an angel though, he thought, as he brushed his teeth. People always listened to angels in the Bible, didn't they? That would do the trick—a bloke in white robes with wings. He'd put the fear of God into him. He smiled and turned off the light.

Pity angels didn't exist.

~ 12 ~

CIRCLES

If there is a meaning in life at all, then there must be a meaning in suffering.
~ Viktor Frankl

February 12, 1971

A little piece of heaven dropped into a back yard in Southern California. Joy swirled across the lawn as two young beauties raced around in circles, and fell over, giggling until their sides hurt. Evelyn ran over to the spigot on the garage wall and turned on the sprinkler. They stood in front of it, waiting for it to lean in their direction; the moment the water touched them, they hopped on one foot, trying to back away. Katie started dancing about in a puddle, flicking mud at the fence.

"No, Katie!" shouted Evelyn. "Dad won't like that." Her little sister kept tossing mud about. The four-year age gap most certainly did *not* result in any kind of deference or respect. Nevertheless, Evelyn doted on her, even when she was defacing the neighbor's car or feeding sausages to the goldfish. "Come on," she insisted. "Let's get our dolls." They ran over to a tub sitting on the patio. Katie tipped it over. Dolls, action figures, and soft toys went everywhere.

Katie threw her favorite doll onto the top of the jungle gym. "Mine's landed on the moon! She's married to Mr. Neil and she's visiting him," she squealed.

"No, she isn't. Neil was mean to her, so she likes Buzz now." Evelyn threw a Barbie doll up on top. "Mine's called Amelia, and she's a great pilot who's exploring the world. She doesn't need a man!"

"Yes she does!"

"No she doesn't!"

"Does too! Mine's married to the number one spaceman. And

yours is married to yucky Buzz. He tells his wife to stay in the kitchen! Or go flying into a tree!" Katie said, as she climbed up and grabbed Evelyn's doll by one of her unnaturally long legs. With a flourish, she threw it into the avocado tree.

"Stop that!"

Fortunately, at ten years old, Evelyn was tall enough to reach it. She cradled the doll, picked up a small yellow comb and started combing its long, blond hair. She loved the plastic figure with its permanent smile. It was happy. All the time. She liked that.

"I'm cold," said Katie, trotting over to the back door. Evelyn turned off the sprinkler and followed her into the house.

"Come on, you two," said Bonnie. "Let's towel you down. Dad's gonna be home soon and we're going out."

Evelyn asked, "Who's taking care of us?"

"Uncle Kenny." The two girls started whining immediately. Katie began to cry.

"Please, Mom. Please not him. I don't like him. He's creepy."

"He's not creepy. He's family, and it's just this once. Sandy's out of town this week. Anyway, there'll be popcorn and I'll tell him you can watch *The Brady Bunch* or *Scooby-Doo*."

"*Scooby-Doo! Scooby-Doo!*" shouted Katie.

The front door banged. Evelyn watched her dad walk in and collapse into his La-Z-Boy. Her mom pulled a beer out of the fridge and handed it to him without saying anything. When he went straight to the La-Z-Boy, that meant he didn't want to be disturbed. The girls needed reminding sometimes. Clearly, Katie hadn't been listening the last time; she jumped straight onto his lap.

"Hey there, sweet pea. Your hair's all wet." He looked at her fingers. Mud was still buried under the nails. "You been diggin' up my yard again?" Evelyn, who was sitting on the couch, stiffened. She knew what was coming. "Goddarn it, Evie, I thought I told you two not to go diggin' up the yard and tossin' mud about." She was always held responsible for both of them.

"Sorry, Dad. I couldn't get to her in time."

"Well, that's not good enough. No TV tonight!"

"But Wayne," called her mom from the kitchen. "I just told 'em they could watch. Kenny's over an' all."

"No!" he shouted. "No TV!" He got up and marched off to the bedroom.

Evelyn fought back the tears as hard as she could. There was no point in arguing. She'd tried that many times. Her dad just dug his heels in. It was better to lay low; the less said, the better. She watched her mom washing dishes at the sink. The salad bowl was taking a beating. Her mom wiped a tear from her eye, threw a dish towel into a drawer, and ran to the bathroom.

Evelyn looked up at the mantel. The whistle sitting in the glass display case caught her eye. She got up from the couch and peered at it. She didn't know why, but she had a sudden urge to hold it. Looking around nervously, she opened the small glass door with trembling fingers. Reaching in, she pulled out the brass whistle with the word "Titanic" engraved on the side. She liked how heavy it felt.

The bathroom door banged. She was about to put the whistle back, when she heard footsteps. Panic set in, so instead, she dropped the whistle into her pocket and jumped onto the couch. Her heart was thumping in her ears. I'll put it back when Mom and Dad have left, she thought. No harm done.

Her parents entered the living room looking fantastic. Evelyn liked it when they wore their best clothes. It always made them happier. Dad wore a patterned shirt, dark slacks, and loafers. His leather jacket was slightly ripped at the elbow, but Mom said they couldn't afford another. She had done her best to sew it up. Her father's hair was greased back with tons of gel from a round tub in the bathroom. Evelyn sometimes stole a little to put on Barbie's hair. She looked up at her mom and started jumping up and down in delight. Her mom's hair would make all the men look at her, she was sure of it. One of her favorite sounds was the whoosh from the hairspray aerosol can. Once, she'd counted up to a hundred or thereabouts before the hiss from the can had stopped. She watched her mom pat the sides of her beehive, which stood at least eight inches above her head.

"You look beautiful, Mom!"

"Thank you, honey."

Circles

A car honked its horn on the driveway. Evelyn watched her mom tottering down the path toward Uncle Kenny, who was sitting in his car, chewing a matchstick. He often had a matchstick in his mouth. She listened to their voices. Uncle Kenny was getting upset. So was Mom. Her stomach started to tighten. She hated it when her uncle was rude. For one thing, it made him bad-tempered, so instead of making popcorn and letting them watch TV, he'd just sit on the couch, demanding beers from the fridge and watching football.

His car left with an ear-piercing skid on the sidewalk.

Bonnie marched in and slammed the door.

"Great." She started speaking to the room. "Just great. When I don't want him in my house, he stays until late, drinking beer, and now when I need him, he stands me up. Right. I didn't want to do this, because these folks are real nice, but it's our only hope." Evelyn's mom took off her shoes, put on some sneakers, and jogged across the street. She waved her arms about, gesturing toward her house in front of a fat man who'd opened the door. He disappeared inside his house, but seconds later, he was walking out carrying his jacket. Her mom had to step back as he came forward. She looked flustered. That was probably because they were late for the double bill at the drive-thru. Her parents loved double bills. They often held hands after coming home from the drive-thru.

The two adults walked across the road. Evelyn darted back inside and hid in the kitchen. "Girls?" said Bonnie loudly. "Mr. Henderson is gonna take care of you tonight, ya hear?"

Katie ran out of her room and launched herself at the rotund man. He picked her up and swung her round in the air.

"I love going in circles! Again, again!" Katie's high-pitched voice filled the room. The man with dimples beamed and completed several more revolutions. Evelyn breathed a huge sigh of relief. No Kenny. Thank God in heaven it wasn't Kenny. Once her parents had left, Mr. Henderson made popcorn. He'd played board games last time, but today he turned the dial on the TV, and installed himself on the couch with the bowl of popcorn balanced on his belly. Lines appeared on the screen. Next it went fuzzy. Evelyn got up and smacked it on the side. The screen went black, then broke into a picture. They all cheered.

"Dad told us we couldn't watch TV," said Katie sadly.

"Dad's not here, though, is he?" Mr. Henderson looked at them with a conspiratorial glint in his eye. He took off his glasses and cleaned them with a cloth he kept in his pocket.

Evelyn folded her arms, her expression serious. "He'll find out and we'll get in trouble."

"No!" said Mr. Henderson loudly. The girls looked a little shocked. Evelyn watched him loosen his tie; she reached out and grabbed Katie's hand. "Sorry," he continued. "Sorry. I mean, no, you won't be in trouble. I'll tell him it was *my* decision. Now let's all calm down, shall we? Have some popcorn." They watched *Jeopardy!* followed by *Little House on the Prairie*. As the credits were rolling, Katie shouted out, "Do Donald Duck! Do Donald Duck!" Evelyn watched the big man's knuckles go white and his jaw clench. His reaction made her stomach tighten.

"On one condition." He took a deep breath. "That you show me your basement. You do have a basement, don't you?" Evelyn told everyone who cared to ask that their house was one of the only ones in their neighborhood to have a basement. While her father droned on to the male visitors about lax building regulations in the fifties, she would grab the hand of one of the ladies and show her where she and Katie liked to build their den.

"Let me get the key!" Katie started jumping up and down. "I'll get it! I'll get it!" She pulled out the step stool, climbed up, and pried open a tin. With great care, she took out a key and ran to a door in the hallway. "This way, Mr. Henderson." The three of them went down the stairs.

Evelyn found the light switch by the door. "It's a bit messy, I'm afraid." She suddenly felt responsible for the state of the house.

"Oh, I like it. I like it a lot." The big man picked Katie up and whirled her around in a circle again, making her shriek with delight.

Evelyn watched without smiling.

"Do Donald Duck!" shouted Katie. Mr. Henderson began quacking and shuffling around, beating his arms against his sides. When he'd finished, he collapsed into an old couch and, quite inexplicably, began to weep. Evelyn stopped breathing and just stared at him. She didn't know what to do. Katie jumped on his lap and asked, "What's the matter, Mr. Henderson? Don't cry. We'll take care of you!"

She gave him a big hug.

He looked at them both. "Yes, you will, won't you?" he said, blowing his nose into his handkerchief. "Right, Katie, it's your bedtime." They walked back up to the bathroom, all three of them. Evelyn followed behind, watching every move, yet not really knowing why. She was scared, but couldn't work out what was making her frightened. So the babysitter had cried. Why was that scary? She didn't know what to do, so she watched as her sister closed her eyes and said her prayers. Mr. Henderson closed the door. Normally, Katie liked it open, but for some reason, she didn't complain.

The large man looked down at Evelyn with a faint smile on his face. She noticed beads of sweat rolling down through his sideburns. A couple of droplets reached his chin and fell off. He rubbed his hands together. She felt a bit dizzy as she looked up at him, suddenly wanting her mother more than anything. Turning tail, she ran into her room and closed the door; she lay on her bed trembling, curled up in a ball.

A while later, there was a knock on the door. She froze. Mr. Henderson came in and sat down on the end of the bed. He looked huge in her small room. A dish towel was draped over his shoulder; he must have been drying the dishes. Mom would like that. He took off his glasses and put them on upside down, which made him look silly. When he bobbed his head from side to side, Evelyn couldn't resist. She began to laugh. He made a funny sound by expelling air from his mouth by pushing his tongue forward. She giggled some more.

"Story?" he said, grinning. "I saw some books in the basement." Evelyn hesitated, but that's all she did. She didn't know how to say no. It was too difficult. He seemed so big and he was funny. She wanted to say no, but the words wouldn't come out. When they reached the basement, she walked down ahead of him, wondering where the storybooks were. She looked around. There weren't any.

"Aren't we going to read a book?" she said, perching on the edge of the couch. Turning her head, she watched him follow her down into the basement.

Mr. Henderson descended, passing first into the second circle of hell, reserved for those who permit their lust to run rampant and unchecked. His conscience dulled by urges he willingly embraced, he made his way further down toward the seventh circle, where his violence reaped an eternal consequence. Passing through the eighth circle, he rested in the ninth, sated by his treachery and lies, wrapped in Satan's arms.

The air was cold.

Evelyn shivered, before her feminine beauty was ripped asunder. Gossamer-thin, she was torn apart, fragments sent flying into all four corners of the room. In her distress, she reached for the whistle and blew with all her might. No sound emerged. Nothing. She blew again. Silence. A silence that rang so loudly in her ears, she thought her head would explode. It did not. Instead, a chasm opened up inside large enough to devour her. The effect was as immeasurable as the full scope of the night sky, the gruesome act a giant destroying all attempts at meaning. For every victim of such a crime, the trauma slayed all argument.

And it took just three minutes.

Later, as Evelyn lay on her bed, shaking, Mr. Henderson noticed blood drops on the carpet. He found a bottle of bleach and dabbed each drop several times, draining the shag pile carpet of its dye.

"Whiter than snow," he whispered. "Make me whiter than snow."

When he was done, he went down into the basement and straightened the furniture. Afterward, he hummed to himself as he finished up some dishes in the kitchen. On his way back to the bathroom, he glanced down at the carpet. Apart from a few small white patches, there wasn't a single trace of what had taken place.

The only blood left was staining Evelyn's sheets.

~ 13 ~

TO MY LOVE, WHO LOVES BETTER THAN I

Memory is the scribe of the soul.
~ Aristotle

February 22, 2005

Aidan hurried along platform 2 of West Kensington Tube station on a cold Tuesday morning.

"Billy!" he said, trying to locate a better signal for his cell phone. "I don't care if the name sounds like a rash in the nether regions, if he's fast, I'm putting money on him. I hear he likes the running soft and it's been raining for weeks, so come on, put a grand on Tickety-Boo, will you? What's that? . . . Which bill? . . . I'm losing you . . ."

He hung up just as the train arrived. After boarding, he found a seat in the corner, which was a rare treat. He pulled out his book, *The Four Loves* by C. S. Lewis. For some inexplicable reason, he'd grabbed it off the shelf that morning. Flicking open the cover, he gazed down at the handwriting that spiraled across the first page. *To my love, who loves better than I, whom I love more than I know, and who is known by One who loves better than all. From his love, Naomi.*

He turned the page quickly.

The journey took twenty minutes, barely enough time to read a chapter. Aidan glanced at his watch as he climbed the escalator at Temple Tube station. He felt late. He was late. His anxiety decreased, however, as he crossed the threshold of number 43, the office music of telephones and rapped keyboards enveloping him like a well-worn sweater on a cold day.

"Morning, sir," said Harry.

"Morning, all," said Aidan, heading for his office, which he shared with another barrister. When he arrived, he sat down at his desk and hit the power button on his computer. "Does your PC take several decades to start?"

The man sitting opposite replied in a monotone without looking up. "Boot up."

"Excuse me?"

"Computers boot up, Aidan. They don't start."

Gordon Roper was an effete man in his mid-fifties whose chance to make silk had passed him by a long time ago. His greasy hair fell across a shiny scalp in long flowing strands that he tucked behind his left ear. He lived alone and managed to make a pint of milk last three days. He owned a goldfish—easy to maintain and very undemanding—and liked soft pastel colors. In addition, he collected stamps—especially penny blacks—polished his shoes on Sunday evenings, and on Saturdays, without fail, he watched a new show called *Strictly Come Dancing*. On occasion, he could be seen through his net curtains doing the waltz with an imaginary partner. In the office, he'd given up complaining about the lousy briefs that regularly found their way into his pigeonhole.

Harry had his number; resistance was futile.

"Right," said Aidan. "Boot up . . . Why don't the nerds at Microsoft speak English?"

Harry walked in, put his arm on Aidan's shoulder and gave Gordon a look. A minute later, the two of them were alone. "Did I ever tell you the one about Peter de Souza?" he said. Aidan shook his head.

The senior clerk pulled up a chair and leaned in close. "Barrister I knew once. Anyway, his Head of Chambers discovered one day that he had a nasty little habit. He was into the dogs, see. Not the fancy ones that run around tracks, but the ones that fight. Illegal it is now. Dangerous dogs—very hush-hush, if you know what I mean. Any barrister would lose their license if they were arrested at a gig like that. All those criminals in one place—it's getting a little close to the clientele. So, you know what the Head of Chambers did when he found out? Told good old de Souza he had to find a new owner. A new place to park his briefs. So de Souza, bless him, left his nearest and dearest, the people he'd worked with for twenty years. But when he got to his new place—funny thing—there was no little cubby with his name on it. His new home turned out to be an establishment that wasn't too fond of his habits, if you know what I mean. Poor man. Never practiced again." He looked Aidan in the eye. "Sad story. Don't want yours ending like that." He handed him a copy of *The Racing Post*. "And one more thing. Your chambers fees are overdue. Again."

He left the office.

Aidan loosened his collar and threw the magazine in the bin. His hands were shaking, his heart rate kicking along at a tempo normally reserved for vigorous exercise. It took a number of deep breaths before he'd gained a measure of control.

Harry returned and dumped a brief on Gordon's desk; he called him in. "Two o'clock at Camberwell Mags for you, sir. A bit of petty larceny that's right up your street." Turning tail, he made a hasty exit, following closely behind Tanya, the junior barrister whose perfume and swaying hips induced what he considered to be the legal limit of arousal permissible in an office setting.

Aidan rolled his eyes as he watched Harry pursue his quarry down the corridor. Later, after several phone calls and numerous interruptions, he packed his briefcase and picked up his umbrella. "It wasn't me, by the way, Gordon," he said, pulling on his overcoat.

The person who'd put a pink shirt with puffy sleeves on Gordon's chair had never been identified. Harry interrogated every clerk, and had even grilled the cleaners, but no one confessed to the crime. Gordon didn't know how they'd discovered his penchant for ballroom dancing, but somehow it had come out. Gary and Steve, the youngest clerks, had spotted him eyeing himself sideways in the mirror, and concluded that an alter ego lay hidden. The shirt had hit the spot better than a cold lemonade on a hot day.

"Of course it wasn't you, Aidan." The balding man started rifling through a sheaf of papers with great intensity. Aidan winced as he left behind the sound of ripping pages.

The first day of any trial always contained a frisson of excitement. Aidan arrived at Inner London Crown Court a little early, so he bought himself a coffee at a stall on the corner. When he entered the court building shortly before 9 a.m., he experienced the same thrill he always felt when preparing to defend: a slight constriction in the throat, a quickening of the heartbeat, and clammy hands. He adjusted his wig and walked purposefully to Court Two, filing in right behind Quentin Molsberry.

The courtroom was largely built of oak. The jury box, the witness box, the advocates' benches, even the public gallery, they were all made from oak. England's national tree was used to construct the majority of the older courtrooms around the country, and Inner London Crown Court dated from the eighteenth century.

The main doors banged shut; battle was joined.

"All rise!" announced the clerk. There was a rumble of chairs being pushed back as the main attraction walked in. Judge Prendergast appeared, wearing the traditional garb—a red sash stretching diagonally across his black and purple robes. He was a bit doddery, but no barrister was fooled by his demeanor. He might be pushing eighty, but he had a sharp mind and a sharper tongue.

Aidan's junior, Fiona, arrived a little breathless and leaned across. "Sorry I'm late," she whispered.

"Don't worry," he said, keeping his eye on the judge. "We're good to go."

Fiona was a mousy woman in her early forties. She wore her hair in a bun and her horn-rimmed spectacles obscured her eyes, which rarely settled on another person's face. Aidan thought she was aging prematurely but he liked and respected her. She was calm, efficient, and though she could be reticent—not the most desirable character trait for a barrister—she was also a stickler for detail. During the past year, she had discovered several useful precedents that had helped him considerably. But perhaps her most important quality was her unspoken belief in him. That kind of support was invaluable and he knew it.

"The Crown calls Tatiana Kopkalic!"

A woman entered wearing heavy makeup. Tall, with high heels, she sported a fuchsia business suit that hugged her curves. All eyes turned toward her. She took her time sitting down, clearly enjoying the attention. She tilted her head to one side.

"An interpreter is available, Ms. Kopkalic," said the judge.

The interpreter—a middle-aged woman in a brown cardigan who

sat by her side—was about to open her mouth to translate, when Tatiana spoke up. "I not need interpreter. I speak English." The woman in brown seemed taken aback but the judge acquiesced. "If you say so," he said. "Mr. Molsberry, your witness."

After some preliminary questions, the QC hooked his thumbs into his robe and said, "Ms. Kopkalic, please tell the court about your plans last year to move to the UK."

Tatiana described her arrival in the country, nine months earlier. She went over in minute detail the various people who had lured her from Serbia during 2004. They included some of her closest friends and relatives. It was traumatic to listen to the deception, the way in which she'd been let down repeatedly by those she thought she could trust.

"Describe your life in this den of iniquity," said Molsberry bombastically. "Especially your relationship with Dragan Bakic."

The judge explained that the prosecution was referring to the brothel where she'd been held. Once she understood this, Tatiana began her story. Slowly and in simple language, she revealed a life of unspeakable horror. Man after man was brought to her room, sometimes twenty or thirty a day. Some were violent; none offered to help her. She was threatened by several Serbian men and beaten regularly. The defendant was a man who slept with all the girls and was apparently very fond of his keys.

"Was Dragan ever violent?"

She looked across at the jury. "Every night, he drink a lot. And take many drug. He also choose woman for beat and sometimes rape."

"Did he ever rape you?"

Aidan rose to his feet. "Your honor, I wonder if the question might be rephrased, so as to avoid leading the witness." Well, he had to draw a line somewhere.

Molsberry scowled and adjusted his wig. "My learned friend doesn't wish me to ask if the defendant raped you, so I will simply ask about your treatment, Ms. Kopkalic. How did he treat you?"

The judge grunted and was about to intervene, when Tatiana's voice rang out. "He raping me twice."

Molsberry looked at the jury and paused, allowing the answer to sink in. He turned to Tatiana. "Can you remember when?"

"November and Christmas Day. He drink much wine and put on party hat. All girls laughing in kitchen and making joke. He come to my room later for rape me."

"Did you tell anyone about the rape?"

"No. I was scared. I waited for chance to take keys."

Tatiana recounted how she eventually made the break, escaping from the brothel in King's Cross the day after Dorina had managed to break out of the house in Camden Town.

The court adjourned for the day.

When Aidan walked in through the front door that night, he was tired. Like most nights. He peeled off his coat and pressed play on the answering machine. There was a message from his bookie, who threw some large numbers at him. He promptly hit the delete key and headed for the kitchen, where he poured himself a glass of wine. After some deft knifework worthy of a TV chef, he had assembled various impressive-looking piles of vegetables ready for steaming or frying, he couldn't decide which.

He was reaching for a cookbook when Simon and Beth walked in. The pair immediately began talking at the same time, the volume increasing as they tried to be heard. Simon grabbed a bottle of wine off the shelf and started looking for a corkscrew.

"Stop!" shouted Aidan. "One at a time, please."

Conversation settled down to a happy rhythm, Simon launching into an anecdote that had his father guffawing at all the right moments. Apparently, a newsreader with an upset stomach had almost missed the news at the top of the hour, arriving just in time to grab some papers and throw himself into the broadcasting suite. He started with the racing from Doncaster and finished with an important item about unemployment, intermittently mouthing his desperation from behind several panes of soundproof glass. Aidan never knew such behavior could happen at the BBC.

When Simon was finished, Beth bemoaned some of the changes taking place at Marks & Spencer, where she worked as a buyer. She waved her wine glass around as she lamented the choices made by a supervisor named Stanley, whose fashion sense was "nothing short of atrocious," given that he was responsible for much of what the nation wore up and down the high street each week.

After dinner, they discussed the future of David Cameron, a politician whose career appeared to be on the rise. Deemed a bright prospect, he was challenging for the Conservative Party leadership, though Beth thought David Davis was probably a shoo-in. Aidan watched her gesticulate wildly as she spoke, a small indulgent smile slowly making its way across his face. The recollection of his son's spat with his wife already seemed long distant, a dull blemish on an otherwise sunny landscape. Beth's anger had quickly dissolved under the weight of time and her innate knowledge of her husband. During a brief respite when they were alone, she confessed to her father-in-law that only a fool would peg Simon as a philanderer. He certainly wasn't a man who kept thongs as trophies.

Aidan lifted the port bottle and poured his son another glass. He walked through to the kitchen and set about doing the dishes. As he scrubbed, he listened to the voices wafting in from the living room, sounds that brought a confluence of contradictory emotions.

Agony and ecstasy.

He dried his hands on a dish towel and picked up the book he'd been reading on the Tube. He flipped open the cover and read the familiar writing. *To my love, who loves better than I, whom I love more than I know, and who is known by One who loves better than all. From his love, Naomi.* Her face was a transport to ecstasy. He longed to remain there, soothed by the cherished image he held in his mind's eye. But it was impossible.

From the living room, he could hear Simon's laugh followed by a high-pitched giggle from his daughter-in-law. Their intimacy, which brought him such joy, was also a regular reminder of that which he no longer possessed. The gnawing emptiness created by his wife's absence was still with him.

He closed his eyes and called up her smiling face. She was with him in court and on the train. He saw her in chambers and across the table in the evenings. She was an abiding presence in his soul and always first among his memories. He still talked to her at night, though she no longer held him under the covers. A wardrobe in the corner of his bedroom still held many of her clothes. And when he occasionally opened the door, he was sure he could still detect her familiar scent. He carried her with him wherever he went, and time, which was supposed to be a healer, had only dulled the pain. It had yet to extinguish it. The aching loss throbbed away deep inside, and Simon and Beth's joy unintentionally increased the intensity.

He crossed the hall and popped his head into the living room. "I'm going to bed," he said. He walked over and kissed them both on the top of the head. "No more drinking with squaddies." They both laughed.

"Oh, I'm already a pacifist, Dad."

"No need for that, Simon," he called out, already making his way upstairs. "Just love your wife. Just . . . love your wife."

~ 14 ~

BAD KARMA

Every sin carries its own punishment.
~ American proverb

February 23, 2005

The following day, nearing 4 p.m., Miloš entered Evelyn's office and sat down. She let him sit there for a minute while she finished up some notes on the previous patient.

"Be right with you," she said over her shoulder. When she spun round on her swivel chair to look at him, she thought he looked worried. There were dark bags under his eyes, and he sat tapping his foot nervously against his chair leg. "Good afternoon, Miloš. How's things with you?"

The young man shrugged.

"You seeing a psychologist as I recommended?"

"I have appointment."

"Excellent. Now why don't we take a look at my handiwork?" She picked up Miloš's hand and inspected the stitches on each wrist. "Time for these to come out, I think. You're healing up nicely." She put on some gloves and, with some surgical scissors, snipped each stitch, pulling them out one by one. The scars were pink, without any sign of infection, which was pleasing. She picked up his left arm and took a look at his cast. "I see you have some supporters who er"—she paused as she read—"appear to watch a lot of TV. Lots of girls' names too." Miloš smiled sheepishly. "Girlfriend?" He pointed at a name. "Excellent. Perhaps when you're feeling down, you should take a look at your cast."

She stood up to inspect the wounds on his head. They were almost healed, with some scabs about to drop off. After checking the bruising on his left flank, she sat down and updated his file. His thigh was an ugly purple and still tender, but apart from that, it was fine.

"Well, Miloš, you're good to go."

The sun was setting as Evelyn left the hospital. She flipped down the sun visor, headed for the beach, and parked the car. Pulling on her Rollerblades, she set off from Torrance toward El Segundo. The wind in her face and the exertion blew time and her worries into next week. She pumped her arms, leaving test results and sick patients trailing in the dust. On her way back, she swung by The Lighthouse for a drink. There were some familiar faces there from work, but she was tired so she left early.

Once home, she opened the door and turned on the light.

She dropped her bag.

The first thing to hit her was the smell. Not only had the thieves trashed the place, they'd emptied the contents of her refrigerator onto the floor. After a warm day, the place stank. Evelyn wanted to throw up. She wandered around in a daze, barely able to take in what she was seeing. In her bedroom, the dresser was on its side with a crack down the back. She pushed it upright and checked in the drawers. The only jewelry left was the odd piece of costume jewelry she kept for fancy dress parties. All her expensive items were gone, including the ring her mother had given her to commemorate Jasmine's birth.

She opened the bathroom door. It looked like someone had taken a hammer to the place. All the tiling had been smashed, as well as the mirrors. Broken glass was everywhere. She closed the door and went to the kitchen, where it looked like the same person had been at work. Most of her glass and flatware had been smashed; ceramic shards crunched under her feet. The living room was little better. The TV was gone. In fact, all her electronic items had been stolen. She looked for her photos. Those were also missing. The shock hit her in the stomach. All her memories stolen by mindless thieves. Collapsing onto the couch, she grabbed the phone and dialed 911.

Tears followed shortly afterward.

It took quite a while to complete her statement for the police. After the two officers had left, she sank into an armchair, exhausted. The kitchen items could be replaced. And no doubt a professional cleaning company would be able to eliminate the stink from the place. But the photos were irreplaceable. How could they steal those? They meant nothing to them. Nothing! She picked up the phone. "Bridget? Can you come? I need you."

Her best friend drove over and sat with her in the dark, holding her. Listening to Evelyn pour out the story, Bridget couldn't help expressing a desire to do nasty things to the perpetrators, which somehow lightened the mood.

It was late. "Come on," said Bridget. "It smells in here. I'll make up a bed for you at my place."

The following day, after work, Evelyn drove up the 110 toward downtown. She found a parking spot, and made her way over to the Staples Center, where she met Bridget in the nosebleed section. They'd known each other since pre-med, Bridget choosing to go into pediatrics, while Evelyn had taken the surgical route. A love of volleyball and medicine had cemented their friendship, which was still strong after twenty-five years.

"Listen up, you're gonna like this one," said Bridget. "A mom comes in the other day and dumps her five-year-old on the table and says, 'Jimmy, show the doctor.'" She offered Evelyn a pretzel. "So there we are, the three of us staring at each other in the consulting room. Complete silence. I mean, the kid's chocolate-box sweet but he won't open his mouth, so I say, 'You know, Jimmy, I got a candy with your name on it, but you gotta tell me what happened.' And I've just finished speaking when his mom says, 'Show her your nose.' So, I get down and look up one of his nostrils. I lie him down, and I'm not kidding, it must've taken ten minutes. At least. Finally, I manage to extricate a small plastic tennis ball. It even had little curved grooves to make it look realistic. I sit him up and he just lies right back down. So I get out my flashlight and I take a look up the other nostril."

"Let me guess. A baseball."

"No, actually. Same sport, but this time it was a tiny, red tennis racket. Took me fifteen minutes. So he's squealing and carrying on, and his mom starts sniveling, 'I am so sorry about this. I don't know what got into him.' And I just couldn't help myself. I think it was her insipid voice, coz I just turned and said, 'Tennis equipment, Mrs. Baker—Tennis equipment!'" She started laughing. "So they're leaving and I notice he's scratching his ear, and I say under my breath, 'Jimmy, how's your ear?' Nothing. So, back on the table, and this time it's a piece of thread. He'd shoved a mini tennis net down there. The kid had turned himself into an entire tennis tournament. I'm telling ya, I thought I'd have to look up his rear end and pull out the umpire's chair."

By the time she was finished, both women were crying with laughter. Once they'd calmed down, Bridget said, "You hungry?" Evelyn nodded. She got up and quickly returned with two hot dogs. It was exactly the kind of food they told their patients to avoid, but they were soon enjoying the dogs like guilty schoolkids.

"Yo," said a man squeezing into the row past a couple of people who looked like they should pay for three seats. Reggie, a paramedic who worked in the South Bay, was tall and bald. A shining scalp had become almost de rigueur among African Americans ever since Michael Jordan's rise to fame. Reggie exuded energy, and his good looks had landed him occasional work in commercials.

"Hey!" said the women.

He sat down and began slurping his Big Gulp. Evelyn lost sight of his face. "Reggie! You trying to kill yourself? You could irrigate the Midwest with that thing."

"I'm thirsty." He sucked back as much liquid as he could manage before coming up for air. "Aaaah!" he said, giving her a peck on the cheek as a peace offering.

"You do realize you're ingesting enough sugar there to frost a couple dozen cakes."

He turned to Bridget. "Can you believe this? At work, I got doctors givin' me orders. Now I'm here to watch Kobe do his thing, and I got you guys, ketchup on your face, soundin' like my mother." He took a huge bite from his burger.

"Reggie," said Bridget. "We love you, man. You know that. It's why we give you such a hard time!" She laughed as she watched her friend popping Skittles into his mouth five at a time. She turned to

Evelyn. "Been thinking about your break-in, Evie. I reckon it's bad karma."

"Bad karma? Come on."

"It's just an expression, but it fits sometimes. Karma's a way of making sense of the world when it seems crazy."

"Bridge," said Evelyn. "That's just hogwash, and you know it."

They watched the tip-off and the first few lazy shooting attempts by each team. "Listen," said Reggie, without taking his eyes off the game. "I don't believe in karma, but there's gotta be somethin' out there. My grandma says we get our just deserts. Sin will find you out. Bad stuff happening is like the universe telling you you're on the wrong track."

Evelyn was about to respond, when the man in front of her turned round. He was in his sixties, balding, and wore glasses.

"Excuse me," he said. "I couldn't help overhearing your conversation just now. I work at UCLA. Anthropology. See, we've known for a long time that people are programmed to expect a just world. We've evolved to look for fairness. It's in our genes." They looked down at the man, the game momentarily forgotten. "We *assume*," he continued, "the presence of other minds that give order to the world; so when bad stuff happens, we instinctively look for the person or persons responsible. When we're young, it's our parents. Later on our teachers, and then the government. Finally, we look to God to deliver justice. You won't find one human society that doesn't invent some kind of deity to explain life. They *all* do it. Makes us feel life is meaningful, when in fact it's random." He picked up his coat. "Enjoy the game."

Evelyn shivered, wondering why the air felt cold. It seemed even stranger when the temperature rose shortly after he'd left. They all stared at each other. Eventually, Bridget spoke first. "I dunno, Evie. I'm not sure I go with all that evolutionary stuff. I'm telling you, it's bad karma."

The ref blew his whistle.

The Lakers beat the Jazz 102-95, courtesy of a forty-point haul by Kobe Bryant. Somehow it wasn't the same, though. Not without Shaq. They filed out with the rest of the crowd toward the parking lot. Evelyn said goodbye to her friends and found her car. Their conversation was still rattling around in her head as she drove home.

Karma. The belief that cause and effect function in the universe. Some traditions included the idea that a deity played some kind of role, perhaps as the one who ensured we receive the fruits of karma. She remembered the class she'd taken on comparative religion. Perhaps the Merovingian was right. Causality. Cause. Effect. The only universal truth. What had Reggie's grandma said? We get our just deserts.

She thought back to her childhood days when she'd believed. She remembered how her mom had bowed her head by their bedside. They used to hold hands, and her mom would pray and leave space for her girls to join in. Evelyn had always found that hard to do. Not like Katie whose prayers were often silly and made her laugh.

But that was all before Mr. Henderson.

After that, she just used to mutter a few words, and over time, her mom had stopped asking. Even so, she remembered Thanksgivings like they were yesterday. She loved the way her grandma told the *Titanic* story, the rise and fall of her voice. And though she struggled, in her heart she made a desperate attempt to join in with the prayer. She tried to believe; she wanted to believe. In fact, every time they prayed, she wished it were true. Closing her eyes, she imagined a big Santa Claus figure with a huge white beard hugging her and telling her everything was going to be all right. But no matter how hard she tried, she knew inside it wasn't true. And thinking of a large man turned out to be a really bad idea.

Evelyn put her key in the lock and opened the door. "Please, no more break-ins," she said out loud, not caring who might hear. The house was still a mess, but no one had broken in. She was about to say "thank God," but stopped herself.

The irony of it made her smile.

~ 15 ~

GREATER GOODS

I hate war as only a soldier who lived it can. Yet there is one thing to be said on the credit side. Victory required a mighty manifestation of the most ennobling virtues of man: Faith, courage, fortitude, sacrifice.
~ General Dwight D. Eisenhower. On a plaque below the cliffs of Vierville-sur-Mer, Normandy, France

February 24, 2005

Evelyn awoke to find herself upstairs on the landing, seated near a huge window with a view over the ocean. Wind-whipped waves were breaking on a sandbar about a hundred yards offshore. At first, her heart sank. Not again. Apparently jumping off a cliff wasn't enough to avoid the guys with the shiny faces. But it had been several days since her last visit, and as much as she tried to resist, she couldn't help drinking in the beauty of the place. On the wall opposite hung a couple of Turners, and further down, *The Hay Wain* by Constable. Must be for that English guy.

She charged down the stairs two at a time. When she reached the bottom, she marched into the Descartes Room. Aidan was sitting at the table reading a book. He looked up when she came in, but didn't say anything. She ignored him and turned to go, almost bumping into Korazin, who was carrying a tray of drinks.

"Ah, Evelyn. So glad you could make it." He grinned broadly. "Do join us."

He kept walking, so she found herself speaking to his back. "Did you hear about the break-in last week?" The lucidus didn't reply.

Gamaliel came in through a side door and poured them each a glass of juice. He took his seat at the end of the table. "Evelyn, a pleasure as always," he said. "Yes, a lucidus did inform us of the unfortunate events of the past week. May we express our sympathy?

It has pained us a great deal to watch this evil come upon you."

As she sat down, she jabbed her finger at the lucidus. "Sympathy? I don't need sympathy. I need protection! Can't you do that? Since you insist on bringing me back here, surely I should get some benefits."

"Benefits, you say?"

"Yeah, benefits."

"Oh, you're receiving them, I can assure you. Though they're probably not the ones you're expecting." The tall lucidus stood up and went to stand near the French doors. "Evelyn, I think the word you're looking for is 'shortcut.'"

"Oh, give me strength! I'm not looking for shortcuts, just a little less agony. And, you know, if you want to resume our debate, fine." She put up both her hands. "I concede the point from last time. Most of us accept a little pain. It's part of life. Happy now?"

Gamaliel walked over to the table and began refilling the glasses; he passed them round and took his seat. "As I'm sure you're aware, my happiness is of little consequence in the grand scheme of things. But let us return to those benefits. We call them greater goods. Have you never considered the good that arises from the existence of evil?"

"Seriously?" said Evelyn. "An enormous amount of evil doesn't lead to any good at all! It's just completely random. Whole villages are swept away during a flood. Millions die from influenza. On and on it goes. What so-called 'good' arises from such devastation? Also, why is a creator limited to such a random system? The reality is, most people never learn a thing. The vast majority die in ignorance. Right, Aidan?"

The Englishman shrugged; he picked at a pastry in front of him but remained silent.

"You like kitchen sinks?" said Korazin.

"Not especially." She hesitated. "Why?"

"Because it feels like you just threw one."

"And? Can you catch it?" She couldn't help liking the lucidus who sat across from her. Even when they disagreed, she felt he respected her and was listening to what she had to say.

"Oh, I can catch it, I think," he said. "Although you threw me some pretty heavy stuff there." He rose from his seat and poured himself a glass of water from a pitcher on the sideboard. "We're all ears, aren't we, Gamaliel?" he said, sitting down to face Evelyn. She stared at him, nonplussed. "How would *you* set things up?"

Both lucidi folded their arms, waiting.

"Hey," she said. "I never claimed to know how to set the world straight. I am simply arguing that if a creator can create goodness in his creatures by means *other* than horrendous suffering, then given *his* goodness, he would have chosen those means."

"Yet he didn't."

"No."

"And your solution?"

"I, I . . . don't have one, but that's hardly the point."

"I'm afraid this time it's entirely the point, my dear," said Gamaliel gently. "You see, a different world isn't difficult to imagine. But what makes yours superior to anyone else's? You think you know how far to turn down the dial?" He paused.

"I didn't claim I knew. I just . . ." Evelyn shrugged.

"It's easy to critique, isn't it? And when you're in pain, the arguments come thick and fast. We get that, we really do. But once you step back, well, it's not so easy to formulate an alternative." Gamaliel sipped from his glass. "We've all done it, Evelyn. We've all wished for more wisdom. That's what Lucifer offered in the Garden, except it was a lie. Humanity didn't hunger for wisdom, but control—a power grab, and it led to hell. It turns out, you see, that when you're faced with untold suffering, what you need isn't greater knowledge, but more faith. It leads to surrender, an act that strengthens the soul."

He rose from his seat, ran his fingers through his hair, and cleared his throat. His deep voice filled the room.

Imagine a world without suffering or need
Gone the grasping, the greed
No heartache and hurting
Neither sickness nor strife
Gone the groaning, the grieving
Imagine yourself with a new kind of life.

Yet the flowering lotus a subtle delusion
No striving, no thriving, no high aspiration
The bravery, fortitude, bottle, and mettle
Emerge from the mud, blood, and whine from the muzzle.

From the hard-hearted husband with no thought of other
Grows the long-suff'ring wife, the rock solid mother
In the firm, field, and fact'ry, surrounded by lies
Toils the unyielding lab'rer, eyes on heaven, the prize.

The elderly couple with rheum in their eyes
The yesterdays fading, remembering sighs
Pearl deeply discovered, yours and mine intertwine
A branch bursting forth from the root of the vine.

Imagine a world with a dearth of variety
No profit from pain, no growth to maturity
No tears wept for joy, no cries of despair
A seed without harvest, the wind without air.

No vices, no virtues, no chance to grow up
Divorced from the soil that nurtures the crop
Farewell overcomers, bereft of the should
No evil to conquer, devoid of the good.

The poem instilled quiet around the table. After listening to a second recitation, both Aidan and Evelyn sat for a while, tossing the words around in their minds, seeking meaning. When Korazin opened a window, they could hear the surf pounding the beach. Evelyn caught sight of a pair of gulls riding a thermal just above the cliffs. Their feathers quivering in the wind, they plunged down toward their nests.

Aidan checked back into the conversation. "I suppose you'll roll out the megaphone next," he said abruptly. Neither lucidus responded.

"That's like a bullhorn, right?" asked Evelyn.

"C. S. Lewis," said Aidan flatly.

She waited for more but he just picked at his food distractedly. Conflicting emotions wrestled inside her. She was irritated that he wasn't pulling his weight, but at the same time she felt drawn to the man, who was clearly in distress.

"O-kay," she said at last. "So give me the megaphone idea."

"Can't remember the quote exactly," replied Aidan. "Something about the Almighty using our pain like a megaphone to get our attention, I think. It's effective. Apparently." His voice dripped with sarcasm, which Evelyn chose to ignore.

"Do you buy this idea?" She turned toward Korazin.

"Well, let me say this," said the lucidus. "It is extremely rare for a person to come to a knowledge of the Father through intellectual inquiry. C. S. Lewis is an exception, not the rule. By contrast, suffering concentrates the mind on the deeper questions of life, which is as it should be." He paused for a moment. "Now tell me, how good is your bowline?"

Evelyn furrowed her brow. "My bowline? Whoa, that came out of left field. Um, let me see. That's a knot used on boats, right?" Korazin nodded. She glanced across the table. "You do much sailing, Aidan?"

"I used to sail with my dad," he replied without looking up.

She ignored his rudeness and turned to face Korazin. "You know, I could do with getting out of here. Can't sail worth a damn, but I'm ready to learn, if that's what you're offering."

"We depart in half an hour," announced the lucidus.

Later, when Evelyn and Aidan walked into the Descartes Room, they found both lucidi already decked out in yellow oilskins. "Right," said Korazin. "We've only ventured to this location once. Try not to go swimming. If you do fall in, it might be a good idea if you were wearing one of these." He gave them each a life jacket. They put them over their heads. "Ready?"

"Where are we going?" asked Aidan.

"North Pacific."

"Listen." He started taking off his life jacket. "I think I'm going to give this one a miss."

Evelyn suddenly felt abandoned. "Aidan, I need you," she

whispered in his ear, grabbing him by the arm.

"I'm sorry . . . I, I'm just not up to it. I can't do this right now." He turned and hugged her, holding her tightly. "You go. You'll be fine without me."

She turned to Korazin. "Right, captain, you'll have to make do with just one crew member today. That enough for you?"

"Shipshape?" He grinned.

"Just give the order."

He went to the sideboard and poured three glasses of water.

"Ready? Down the hatch!" he quipped.

Together they drank.

Seconds later, the three of them fell into the bottom of a wooden skiff pitching violently in choppy water. Evelyn found herself rolling around near the bow, a length of rope entangling her legs. She quickly extricated herself and clambered back toward the stern. Once there, she sat on a bench out of the way of the lucidi, who were working swiftly to pull up the sail and get the boat moving. The skiff was about eighteen feet long, quite sturdy, and although the sea was rough, it was far safer under sail than simply bobbing up and down on the ocean. Gamaliel pulled in a sheet and wrapped it round a cleat.

"Heads down. Going about!" announced Korazin in a loud voice, and pushed the tiller away from him. The boom swung across, surprising Evelyn, who ducked just in time. They tacked again, making steady progress, as she took in her new surroundings, lapping up every detail.

She shouted over the wind. "So where are we?"

"Pacific Ocean. West of Hawaii. The year's 1942."

"What are we doing here?"

"You'll see," shouted Gamaliel, who was tidying up the ropes in the bottom of the boat. Korazin changed course, and as they began to surf down the swell, Evelyn spotted something on the starboard bow. It looked like an airplane.

Korazin brought the boat in close, so they could see what was going on. "Looks like they just put her down. Last time, we arrived in time to see the landing. Not easy, but Cherry's quite a pilot."

"So what's going on?"

Gamaliel filled her in.

Eight men were climbing along the wings of the plane. Reaching the ends, they clambered into small life rafts—three in all. They were all servicemen of the US Army Air Corps Transport Command. Bill Cherry was the captain during the flight, but the de facto leader of the group was Eddie Rickenbacker, a war hero who had shot down a record twenty-six enemy aircraft during World War I. The airmen were on a routine run delivering a B-17 Flying Fortress to one of the Pacific islands when they ran out of fuel and were forced to ditch.

Evelyn was surprised by how little they seemed to be taking with them. One of the men was handing out small orange segments. Each man sucked on the juice eagerly and licked his lips.

"That's it?" she said. "That's all they have?"

"And no water," said Korazin. "Here, you should drink. It's easy to become dehydrated." Evelyn took a long swig from her water bottle. She spat out a mouthful and sprang back from the side.

"What?" She began coughing and spluttering. "Are those what I think they are?" Dark shapes moved beneath the boat, gliding noiselessly toward the rafts.

"Quite probably," said Korazin calmly.

The sharks circled about, surfacing periodically, their dorsal fins cutting through the water. In the rafts, the men openly discussed whether to attempt a kill, but decided against it, concluding that blood in the water was to be avoided at all costs. Korazin took the boat in a full circle around the servicemen, who now watched as their plane sank beneath the waves. There was a sucking sound as it disappeared, leaving just bubbles and swirling eddies in its wake.

"They're on their own now, that's for sure," said Evelyn.

"Oh, they're never really on their own," replied Gamaliel, securing a line. "Now hold on, because when the mezcla shifts, we can hit a rogue wave." He chuckled to himself and his face shone brightly. "There is no reason to be alarmed!"

"Right," said Korazin. "Let's jump forward to the first night." The boat pitched off the top of a wave and fell a couple of feet down a trough. He struggled to hold the tiller. The wind had dropped significantly and the only light came from the moon and the stars.

"Now there's a sight you don't see in the city." Evelyn stared up into the sky, her mouth open in wonder at the heavens. "Ooh, it's chilly." Gamaliel pulled out a thick sweater and a waterproof from a hold, handing them to his guest. She watched the rafts and clapped her hands together to generate heat in her fingers. The men nearby in the rafts were hugging their knees to their chests to keep warm. Water lapped across them, preventing them from getting comfortable, and never allowing them to sleep for very long.

The mezcla shifted again. Night became day.

The sudden change from darkness to light caused Evelyn to close her eyes tight against the glare. It took minutes before she'd adjusted to the intense sunlight. When she had, she became aware of how hot she felt. She peeled off her heavy clothing and stowed it under her seat.

Their boat drew up alongside the rafts. Evelyn couldn't believe how small they were. Two of them were about two and a half feet by five and a half feet; the third, shaped like a donut, was even smaller. The men were trying to shelter from the sun, their shirts draped over their faces. One was reading a small book.

The mezcla shifted again, sending the boat smashing into another wave. Evelyn gave a yelp of surprise. "Day four now, I think," said Gamaliel, smiling his encouragement.

The men looked awful. Their skin was burned to a crisp and they lay in a stupor, barely moving at all. Most covered their heads with their shirts, but the sun was merciless. Every exposed piece of flesh had turned an angry red; some had even blistered.

Suddenly a bird landed on the head of one of the men. They all sat up and froze. Evelyn was immobile, her eyes fixed on the man, who slowly raised his hands, inch by inch. With a quick motion, he grabbed it and killed it. A cheer went up. There was no way to cook it so they ate it raw. Their spirits lifted, even though they still had no water.

The mezcla shifted to the evening.

"Watch that man there," said Korazin, pointing. "His name is Lieutenant James Whittaker."

Cherry's voice began echoing across the water. "Therefore, take ye no thought, saying: What shall we eat? Or what shall we drink? Or wherewithal shall we be clothed? For these are things the heathen seeketh. For your Heavenly Father knoweth that ye have need of all these things. But seek ye first the Kingdom of God, and His righteousness; and all these things shall be added unto thee. Take therefore no thought for the morrow; for the morrow shall take thought for the things of itself."

"Whittaker doesn't look convinced," said Evelyn.

"No, he doesn't. He had a religious upbringing but it didn't stick. All this is new to him." The mezcla shifted again. She could hear the Lord's Prayer drifting across the water. This time, however, the lieutenant joined in. He appeared to know the beginning and the end. His amen was one of the loudest.

Cherry's voice rolled across the waves. "Old Master," he said. His tone was filled with reverence and deference. He spoke as though to an esteemed schoolteacher. "We know there's no guarantee we'll eat in the morning. But we're in an awful fix, you know. We sure are counting on a little something by day after tomorrow, at least. See what you can do for us, Old Master." The men grunted their assent.

Evelyn strained to hear the closing amen. "That's quite a prayer."

"Yes it is. These prayers taught Whittaker to trust his Father. By his own admission, he was self-sufficient, self-reliant. He thought he was far too tough for hymns and meetings." The men's bodies sagged against the sides of the rafts. "Lack of water," continued the lucidus. "Right now, dehydration is what's killing them."

The Lord's Prayer was once again audible, the faces of the men reflecting a whole gamut of emotions. Some were hopeful, others in despair.

"Old Master," said Cherry, "we called on you for food and you delivered. We ask you now for water. We've done the best we can. If you don't make up your mind to help us pretty soon, I guess that's all there'll be to it. The next move is up to you, Old Master." His voice was neither pleading nor pitiful. It was matter-of-fact, as though he was addressing someone sitting right next to him.

As Evelyn and the lucidi watched, a raincloud built in the east.

Moments later, the heavens opened and tropical rain fell in sheets, soaking them all in soft, warm rain. The men's life jackets were inflatable, so they wrung out their shirts into them, attempting to capture as much water as they could. They let out hoots of laughter and slapped each other on the back.

"Looks like the rain arrived just in time," said Evelyn.

The relief was short-lived, however. The mezcla shifted once more, and they found themselves in the middle of a sweltering hot day. Their clothes were soon bone dry. Whenever the men adjusted position in the rafts, their bodies brushed up against each other. The slightest contact with another man's bright red rash caused him to cry out in pain.

The following day, clouds appeared on the horizon, gathering pace toward them. A dark shadow on the water indicated the presence of a squall edging closer. The prospect of rain triggered a hubbub of excitement among the men; they began whooping and laughing.

Their joy was premature.

For no apparent reason, the squall stopped and began moving away. Their faces were haggard with disbelief.

A voice rang out over the water. It was Whittaker.

"God," he prayed. "You know what that water means to us. The wind has blown it away. It is in your power, God, to send back that rain. It's nothing to you, but it means life to us. Please. Order the wind to blow back that rain to us." Every eye was fixed on the squall as it stopped in its tracks. At an excruciatingly slow pace, it changed direction, heading back toward the rafts. The wind direction never changed. The squall simply moved against the wind toward the men. When it arrived, it brought a deluge larger and more gratefully received than the last. Every man celebrated as the water washed the salt out of his wounds.

Their joy was unrestrained. But it did not last long.

After the next shift in the mezcla, they sat in the doldrums in the stifling heat. The surrounding water was flat calm, with barely a ripple disturbing the surface. Gradually, the men started to lose touch with reality. Evelyn could see Whittaker slumped against the side of his raft, his eyes at half-mast, delirium playing havoc with his mind.

Yet the following day, it was he who led the service.

"He's our guy, isn't he?" she said. "The soldier who started out not knowing any of the prayers. And now he's leading?"

"Please, Lord." The lieutenant started praying. "You know how bad this looks for us. We've made it this far. We've done the best we can, but we need your help again. Please remember us. Amen." He looked up into the sky; it was cloudless and intolerably bright.

Late in the afternoon, as the men chatted away to Davy Jones, his locker, and various fictitious characters, a dull drone started throbbing in the distance.

Bill Cherry sat up. "I hear an engine!" he shouted. "I hear an engine!" All their faces turned in the direction of the noise. A Navy Kingfisher emerged from the haze, five miles to the north of their position, too far away to signal. The men flapped their arms wildly, but to no avail. As the plane's engine faded to a low hum, the men were devastated. They shrank back, cursing their luck.

The following day, they cut the rafts adrift.

Gamaliel set a course to follow closely behind Whittaker and two other men. The mezcla shifted, reaching the twentieth day of the ordeal.

"Is that land?" said Evelyn. The serviceman pulled out the oars and began pulling as hard as he could toward a line of palm trees on the horizon. "The other two aren't helping! They're not gonna make it."

"Just wait, Evelyn."

Without warning, the wind shifted and the current began to move the raft further away from the land. As Evelyn watched the island slip by like a huge ocean liner, sharks carved in and out between the skiff and the raft. Not far off, Whittaker stared up into the sky, shouting over the wind. "God, I'm finished! I can't do any more. You hear? It's just me now but I can't row against this current on my own. I'm gonna need some of that strength you got, to help me. *Please. Help me!*"

A rainstorm blew in and soaked them all. The island disappeared. Whittaker picked up an oar and slashed at the sharks circling the little raft, causing them to retreat for a while. Blinking away the rain, he expended the last of his energy, until he was about to drop. Evelyn pulled on a waterproof and drank from her bottle. When she looked again, she noticed someone sitting behind the man with the oars. She turned to Gamaliel. "What's going on? Who's that?"

The lucidus squinted at the raft. "I believe that's Nathaniel. Let me see." He shaded his eyes with his hand. "Yes, that's definitely Nathaniel." A small smile settled on his face.

A tall figure sat behind Whittaker and although the serviceman's arms appeared to pull the oars back, they were limp, the strength gone. The force of each pull was exerted by the lucidus behind. The raft inched its way toward land; it bumped over a sandbank and crashed onto the beach. Evelyn watched, riveted. When the men reached the shore, they crawled their way to safety and lay, exhausted, beneath a coconut tree.

"Three weeks. They lasted three weeks out there," said Gamaliel as he brought the skiff in carefully, making land shortly afterward. The three of them sat under a palm tree and looked out across the ocean, sipping from their water bottles. Evelyn cracked open an orange and offered a slice to Korazin.

"Thank you," he said, looking down the beach. "You know, we're right down at the tip of this island. They nearly missed it. They *would* have missed it actually, without some help."

Nearby, two of the survivors bowed their heads. The third man lay unconscious between them. "We give you thanks, O Lord, for saving us," said Whittaker. "We're different men to the ones who landed on the ocean three weeks ago. We wouldn't wish this on anyone, but you have used it to change us. Please keep Jimmy alive here. He's real bad, Lord, and he needs help. Amen."

Evelyn's head was full of questions, but they all faded away as she watched the serviceman leaning over his friend. He lifted the man's head and brought half a coconut up to the man's lips.

"Well done, Jimmy," said Whittaker, as the man began sucking on the edge of the shell. "Well done, son."

When they arrived back in the Descartes Room, Aidan was sitting near the French doors. He looked up when they came in, his face expressionless. Evelyn went over and sat down opposite him.

"Well, you missed something really special."

"Oh yeah?" He sounded angry.

"Hey, watch your tone!"

He scowled. "So what happened? Where did you go?"

The lucidi took their places. She hesitated before speaking. "Well, we wound up in the Pacific right near a plane after it crash-landed. 1942, during the war. Eight army guys got into these rafts and they somehow survived for three weeks."

"I'm guessing they had water then."

"Actually, no. But it rained, and you know, I can't explain it, they prayed and stuff happened. Heck, I don't know what to make of it, but it was one of the most incredible things I've ever seen. You shoulda been there."

"Well that's just great, isn't it? They pray and whoopee do, the Almighty comes riding in on his charger and everything turns out just fine. I am so pleased for these guys, whoever they were."

"Aidan!" said Evelyn. "Stop!"

"Stop? You want me to stop? Do I seem upset, is that it? Well, my apologies for the negativity, but you'll excuse me if I don't find this story so heartwarming." He got up and began pacing up and down. "See, I did a little praying of my own, remember?" He jabbed his finger at Gamaliel. "Were you on duty that day? *Were you?*" Evelyn looked at the lucidus, confused. "Mind you, you're not really the person in charge, are you? You're just a minion. Isn't that what we all are? Minions? Just pieces being moved around like pawns on a chess board?"

"Aidan!" said Evelyn.

"*Shut up!* I'm talking to him now. And this other guy. What did you do just now? You went to watch a nice, happy, feel-good story about some guys who prayed and big daddy up there deigned to reach down and do something. But hold on a moment. Didn't you say it took three weeks? So he had them all sitting about, getting burned up, dying of hunger and thirst—and what, he steps in and we're supposed to stand up and applaud? Is that it? Well, where was he when *we* needed him? *Where was he?*"

He slumped into a chair and held his head in his hands. The memories came flooding back, pounding on his forehead. Korazin went and sat down next to him, placing a hand on his shoulder. The touch caused a jolt to go through Aidan's body. It was followed by a warm, soothing sensation that brought comfort into the dark recesses of his heart. However, once the lucidus moved aside, the pain seeped back again.

Aidan got up, went to the French doors and looked out over the ocean. With eyes closed, he walked back into a warm, spring morning.

The apple trees were starting to blossom, their branches bursting with a profusion of light pink petals. They had stopped off overnight at Bruce's place on their way down to Devon. At the last minute, Bruce had told them he wanted to join them. He hadn't seen his nephew in a while, so why not? Simon had been staying with his grandparents in Tavistock for a few days, and his parents were eager to pick him up. Now with uncle in tow. As they finished packing the car, Bruce rattled on about the new digital technology they were installing at the BBC. Aidan's predictably flippant response incurred a despairing shake of the head from his brother.

"I realize, you idiot," he said, "that computers and surfing don't mix. You're such a Luddite, Aidan. It's time for you to pack up your Morse code and join us in the nineties!"

After climbing into the car, Aidan remembered how odd it felt to be sitting in the back. He hardly ever sat there. Driving along, the noise in the car was deafening. Bruce started singing "She Bangs the Drums" by The Stone Roses, while Naomi ignored him, raising her voice to ask Aidan if they could give the awkward new couple at church a place to stay. Aidan unbuckled his seat belt and shifted to the middle in an effort to hear her voice.

They were passing Salisbury on the A303 when it happened. He recalled the red lettering on the front of the truck as it came toward them. Its approach stimulated a scream in his head that never made it to his vocal cords. When the massive vehicle struck their car, all he could remember was the sensation of flying through the air.

After that, he blacked out.

When he regained consciousness, he was lying on his front, his cheek pressed against the tarmac, a piece of metal sticking out of his leg. As the shock wore off, everything started to hurt, especially his left leg. Blood oozed out of a deep gash in his thigh, soaking his clothing and dripping onto the road. He tore off a shirt sleeve and wrapped it around the injury. Sitting up, he breathed in a mouthful of black smoke coming from the overturned truck. It made him retch.

He turned to Korazin and spoke, his voice barely audible. "I prayed. You know that, don't you?" The lucidus didn't respond. "When they were lying on the side of the road, I prayed like never before. I knew Bruce hadn't made it—no one survives injuries like that—but Naomi was still conscious. She was so happy that day, wasn't she?" His hollow laugh echoed around the room. "And remember Bruce's hair? He'd dyed it pink, the stupid bugger." He bowed his head and started laughing, a pitiful sound that rapidly turned into sobbing. Evelyn watched him, powerless in her isolation, while the lucidi sat calmly, waiting for him to regain his composure.

Aidan continued to address Korazin, his voice brittle. "Since I arrived here, I've been meaning to ask you, just in case, you know, you have a hotline to the throne room. Why? Tell me that. *Why?* Because surely a woman as gorgeous . . . and virtuous . . . and loved as she was, she'd be an asset to the world, wouldn't she? She was only thirty-three, for crying out loud! And what about Bruce?" he shouted. "*Why him and not me? It's not right. It's not fair!*" He stormed out of the room, slamming the door behind him.

Evelyn looked at the two lucidi, who sat motionless in their seats. "What's wrong with you?" she blurted out. "Why don't you do something?" Neither said a word. "Have you no compassion?" She was shaking with pent-up emotion.

Aidan sat on a rock a few yards from the cliff edge. He was convinced he'd blown it. Surely they would never invite him back now. Not after all the shouting. He picked up a stone and threw it over the edge. It clattered on the rocks below. All his emotions were jumbled up. His grief gnawed at his insides, but overlaid upon it was a burning rage at the lucidi. He wanted to physically assault these representatives of the Almighty, but not until he'd sat down and asked them a whole heap of questions. It made no sense at all. He had no answers so he simply wept until there were no more tears to weep. He was mad, intrigued, confused, but most of all lost. Desperately lost. Gaining hold of his thoughts was like lassoing a whirlwind.

He looked down toward the far end of the beach, where the breakers were pummeling a pile of boulders. The spray caught the sun, sending shafts of light in all directions. One of the waves rose sharply; Aidan caught sight of a small school of dolphins riding inside, skimming down the face toward the shoreline. He felt himself trapped between the beauty of where he sat and the agony raging within. He closed his eyes, enjoying the breeze blowing up from below the cliffs. Evelyn's arrival interrupted his thoughts. Without saying anything, she perched herself on a rock nearby and waited. The silence they shared began to alleviate some of his pain.

"She sounds like quite a woman," she said eventually. "I'm very sorry for your loss."

Aidan didn't reply. The sun was setting on the horizon. He could smell the salt in the air. A pink, mackerel sky swept down to the ocean, where he spotted a flock of pelicans flying in formation. They skimmed the surface with their bellies; one of them suddenly folded its wings and dived, emerging with a fish in its beak. The bird's throat bulged as it swallowed.

He looked across at her. "I apologize."

"What for?"

"For telling you to shut up. I don't do that."

"Yes, you do. Stop apologizing and being so . . . polite and English."

He couldn't help smiling. "You Americans. You're so direct."

"Were you married long?"

"Twelve years." He sighed.

He was about to speak when she said, "Listen, Aidan, I'm sorry. I'm a pushy American and I'm invading your space. Forget I asked."

"No, no, it's fine," he lied, looking away.

"Seemed pretty raw back there."

He paused, withdrawing into the safety of silence. His habit was to retreat, to use his wife's death as a defense against intimacy. Such a loss, even when wielded poorly, was always effective. But on this occasion, he couldn't help but change tack. The woman by his side simply compelled his attention. He glanced across at her again.

Evelyn met his gaze. "You know, I should leave you. I'm really sorry. No one should gatecrash another person's grief. I'll, er, I'll see you later."

As she got up, he reached across and grabbed her arm. "No," he said. "Please don't go. Don't do that." He released her arm.

She sat back down.

They watched the sun's last hurrah—a pink and vermilion spray across the darkening sky. The wind had died down and the light was fading fast; the air was cooling. Above them, the stars were starting to flicker. Evelyn draped her sweater over her shoulders. "I don't know if you heard," Aidan looked quizzical. "I got a little upset too." She paused. "Let's just say there's no point in jumping off the cliff."

"Wow." His mood lightened. "No cliff-jumping. Duly noted."

They looked at each other, smiling.

Aidan talked about his marriage, its pleasures and pains. He hadn't unloaded to anyone since Naomi's death. Confiding in another woman made him feel a touch guilty, though the words flowed like water. With each passing minute the weight seemed to fall away.

"Are your parents still alive?" said Evelyn.

"My father is. Mother died a few years ago. Funeral for ten people. I have two aunts but neither showed up." He kicked some tussock grasses growing nearby.

Evelyn couldn't resist. "Do you remember anything when you wake up?"

"Well," he said, taking a moment to think about it. "I remember the *Pietà* in my dreams . . . and the ocean sometimes . . ."

She hesitated. "And me?"

"I've dreamed of you twice, I think. My dreams are mostly about the atmosphere, how I feel. I wake up knowing I've been happy or fearful or excited."

"And the dreams I'm in?" She looked him full in the face.

He wanted to meet her gaze but, instead, looked down at the ground. "Americans," he declared, grinning. "Come on, it's getting late."

~ 16 ~

DORINA

*People were created to be loved. Things were created
to be used. The reason why the world is in chaos
is because things are being loved
and people are being used.*
~ Dalai Lama

February 25, 2005

Dorina lay in bed, gazing at the ceiling. The dawn sun penetrated the threadbare curtains, bathing the room in a cool, blue light. Sleep eluded her; she'd been awake since six, painfully trawling through memories that refused to remain buried. The knowledge that they would be picked over later that day caused them to surface and sear her soul. She watched her breath condense above her, and shivered. The only radiator in the room was broken. Turning over, she looked at her alarm clock.

It was still early. 7:15 a.m.

She rolled out of bed, stretched, and grabbed a towel off the back of the door. The bathroom she shared with the other girls was three doors down. Once inside, she peered at herself in the mirror. A young woman in her mid-twenties stared back. She was medium height, around five feet five, pretty with dark brown eyes, and at one time, long, lustrous dark curls. She'd shorn them off months ago. She ran her hand through what was left. A short, heavyset man with no neck used to come in wearing an Arsenal shirt. He enjoyed tugging on her hair during sex, which hurt. So she'd cut it off.

Dorina showered, using excessive amounts of cheap soap provided by the shelter. Afterward, she brushed her teeth. She brushed them a lot. It was a way to feel clean again. The dirt never seemed to wash away completely, but showering and teeth cleaning made her feel better. She looked in the mirror again. The blank stare was still there. At one time she thought her smile was gone forever.

At first, when they shoved her into the car, she didn't do anything. Something was obviously wrong, but instead of fighting, she decided to wait for a second chance. But, of course, there were no second chances. The moment they pushed her through the front door of a little house in King's Cross, she knew she'd made the worst mistake of her life.

The place was roasting. Wet laundry hung on every radiator, sending a damp fog down the narrow, dark passageway and into the front room. On the couch, two girls were slouching, reading magazines. Photographs of women with their legs apart or on all fours, looking back at the camera, covered the walls. On TV, a porn film was running. The girls ignored it, and when she came into the room, they didn't even glance in her direction. When they did speak to her later, they refused to make eye contact. Dorina noticed how young they were. She felt like an old lady by comparison. And she was just twenty-four.

"What's your name?" she asked a girl who looked like a china doll. The girl wore a tight, pink PVC skirt and a lime-green halter top made of cheap polyester. Her fake eyelashes were so heavy with mascara she was struggling to open her eyes fully. Or maybe that was due to the drugs. The track marks up one of her arms looked new; dried blood was caked near the elbow. Her jaw moved in a circular motion, chewing gum.

"Petra," said the girl, looking away. Dorina wondered what her real name was.

"How old are you?"

"Fifteen."

"Where are you from?" Dorina's English was limited when she arrived. She had been looking forward to improving it in a vibrant, cosmopolitan city.

"Albania," came the reply. The brothel contained a mixture of Eastern European girls, along with some from North Africa. Most of them were drug addicts. One girl, called Mika, told her that her family would kill her if she went home. Dorina wondered what her own mother would do. They hadn't exactly parted as friends. She had turned down the best offer she was ever likely to receive, and for what? To be with Razvan. The bastard. That was one word she knew in English. In fact, she had learned quite a few swear words. Make them feel like they're giving you pleasure, then it's over so much more quickly. That's what they told her, so that's what she did. She moaned and whispered the words they used beginning with F, C, and A. She didn't care what they meant, as long as they got it over with as fast as possible.

When Dorina first arrived, they tossed her into a room on the second floor. Goran, his fat arms covered with tattoos, pressed her down on the bed and grabbed her hair.

"Four thousand pounds. You owing us money. Four thousand."

He ripped off her dress and raped her. Jakov followed, spitting on her as he left. She had no passport, no money, and no hope of getting out. No wonder she cried herself to sleep at night.

The passing of the hours, days, and weeks was hard to keep track of, but one morning they had moved her to a different brothel. In Camden Town. A large black car drew up outside and she was marched out the front door. "If you shouting, we raping." Goran and Jakov knew the technical term for their crime, and didn't mind using it. When they reached the other house, they dragged her out the back of the car and shoved her toward the door. Five seconds in the open air was all she had before the darkness returned. She remembered looking up as she walked in. Fluffy white clouds, like pillows, floated in an ocean of blue. The image remained with her for the next few months. It was a picture of space, of freedom. And she clung to it like nothing else.

Dorina walked downstairs, made a cup of tea, and went to sit in the living room. It was filled with shabby brown chairs, many held together by duct tape. She took note of the unsavory décor. The carpet was covered in orange and brown swirls and the curtains were made of purple polyester. Poor color schemes always caught her eye. Back home, she had an eye for design. She used to enjoy dressmaking.

Her drawings had even caught the eye of a local businessman, who invited her to the workshop above his clothing store. She received a letter inviting her to a second meeting on the day Razvan called from England. She was in love, so what was there to decide?

She picked up *Hello!* magazine and flicked through the pages. Shiny, happy people with spray tans held well-fed babies while flashing their white teeth at the camera. She turned to a page showing the Beckhams "at home." "Beckingham Palace," the report was headlined. Victoria Beckham's tanned face wore a blank expression. Dorina thought she looked sad. She wondered if the Beckhams were in love, wondered if all that money had helped them find happiness.

Penelope, the lady who ran the shelter, came in. "You okay?" she said. "They'll come for you at 9:30 a.m." In court the previous day, they'd asked her if the defendant, Dragan Bakic, had raped her. She'd been tempted to lie, to hold him responsible for what Goran and Jakov had done to her. But she couldn't. She'd never heard of him raping any of the girls.

A couple of hours later, Dorina was sitting in the witness box, looking at a man in a wig who was rocking from foot to foot. He told her the ordeal was almost over. She hoped he was telling the truth.

"Please tell the court, Ms. Ibanescu," said Molsberry rather grandly, "about the conditions in the brothel where you worked."

"The house was horrible," she said. "Dirty. Dark. Girls, they walk with no clothes sometimes. The bathroom so disgusting. I sleep in small room in . . ." She pointed up.

"In the attic? The roof?"

"Yes. In attic. In first month, they lock door. Give me bucket for toilet. Send men to my room. One I fight. He get angry. Rape me. Then I decide, better not stop them. So I lie on bed. Let men having sex with me. When they leave, I cry. I cry all day."

"Did you ever see Razvan again?" asked Molsberry.

"No." She paused. "When I live in brothel, I wanting to die. I steal knife from kitchen. I want to cut arms. Next day, very late, Besiana from Russia, she come to my room. She sit on bed with me. She is crying. I put my arm on her shoulder, give her paper tissue for wipe nose. It make me feeling good, doing something for help. I am not bad person. I am here for helping people. She tell joke and I laugh. We both laugh and cry." She wiped a couple of tears from her cheek. "In my country, in Romania, I make dresses. I'm not prostitute. I'm good person. I want to go home. Live better life. I want to see my mother."

She began to weep.

The court adjourned for the day.

After work, Aidan found Edward and Sean tucked away in the corner of The Old Oak on North End Road in West Kensington. They were both friends from Oxford University, each the polar opposite of the other. Sean, an Irishman, was an artist who rented a two-bedroom flat in Pimlico with his wife. He was quiet and declined to own up to his double first. He'd started off in finance, earned piles of money, and then without notice, he'd "retired" at age thirty-four. Now he devoted himself to his true passion, which involved daubing canvases with brightly colored paints; they sold for handsome sums to yuppies who liked "urban art."

"What'll it be, gentlemen?" said Sean.

"Pint of Harp," said Aidan, removing his jacket. Sean raised his eyebrows. Aidan rarely drank lager. He was normally a real ale man.

"The usual," said the man filling the corner seat, already nursing what looked like a double whisky.

Edward was a QC whose time was spent largely at The Old Bailey. He was conservative—according to Sean, further right than Genghis Khan—and enjoyed the cut and thrust of advocacy better than sex. At least, that's what he claimed when he wanted to shock a judge. He wore cufflinks in expensive double-cuff shirts, and owned a variety of jackets custom-made for him by his favorite tailor in Savile Row. He was large of both body and personality. Aidan had been his opposite number on numerous occasions and found him to be pugnacious but fair. He also discovered that whatever offenses might have been suffered during the day were soon forgotten once they were quaffing their pints in one of London's better establishments.

Sean returned bearing liquid refreshment, to be greeted by Edward's opening salvo. "I saw one of your efforts in the Barbican the other day, old chap!" said the barrister. "You've got a nerve!" The conversation was soon replete with jovial remarks, as they cross-examined each other on the general furniture that comprised a day in court or in front of an easel.

"You'll like this one, Aidan," said Edward. "I'm a vicar. I live in a nicely appointed detached house in Surrey. Two kids in primary. Wife who bakes for Britain. Laura Ashley dresses. I got a first from Cambridge. I enjoy crosswords. The Times, of course. I play golf with the judge and I have a terrific baritone voice. I am squeaky clean."

"And what? You got a little hot under the collar with the confirmation candidates?" said Sean.

"Close. Sixteen-year-old alleging inappropriate sexual advances."

"Well, here's what you're facing, reverend," said Aidan. "I'm on your jury. I'm a builder. I had always wanted to go to university but I went to Catholic school, and the priest, he did bad things to me. Messed me up. So when I look at your vicar, what do I see? An evil man in a dress. Unavoidable. But next to me in the jury box is a housewife who decorates the church every Saturday. Ready for the Sunday services. She's in her sixties and the vicar says thank you every time. Without fail. Never flirts, straight up, a real gent. Not like her husband, who ignores her most of the time. So when she looks at him, she sees a good man, right? How could he be anything else?" He paused. "Inputs and outputs . . . We see what we expect to see, what we're programmed to see." He stood up suddenly and smacked his forehead. "Ha ha! That's it, Ed, you little beauty. Ha ha!"

He sat back down. His friends looked at him with blank expressions. He continued, "You wanna know? Okay. I'm defending a big man with tattoos and the jury see what they *expect* to see. Of course they do. Thing is, they're looking at the wrong man." He paused. "Ed, I salute you. Glenfiddich, isn't it? "

He started to get up.

"And what about me?" said Edward. "Am I guilty?"

"No idea, but if the majority of the jury were screwed up by men wearing fancy dress on Sundays, you're in trouble."

"Hmm. My own fancy dress in court probably doesn't help either, does it?"

When Aidan arrived home that evening, he muttered thanks under his breath to Carmen, his cleaner, for doing the shopping. He rustled up a dish of something with eggs and vegetables, and made his way to the living room, where he ensconced himself in an armchair. With his dinner balanced precariously on his lap, he switched on the TV. A new show called *The Apprentice* was on. A chap named Tim talked a lot and started to get upset, so Aidan pressed mute.

He was just bringing his fork up to his mouth when Simon walked in and made his way to the kitchen. He'd forgotten his son often stayed over when Beth was away on business.

"Hi, Dad," he called. Aidan could hear him rummaging through papers. "Hey, what's the deal with all these overdue bills?"

His voice was good-humored, but to Aidan's ears it rankled. "None of your business," he replied tetchily. "Leave them alone! Now why don't you get something to eat? I think there are still eggs in the fridge."

Simon emerged from the kitchen a little later with some cheese on toast and a glass of milk. After dinner, Aidan pulled out a mahogany chess set he'd purloined from his father and laid out the pieces. While casually reading the paper, Simon had his father in full retreat within a few moves. His son's nonchalance irritated Aidan, yet made him glow with pride in equal measure.

Aidan said, "Come on, have a nightcap before you hit the sack." He poured them both a whisky. Simon stood up and started perusing the photographs on the mantel. Most included either him or his parents. On holiday. With friends. The usual family stuff.

"Simon," said Aidan, putting down his glass. "Do you dream much?"

"Dream?"

"Yes, dream. What are your dreams like?"

"Oh, you know, probably the same as anybody else's. I feature fairly prominently, of course." He laughed. "I drive a Lamborghini, meet politicians, read the news on TV. That kind of thing. You want to know if I dream in color, right? Or if I fly? No to both of those, sorry." He sank into an armchair.

"Ever had a dream that repeats itself?"

"Similar dreams maybe, but never the same one. Why?"

"Well . . . I keep seeing the same person in mine."

"Mum?"

"No, not Mum. A different woman. I see her across a table most often. And sometimes we're sitting near a cliff. Crazy, right?"

"No, not at all. It's probably something going on in your brain. Some kind of neuron firing repeatedly when you sleep. Can you control what's happening? Can you stop it and make decisions consciously?"

"Well, when I wake up, I can remember making real decisions, but—"

"A lucid dream."

"What's that?"

"It's when you're consciously aware that you're dreaming, and you can determine the course of the dream. At least, your part in it. It either starts as a normal dream and changes, or you can go straight from being awake to dreaming, without really losing consciousness. They've proved it using rapid eye movements. I saw a documentary once."

"No," said Aidan doubtfully. "That's not it. This is different. When I wake up, it's like I was right there. Physically there. Colors you can't imagine."

"That's what they're like apparently. Extra vivid."

"Hmm. I'm not sure. Maybe."

"So, tell me about the woman," said Simon. "What's she like? Is she like Mum?"

"No. Nothing like her. She's American."

"American? How do you know?"

"We talk. I can't remember it all, but we talk. It's all a bit vague. Stuff about her relatives, I think." He twirled the ice about in the bottom of his glass, then poured himself a thimbleful more whisky. His face broke into a small smile.

"You like her, don't you? You son of a gun!"

Aidan tried to stop smiling but couldn't. "She seems real, Simon. Like you or me."

"Do you see her every night?"

"No. Not every night. Just sometimes." He looked up at the ceiling, his eyelids beginning to droop.

Simon sat forward and tapped his father on the leg. "Dad? You look bushed. You should get to bed. Who knows? Tonight you might find yourself chatting to a tasty blond from California."

"I didn't say anything about California."

"No, you didn't." He hesitated. "But she's obviously cute, and isn't it an article of faith in America that the girls from California are the pretty ones? I think The Beach Boys established that doctrine in the sixties."

"Sounds like you're mixing your theology with your imagination."

"Quite possibly." Simon smiled and rose to his feet. He went to the kitchen and put his plate in the dishwasher. Before going upstairs, he poked his head into the living room. "Dad?" Aidan looked up. "Thanks . . . Really."

"For what?"

"Oh, I dunno . . . Everything."

~ 17 ~

LOVE THY NEIGHBOR

*Loneliness and the feeling of being unwanted
is the most terrible poverty.*
~ Mother Teresa

February 26, 2005

Evelyn ran down to the boardwalk with Søren by her side. The Westie's legs moved back and forth at a furious pace just to keep up. She smiled down at him.

"Come on, lazybones. Let's show 'em all what shape you're in!"

They took off toward Manhattan Beach. Søren trotted along happily for a while, but he preferred water to asphalt on his paws, so he charged off to the shoreline. Evelyn felt the pull of the ocean and followed him, conscious that dogs weren't really allowed on the beach. It would have to be a quick stop. The surf was up, waves crashing on the beach with a steady rhythm. She sank down on the sand, watching her dog chasing sandpipers through the shallows. Further out, surfers sat with their boards poking out of the water like shark fins. They peered into the distance waiting for the next wave. When it arrived, a tall blond youth caught it briefly and completed a couple of cutbacks. He sank into the foam, climbed back on, and paddled out to his friends.

Søren began digging a hole.

"Come on, you—time to get home," said Evelyn.

She chose a route that took her through the canals, narrowly avoiding a couple of rollerbladers on the way. She loved running along the canals. Of course, the connection with the Italian city was tenuous at best. Venice Beach didn't have a fresco to its name; it wasn't sinking into oblivion with an expiration date within spitting distance; nor did its waterways emit a rank odor during the summer months.

"Get your heart rate up, you little mutt?" she said to Søren as she walked through the front door. The dog scampered over to his water bowl, plunged his nose into it, and squirted liquid out of his nostrils onto the floor. Evelyn filled a glass with water, drained it in one gulp, and pulled out the coffee grinder. As the coffee started to brew, she fell onto the couch and reached back to turn on the radio. *From WBEZ Chicago, it's* This American Life *distributed by Public Radio International. I'm Ira Glass . . .*

Closing her eyes, she was about to tune into the program, when she heard shouting outside. She got up and looked out the front window.

A huge moving truck had pulled up in front of the neighbor's house. Delivery guys were hollering at each other from one end of the vehicle to the other. Boxes sat in the front yard, observed by a skinny man in his fifties, a cigarette in his mouth, who was sitting on an upturned box watching the proceedings. Occasionally, he barked out instructions. The new neighbor, no doubt. The word "ENGLAND" was splashed across the side of the truck. It seemed to jump out at her. She stared at the bold red lettering, mining her memories for significance, but they didn't coalesce into anything meaningful.

Four men were manhandling a couch out of the back of the truck. They each tugged in different directions until one of them fell over. Evelyn stifled some laughter. It looked like an episode of *Laurel and Hardy*, especially when one of the men started bawling out his companions. Red-faced, they dusted themselves down and started again. After some mild cussing, the couch began swaying into the house, its fabric scuffing against the doorframe. The sound of ripping material made Evelyn cringe.

She grabbed her keys and headed for the store.

Once home, with shelves stocked for the week, she sank into an armchair and picked up her book. The name on the cover induced a spark of recognition, as though the word *Fatherland* had some meaning beyond naming the book. She dug around in her mind but couldn't come up with anything. It was frustrating. As she was turning her attention back to her book, she caught sight of her new neighbor entering his house. For a moment, he stood facing Evelyn's house. She thought he looked lonely.

Clouds of cookie mix soon filled the kitchen.

It was early evening when she walked over and pressed a rusty doorbell. A middle-aged man wearing a pair of beige polyester slacks, a brown jacket, and loafers, opened the door. He was tall and skinny, his hair was thinning, and dandruff was collecting on his collar. Sweat lined his upper lip, where a thin mustache struggled to sprout.

"Hi!" she said. "Hope your movers didn't break too much this morning. My name's Evelyn. I live, er, just right there." She stood pointing at her house and feeling a little foolish.

"Right, right." The man's voice was unusually high-pitched. "Duncan. Duncan Fowler. Pleased to meet you."

She was about to offer her hand for a handshake, but thought better of it. "Listen, I baked you some cookies earlier today. Neighborly thing to do 'n' all. But I don't want to interrupt your unpacking or anything."

She handed him the plate and turned to go.

"Don't leave. Please. Come right in." He held the door wide open and ushered with his left arm. The offer caught her off guard. There was something about greeting a new neighbor that made her doubly nervous. As though there was more at stake than just a routine social call. A small smile crossed his face. She found it impossible to refuse.

As she walked forward, she felt like a kid at the top of a waterslide. Once she had forward motion, there was nothing she could do to stop herself. It made her feel a little sick inside. Walking through to the kitchen, she glanced around the living room. Over in the corner were several large display cases full of butterflies. Magnifying glasses, dozens of them, were strewn across an old bucket chair near a hutch lying on its side. The deliverymen hadn't bothered to set it the right way up. In a container in the corner, she spotted some odd-looking gray objects, like stretched canvas. She didn't realize it but they were the dried, treated internal organs of various cats whose lives had been ended in a backwoods in West Virginia. Duncan saw her look but didn't enlighten her.

On the windowsill stood a photograph in a silver frame, newly polished. It showed her host with an old woman who looked strikingly similar to him. That must be his mom. How nice. In the photo, Duncan was smiling, but the tall, erect woman by his side looked like she wanted to do physical harm to the photographer. Her brow was creased, the corners of her mouth were turned down, and her lips were pursed. Evelyn noticed that although they stood next to each other, there was a gap of about a foot between them. The pose was awkward, uncomfortable.

Next to the kitchen door, an enormous hunting rifle stood leaning against the wall. Evelyn, who was a couple of steps behind Duncan, recoiled slightly when she saw it. He didn't notice her reaction, just kept making his way through to the kitchen. On the counters lay more tins of tuna than she'd ever seen. They were stacked in piles of five and six on every available surface.

"That's a lot of canned fish," she said, immediately regretting it.

He ignored her comment. "Coffee? Tea?" He started pulling some chipped cups out of a crate.

"Oh, just water for me, thanks," she said, already anxious to make the visit a short one.

"I sure like this city." Duncan described his move from West Virginia to LA and his new job in maintenance with the city. He was fifty-five, single, no kids, and enjoyed remote-controlled aircraft. Apparently, there were some ideal locations for flying them out in the desert. Thermals, he said. It was all about the thermals. Evelyn nodded encouragingly to convey interest and comprehension but was rapidly feeling nauseous inside the tiny kitchen.

She spotted what looked like a wing outside, an observation that at least removed her from the kitchen. They walked out onto the deck, where Duncan picked up his pride and joy. She had never known there was so much to learn about operating a remote-controlled glider. He spoke quickly, hardly needing to breathe. As he became increasingly animated, Evelyn despaired of finding an opening to make her apologies and leave. His whiny voice was giving her a headache.

"You like Letterman?" he asked. "I like 'im. He's real funny, ain't he? Man, I'm tellin' ya, when he gets started, he just kills, just kills me." He roared with laughter, oblivious of whether his guest was joining in. His hilarity made her feel queasy.

"You know, Duncan . . . Duncan? Listen, I really have to go."

"You're leavin'? Already?" He put on a look of disappointment. "You guys on the West Coast, you don't know nothin' about hospitality. Have ya been to the South? Have ya? I'm tellin' ya, it's hotter than a Penthouse chick in a sauna." He guffawed thickly; she grimaced. "That's why I moved. My momma told me the rents were too high in California, but she don't know ****!" He cursed his mom, becoming quite worked up; he wiped sweat from his forehead.

Evelyn decided enough was enough and started making her way back through the house. "Duncan . . ." She began speaking quickly in an effort to prevent any interruptions. "You have been so hospitable but, you know, I don't wanna stop you getting all tidied up here, so I am just going to wish you a very good evening."

At the front door, she turned to face her host. "That's a beautiful plant," she said, pointing at a spider plant in urgent need of repotting. As he turned to look at it, she opened the screen door and stepped onto the porch. The prospect of shaking his hand was mildly repulsive so she started backing up. Duncan, however, thrust out his hand. There was no escape. Unsurprisingly, his handshake was a wet fish. Evelyn had expected that. What she hadn't expected was the withdrawing of his index finger along her palm as he let go. It made her shiver.

"Sure nice of you to visit, Evelyn," he said in a languid drawl. "Come again. Perhaps we could—"

"Thank you, Duncan," she interrupted. "Sorry. I need to go now. You've been very kind. Enjoy the cookies." She turned and walked as slowly as she could manage toward her home. The urge to run was intense. After a couple of yards, she was tempted to look over her shoulder but, instinctively, she knew that was a bad idea. Reaching her front door, however, she risked a quick glance in his direction. He wasn't looking at her at all. He was leaning casually against the doorframe, stroking his index finger up and down his palm. He sniffed it and put it in his mouth.

Evelyn entered her house and bolted the door.
She shuddered and went to the shower.

The following day, Evelyn extracted a metal post from a construction worker's thigh, then managed to ensure a baby survived past her first birthday. It was past six by the time she was driving home. The commute was relatively pain-free. NPR's Robert Siegel continued as a soundtrack in her head as she turned off the ignition and opened the car door. She grabbed her bag, already thinking of dinner.

As she put her key into the lock, she looked to her right. The broom she used at the weekend for sweeping the porch wasn't where she'd left it. She didn't give it a second thought, just pushed open the door and stepped over the threshold.

She stopped.

On the floor of her living room sat dozens of plant pots containing small spider plants. They were arranged in the shape of a love heart. In the center of the heart lay a pink sheet of paper with the words "Dinner Saturday? D."

Evelyn sank to her knees.

~ 18 ~

MESSING ABOUT IN BOATS

The beauty of a woman is not in the clothes she wears, the figure that she carries, or the way she combs her hair. The beauty of a woman is seen in her eyes, because that is the doorway to her heart, the place where love resides. True beauty in a woman is reflected in her soul.
~ Audrey Hepburn

March 1, 2005

Aidan stood in the hall, drying his hair in front of a mirror. The discovery that the Viatici House possessed a pool was, he felt, a just reward for half an hour's intense discussion with the lucidi, which had left him with a mild headache. The swim, however, had worked better than aspirin. Refreshed, he had emerged from the pool wishing he could bring the salubrious effects of his swim back to his earthly body. The thought made him smile.

He threw the towel on a nearby chair and turned to look up the staircase. As soon as he saw Evelyn crossing the landing, he caught his breath. She seemed to grow lovelier with every passing visit.

"Feeling better?" he called up.

"Much." She came down the stairs, passed by the *Pietà* and walked out through the bifold doors onto the balcony. Aidan joined her, leaning against the railing. They squinted as they looked out over the ocean. The sun was still high in the sky and the surface sparkled with its reflection. Motorboats bobbed on the water, fishing poles dangling off their sterns. He wondered what it was like to be a lucidus fisherman—wondered if bodily life was a wrench from the ethereal, or whatever it was lucidi experienced when they weren't in the Espacio. They stood a little closer than normal, their arms touching. Though neither acknowledged the physical contact, they were both aware of their proximity.

"Wanna steal a boat and go sailing?" said Aidan. "Apparently, there's a fishing village round that headland." He pointed up the coast.

"Sailing? Sure. Did you say steal?"

"Okay, borrow. It's worth a shot, surely. Heck, they let you jump off a cliff. What's the worst that can happen?"

They left the house and found a path that meandered through some dense brush. Reaching some rickety wooden stairs, they descended to a small country lane lined with tall hedges and wildflowers.

"This is unreal," said Aidan as they made their way down the hill. "I think I'm in Cornwall, and if I'm not mistaken, it looks like we're about to reach . . . Goodness, this place could be Mevagissey."

"Mevagissey?"

"Cornish fishing village. Picture-perfect. We used to go there on holiday." They entered the village and walked down narrow cobbled streets toward the quay. Fishing vessels of various shapes and sizes were moored in the harbor and against the dockside. The village itself appeared to be sparsely populated. Aidan found it hard not to stare, though, at the few lucidi who strolled up and down. Their faces glowed more brightly as they became aware of his gaze, almost as though they were embarrassed.

When they reached the end of the quay, a lucidus approached them. He wore a long, dark blue coat and a flat cap. "Few can resist the pull of the ocean," he said grandly. "Especially those who know a thing or two about handling a boat. I have just the thing."

The lucidus climbed down into a small dinghy that squeaked against the fenders attached to mooring rings on the stone wall. He untied a rope, gesturing for them to follow. Once they were on board, he gunned the engine and they began motoring out into the harbor. They pulled up next to a forty-foot sloop lying a hundred yards offshore. After climbing aboard, they were followed by the lucidus, who swung himself over the side in one fluid motion.

"Wow, this is quite a boat," said Evelyn, stepping down into the seating area near the stern. The sloop was beautifully maintained with immaculate decking and shiny winches. Even the ropes were folded neatly in bundles draped over the side railings.

"Not too shabby," whispered Aidan under his breath as he followed the lucidus below. They spent the next ten minutes going over the specs before examining the charts that covered the local area. Aidan had dozens of questions about the coast, and whether the Viatici House was on an island or a vast land mass, but he held himself back. The questions were still bubbling away as he came back on deck.

"I hope you know what you're doing," said Evelyn. "Because I am no sailor."

"You can follow directions, though, right?"

"Of course, but don't treat me like an idiot."

Once the lucidus had untied the boat from the buoy, he climbed down into the dinghy and pushed off. He turned on the engine and revved it with great enthusiasm, causing the bow to rear up like a startled horse.

"He certainly enjoys his job," said Aidan as he watched the lucidus slalom his way through a cluster of boats moored nearby.

Evelyn put on a life jacket she'd found in one of the holds, and gave one to Aidan. "Here. Let's stay alive. I've already died once!" She laughed.

They motored out toward the entrance of the bay, and when they'd reached open water, she untied the mainsail cover. Aidan started hauling up the sail; in seconds it was working its way up the mast, crunching and flapping until it ballooned out, filling with wind. He cut the engine and asked Evelyn to come back and turn a winch.

"Ooh, it's a genoa," he said as a large sail unfurled from the forestay. "Very nice. That should give us some speed." They watched it billow out and catch the wind. The boat keeled and drove into the swell, sending spray crashing over the decks. He set a course down the coast, a little nervous of what lay further out.

"He showed me the charts, but I'm a bit worried about sailing off the edge."

Evelyn laughed. "Yeah. There are probably dragons and sea serpents out there."

"Well, you never know! Can you find me something to drink down there? I think I saw a fridge. A beer, if you can find one." He leaned back and closed his eyes, enjoying the wind buffeting the side of his head.

Evelyn emerged from below with a bottle of Becks and a can of Coke. "Didn't you sail with your dad?" she said, passing him the bottle.

"Yup, but he never taught me a thing. Hours and hours on a boat during childhood, and I couldn't tie a knot until I left home. I ended up taking lessons in my early thirties, would you believe it?"

Aidan looked up at the anemometer on top of the mast, trying to gauge whether they needed to pull in the mainsail a little more. Spray drenched his face, but he was beaming from ear to ear, filling his lungs with cool fresh air. As the wind picked up, it made conversation difficult, but Evelyn didn't mind. She took pleasure in watching him, knowing he was oblivious to her gaze, his concentration on other things. She liked to see him happy, liked being near him when he was enjoying himself.

"Right, let's let out these sails, shall we?" he said. "I want to see what it's like further up the coast." He turned the helm and they released the sheets. The boat immediately stopped fighting. They aimed for a point just north of the headland; within seconds, the boat was surfing along, rising and falling on the swell. "You wanna helm? It's easy. I'll show you."

Evelyn got up and stood next to Aidan. He moved to the side, making room for her. She felt like a schoolgirl waiting to be kissed, but nothing happened. He didn't caress her shoulders or put his hands on hers. Neither did he stand particularly close. In fact, he didn't touch her at all. When he went and sat on one of the benches, she felt his absence next to her, a gap where he should have been.

"See that point, just to the left of those cliffs?" He pointed. "Just hold her steady. Small adjustments, that's all it takes." He smiled encouragingly at her.

They rounded the headland and came in sight of a bay. As they sailed toward it, the wind dropped considerably. They passed beneath the cliffs and Aidan began to pull down the sails. The beach ahead was deserted.

"Let's anchor here, shall we?" he said. "Here's as good as anywhere. Coming in for a dip?" The sun was still up, although clouds were starting to gather over land.

They lowered the anchor.

Evelyn went down below and put on her swimsuit. She gasped when she caught sight of herself in the mirror. She peered at her face closely, running her hand down her cheek. As she moved her hands down her sides and across her belly, the contours felt familiar. The main differences, it seemed, were her hair and feet. The hair was darker and thicker, and her feet looked a size too large. There were moles on her neck too that she didn't have at home. Her face, on the other hand, appeared to be almost identical. Perhaps even a little prettier than at home. The thought amused her as she made her way up on deck.

Aidan was wearing Bermudas, clinging to the rigging twenty feet up. "Me, Tarzan!" he shouted. "You, Jane!"

Evelyn began climbing up the net that straddled the stays in the midsection of the boat. When she reached him, her feet ached but the height was exhilarating.

"Quite a view," he said as she stepped across toward him. She briefly lost her footing, but was instantly caught by Aidan, who reached out, wrapping his arm around her waist to hold her up.

"Whoa there, Evie!" She was breathing hard as she moved close to him, looking up into his face. The urge to kiss him was intense. He, on the other hand, appeared unaffected by her proximity, maneuvering himself until he was facing out toward the ocean. Reaching back, he grasped the netting with both hands, leaning his body forward and flexing his knees. Even here, she thought, the man's still got to do his thing. Well, if he must, he must.

"Go on, Tarzan. Swan dive."

He laughed and leaped forward, arms flailing. When he surfaced, he beat his chest vigorously. The Tarzan remark had clearly hit the spot. "Come on—jump!" he shouted. "It's like a bath in here!"

Evelyn leaped feet first, her cheeks streaming with tears as she entered the ocean with pointed toes. Aidan was right. The water was beautifully warm. After swimming together round the boat, he climbed up on board, emerging from the cabin a few moments later holding a couple of masks and snorkels. They swam over toward the rocks and investigated the shallows, where they discovered tropical fish of infinite shapes and sizes. A stingray passed beneath them, and they watched it with the enthusiasm of infants chancing upon fairies. The sun's rays played on the sandy bottom, sending flecks of light up into their eyes.

Once aboard, there was no need to towel down. It was still warm and they were bone dry within minutes. Their skin tightened, white lines of caked salt appearing on their arms. Evelyn began digging around in the fridge while Aidan pulled out the seat covers and put up the awning. Table laid, they tucked into French bread, Brie, salami, and tomatoes. Aidan poured wine into two glasses, handing one to Evelyn.

"To a place of inexpressible beauty," he announced, "with a woman to match!"

She smiled. "Flattery will get you everywhere, sir!"

They lay back and chatted, falling into each other's lives and soaking each other up. As Evelyn listened, she cast her mind back over their past few visits to the Espacio. Aidan had been unflappable during her outbursts. She was grateful for his steadiness, his reluctance to judge her. She suspected his reticence was due to his loss. He could have pulled away of course, but instead he had opened up—as much as a reserved British man was capable of doing. His demeanor carried some of the stiffness of his culture—he couldn't help being British—but his delight and animation when he spoke of things he enjoyed was so infectious she couldn't help the slow build of attraction that wrapped itself around her heart.

For Evelyn, this was a completely new sensation. She had never loved. She had never been able to trust a man. Until now. She felt sure she was in the company of someone who would treat her kindly, who would listen to her, give her space. If she ever met him, of course. He was also calmly confident of himself when he was holding forth on his favorite subjects. And he was unthreatened by her assertiveness, a rare thing indeed. As the words floated between them—he was apparently a huge Rafael Nadal fan and considered Mike Myers to be a comic genius—it was almost unbearable waiting to discover how he felt.

Aidan got up and went down below, appearing shortly after with more wine and soft drinks. He tossed her a couple of books he'd found. "I remember you like Robert Harris. What about the classics?"

Evelyn picked up *The Return of the Native* and confessed that her literary tastes tended toward the American greats—Steinbeck, Wolfe, Salinger, Harper Lee. As she waxed lyrical on the pathos in *Of Mice and Men*, he leaned back and wondered how a couple of feet could feel like a million miles. Her opinions on Steinbeck were insightful but, in truth, he was distracted. She looked luscious, her skin a burnished bronze and her wet hair sending trickles of water down her arms. Her legs were toned and slender, their length accentuated by the swimsuit she was wearing. But it wasn't just her physical form. She moved with a confident, unruffled grace—a projection of both her femininity and her forceful personality. He couldn't help wondering what she really looked like.

As he listened to her views on 1930s Southern culture portrayed in *To Kill a Mockingbird*, he gradually became aware of the frustration simmering inside. If this was supposed to be a window into the realm of a compassionate creator then something was wrong, because it felt like torture. To fall for someone you had no hope of actually meeting was surely the cruelest joke of all. The only thing worse was his inability to express his feelings. Emotions always turned him to jelly. He wondered if it was the Espacio itself holding him back, restraining him. But, no, that couldn't be the answer. He just needed to step out and—

Her voice caught him off guard. "Tell me more about your family." He looked at her blankly. The moment was gone. He would have to wait for another.

"I'm sorry?"

"Tell me about your dad."

"Oh. My dad?" he said, trying to find his feet. "Well, I think we've come to an understanding. He lives his life and I live mine." He put on his sunglasses, leaned over, and picked up the last piece of bread.

"What does he do?" Evelyn popped a cherry tomato into her mouth.

"Before he retired, he was a circuit judge."

"Sounds important."

"Perhaps. I prefer it dark and dirty." The surprised look on her face amused him. "Prison visits, Evelyn, nothing more." He laughed. "Anyway, truth is, my dad doesn't take much interest. The occasional comment when he's seen my name in the paper, but apart from that, he steers well clear."

"That bad, huh?"

"Oh the well goes *way* deep." He was silent, looking out over the ocean, his thoughts hidden from her.

"What about school?" she said, fishing for a new angle.

"Boarding school from the age of eight."

"How British."

"How Victorian. An antiquated system designed for the sons of army brigadiers serving in India or missionaries toiling in African jungles. More wine?"

She held out her cup. "Sounds miserable."

"Well, I like to think of it as a bygone era, best left forgotten. In fact, speaking of bygone eras, I was intrigued by your great-grandfather's exploits on the *Titanic*. Mine was there too, would you believe it? What are the chances of that?"

"Seriously?"

"I know. Kind of weird, right?"

"Did he make it?"

"No, sadly." He hesitated, staring into her eyes.

"I'm sensing a story."

Aidan sat forward and rested his arms on the table in front of him. "Okay, well, it goes like this. My great-grandfather went by the name of Henry. Henry Manning. And he boarded the *Titanic* in 1912, leaving his wife and young son behind. Henry was a clergyman who planned to make a new life for himself in the New World, as we used to call it. He intended to establish himself before bringing over his family to join him. Most of the details come from my grandpa's cousin Grace, who's in her nineties now. Very gung ho she is and loves to hold forth on family matters. Apparently my great-grandma Edna was never that keen on leaving England. It's a long time ago now, but Aunt Grace got the impression her uncle didn't get on too well with the trouble and strife."

"Trouble and what?"

"Sorry, Cockney rhyming slang. Trouble and strife . . . wife. I'll explain later." He smiled and sipped his wine. "So anyway, Henry was lost in the North Atlantic along with . . . what . . . over fifteen hundred other souls, but that's not the end of it. In the weeks after the ship went down, journalists were crawling all over the story and something came out in the *New York Post* about a cowardly vicar from Devon. Apparently, Henry stabbed a young lad in a fight over a life jacket. Killed him. Mind you, I don't think it was ever really proved.

"Anyway, the story eventually made its way over to England. *The Times* ran a feature on England's *Titanic* murderer—you know what the press is like. For Edna, it was devastating. I'm not sure, but I think she may even have changed her name."

He filled his cup with wine and took a sip.

"You said he had a son," said Evelyn. "Your grandpa, right?"

Aidan nodded.

"Must have been tough for him, losing his dad."

Aidan shrugged. "I wouldn't know. My family isn't that close. Stiff upper lip and all that. It's the English way, I guess." He looked up at the sky, suddenly feeling rather exposed. Twilight had fallen. The sun was already beneath the horizon, its rays daubing the feathery clouds with swathes of orange and pink. "Another swim before we leave?"

"Sure. Why not?"

They swam over to the beach, where they found a spot beneath a coconut tree. Evelyn was giggling at one of Aidan's bad jokes when they heard a call from further down the beach. Aidan turned to Evelyn and was about to speak when the voice rang out again. He groaned. "One day, I'm gonna shove those pills where the sun don't shine."

Evelyn laughed. "And here I was, thinking you English were always so polite!" She started throwing sand at him.

~ 19 ~

A FISHING EXPEDITION

*Human behavior flows from three main sources:
desire, emotion, and knowledge.*
~ Plato

March 2, 2005

Fenwick picked up Aidan and Fiona at 10 a.m. on a cold Wednesday morning. The drive to the Camden Town brothel took them less than half an hour. When they arrived at the house, two policemen met them at the door. The solicitor explained the reason for their visit and they were soon ushered in. Certain sections were cordoned off with blue and white *Do Not Cross* tape.

"Don't touch anything!" an officer called back as they made their way through the hall to a living room. Aidan peered in. Some of the dirty photographs were still on the walls. The carpet was worn and stained. A rickety table sat in the corner, laden with half a dozen empty beer bottles. Next to it was a brown and yellow couch covered with faded purple cushions. The whole place stank of smoke.

They walked on through. Every bedroom in the building contained a small single bed, with barely enough room to put a table or chair next to it. From each ceiling hung a single light bulb without a lampshade. Fenwick and Fiona turned into the kitchen with the policeman, already deep in conversation. Aidan heard Fiona ask some questions about the challenges of modern policing. Nice, should keep the copper talking for hours.

He went on alone to the back of the house. He'd seen drawings showing where Dragan's room was located. When he found it, he stopped at the entrance. A single strip of blue and white police tape was stapled to the doorframe, blocking entry. He ducked under it into the room and looked around. Photos were stuck all over the walls. Motorbikes, footballers, various types of weaponry. A couple of models, pouting. No pornography, though, which was a little surprising. In the corner stood a bedside table. He opened the drawer and pulled out a newspaper and some coupons. Right near the back, he spotted a photograph. He picked it up. The pose was set in front of a tumbledown house with a broad, wooden door and whitewashed walls. The mother—he presumed it was the mother—wore a dark red headscarf and was holding a little boy with tousled blond hair and big blue eyes. He looked about three years old.

The eyes were unmistakable.

Aidan glanced toward the door, and with his heart hammering away in his chest, slipped the photo into his pocket. He poked around behind the bed and in the wardrobe. Nothing. When he came to the sink in the opposite corner, he noticed a newspaper cutting stuck next to the mirror. A bunch of scruffy soldiers grinned at the camera, each brandishing a weapon. He inspected the picture closely, checked to see no one was looking, and removed it. He was slipping it into his inside jacket pocket just as the policeman appeared at the door. "Sir," he said, bristling. "Can't you see the tape?"

"Oh, I'm so sorry. I do apologize." The police officer frowned as Aidan ducked back under the tape and walked off down the corridor to find his colleagues. Once outside, they each thanked the policeman and got back in the car.

"Dynamite, Fiona. Let me guess. The plod droned on about overtime pay. Am I right?"

"That and working nights."

"Excellent."

After work, Aidan alighted from the Tube at West Kensington and made his way down North End Road. The William Hill betting shop a few yards down from the Tube station was a terrible temptation. When he reached it, he hesitated. He ached to try his luck on the Tottenham-Arsenal game at the weekend, but thought better of it. A nice refreshing pint on his mind, he reached The Old Oak and crossed the threshold, where he found Edward and Sean chatting at the bar. After handshakes all round, they found a table in a small alcove, away from the rest of the clientele.

"Read about your case in the papers last week, old chap," said Edward. "I hear you're crossing swords with old Molsberry. His bottom lip still quivering?"

"Like a guitar string!"

They both laughed.

Aidan turned to Sean. "How's the exhibition going? What was it last time? A picture of a skyscraper with the word 'stress' at the bottom, I seem to remember. I swear you could sell fridges to Eskimos."

The Irishman smiled coyly. "Sold a couple last week. The English love 'em. Anyways, I can't complain. Every sale keeps the wolf from the door."

"A wolf, you say, old chap," said Edward, sipping his pint. He grinned, stroking his chin with mock sagacity. They promptly dived into a discussion concerning "The Three Little Pigs," and were instantly divided over the pigs' relative wisdom in selecting appropriate building materials.

"What's wrong with building with straw?" said Aidan. "Building with anything at all is fairly impressive for a pig, I would have thought."

"Oh come on, you plonker," said Sean. "*Straw?* His brothers choose wood and bricks. And he opts for straw! How is that supposed to protect him from the talking wolf?"

"Uh-uh, are you sure he knows about the wolf's verbal aptitude? Because that's not mentioned at the beginning of most versions."

"I think it's assumed," said Edward.

"Well, you shouldn't assume," said Aidan. "I grant you, he's naïve. Pig in a forest. He should have looked down at himself and thought 'I'm made of meat. I should probably be careful about who I mix with. Odds are, someone is going to have a hankering for sausage or bacon and they're going to think, you know, I happen to know a piggy living in a straw house. Hmm, now wouldn't *he* come in handy?'"

"You know," said Sean, "me mam used to tell me a version that went like this. Adapted here slightly by me. Pig One persuades the wolf to go with him to Pig Two's house using the argument, 'He's bound to taste better than me.' So off they go, ambling along through the forest with the pig monologuing, 'You know, Wolf, I shouldn't really be telling you this, but me brother—the one with the power tools—he's buff, he's got muscle. Not like me. I'm just fat. Obese, I suppose you could say. Some people call me lazy. I prefer . . . easygoing. And yes, that *is* reflected in my ample waistline. Me brother, on the other hand, is ripped from all that building he's been doing. All muscly and sinewy. Tough. That's how I'd describe him . . ." He tailed off. "Well, I guess Pig One only had himself to blame, didn't he?"

They all agreed that Pig One wasn't the pick of the litter and probably had it coming.

"But one thing I want an answer to," said Sean. "What's with all the huffing and puffing? What kind of numpty does that?"

Edward didn't hesitate. "He's a wolf. That's what wolves do when—"

"Oh come on!" said the Irishman, interrupting. "Since when do wolves huff and puff? Would you look at yourself, Ed. What do *you* know about aggressive lupine behavior?"

"I'm not finished yet, you Irish pillock. As I was saying, he's a wolf and . . . and *it's in his nature* to act arrogantly before trapping his prey. He's a big bad wolf, remember?"

"Aah, now here I think we have one," said Aidan, slapping his friend on the back. "You're quite right, Ed, but why call the wolf 'bad'? Big, perhaps, if he's larger than the average wolf—but bad? He's a wolf, for crying out loud! We have an inherent contradiction here, surely. You can't in one breath argue that he's 'just a wolf *whose nature* it is to eat pigs' and then call him 'bad.' That simply won't wash. I mean, why should we consider the wolf to be morally culpable for devouring pigs?"

Sean looked straight at Edward; they both burst out laughing.

"I'm serious," said Aidan once they'd calmed down.

"Well, he can talk," said Edward. "And generally, the greater a creature's brain functioning, the more likely we are to assign moral responsibility. For example, children aren't considered as morally responsible as adults. They're not old enough to understand the consequences of their actions."

"Well," said Sean, sitting back and adopting a wry smile, "I hate to agree with the imperialist bugger sitting on my right, but I feel I must."

They embarked on a discussion regarding ethical behavior, straying rather oddly onto the issue of whether a person with Tourette syndrome was responsible for using foul language. When Sean pointed out that the tics exhibited by people with Tourette's were inherited, the conversation drew to a close.

"Right, Ed," said Aidan, slapping a twenty pound note onto the table. "Would you do the honors?" The ample barrister grabbed the note and gathered up the empty pint glasses. Slaloming his way toward the bar, he disappeared into a crowd of bankers with loosened ties and overdeveloped egos.

When he was gone, Sean leaned back and put both hands behind his head. "Well? Have you seen her again?"

Aidan hesitated. "Seen who?"

"You know, the little lady from your dreams."

"Oh," said Aidan, the penny finally dropping. "Yes, but I can't remember what I told you." His various social interactions often blended into one.

"You said she was on a par with Helen of Troy, her hair was dark reddish-brown, and she spoke with an American accent. She sounds like a cross between Michelle Pfeiffer and that woman from the soap commercial."

Aidan thought back over the past few weeks. The dreams hadn't gone away. If anything, they'd intensified. "It's getting worse," he said. "Or better, depending on how I'm feeling. I wake up and smell her on my clothes. How ridiculous is that?" He looked down and smiled.

"You hopeless romantic," said Sean, ruffling his friend's hair.

"Stop it! Sometimes I think I'm heading for a breakdown. I see her at least twice a week, and I've never even met her."

"Listen." The Irishman lowered his voice. "I know a hypnotherapist in North London. A friend of mine paid a visit last month. Might be worth a try." He slid a business card across the table.

Aidan picked it up. "No promises, okay?"

"Ball's in your court, mate." He smiled.

Edward returned, clutching pint glasses. "What did I miss?"

"Nothing," said Aidan. "Nothing at all. Sean here was just bemoaning the Tate Modern's failure to include enough space for new artists. Weren't you, Sean?"

When Aidan arrived home, it was past eleven. As he passed the living room, he noticed his son reclining on the sofa. A touch unsteady on his feet, he grabbed the top of an armchair to stop himself swaying. "Evening," he said groggily. "Beth at a conference again?"

"I told you last week, remember," called Simon.

Aidan was already meandering toward the kitchen, looking for alcohol. His son had obviously performed some light cooking operations but, as usual, had failed to clean up. "Wine?" Aidan called out, mildly irritated, having located a half-empty bottle of plonk.

Simon turned off the TV and joined his father in the kitchen. "Sure. Sounds good," he said. He picked up some papers lying next to the bread bin. Leafing through them for no good reason, he pulled out an information sheet on a one-bedroom flat in Kentish Town.

"What's this? You're not thinking of moving, are you?"

"None of your business," said Aidan, removing the offending sheet of paper from Simon's hand and replacing it with a glass of wine. He didn't appreciate his son delving into his personal papers. He'd never had to hide documents before and he didn't particularly want to start now. Simon picked up some used scratch cards from the counter. "It's not the gambling again, is it?"

"I thought I said it was none of your business," Aidan replied testily. He started washing some stray glasses in the sink.

"Oh, but it *is* my business if my dad's in trouble. It's very much my business."

"Simon, when I want your opinion, I'll give it to you, okay?" He felt bad for sniping at his son, but the young man didn't seem in the mood to let it go.

"Come on, Dad. How bad is it? A few thousand? More?"

Aidan's rising irritation caused him to break a glass. "Damn! Go get some plasters, will you?" Blood was dripping into the sink.

Simon went to the bathroom and returned with a packet of Band-Aids, handing one to his father. "You do know there are organizations that can help."

"I don't need help!" said Aidan, wrapping the Band-Aid round his wounded thumb.

"No, of course you don't. Thing is, you don't even realize that your—" he could barely bring himself to use the word, "*habit* is affecting things around you. Beth and I, we're not idiots. Are we just supposed to ignore the signs?"

"I think we're done here." Aidan was turning a light shade of red. "I'm off to bed." He picked up his jacket and made for the door.

"Fine," said Simon before his father could reach the stairs. "Who's Billy Fischer?"

Aidan stopped and turned to face his son. "How *dare* you?" Silence echoed around the room. It bounced off the walls and crashed through their heads. Aidan whispered, "Have you no respect?"

"That's not fair, Dad. You leave papers all over the place."

"They're none of your business."

"Come on, Dad. You're on repeat!"

Aidan was so angry he declined to speak.

"Listen, Dad," said Simon, lighting the fuse. "You can get help."

"*I don't need help! Now leave me alone!*"

Aidan stormed out of the kitchen, banging the door behind him. Simon let out a sigh and sat down at the table. He drained his glass, his hand trembling, causing the wine to splash onto his upper lip. Upstairs he could hear his father crashing about, throwing objects at the walls. He'd never known him to react in such an extreme way. Putting his head in his hands, he closed his eyes.

And prayed.

~ 20 ~

SREBRENICA

Man can do what he wills but he cannot will what he wills.
~ Arthur Schopenhauer

March 2, 2005

Evelyn woke up sweating. The image was still there, choking her. Mr. Henderson's fat face bore down on her. She could feel his hands clawing at her, tugging at her clothing. Inches away, she could still see the pockmarks dotting his cheeks as the sweat rolled down through his sideburns. She sprang away from where she'd been sleeping, as though to distance herself from what she'd been dreaming. Asleep, the assault lasted seconds. It was the aftermath that lingered.

She got out of bed and stood in front of the mirror, examining herself. She remembered watching her body change over the years, reaching maturity in her late teens. The stench of what he'd done to her never really went away. It just changed its form, wending its way in and out of her pores. As she dreamed, it was her shame that sat most heavily on her soul. She'd reasoned often enough about its absurdity, told herself repeatedly that it wasn't her fault. As an adult, she'd gone to therapists and tried hypnosis, but nothing really worked. He was still there, buried deep, popping up in dreams to violate her again and again. Hammering the shame into her soul so that it would never go away.

She threw a shoe at the mirror.

In the shower, she washed her hair several times before covering herself in lotions and creams. She went to the kitchen and turned on the radio full volume. Anything to silence the lies running through her mind. Søren nuzzled her legs and trotted out into the backyard. Evelyn picked up her coffee and joined him on the patio. Closing her eyes, she enjoyed the warmth of the morning sun on her face.

Time, however, was pressing. She poured some dog food into Søren's bowl, and grabbed her keys off the counter. Arriving slightly late for work, she launched herself into the hurly-burly, reaching midday in a time warp and wondering how she'd got there. For lunch, she munched a sandwich as she browsed through some notes. Work never really stopped. At 12:45 p.m., she buzzed through to reception, looking at a list on her computer screen.

"Candy, you can send the next one in."

Evelyn looked up as Miloš walked in. He seemed subdued.

"Good afternoon, Miloš," she said, wiping mayonnaise from the corner of her mouth. She checked the bruising on his left thigh. There was some discoloration, but no warmth or any other sign of infection.

"I'll be right back." She left the room clutching his file.

After the door closed, Miloš looked around and wondered what he'd done to deserve these visits to the doctor. The guilt lay heavily on his soul, suffocating him until he found himself casting about for distractions. Anything to take his mind off those days in July 1995.

The room felt hot. He loosened his collar.

Eastern Bosnia was often hot during the summer, but in 1995 the heat was oppressive. Even at 9 a.m., moisture rose from the green pastures around Srebrenica, drenching the men in sweat; there was no wind to give them relief. Their pores dribbled salt water that ran down into every orifice they possessed.

By mid-morning of July 11, Miloš's unit was bored stiff. It was taking longer than anticipated to gain entry into the town. The sound of artillery broke the peace every few seconds, a series of cracks that went on for hours. To everyone's relief, at around midday, the firing of heavy weapons came to an end. Bojan, a large brawny man with a snake tattoo running up his neck came and sat down next to Miloš, punching his upper arm in a show of mock camaraderie. He started to chatter away, as though eager to divulge his brain's entire back catalog. So the man was a bit nervous. Well, weren't they all?

In Miloš's case, he just wanted to get started.

It was time to teach the world a history lesson.

For Srebrenica wasn't just another town. It was both strategic and a symbol. Fought over for centuries, it had changed hands multiple times. The Ottoman Turks ruled Serbia and Bosnia for five hundred years, only relinquishing power in 1918 after the First World War. The Bosniaks—Bosnia's Muslims—were descendants of the Slavs, who had converted to Islam under Turkish rule. They were therefore considered traitors. That was the propaganda. It was taught in school and drilled in the army. Miloš was no different to all the other men who sat on the hillside that afternoon, drinking from their water bottles and joking with each other.

He was a product of his culture.

At just after midday, the CO, Duan, stood up and put his walkie-talkie to his ear. Seconds later, he snapped the antenna down inside the device. "We're moving in!"

The men grabbed their packs and began walking down the hill. As they emerged from the wood, they crossed the Ćićevac, the stream that ran to the west of the town. It didn't take long before they were walking up Maršala Tita, the main street. In front of them, a T-54 tank was rolling along, soldiers seated on the front with Uzis over their shoulders. Dutchbat, the United Nations peacekeeping contingent responsible for maintaining Srebrenica as a "safe area," never once fired on them. Apparently, some of the Serbian brigades arriving from the west had taken fire, but Srebrenica fell with barely any resistance at all.

Two F-16s from the Royal Dutch Air Force buzzed overhead, their engines thundering in the men's ears. The warplanes circled back and careened over the hills to the east, then headed north. They were heading for Potočari. The men entering Srebrenica heard a soft thud. The planes were back, lower this time, which had them all cowering. Another thud was heard from the hills to the east, and with a roar, they were gone. The best the UN could come up with to protect the civilians of Srebrenica was one smoke bomb—and even that missed its target. Within the space of a few hours, Srebrenica had been transformed from "a safe area" into something quite the reverse.

Further up the road, Miloš spotted movement. The town's whole population was making its way to the UN base. Miloš was draining his water bottle when he heard cheering from further back down the street. A big burly man strode forward, his chest puffed out like an emperor penguin. In front of him, scurrying backward, was a man trying not to trip up on the cables that draped, spaghetti-like, out the back of his camera.

Ratko Mladić, the leader of the Bosnian Serbs, had been dreaming of this moment for months. He and his enormous ego were going to remember this for the rest of his life. "On to Potočari!" he announced dramatically, speaking directly into the camera and jabbing his finger at the lens. "Here we are in Srebrenica on July 11, 1995," he continued, "on the eve of yet another great Serbian holiday. We present this city to the Serbian people as a gift. Finally, after the rebellion of the Dahijas, the time has come to take revenge on the Turks in this region." His reference to the Dahijas invoked a conflict almost two hundred years old, when the Serbs rose up against the Turks, only to be brutally crushed.

Now it was payback time.

Up the road, something approaching panic was taking place. The town's population had been desperately seeking protection in the UN base that was administered by the Dutch. Over five thousand people were both inside and outside the base, but the Dutch peacekeepers were overwhelmed, unable to cope with a fluid situation that was spiraling out of control. They barked orders at people who ignored them or raised their fists in anger, spitting back expletives. As the Serbs advanced, the peacekeepers urged people to head north to Potočari.

In dribs and drabs, men and women piled onto the few vehicles going in that direction. By 4 p.m., the road to Potočari was filled with a solid wall of refugees. Thousands of Muslim women, dressed in bright red and green *dimijes*—traditional pantaloons—trudged along, many of them carrying children or leading them by the hand. Weeping and wailing rose up from the crowd as it made its way toward the Dutch headquarters. Now and then, a woman fainted and had to be helped up by friends or relatives. Occasionally, those who fainted or couldn't walk fast enough were left on the side of the road, abandoned by others too frightened to lose contact with their families.

The brutality began in earnest the following day. It was stifling hot again and Miloš's unit was restless and uncomfortable. Five thousand people had managed to find their way inside the Dutch base, with another twenty thousand surviving outside with no running water and little food. The smell of fear mixed with the stench of sweat, urine, and feces. Conditions were deteriorating hourly. Later that afternoon, buses arrived to take away the men. The Dutch tried to complain but the Serbs ignored them. Men of all ages, young and old, were ordered to get on the buses. They had no option. Most complied without a backward glance, leaving their women looking up wide-eyed and terrified.

The sun was retreating behind the hills when Miloš's unit was ordered to deal with a warehouse full of Muslim men. He remembered it well. The floor was dense with humanity, men and boys sitting with their knees drawn up and heads bowed. There were no orders. The soldiers simply released their visceral hatred with their rifle butts. Many laughed and cursed their victims, reveling in their barbarism. Miloš breathed in the atmosphere and joined in lustily. He beat and kicked, and felt powerful and strong, unable to perceive the hardening of his soul, as it calcified until he was barely human.

When Evelyn entered the room, the images were still flashing across his mind, taunting him until he was sweating not from the heat but from the effort he was exerting to repel them.

"Are you okay?" she said.

"Yes, I . . . ." A sudden powerful urge to seek absolution from someone, anyone, came over him. He was too ashamed to go to a priest. Perhaps a doctor would understand. No. How could she? She couldn't possibly imagine the horror of his crimes. And she certainly couldn't give him absolution. You needed a priest for that.

"Miloš? What's wrong?"

He was gripping the arms of his chair as though clinging on for dear life. "Nothing!" he blurted out. "I'm okay."

When she asked Miloš one more time how he was doing, he lied again. There was still part of him that wanted to die.

A few days later, Evelyn was sitting on the porch drinking coffee with Bridget. Søren lay nearby, occasionally twitching. She got up and went inside, emerging soon after with the coffee pot in one hand and a packet of Chips Ahoy! in the other. "Want another cup?" Her friend held out her mug. "So, Evie," she said, "what's the deal with all these ladders you keep leaving about?" She waved her hand at a stepladder leaning by the front door. Another lay further down the porch.

"Mine broke, had to borrow one. Then that one broke . . . it's a long story. I was thinking of using one as décor!" Her friend pulled a face. "Hey, Bridge," she said, changing the subject, "what are your dreams like?"

Bridget thought for a moment. "Er, I fly, I play Beethoven. You?"

"I had a dream about a week ago," Evelyn said, sitting down. "A really odd one. When I woke up, my forehead was hurting. It was sensitive to the touch, but there was no inflammation."

"That's just from lying under the duvet."

"No, no. My skin felt kinda hot, like I'd been sunbathing."

"Some kind of psychosomatic effect from a dream? What did you dream about?"

Evelyn smiled sheepishly. "A man."

"And you woke up feeling . . . hot?" They both started laughing. "That's not hard to figure out!"

"Stop it, Bridge. It wasn't like that." Evelyn blushed. "Well, maybe a little." She composed herself. "He was a British man, actually. Very polite."

Bridget sat forward. "British? Did he pour you tea, madam?"

"Just juice."

"I suppose he was tall, dark, and handsome."

"He was an attorney and I don't even know how I know that." Evelyn laughed.

"So you got the hots for a British lawyer, who doesn't? Was there chemistry?" Evelyn's face flushed again. She couldn't help smiling. "Holy cow," said Bridget, sniggering, "you're in trouble. Pity he's just a product of your overactive imagination."

"I know. Too bad, huh?"

A car pulled up outside the neighbor's house and Duncan got out. Walking up to his front door he glared at the women, but said nothing. Evelyn stiffened, pulling Søren into her lap.

"What's his problem?" said Bridget.

"Didn't I tell you?"

On discovering the plants in her living room, Evelyn had acted swiftly to remove them. She picked them up one by one and deposited them in the backyard. She checked the side door, and sure enough, it was unlocked. Once he'd found an entry point that didn't require breaking glass, he must have decided to take a chance. To him, it was romantic. What woman wouldn't want to find a room full of plants and an invitation to dinner? The fact that he'd committed a misdemeanor by breaking into her house apparently didn't occur to him. But then he was clearly a man who struggled to connect with people.

She had a decision to make.

Evelyn had met similar men in her consulting office. They saw themselves as hopelessly misunderstood and were easily offended. To Duncan, the world was a confusing, vengeful place, full of people who were out to get him. Perhaps if she'd given the situation a little more thought, she wouldn't have responded as she had. For, instead of going over and letting him down gently, she'd written him a note. The idea of facing him was too much. And in any case, she was busy; she didn't have time for such people.

The note was short and perfunctory. Despite some pleasantries at the beginning, there was no getting past the starkness of the rejection. Somehow, she'd hoped the whole thing would go away. So she'd placed him in the out-box. The note was slipped under his door. No further action necessary.

She should have known better.

A series of hostile behaviors followed, involving the contents of her trash can, which were strewn all over the front yard. It happened twice. A couple of days later, he keyed her car, which made her furious. The ensuing face-to-face row on his doorstep didn't help matters. It produced the worst headache she'd ever had.

Evelyn ran back into the house, emerging a minute later with a piece of cardboard. A message was scrawled across it in crude red letters. WE ALL GOT TO MAKE SACRIFICES. Bridget read it out flatly, turning the cardboard over and examining both sides.

"Left against my back door."

"You call the police?"

"Yup, but he's good. No prints."

"Evie, you need to think about moving. Really."

She sighed and stared at the ground. "I know . . . I'm just not quite there yet."

Later that evening, Evelyn was finishing up some cleaning in her room when she felt an itch on her leg. She scratched it, standing with her back to the mirror. Twisting her head to look over her shoulder, she strained to see the back of her leg. A rash was spreading down her calf from behind her knee. It looked like lichen planus, although she'd need a second opinion from someone at work. She went to the bathroom and pulled out a bottle of calamine lotion. It felt good as she rubbed it on and lay back on the bed.

The phone went. "Mom?"

Evelyn sat up. "Jasmine? Is that you?"

"Mom. I'm, er, I need help."

"What happened? Where are you?"

"I'm in a jail cell in Torrance. I need you to post bail. It's closed now, but can you come tomorrow?"

"Jail? What happened? What—"

"Mom, just post bail, okay?"

"Sure, honey. How much do you need?"

The line went dead.

~ 21 ~

SIDNEY

Just as the feet carry the body,
the affections carry the soul.
~ Catherine of Siena

March 4, 2005

Aidan arrived at work and started shaking out his umbrella. He'd managed to dodge the puddles and keep his top half dry. That was always the way with umbrellas. By the time he got to work, his trousers were soaked but heck, at least he wasn't combing back his wet hair like Tanya, the new junior barrister. She'd also arrived at the office dripping wet, and was causing all manner of furtive glances among the male staff.

He picked up some papers from his pigeonhole. One was a scribbled note with the words "Gamblers Anonymous" on it, written in Harry's unmistakable handwriting. Aidan frowned and went to his desk. Gordon, sitting opposite, looked perkier than normal. He even said good morning, which was a step up from the reluctant grunt that normally came from his side of the room. Recently, there'd been a new spring in his step. He'd started greeting the clerks, and had even commented on the football, a game he despised. Some of the staff thought he'd found love, but when quizzed, he'd played the innocent. Aidan had decided not to inquire. Anyone with news good enough to change behavior couldn't possibly keep it in forever.

Harry walked in making a fruitless attempt to repress a grin. Both barristers looked up. He leaned lazily against the wall, crossing his legs. "So which of you two gentlemen is on a murder case next month?"

They looked at each other blankly.

Aidan said, "Harry, as usual, we're in your capable hands."

"You are right on the money, sir. So, Spencers called. They want a defense barrister," he paused for dramatic effect, "with a track record of resounding success going back many long years." He performed a drumroll with his forefingers on the bookcase next to him. "Which means, Mr. G. Roper, that you—yes, you—are the lucky winner of today's *Who Wants to Be a Millionaire—The Barrister Edition!*"

Gordon couldn't help breaking into a smile. A murder. A murder! He hadn't defended a murder suspect since his early days, years back. Aidan looked suitably impressed.

"I'm telling you, Gordon," said Harry, "things are looking up for you, my friend. Or perhaps someone is looking down. Who knows? Just make sure you dance to the Spencers tune the way only *you* know how." He planted the brief on Gordon's desk and darted out of the room.

When Aidan arrived in court later that morning, he was met by a flustered Fenwick, and Fiona, dressed immaculately as always. The judge entered the courtroom, catching the court clerk by surprise. She leaped to her feet and announced loudly, "All rise!"

Aidan looked across at Molsberry. They exchanged polite nods that temporarily broke the ice. He hoped warmer climes were ahead. A prosecution witness entered—a scientist who was there to provide testimony on a variety of forensic evidence. The court was soon filled with bold statements about DNA and percentages of certainty, illustrated on poster boards that looked highly impressive.

Dragan sat with slumped shoulders, his eyes glazed over. An IT expert entered the witness box next. He managed to wow the jury with names discovered on a variety of texts and emails, all linking the defendant to organized crime. Aidan's attempts to undermine the evidence were weak at best and he knew it. Things were not looking good, and they weren't improved by a moment's hesitation when he glanced across at the jury.

He took a second look.

At the end of the front row sat a woman he recognized. He felt his chest tighten. Surely not. He rubbed his eyes and looked down into his lap. When he looked back at the jury, she was still there, a small smile on her lips. She wore a baseball cap with a capital *A* on the front. The *A* had a halo round the peak. He stared at the woman, mouth open.

"Mr. Manning?" said the judge. "We haven't got all day."

"Yes, your honor," he stammered, fussing with his papers like an absent-minded professor. The woman rose from her seat and left through a door to the rear of the courtroom. He watched her go. When he looked back at the jury, an elderly Afro-Caribbean man with a salt-and-pepper beard was sitting at the end of the front row. He'd been there all the way through the trial. Aidan turned his attention to the witness, who stood, waiting. He grabbed a random piece of paper from the desk in front of him and cleared his throat.

His first couple of questions made no sense at all.

The court adjourned at midday, the same time as the judge decided a pint would go down well with his roast beef and Yorkshire pudding. Aidan breathed a sigh of relief. He wanted a drink—a stiff one—even though he didn't normally imbibe at lunchtimes. He headed for the lobby. As he was nearing the exit, Molsberry swept across the tiled floor, brandishing a piece of paper. Aidan felt in the mood to ignore the man, but his inner sense of decorum got the better of him.

He turned and faced his adversary. The QC looked furious. "Here you are, Manning," he said, handing him a sheet of paper. "Mind you, after that performance this morning, you don't really deserve it. What are you? A charmed man?" Aidan thanked him as he glanced down at the document. Must be good, he thought. Must be very good.

"Many thanks, Quentin," he replied. "I appreciate your following the rules. Not always easy." He scanned the page. Molsberry was right. He didn't deserve it.

The QC detected sarcasm where there wasn't any, scowling as he left, but Aidan meant exactly what he'd said. Disclosure rules required prosecuting counsel to share new information regardless of its potential effect. There was no doubt that he now possessed something capable of turning the case in his favor. That was worth a toast. In fact, later on in The Curtain's Up, a wine bar near his house, Edward thought it was worth champagne.

Sidney

In court the following afternoon, the prosecution recalled Dorina, as they were required to do by law. Fortunately for Aidan, the defense went first, which was highly preferable. No doubt his opponent would undermine her testimony later, but he had to be careful. Dorina was a prosecution witness, and as such, Molsberry needed the jury to find her credible, even though her testimony was now likely to damage his case. He was in an unenviable position, which suited Aidan just fine.

He sat staring at a single sheet of A4. It wasn't much—just a few words—but he knew it had the potential to change everything. He rose to his feet and waited while the clerk handed Dorina a piece of paper.

"Ms. Ibanescu," he began, "that is a statement you made yesterday to the police, I understand."

"Yes, it is."

"Would you like to tell the court what it says? You may read it or just tell us in your own words."

Dorina looked across at the jury. "Yesterday, I was in this building and I see a woman from first brothel. In King Cross. Her name is Tatiana. When I see her, I remember I see her two times. In King Cross house, I was in room every day. I not see very much. But I see this woman. Now I remember. When she look at me, I remember where I first seeing her. She was with men in pub where Razvan sell me." Audible whispers broke out in the public gallery.

"Dorina," said Aidan as gently as he could. "Tell us what happened in the pub, who was there. As much as you remember."

She proceeded to describe what took place on August 29, 2004, when she came to England to start a new life.

Walking into the pub in Camden Town with Razvan, Dorina was intoxicated with emotion. After six months of separation, she was ecstatic at seeing him again. He was everything to her. After sitting down in a corner booth, he got up to buy some drinks. Two large men came in and sat down on either side of her. She wanted to tell them the seats were taken but they were too quick, so she just mumbled "not free" as they squeezed in next to her. When they showed no signs of moving, she knew something was wrong. She began to feel sick.

Razvan came back and pulled up a chair opposite. He seemed to know the men and didn't ask to sit next to her. That's when she began to panic. The men on each side didn't look anything like hotel owners, but there was little she could do. They were huge, wore dark glasses, and talked over her head in Serbo-Croat, a language she recognized but didn't know well. Razvan asked for her passport, and when she refused, they ripped her bag from her grasp. She started shouting at her boyfriend but he just got up and began pacing up and down. The large man on her right pulled out her passport, and was leafing through it when the woman came in. Looking back, it was hardly surprising she'd forgotten her. By that stage, she was scared witless.

Aidan stopped her. Was she absolutely sure the woman she saw yesterday was the woman from the pub? He handed a photo of Tatiana to Dorina, who looked at it quickly and handed it back. Yes, she said, there was no doubt in her mind. After each juror had taken a brief look at it, the photo was returned to the clerk of the court.

Dorina pressed on with her account. It was all coming back to her now. She remembered Tatiana kissing one of the men on the cheek as they all walked out. She apologized to the court for not remembering this information when she first gave her statement. Aidan assured her that traumatic experiences could play havoc with one's memory and that everyone in the court—the jury, the judge, even the prosecutor—understood perfectly well. "Do go on," he said.

"The woman, Tatiana, she kiss Jakov. He rape me in King's Cross house."

"Did you see Dragan?"

"Yes. He was driver. They push me into back of the car. They shout at Dragan to drive quick. So he drive very speed. We arrive to the house very quick. I walk into house and prisoner there for long time. I already tell story."

"Yes, you did, Dorina. Just a few more questions and this will all be over." When she smiled weakly, the jury looked like they wanted to honor her with a knighthood. "What happened in the car on the way to the house?"

She paused and thought. "They argue and Jakov, he hit Dragan on the head."

"What else do you know about the operation they ran? Was Dragan in charge?"

Her answer came instantly. "No. Zora was in charge." Loud murmurs rippled around the courtroom. Journalists began scribbling frantically on their pads.

"Order! Order!" said the judge loudly. He turned to the witness. "Ms. Ibanescu, did you mention this in your original statement?"

Dorina shook her head. "The police only ask me about Dragan."

It sounded like a clear case of evasion, but Dorina had earned sufficient sympathy to overcome any sense of unease. Furthermore, anyone who knew police procedure could join the dots. Once they had their suspect, the police often jumped to their own conclusions. No wonder they hadn't dug any deeper. Evidence was gathered that established Dragan's guilt. No further questions were asked.

"Mr. Manning, you may continue," said the judge.

"Dorina, do tell the court about Zora."

She suddenly seemed unsure of herself. Aidan stopped. He thought it might be worth doing some digging, so he asked for an adjournment. The judge looked at his watch. It was a little early, but the old man had a hankering for a sherry.

Court was adjourned. The public gallery burst into life again. Aidan looked over at Dragan.

He'd seen the expression many times before.

The big man was terrified.

Aidan made some notes, underlining the word "Zora." After Fenwick and Fiona had left, he pulled out his diary. As he opened it, a piece of card with gold embossed writing fell out into his lap.

Sidney Manning requests the pleasure of your company.

It was an invitation to his grandfather's ninety-eighth birthday celebration.

He picked it up and looked at it, running his fingers over the raised type. He hadn't seen his grandfather for over a year. Holding the card, the dread weight of familial guilt descended on his soul. He hesitated, feeling the loss of family connection, keenly aware of his own share of responsibility. He'd never really made any effort.

Examining the invitation, he noticed some spidery writing at the bottom that read, "Aidan, I do hope you can make an appearance. Aunt Grace." Make an appearance. So that's how they viewed him. He looked at his watch. Of course he could make an appearance. Pulling out his cell phone, he tapped in the number on the card. He didn't deserve it, but Aunt Grace informed him a place setting could be arranged.

Dress nicely, she said.

Which meant a dinner jacket.

Arriving at The Savoy later that night, Aidan found the private dining room already full of people. Aunt Grace rose to greet him, looking like a dowager duchess. She was in her mid-nineties, but she walked with her head held high and her shoulders back. He thought she looked resplendent in a maroon dress, with a dark purple collar, a mélange of colors she carried off with aplomb. When she reached Aidan, she placed her hands on his shoulders and kissed him on both cheeks.

"Aidan, my dear. What an honor. I've saved you a seat next to me. Do you know everyone?"

He looked at the assembled company and realized several relatives had either grown beards or developed a penchant for heavy makeup. He found himself sweating whenever his memory was unable to match faces with names. He felt certain that at least two of his cousins were named Jane, but one of them looked confused when he greeted her, so as he went down the row, he began compensating by nodding a lot and saying "You look well" a little too loudly.

At the end of the table sat his grandfather.

When he spotted his grandson, Sidney's face lit up. Aidan's guilt deepened in response to the old man's evident delight. He knew he should have visited him more. Especially since he lived in a nursing home not five miles from his house. Sidney was turning ninety-eight, but like Aunt Grace, he looked much younger. His dark suit contrasted with his silver hair and he sat hunch-shouldered. Yet as Aidan approached, he turned briskly in his chair, leaned back, and peered up at his grandson, a smile breaking across his face.

"Grandpa!" said Aidan, handing over the small package he'd just had wrapped in Selfridges an hour before. He rarely wore cufflinks himself but he knew that old men often wore shirts that needed them. "How very good to see you. Happy birthday!"

Sidney didn't rise, but clasped his grandson's hands tightly, looking up at him with a fondness that Aidan knew he didn't deserve. He could barely meet the old man's gaze. Shame sat heavily on his soul. He attempted a smile before taking his place at the far end of the table next to Aunt Grace.

The meal was delicious. Aidan ordered seafood—oysters, prawns, and salmon. He knew fish was good for him and he rarely cooked it at home. On his right was Colin, recently married into the family via a cousin. Aidan listened as carefully as he could to a man who appeared to prefer his trade union to his own family. Nodding sagely at appropriate moments, Aidan amused himself with the thought that their conversation was taking place in The Savoy of all places. No doubt, come the revolution, the place would be turned into low-cost housing for the masses. Colin's denunciation of New Labour was in full flow, when the poor man was cut short by his phone. As he rose to take the call, Aidan uttered a prayer of thanks for small mercies.

He turned toward his grandfather's cousin, the woman the family called Aunt Grace. Was she well nowadays? Yes, quite well. And Grandpa? Also doing well, though not as mobile as he used to be. You should visit more often. You know he'd like to see his grandson. And stop telling us we're doing well for our age. It's all in the mind. If you say so, thought Aidan, but didn't reply.

He hesitated, caught between the desire to discover more about the family and the shame of knowing so little. "It's a funny thing, Aunt Grace," he said. "I had a dream the other night, and it's hard to explain, but I was talking to someone about the family."

"Oh yes?" She put down her glass and leaned forward.

"I was telling someone about my grandfather and I realized how little I knew. It's silly, really." He glanced down at his plate. His great-aunt looked at him affectionately. She had always shown a keen interest in her cousin's family. Her connection with Sidney ran very deep. Gifts for Aidan at birthdays, attendance at school plays—she showed more interest than his actual grandmother. He remembered her kindness after the death of Naomi and Bruce. She did more than send a card. She visited often.

"You know Sidney came to live with us, don't you?"

He paused, racking his brains. "Er, no. I don't think I do. When was that?"

Aunt Grace launched in.

Edna Manning took the death of her husband, Henry, in 1912, very hard. Her quiet stoicism failed to cope adequately with the loss of the home's breadwinner. Yet beneath the grief boiled a good dose of anger. Grace knew this from her aunt's occasional visits when she was young. She often snapped at her for the most minor of infractions, like a dirty pinafore or being too familiar with the servants.

Then came the news that left a deep-seated scar inside all of them. Her mother, Mildred, sat her down one day and explained that the boy she called her brother was, in fact, her cousin. Aunt Edna's son. Grace couldn't quite take it in. As for Sidney, he started wetting his bed soon afterward.

What a shy boy he was. He spent most of his time playing with pieces of metal round the back of a builders' merchants. She could still remember the pride on his face as he walked in one day with what looked like an iron bird.

"When did he come to live with you?" asked Aidan.

"When I was two, according to Mother."

"You didn't believe her?"

"Oh, I believed her. In fact, much of this comes from my mother, but looking back, my dear, I can hardly bear to think of it."

Aidan looked down toward the end of the table, where his grandpa was bringing a quivering spoon up to his mouth. The people on either side of him were busy talking to each other across the table.

"So, what was it like growing up with him? Did you get on?"

"Oh, I didn't grow up with him."

Grace recalled Aunt Edna's visit with a mixture of fear and loathing.

Sidney

According to her mother, it took place just after the outbreak of war. She remembered the bewildered look on Sidney's face, the staccato shrillness of her aunt's voice. Sidney was leaving, a departure that was tearing her family apart. And no one was doing anything to stop it. So she just stood there crying.

A stronger character might have thrown a tantrum, but Sidney just got up meekly and did as he was told. He was defenseless and so very alone. He'd hardly seen his mother during the previous two years, and now her first words came out as a command. The blood drained from his face, turning him chalky and pale during his forced march out to the Daimler. The iron bird he was dragging along behind him was snatched from his grasp and discarded in the flowerbed. Grace never forgot her last glimpse of Sidney—forehead pressed against the back window, a look of utter dejection on his face.

"So let me get this straight," said Aidan. "My great-grandma dispensed with her son just after the death of her husband on the *Titanic*, but decided to take him back when he was . . ."

"Seven and a half."

"So he lost his father and his home when he was . . ."

"Five."

"And he lost touch with his closest relatives—his cousin and his aunt—when he was seven and a half."

"Yes. I'm afraid so."

Aidan looked down the table toward his grandfather. He was wiping a dribble of soup from his chin. When he put his napkin down, a woman to his right picked it up and leaned forward. Without asking, she wiped away a stray splash he'd missed, a task completed with such speed and efficiency it was surely borne of familiarity. In the time it took to hail a cab, she had turned away, oblivious to the elderly man's smile of thanks, offered too slowly to be noticed. Aidan was heartened to see the woman replaced by a jolly, buxom lady, who appeared voluble if nothing else.

He turned back to his aunt. "So that story about my great-grandfather Henry—is that true? I heard once that Uncle Joe was all cock-a-hoop when he discovered some old newspaper clippings. Apparently, he was telling everyone that Henry was guilty of murder.

Makes me really mad. How could he possibly know?"

Aunt Grace's face darkened. "Oh, don't you worry about Uncle Joe, he's all hot air. In any case, you're right—how can we know? What I *can* tell you is that my mother defended Henry to her dying day. She was adamant her brother-in-law was a man of honor." She looked down and began cleaning her glasses. "I like to think that honor and duty still exist, don't you?"

"Of course," said Aidan.

She glanced up. "However, before we make a start on what you've been up to, I want to finish by letting you in on a secret." She looked around furtively, playfully, then fixed him with a steady gaze, a small smile on her lips. "Our family has suffered enough to make one despair. But such a reaction would be foolish in the extreme. Because one day, the Lord God is going to make everything beautiful again. All the ugliness in this world will be gone. You know that, don't you? It will be a day of great celebration. It's not too late to return, my dear boy. Prodigal sons have a habit of turning up at banquets, you know. And if you look around, I think you'll find this is a banquet."

The glint in her eye was infectious, her smile warm and generous. Aidan looked down, folding and unfolding his napkin. He felt a pang of jealousy for a belief solid enough to define a person's life. Grace led prayers at the old people's home where she lived, and had gently chastised him after he'd lost his faith. Yet she never scolded him. She always remembered his birthday, always listened, always loved.

He looked up into her eyes; deep within his soul, he felt both shame and longing. That he had drifted so far from the steady mooring of his faith was the cause of his shame. His longing, however, was weak and ill-defined. Deep in his heart, his desires and priorities were a confusing mixture, each of them competing for his affection. In the confusion, he had become unable to identify what mattered most. It left him feeling disoriented, a sensation accentuated by the strength of his aunt's faith.

He picked up his fork and started dissecting his salmon.

The evening swept by on a diet of rich food and expensive-tasting wines. Aidan circulated and made a valiant attempt to feign interest in the petty slights that preoccupied an alarming number of his relatives. Some had seen his name in the newspapers and assumed he was some kind of legal celebrity. When informed that he was merely a humble barrister, a rotund woman bedecked in purples and pinks retorted sharply, "Not even a QC?" If he'd cared, he would have been offended. As it was, he was merely bemused.

Proceedings drew to a close with a whimper rather than a bang. The guests gradually donned coats, cheeks were pecked, and unsteady legs bore their owners in the direction of home. As Aidan extricated himself from a tearful woman who had been tugging on his sleeve every few seconds, he noticed his grandfather sitting alone, unattended. He wandered over, taking a seat by his side.

The elderly man was engaged in lighting his pipe, repeatedly aerating the stem in an effort to ignite the tobacco. The put-putting sound he made dragged Aidan back to his childhood. The redolent odor of the pipe smoke transported him to a dimly lit drawing room filled with mahogany antiques, where an ivory chess set was laid out between him and his grandfather. He could almost detect the same musty smell of the house as he stoked his memories.

Sidney looked up.

"Hi, Grandpa," began Aidan. "Did you have a good evening?"

The old man's watery eyes brightened. "Delightful, my boy. So glad you could make it." He tossed a match into a nearby ashtray, sat back, and peered at his grandson. Apparently, the care worker, Victoria, was taking her time to find the car.

"I'm sorry for not visiting more," said Aidan. "But if you're free next week, I—"

Sidney interrupted. "Any time you like, my boy. Any time. No need to call." He seemed distracted, his eyes staring beyond his grandson into the middle distance. "You know, I was just telling Brenda about the time when your father came home from school without his winter coat."

The change of subject caught him off guard, but Aidan expertly followed his grandfather's stream of consciousness. "Dad still forgets things, Grandpa. Probably forgot about this evening, you know how he is."

"When Rosemary found out," continued the old man, "I thought she might explode on the spot. Oh, she was hopping mad." He cracked a small smile. Aidan had never liked his grandma very much. She was cold and harsh, quick with correction—the complete opposite of Aunt Grace. "Did he often forget his coat?" he said.

"No, just the once, but his mother never let him forget it, poor boy. Fearsome she was, quite fearsome." His grandparents' divorce was rarely mentioned at home. In fact, Aidan was only informed a year after they had gone their separate ways.

As they waited for Victoria to return, they fell into a conversation about cricket. Aidan much preferred tennis, but knew enough about cover drives and off breaks to fill the space vacated by the care worker's delay. Suddenly, the discussion took an unexpected turn, Sidney veering back through time to England's Test series with India in 1946. "He would have enjoyed the match that summer," said the old man, tapping his pipe on the ashtray. "That was a pity, that was."

Aidan leaned forward. "Sorry, Grandpa, I've lost you. Which match? Who would have enjoyed it?"

"Your father. A wonderful match at Lords, it was. We drove up. Aunt Mildred and Gracie met us there. Alec Bedser took eleven wickets, I seem to remember. Jolly good." He twisted in his seat and tried to look over his shoulder. "Is Victoria here yet? Where is that woman?" He continued tapping his pipe against the ashtray.

"Hold on, Grandpa. You said my dad missed the match. What was that all about?"

Sidney didn't look up, still preoccupied with the pipe. "Oh, it was during the summer holidays. He was at school. Rosemary's idea, of course. Too busy, she said. And, er, well—those matrons, they mothered him like nobody's business. Only left him there once, but such a pity he couldn't see Bedser in full flow."

He launched into a fond recollection of the famous bowler's inswingers, but Aidan was hardly listening. Instead of wickets, whites, and willow, all he could see was a small plastic box he used to own, with little cars that moved forward at the tap of a button; that and bloody swirls that stained the pristine white sheets of a school bunk bed. It was not a legend of the game he saw, but a jagged pin jabbed into a bloody knee. The repetitive twisting of the metal in the flesh caused the blood to flow freely, until it stained not only his leg and the sheets but dripped down onto the wooden floor. His grandfather's undulating voice drew up his past like a hot, damp cloth draws an infection to the skin's surface. The memories caught him by surprise, searing his soul, and almost flowing down his cheeks.

Aidan coughed and removed the image by changing the subject. He interrupted abruptly. "Do you remember your own father?" he asked. "Your own father, Henry. Do you remember him at all?"

Sidney hesitated, once again staring past his grandson. "He went down with the *Titanic*, you know that. Why would I remember him?" He harrumphed irritably as he fussed with his pipe, attempting to put it away in a cloth bag. Just then, Victoria arrived with a wheelchair. Sidney waved it away, struggling to pull on his coat. It came as no surprise when he grabbed his walking stick and, instead of saying goodbye, departed without so much as a backward glance.

Aidan arrived home after midnight.

He picked up an envelope leaning against the carriage clock in the hall. His name was handwritten on it. Inside was a card with his father's name embossed in gold lettering in the corner. The handwriting was familiar. *Cemetery. Next Friday. 5 p.m. work for you?* Why didn't he just call? Of course 5 p.m. would work.

In the kitchen, he found the rest of his mail on the counter, arranged neatly by Carmen. When she suspected bad news, she hid the offending item at the bottom of the pile, as though to soften the blow. A brown envelope stared up at him. Red letters on the outside didn't augur well for what was inside. Sure enough, it was a bill gathering pace, amassing interest at an alarming rate.

He shoved it into a "bill tidy" that Beth had given him for Christmas. A metal device for holding papers together, it gave the owner the misleading impression that orderliness equated to financial discipline. He poured himself a glass of wine and returned to the living room where he collapsed into an armchair. He opened up his laptop and pressed the power button.

Just one game.

It was always just one game.

That was the problem. Had been from the very beginning.

After Naomi died, he began inhabiting the William Hill betting shop a mile away from his house, later on graduating to his own personal bookie, a man he'd found in the *Racing Post*. At first, gambling was a distraction. It helped ease the pain of his loss, generating endorphins he hoped would combat whatever was driving him into sad, lonely places. For a number of years, he had it under control. He dabbled more than anything else. The numbers were manageable, the losses minimal. He even thought he knew how to beat the system, a fantasy entertained by gamblers the world over.

Sadly, however, he'd started to win.

Winning was fatal. It made him feel inviolate, as though he was destined to pick the right numbers, the right horse, or the right team. Six months ago, he'd branched out into bets on sporting events he knew little about. Again, he won and the numbers he played with started growing zeros on the end. But inevitably, his luck had turned. And it had turned a long time before he faced up to it. The zeros were still there, but now they were the wrong color. He borrowed to make his payments, but the story was stuttering to a close.

Billy, his bookie, wasn't nearly as friendly as he used to be.

He'd gone off him completely.

Aidan surveyed his living room. He liked living in West Kensington. He enjoyed the middle-class affluence in which he was cocooned, protected from the harsher elements of the city. He would miss it. Even as he clicked on roulettewinbig.com, he persuaded himself he was doing just fine. The bedsit he'd visited the other day was a little dirty, and he'd have to sell most of his furniture, but somehow he'd manage.

He had to manage.

Just one more game and then he'd stop. He was feeling lucky. He'd won the last two times with odd numbers plus his birth date.

Play Now!

Surely his luck wouldn't desert him.

~ 22 ~

FREEDOM

All theory is against freedom of the will; all experience for it.
~ Samuel Johnson

It is for freedom that Christ has set us free.
~ Galatians 5:1a

March 6, 2005

The heat hit Evelyn like she'd walked into an oven. She started sweating instantly, perspiration trickling down her back. Putting on a pair of sunglasses, she turned and started following behind Aidan. Her mind was on other things, but she still enjoyed watching him walk. She liked the firm set of his shoulders and the confidence in his stride. His back was broad and strong. She could see his muscles tighten beneath the thin white shirt that stuck to him as he navigated the narrow, muddy path in front of him.

Aidan was taking care not to slip, but he was also fascinated by his surroundings. Looking around, he used his hand to shade his eyes as he took in the sight of thousands of cotton plants covering the fields for miles around. The bushes, about five feet high, were covered in white bolls. He knelt down to pull a stone out of his boot. As he rose, his eyes came level with the tops of the plants. A vast, snow-covered landscape stretched out into the distance—a display so arresting he stopped momentarily to take it in. As he watched, a Black man, his torso naked and shiny with sweat, stood up no further than fifty feet away, as though rising from within an endless white comforter.

Aidan hurried after the others.

Their arrival in the mezcla had been sudden. He sometimes found the adjustment hard. It wasn't that long ago he'd been on the phone to Simon. Now he was back in the nineteenth century, traipsing after Korazin in sweltering heat.

"Not far now, everyone," said Korazin, who led the pack. "We're meeting up with Jeremiah, a lucidus who spent centuries in the Deep South." They kept walking until they saw a group of slaves off to their right. Some of them were naked. Others wore a filthy white shirt or a pair of threadbare pants. None wore both. They had sacks over their backs and were picking the bolls as fast as they could. A woman near the back looked like she was pregnant. Blood appeared to be running down her legs. One of the overseers was cursing a couple of men for no discernible reason. He carried a long bullwhip and lashed the back of one of the men. The crack was like a gunshot. It made Evelyn jump.

As they neared the end of the row, they came across a tall broad-shouldered man who was standing, waiting. Any illusion of his being a slave vanished the instant he smiled. His white teeth shone brightly, and though his black face didn't exactly change color, it seemed to glimmer in the evening light, while his green eyes glowed in their sockets. "Jeremiah, at your service," he said, bowing. "Good to meet you folks."

Korazin turned to his guests. "Jeremiah here will be our guide."

The lucidus stepped forward. "Why don't we begin with this group behind you?" he said, his voice deep and resonant. They turned to watch the band of slaves they'd just passed, moving slowly through the field. Now and again, they heard the crack of the whip. "A slave could receive a lash for almost any reason at all. For drinking too long at the dipper; for not picking enough cotton. For almost any infraction. One slave wrote that his plantation rang to the sound of the whip and shrieking from morning till night. And it wasn't a mere one or two blows. Twenty-five lashes were not uncommon for breaking a branch in the field or when dry leaves were caught in the bolls."

Aidan stood watching the scene with a mixture of fascination and horror. He knew there was nothing he could do, but he couldn't avoid the desire to intervene. "I saw *Amistad*," he said. "That was pretty shocking."

"The movie barely scratched the surface, Aidan," said Jeremiah. "Its depiction was harrowing, yet it couldn't hope to convey the scale of human misery experienced in reality. Slaves were packed into the most squalid conditions imaginable. Slave traders attempted to maximize their profits by stuffing their ships to capacity and beyond. The amount of room below decks was so paltry, the slaves could not stand, nor could they crouch down properly. They lay in rows, but were often forced to lie upon each other. Many suffocated. Human waste and vomit washed over their bodies, and each morning, if they were fortunate, the dead were removed and thrown overboard. The smells were beyond description. Food was tossed down randomly. Many died of hunger and disease, while still more died of thirst. Death was a relief to many."

The mezcla jumped, and with it, the surroundings.

They found themselves to one side of a bustling town square. Women in long dresses were accompanied by men in smart suits, some in top hats. In front of a bell tower, a wooden platform had been set up. Slaves were being marched up in chains and advertised to the assembled crowd, who gathered round, looking up. Evelyn ignored the man who was extolling the physical prowess of the slave on the platform. She was drawn to the sight of a woman near the back, who was weeping bitterly.

Turning to Jeremiah, she said, pointing, "Who's she?"

"Well, back then, she didn't have a name. We call her Beatrice now. She chose the name herself. As you can see, she is distraught. And understandably so. Her two children will be sold today. Her master will not even give her the chance to say goodbye. We are in Virginia, the slave-breeding state where plantation owners had a penchant for women who could produce the next generation. The more fecund, the better; it was good business for them. Either the children grew up to work on the plantation or they were sold. As in the scene you're viewing today."

A shriek sounded from near the platform. Two small children, a boy and a girl, aged about four and five, were led up and ordered to stand still. Their mother was restrained by two women who attempted to comfort her in her grief. Aidan and Evelyn watched in disbelief as various men in fine clothing communicated their bids by waving papers in the air. They were unperturbed by the loud wailing that continued in the background.

The young faces, shining with life, caught Evelyn's immediate attention. The boy was grinning broadly, while his sister looked at their mother and called out "Mama" in a high-pitched voice. They had no idea what was happening to them, they were just enjoying the attention. A moment later, they both started waving to one of the bidders, huge smiles on their faces. In horror, Evelyn realized the children thought they were playing a game. She found the pathos too much to bear.

"Please," she said, turning to Jeremiah. "Can we go now?"

"Certainly."

The mezcla shifted and they found themselves in the fields again. Various groups of slaves were out picking cotton. Baskets stood at the ends of the rows, and each slave had a large sack draped around their shoulders. They were picking feverishly in the midday heat.

"They worked hard," said Jeremiah, "because to fall short of the required weight resulted in a whipping. After they finished in the fields, they had other chores to complete. Feeding the mules, cutting wood, that kind of thing." The lucidus was quiet, giving them time to observe. At close quarters, the pain written on the array of faces before them was almost too much to bear. Evelyn couldn't help grimacing every time she heard the whip. There was no getting used to it.

Jeremiah sensed her discomfort. "Not long now, Evelyn," he said, his voice softening. "We ain't here to shock you." His face shone with tenderness and concern. They expected more but it was a while before he spoke again. The silence among them was reflective and thoughtful, broken at last by the lucidus' deep voice. "It's worth asking yourself which was worse: the agony of physical suffering or the anguish experienced by a soul deprived of liberty?" He allowed his question to settle on their hearts. "Now there's a question to confound us all."

The mezcla shifted again and they found themselves in the wood at night. Aidan and Evelyn were immediately aware of a thumping beat not far away. They walked toward the sound, which grew louder as they approached. Arriving at a small clearing, they came upon a large group of slaves, sitting on logs around a roaring fire. They were all laughing and joking as they banged on drums and a variety of homemade instruments.

Jeremiah faced his guests and smiled. "It's a mercy, isn't it, to see them squeeze a little joy out of life? Holidays, especially between Christmas and New Year, were a time when the masters gave them longer periods of rest." The music's mood changed from a rhythmic beat to a slower, richer sound.

I looked over Jordan
And what did I see
Coming for to carry me home
A band of angels
Coming after me
Coming for to carry me home

Swing low, sweet chariot
Coming for to carry me home
Swing low, sweet chariot
Coming for to carry me home.

As the song came to an end, Jeremiah turned to his guests. "Not all slaves were believers, of course, but many were. They clung to the Father's promises in no small part because they had nothing else left. They believed not only that the Father cherished each of them individually, but they also held onto the hope that one day, he would deliver justice for them all. And they sang of heaven almost as if they could taste it. They imbued their suffering with meaning while also raging against it, a delicate balance not always achieved." There was melancholy in his voice as he finished speaking.

Korazin stepped forward and embraced Jeremiah. "It's been an honor to spend time with you, my friend. As always."

The Black lucidus stepped back, bowing. "The honor is all mine." He turned and walked away.

Korazin handed out water bottles.
Together they drank.

Evelyn found herself sitting alone at a table down in the herb garden. The weather was warm. Cirrus clouds floated high overhead, and a gentle breeze was rustling the hedges bordering the garden. Through the archway opposite, she could see the ocean, blinking in the sunlight. When Aidan arrived shortly after, he was carrying a pitcher of water and some glasses. He served her a glass of water and sat down. Though she smiled up at him, her mind was elsewhere. She couldn't help speculating on what had happened to Jasmine. And deeper down, she nursed a real fear that Duncan was seriously dangerous. The anxiety was giving her a stomachache, even in the Espacio.

Gamaliel arrived with a woman beside him. Except that she wasn't really a woman—her glowing face gave that away. The introductions were quick and businesslike. Her name was Aliza. She was dressed simply in a dark green summer dress that brought out the emerald in her eyes. Evelyn recognized her from the first day, when she'd brought in some food. Aliza smiled and took her seat, folding her hands in her lap. Initially, there was something about her that Evelyn couldn't quite put her finger on. But then it struck her. The lucidus oozed serenity. She had peace. Yes, that was it. Peace.

Korazin arrived with the inevitable tray of food and drink. Chips and salsa. Juice. Nuts. Fruit. He picked up an apple, smiled, and left.

Gamaliel sat quietly, his expression inscrutable; Aliza closed her eyes, enjoying the sun on her face. The lucidi never seemed to be in a hurry. After a minute or two, Evelyn spoke first. "Okay, so slavery in the Southern states. A horror show, obviously, but we're not here to discuss nineteenth century conditions in the Virginia cotton fields, are we?"

The face of the tall lucidus shone a little more brightly. "As always, my dear, your neurons are firing as explosively as ever." He smiled.

"You lost me," said Aidan.

"Freedom," said Evelyn. "But not the political or religious kind, right? I'm guessing we've moved onto freedom of the will. Free will."

Gamaliel nodded. "A common response to the problem of evil."

"But we don't all have the same opportunities, the same amount of freedom, do we?" There was an edge to her voice. "Just tossing the word 'freedom' around is hardly an answer."

"Very astute." Aliza poured herself a glass of water. "You are free to the extent that you can direct your behavior, but you're still you. You can't simply become someone you're not. No act of the will can achieve that."

"Sounds fatalistic," said Aidan.

"It does, doesn't it? Not only that, you all feel like actors in your own play, don't you? But since when is the main character also the writer? After all, Hamlet didn't write a play about a Danish prince. That was Shakespeare, as you well know. All the world might be a stage, but if it is, then are you just players in someone else's play?"

"You're depressing me," said Aidan.

"So we're not free at all?" asked Evelyn.

"Do you feel free?"

"Of course."

"Then embrace it." Aliza sat forward, her face shining with intensity. "Hold tight to the belief that freedom matters, whatever the implications. You should go with your gut instinct. That you're free. And this means that, in reality, there is still plenty of scope for change. *That's* what counts."

Gamaliel smoothed back his silver hair. "Freedom," he announced. "Ah, yes. The freedom to change and grow. Freedom, even given its limitations, Evelyn, is still the fresh air in which human beings flourish best. Adventure, ambition, discovery, the building of empires and democracies, not to mention all those virtues we have already mentioned such as compassion, fortitude, tenacity—they're impossible without freedom. Freedom . . . of the will. Because it's the will—the human heart—that concerns us most. Why? Because the human heart is the part of you that controls the affections. It's with the heart that you love, and love is more important than anything else. It cannot develop and grow without the oxygen of freedom.

"Unfortunately, this means humans must be allowed to fail and disappoint. That's why during this current era, true freedom will always presuppose the existence of evil. Without it, choice is drained of meaning. Indeed, the very essence of freedom is expressed by the contrary inclinations that fight within the human soul. It's by recognizing evil and resisting it, *even within yourself*, that true virtue is produced. In the absence of evil, the human soul is denied the possibility of true spiritual growth."

Gamaliel offered Aidan and Evelyn a glass of juice. They accepted. Aidan was thankful for the respite that went with pouring liquid into glasses. He murmured his thanks.

Evelyn took a sip from her glass with trembling hands. She started shaking her head. Her voice cracked as she spoke. "I'm afraid there's a terrible imbalance at the center of this discussion. Why—" She paused, unable to complete her sentence. Neither lucidus spoke. They waited for her to continue. Aidan looked across at her, unsure why she was at a loss for words. "Why," she said, "does a rapist's freedom outweigh the value . . . ," her voice was trembling, ". . . of a little girl who *should* be free to remain safe in her own home? It doesn't make any sense."

There was quiet around the table. No one spoke. She began to weep. Bowing her head, she covered her face with her hands.

Tears ran down Gamaliel's face as he looked at her.

Aliza spoke first. "Aidan, Gamaliel, would you excuse us?"

After they'd left, Aliza came and sat next to Evelyn, moving close and wrapping her arms around her. The body of the lucidus exuded a warmth that spread out and touched her. Affection engulfed her, a feeling of wellbeing that ran right through her, comforting her. It held her tight, made her feel secure. And though her body shook, her soul soaked up kindness like a sponge. She unashamedly received the love that was offered.

The fissures inside her began to close.

Slowly at first, it began to dawn on Evelyn that the lucidus' embrace carried the presence of the Father. Her touch communicated his love. Her awareness of what was happening took place not in her intellect but deep within her spirit, in the very center of her being. And adequate words could not be found to describe it.

Gradually, the sobbing subsided. She took hold of the tablecloth and blew her nose with it. "Hope you don't mind," she said, folding up the fabric and pushing it back on the table.

"Be my guest," said Aliza, smiling.

While Evelyn made use of a napkin to dry her face, the lucidus waited for her to compose herself. "There's somewhere I'd like to take you. If you're up for it, of course."

"Sure. But Aidan?"

"Oh, he'll be fine. Korazin was talking about tennis. They're probably already into the first set."

She smiled and rose to her feet.

The pair met later in front of the Viatici House. Aliza was dressed in black cycling shorts and a yellow top, her hair tied back securely in a braid.

"Ready?" she said. They set off, relishing the warmth of the sun on their backs and the wind in their faces. Aliza looked like she was in the body of a fifty-year old, but she was fit and she set a fast pace. The route led them up past cornfields and vast acres filled with sunflowers. Evelyn settled into a steady rhythm, glancing occasionally at her companion. The lucidus, a small smile on her face, powered forward abruptly, calling back, "Show me what you got, Evie!"

Evelyn laughed and gave chase, rising from her saddle and giving the pedals maximum effort. As the slope flattened out, they entered a pine forest. They slowed as the path narrowed, enjoying the immediate drop in temperature that cooled their bodies. The forest floor was covered in pine needles that crunched under their bike wheels. After passing a huge fallen tree trunk, covered in moss, the path led out into a clearing with a lake directly ahead. Its surface was a mirror.

They reached the shore and laid down their bikes.

"Come," said Aliza. "Come and sit on this rock." A huge slab of limestone jutted out into the lake, creating a promontory. They walked out and sat down. Evelyn peered down into the dark water below.

"So how have you enjoyed your visits?" The lucidus looked down, giving her space.

"Oh. Fine. Well, you probably heard about the start. Not auspicious, I know. But since then, I've enjoyed the guys. Korazin, in particular. He's quite a character."

"He is, isn't he?"

"Gamaliel reminds me of my granddad." She paused. "I do have a question, though. All this talk about suffering and the arguments they keep piling up—I'm not sure what that's supposed to prove. As soon as I wake up, I'm back at square one. Struggling with a creep who lives across the street, a daughter who hates me and, well, still just my dog for company."

"Were you hoping for answers?"

"Er, an explanation maybe?" She hesitated. "At first, and now . . . an apology. I'm still so angry. It just won't go away." Her voice cracked. She tried to maintain her composure but it was impossible. Memories simmered inside and streamed hotly down her cheeks. The tears spilled off the end of her nose and landed in the water. Spreading out in a large circle, they formed a huge diaphanous sheet. The surface was a little hazy, but in time, she made out her reflection staring up at her. The lucidus by her side smiled up from the lake, calm and reassuring.

"Wow," she said. "I feel like Alice."

Aliza smiled fondly at her. A doe tiptoed forward from behind a tree, hesitantly lowering its head to drink from the lake. Placing its front hooves apart, it lapped briefly from the shallows. Sensing danger, it straightened, its eyes darting around, nose twitching. They both watched it skip back into the forest.

The animal's departure dropped Evelyn back into her memories. "I wanted to tell my mom," she said softly. "But I couldn't, I just couldn't. I was too scared. He'd threatened Katie and I was ten years old, what was I supposed to do?" Her voice trailed away. "But you know, coming here, it's been indescribable. What a liberation! I knew as soon as I got here that something was different. I was angry—who wouldn't be—but when I woke up the first few times, I knew, I just knew something was happening to me, something wonderful and strange. As for this body you've given me, it has one *huge* advantage. No one has ever violated it, or touched it without my permission. It feels clean and new and . . . pure. It's just wonderful." She looked across at Aliza and attempted a smile. "I would do almost anything to be in this body when I wake up." Her face fell. "But that's not possible, is it?"

Aliza shook her head.

Quiet descended.

Evelyn's loneliness beat in her chest and head, crowding out her thoughts. She felt herself diminished, and spoke to battle the vacant spaces inside. "It hurts when I go back to my body. You know that, don't you?" As Evelyn stared down, wandering alone into far-off places, the surface of the lake began to cloud. A thin silver film began to spread across the expanse, shimmering in the dappled light. It hooked her back into the present. She looked across at Aliza.

"Just wait," said the lucidus.

The cloudy covering settled into an image. A little girl smiled up at them both. She stood awkwardly, hands clasped together in front, weight shifting from foot to foot. Evelyn's voice came out as a whisper. "I look about ten."

The young girl looked up, her face breaking into a smile, radiating life and vigor. Her hair was curly and auburn; her eyes sparkled with joy. Bubbling up from within the lake burst laughter, far off but distinct. Innocence and beauty broke over Evelyn, flooding her with huge, racking sobs that shook her without mercy. She was defenseless, weeping unashamedly. The outpouring seemed to drain and, at the same time, soothe the pain inside. A measure of healing was dispensed through the tears. Wiping them away, she murmured in a small voice, "Just look at me. I was beautiful. And vulnerable. It's not fair. Little girls should be playing hopscotch and tag and making mud pies. And I was—" She couldn't finish. As she peered down, the images began to shift. Another little girl came up and stood next to her, reaching for her hand.

"Katie, right?" asked Evelyn, but she already knew the answer. "I used to laugh a lot." She looked down at herself rolling on the grass with her sister.

From out of nowhere, a man's face appeared. He was balding and portly. Evelyn stiffened. She grabbed Aliza's arm and held on, unaware of how hard she was squeezing.

"What's he doing there?" she said, looking away.

"Don't be frightened, dear one. It's just a memory."

Evelyn allowed herself a quick glimpse of Mr. Henderson. He was wearing a grubby raincoat and dull brown shoes. An air of uncertainty shrouded him, so that, above all, he seemed lost. She looked again, this time for longer, her eyes widening with incredulity as she watched him start to shrink. His coat soon towered over his head, while his arms disappeared up the sleeves.

"What's happening?" she said. "This can't be a memory."

"You're projecting—taking back some control." The lucidus paused. "But what do *you* see?"

Evelyn stared more closely. "I've lost him. He must be somewhere inside his coat." The fabric of the coat twitched, as though inhabited by a small animal, the whole scene mildly comical.

"Feels good, right?" said Aliza. Evelyn couldn't help smiling. "It's okay to be angry, you know. Never confuse anger with hatred, my dear. They are not the same. Anger can invigorate and motivate. By contrast, hatred is self-destructive and poisonous, relentlessly strangling the life out of a person. Hatred separates people and does violence to the soul."

She stood up.

They mounted their bikes again, and followed a path round to the far side of the lake. As they were leaving, Evelyn stopped and looked back. The water's surface had lost its sheen. The images from within had disappeared. A duck flew down, spread its feet, and landed in a glorious riot of water and flapping wings.

The mirror was gone.

She turned and pedaled after Aliza. The path became narrower the further up they climbed, and the pine trees thinned as the trail left the forest. Navigating their way through rocky terrain, they finally came up to the edge of a cliff and were met by a sight to stun the eyes and stop the breath. For hundreds of miles, mountains stretched out in front of them. Evelyn thought the rock face opposite was at least four or five thousand feet tall. It looked even taller than El Capitan. The path hugged the cliff edge and the climb was steep, but at last they reached the top. Laying down their bikes, they went to sit down, dangling their legs over the edge. They both sheltered their eyes as they took in the view.

"You come up here often?" said Evelyn. The lucidus nodded. "I'm supposed to forgive him, aren't I? That's what religious types always say."

"So dump the religious language."

"What?"

"Dump it. If the word 'forgiveness' isn't helping, choose something different."

"Like what?"

"Like . . . letting go. Let him go, Evelyn. The tighter you hold on, the more it hurts. Your anger may never go away. Ever. But right now every time you feel angry, you embrace it. It's like you're clutching a warm blanket, using it to comfort yourself. Except it's not comforting at all. It's hurting." She paused. "It can sometimes be helpful to remind yourself what forgiveness *isn't*."

"What forgiveness *isn't*? You lost me."

"It isn't forgetting," said Aliza. "And it isn't excusing. You are not required to understand the other person's actions. Nor do you have to wish them well. You don't have to do any of that. Forgiveness is letting go, and it's a slow process—which is often left incomplete."

They sat in silence for a while. Evelyn leaned against the lucidus and soaked up her care. The curative touch of the divine flooded her body, her soul.

"Religious type, was it?" Aliza sat back and fixed Evelyn with her emerald eyes. "Hmm," she said thoughtfully. "Nope. Never been a fan of religion. Come on. It's time to go." She passed her guest a water bottle.

They both drank.

It was just as hot as last time, but on this occasion, the discomfort was caused primarily by the humidity. On arrival, they started sweating instantly. The fields were fleeced with cotton bolls, as wondrous a sight as when they'd first arrived. Placing her hand on her forehead to shade her eyes, Evelyn squinted out at the fields. She wondered where Aidan might be and turned back to ask Aliza.

The lucidus was gone.

She let out a short gasp. "She can't have left me, surely," she said under her breath.

But she had. Evelyn was on her own.

She looked about, trying to get her bearings. To calm down, she reminded herself that the lucidi had never hurt nor abandoned her. In fact, they had done nothing but care for her. The urge to panic receded, followed by a feeling of mild irritation. She couldn't understand why the lucidus would have deserted her, or what benefit she could derive from wandering around the Deep South on her own.

The heat quickly forced her into action. It was oppressive.

She needed to find some shade.

Spotting a path leading down toward a wood not more than a hundred yards away, she began walking. The track entered a marshy area, and she could hear the sound of water thundering over rocks. A river wasn't far away, but how big it was, she couldn't be sure. Approaching through the trees, she caught sight of moving water, glinting in the sun. It danced and winked at her. The vegetation thickened a little, but she pressed on until a riverbank came into view.

The sight before her filled her with joy and relief. On the bank opposite stood Aidan. He waved, causing her heart to surge with anticipation.

In an instant, the gap between them snapped something inside. The distance tipped Evelyn over the edge. She wanted him more in that moment than she had ever wanted him before. It was absurdly romantic and perhaps rather foolish to clamber over rocks in the middle of a fast-flowing river, but she didn't care. She gave not one thought to the danger, or the possible presence of the lucidi. Nor did she care if she was throwing herself at him. The ache to hold and be held by him was a physical thing. It throbbed in the pit of her stomach, constricted her throat, and gave her pins and needles.

"I think I love you!" she called over the rumble of the rapids, and burst out laughing. "This is insane," she whispered. What a ridiculous thing to say.

"What?" he called back, cupping his ear. "I can't hear you." At least, that's what she thought she heard.

She threw caution to the wind. "I said, I think I love you!"

"I can't hear you," he replied. "I'm coming to get you."

They both jumped into the river at the same time. Although the current was strong, the water only reached their waists. They waded across to some large boulders that stood right in the middle of the river. Aidan arrived first, but slipped as he scrambled up, grazing the palm of his right hand. Blood started to ooze out, but he took no notice. When Evelyn reached him, she sat down by his side, feeling a little foolish. She was trying to balance herself when he moved forward and took her into his arms. In a sweeping motion he'd rehearsed many times in his mind, he pulled her into his lap and looked down into her eyes.

"Frankly, my dear," he said, stifling a laugh.

"Stop, stop," she said, wriggling up.

"What? You don't like my Clark Gable? I thought this was the ideal setting too."

"Oh, go on then." She smiled and lay back down, nuzzling into his arms and enjoying the strength she could feel pressing against her back.

"Now, where was I," he said, "before I was so rudely interrupted? Although, I must say, I don't *give* a damn." Evelyn giggled. "Oh yes, I believe I was about to declare my love for you in the middle of a raging torrent." He looked down at her, whispering softly, "I've waited too long for this. I—"

"Enough," she said, pulling his head down gently. Their lips met. At first, they kissed nervously, tentatively, but their need for each other quickly overwhelmed them. The desire to know and be known could not be held back. They held each other ever more tightly and kissed with one thought only: to communicate their love. Yet without knowing it, they conveyed much more. Each satisfied the other's longing, but their closeness was also like a balm. It eased the profound pain that dwelled in the darkest recesses of their souls. Evelyn's loneliness was like a piece of parched earth upon which Aidan's affection was being poured in a constant, steady stream. She soaked him up and drenched herself in his love until she thought she would drown.

Their mutual healing did not eradicate their pain, but the sharp edges softened and they felt in their spirits a rejuvenation prompted by each other's embrace. Their encounter was viewed in the heavenlies and produced much rejoicing among the lucidi, as did countless other acts of love in countless other lives all over the globe.

They were not unique in their love, yet they felt special.

Chosen. Blessed. Healed. Loved. And so they were.

As they pulled apart, Evelyn noticed Aidan's palm, from which blood was still seeping. "I'm not the only one who's bleeding," he said. She hadn't noticed a sharp gash on her knee.

Korazin and Gamaliel appeared on the bank and started waving. "For you," shouted Korazin, holding up what looked like a first aid kit. Exercising a little more caution than before, Aidan and Evelyn climbed down into the water and waded to the riverbank. They collapsed onto the grass and were soon tending each other's wounds with broad, oversized Band-Aids. Gamaliel handed them each a towel.

"Weren't the last ten minutes supposed to be private?" said Evelyn, dabbing some cotton wool on Aidan's palm.

"Yes, yes. Completely private. We didn't see a thing." Gamaliel winked, unable to hide a grin.

The prospect of returning to earth suddenly filled Evelyn with fear. Surely they would help her find him. Surely. But they wouldn't. She knew it. The thought of waking up and returning home threatened to rob her of her joy. It was too horrible to contemplate. Reaching for Aidan's hand, she held it tightly, as though physical contact could keep him there, an absurd thought but one she clung to for a moment.

The lucidi weren't in a mood for reflection, however. They took off down a path that meandered along the riverbank. "Follow us," called Korazin, leading the way. The day was roasting, and they were all glad to fill their water bottles from a nearby creek. A mile further on, they spotted Jeremiah standing on a rock in the middle of the river, his hands on his hips.

"Greetings!" he called out. They all waved. He flashed them a warm smile and performed a mock salute. "You've come on a good day. A *very* good day, my friends!"

From through the trees, they could hear singing. A group of twelve women, their hips swaying in time to their voices, came walking through the thigh-high grasses.

Tain't no mo' sellin' today.
Tain't no mo' sellin' today
Tain't no mo' pullin' off shirts today.
It's stomp down freedom today.

When they arrived at the riverbank, one of the women started it. The rumpus, that is. She jumped fully clothed into the shallows and began splashing her friends. "I's free! I's free! I's free!" One by one, they all leaped in, hollering and hugging. Evelyn had never seen such joy in all her life. It poured out of the women and filled the air. Jeremiah couldn't contain himself. His face directed a beam of light capable of illuminating a tall building. When the women had worn themselves out and were sitting on the bank, wringing out their dresses, he began to sing. The humans had never heard anything like it before in their lives. Evelyn reached for Aidan's hand and squeezed it. The beauty and resonance of Jeremiah's voice entered them with an almost physical power. They just stood and listened, filled with wonder at what they were hearing.

When he was finished, Korazin said, "The Thirteenth Amendment to the Constitution was a leap forward; a wonderful document. But documents don't change human hearts. The lives of many slaves didn't improve at all. But just look at them. Nothing on this day could dampen their spirits. All that lay in the future."

They watched the former slaves depart. When they turned back to look at Jeremiah, his mood had changed. Fire burned in his eyes. His face darkened and he was trembling.

"Justice delayed is justice betrayed!" His voice boomed out across the water. "The scandal of injustice weighs heavily upon a nation claiming to have been birthed in the cause of liberty. The folks whose clothes we just saw drenched in the joy of proffered freedom will shortly be wrung out with further abuse and the denial of common decency. They will return to their masters and bow their heads once again, not out of institutional servitude, but under the cosh of cruelty and rank violation of the law. Promises made became promises broken. Just as the native populations were lied to, so too Black people found themselves the recipient of fanciful assurances. Land and mules and the means to profit from them were promised, then denied. Sharecropping kept former slaves in poverty, crushed by pernicious 'black codes.'" He stopped for a moment, his chest rising and falling. "Segregation, that hated practice, continued to define the southern states for more than a century, while decent white folks passed by on the other side." He paused. "Passed by . . . on the other side."

They watched the lucidus as he planted his feet apart and set his face toward the heavens. "He seems very . . . animated," said Aidan, turning to Korazin.

"Oh, he hasn't even got started."

Jeremiah stood looking up and let out a primal scream from deep inside. His vocal cords produced the sound of a rushing gale; the trees bent before its power. The shock of it caused the humans to cower. Evelyn held Aidan's hand tightly, standing as close to him as she could.

"Are you sure we're safe here?" She glanced across at Korazin.

"Oh, you're quite safe," he said, his face glowing unusually bright. "Consider yourself an honored guest. There are few who witness Jeremiah in full flow."

When the Black lucidus continued, his voice was low and brooding. "Spare a thought, Lord, for the oppressed of your world. For they will not remain cowering beneath the feet of the tyrant forever. No, sir, they will not. Even today upon the earth there remain injustices to rival the Roman cross and the French guillotine. Slavery still lives in the brothels of East London and the bordellos of Amsterdam. The women and the young are abused by men whose hearts are beholden to their own disgusting passions, driven by the rapacious appetite of an Enemy given free rein for long enough. The dream of your servant, Martin, is mocked by the nightmares of children who live in fear, the little ones who are trafficked and coerced into the slaughter of their own flesh and blood. Such nightmares must end. They *will* end!

"For your old men are dreaming new dreams and your young men possess visions of a better future. But how long, O Lord, must they wait? How long must your people languish in the prisons of China and the camps of North Korea? How much longer must they hide behind the veil in Saudi Arabia and shrink from the secret police in Iran? For you, Father, are a good shepherd, who leads his flock with tender care, who guides his people through dark valleys until they reach the fresh pastures of your holy presence. O Lord, let justice roll on like a river, righteousness like a never-failing stream. Let it run through the streets of Bangkok, along the canals of Venice, down the slopes of Mount Fuji, and into the hearts of men and women who bear your name."

Jeremiah's voice gathered momentum and volume as he moved toward his conclusion.

"Your servant declared long ago that he came not to bring peace but the sword. Yet when will the sword be satisfied? When will it be satiated by the blood of your beloved? When will the Prince of Peace declare 'enough is enough'? For peace is the longing of our hearts. A time when your will is perfected in the lives of your people. When your glory is revealed and the Enemy is defeated. When love and mercy saturate our hearts forevermore. When we gather not simply as lucidi around your throne, but we join with created beings of all kinds, to worship you, O Lord our God, our Fortress and Protector. For you alone are worthy to receive honor, glory, and power. Forever and ever. Amen."

When he'd finished speaking, he knelt down and bowed his head. A low rumbling sound was coming from his mouth as he clenched his fists and beat upon his chest. From out of his back, two wings appeared; he spread them wide. They were dark brown, like the wings of an eagle, dappled with flecks of white. Slowly and deliberately, he rose to his feet. Smaller wings sprouted from his thighs and calves. They beat the air, lifting him up until he hovered ten feet above the river. The air around Aidan and Evelyn vibrated, pressing in on their ears and bringing tears to their eyes.

The lucidus seemed to grow before them.

His face shone like the sun. He opened his mouth wide. First one, then two swords emerged. They flashed from side to side, glinting in the light that emanated from his eyes. Fire poured from his mouth whenever he spoke. His voice was like thunder. It made the ground beneath their feet shudder, as though an earthquake was about to tear the earth apart. Evelyn clung to Aidan, who wrapped his arms around her. The lucidi by their sides simply stood, lost in wonder, their hearts directed to the Father in worship.

As they watched, two spinning wheels appeared from the river. They rose and came to rest on each side of the lucidus, who continued to hover, his enormous wings beating the air in a fluid motion that kept him stationary above the waters. The wheels sparkled like topaz, their rims dazzling the humans, who shielded their eyes from the brilliant light. When Jeremiah beat his wings, he rose higher and, as he did so, the wheels rose with him. When he turned, the wheels turned with him. Lightning flashed in the direction of his gaze and burst through the trees.

As quickly as it started, it ended. The wheels disappeared, the fire and swords were gone, and his face settled down to a gentle glow. He landed on a boulder and folded in his wings. He faced Evelyn, whose heart burned inside her. "Do not be afraid, dear Evelyn," his voice bellowed over the rumble of the rapids, "for every event in your life carries the potential for redemptive growth. Remember that." The words entered her and buried themselves deep inside, settling down in the hiddenmost parts of her being. She looked up at the lucidus, seeking more, but no more came. He had turned his attention to the man standing beside her. "Freedom, Aidan!" he called out. "Grab it! Taste it! Live in it!"

Jeremiah launched himself into the air. Wings erupted from his back, thighs, and calves, thrashing the air. He hovered, lit them all up with a radiant smile, and shot off over the trees.

Feathers floated down like snowflakes.

The lucidus disappeared from sight.

~ 23 ~

AN EMPRESS AMONG BABIES

Children sweeten labours, but they make misfortunes more bitter.
~ Francis Bacon

March 7, 2005

Evelyn parked her car behind the Torrance library, and walked over to the police station. Heat rose off the asphalt, enveloping her as she approached the main doors. Inside, she looked around. Against the wall stood a cabinet containing trophies. One commemorated four officers who had died in the line of duty. Several people sat in the waiting area, holding subdued conversations. A Hispanic police officer with a shiny badge looked up.

"Hi," said Evelyn. "I understand you have a Jasmine Machin in custody. She's my daughter." The woman started tapping a keyboard, while peering at a screen. She pulled out a folder from the file cabinet behind her.

"She posted bail this morning."

The words struck Evelyn's eardrums and registered as a punch in the stomach. "Excuse me? I got a call from her just last night. I don't understand. Who bailed her out?"

The officer hesitated, unsure if she was allowed to give out that information. "A Brian someone. I can't read his writing."

"And you didn't think to call me?" said Evelyn, her voice rising.

"She's an adult, ma'am."

"What was the bail amount?"

The woman scribbled on a Post-it note.

"Five thousand dollars," said Evelyn flatly. "And the reason for the arrest?"

"Looks like a DUI followed by an RTA. Must've hit someone."

The questions tumbled around Evelyn's head, like lottery balls in a metal cage. None of the answers she came up with made any sense. Jasmine drunk at the wheel? And who did she know who could suddenly come up with $5,000? No, it wasn't the amount of money. Of course it wasn't. It hurt because she thought her daughter was turning to her in her hour of need. Turned out a guy named Brian was more important. And who the hell was he? She didn't recognize the name.

She glanced at the Post-it note. Just looking at it hurt.

When her daughter was born, the nurses in Labor & Delivery fell over themselves gawping. They saw babies all the time, but not like this one. She was an empress among babies. Her skin had none of the red blotches many newborns have. She wasn't a cone-head or a puffy-cheeked marshmallow. She wasn't even in one of the two categories that Katie insisted applied to every baby ever born: Winston Churchill or Buddha. No exceptions, said Katie—they're either Winston or Buddha.

Until Jasmine came along.

Her skin was smooth and olive-colored, and she had enormous dark brown eyes that were open from the moment she arrived. She would lie for hours on her side, eyes wide open, just staring at the world. Evelyn remembered her mom's reaction. There were tears of joy followed by a gaping jaw of wonder. Katie was there too, looking like she wanted to give birth herself that very minute.

Jasmine was the result of a foolish fling with a guy named Brandon. Many advised Evelyn to terminate, but she couldn't do it. The life inside her felt far too important to discard. On the day of the birth, Brandon was nowhere to be seen. As she lay in recovery, Evelyn remembered the sadness that ached inside her. The father was supposed to be there. He was supposed to greet his daughter, provide for her. She didn't even have a last name to enter on the birth certificate in the box marked "Father."

The early years involved too many hours spent in day care. UCLA medical school gobbled up Evelyn's life, and when it spat out the bones, it wanted to chew on those too. Grandma put in frequent babysitting shifts, as did Katie, both helping to steady the ship, but the reality was sobering: in the process of juggling single-motherhood with medical school, the ball most often dropped was Jasmine.

By the time she reached her teens, however, Evelyn thought they made a good team. Her hours calmed down and she was able to attend her daughter's basketball games. They even managed some trips up to Big Bear to go snowboarding and mountain biking.

It had all collapsed one semester in the fall, two years ago. Jasmine was in her second year at El Camino, the local junior college, when she met Floyd, a young man Evelyn disliked from the moment she met him. He had bleached blond hair, displayed his boxer shorts to the world, and drove a BMW. Evelyn didn't much care about his clothing or his vehicle, but she did care about the effect he had on her daughter. Jasmine started coming home late and answering back. Then one day she had walked out. She and Floyd had taken an apartment together. Evelyn remembered the day when she had come home to find her daughter's room cleaned out. The emptiness had left a gaping hole not just in her home but also in her soul.

Evelyn walked to her car and climbed in. Folding up the Post-it note, she tucked it in her bag. Hadn't she forgotten something along the way? Surely the note was a sign. Yes, that's what it was. Even though someone else had come to bail her out, Jasmine had called. That was better than nothing. That meant something. By the time Evelyn drove out of the parking lot, she was feeling better.

She grabbed her phone out of her bag and stabbed at some numbers. The speakerphone rang with a high-pitched trilling as she drove down the on-ramp onto the 110. Traffic was doing its thing—looking like mice in a maze. By the time she was nearing the 405, the phone stopped ringing. No answer. When she pulled up on her driveway, she noticed her front door was ajar.

"Please, God. No," she said out loud, her heart racing. Surely Duncan hadn't paid another visit. As soon as she reached the porch, the door swung open. Her sister walked out, arms open wide.

"Surprise!"

"Katie!" she screamed, falling into her arms. They walked into the living room. Her mom rose from the couch to greet her.

"To what do I owe the pleasure?" said Evelyn, turning to her sister. "Have you come in search of voters for your Congressman to devour?" Søren ran up, his tail flicking from side to side. She bent down and ruffled his ears. After pouring him some dog food, she filled his water bowl and began running the coffee grinder.

Katie, it turned out, was in town for a conference. "Do HMOs provide value for money?" Evelyn picked up a brochure and almost burst out laughing.

"No, Evie, don't laugh," said Katie once they'd joined their mom in the living room. "HMOs have distorted the healthcare market. You know that."

"Yes, I do. But answer me this. Who's paying? That's what I wanna know."

Their political views were too similar for a full-scale debate, and they were soon tossing Twinkies at each other. Katie always brought Twinkies with her, along with Wienerschnitzel coupons. Evelyn claimed that some food corporations didn't actually sell food, and Wienerschnitzel was one of them.

"So how's Nicholas? Didn't he—?" said Evelyn, handing round cups of coffee, unaware she'd just touched a nerve. The gloss had come off the boyfriend, though his name was still up in lights on Broadway. After one too many parties at which his eyes and hands had displayed a woeful lack of self-control, Nicholas had proved to be a disappointment. Forty, financially independent, and single again, Katie wore a brave smile that told the world she was okay with that. Most of the time.

"Listen, I got something I gotta do. I'll be back in half an hour."

"But you just arrived—" Katie was already out the door. Evelyn shrugged and started making lunch, watched by her mom, who couldn't stop smiling. To see her daughters together in one place, she thought if she died and went to heaven, the good Lord couldn't possibly improve her condition. She rummaged around in her bag and pulled out her knitting, interrupted by Søren, who started digging for bones at the back of the couch.

Approaching midday, Evelyn's phone rattled in her bag.

"Come out on the porch and look north." Her sister had a strong sense of the dramatic. About two hundred yards away, Jasmine stood on the sidewalk, her head tilted to one side.

Evelyn started to run.

She ran hard, tears streaming down her face. The pounding of her heart echoed the pounding of her feet, each step resounding in her ears. Her embrace, when it came, communicated her long-held desire to extinguish, to asphyxiate all the bitterness and hurt of the past. Their apologies, babbled and meandering, fused together into one long expression of regret. Evelyn closed her eyes, desperately trying to burn the moment into her memory, eager not only to drink in the joy, but to place it in a secure corner of her heart, as protection against future sorrows.

She finally pulled back and took her daughter's face in her hands. Kissing her on both cheeks, their tears mingled even as their souls caressed without words. "No more apologies, my love." She wiped away a tear. "You're back now." The ice, which was melting, washed over their souls, soothing them, healing them, and returning them to health. They breathed in deeply as they walked, arm in arm, back toward the house.

Later that evening, Bridget came over. Evelyn looked around at the four most important people in her life, treasuring the moment. They ate steak and seafood, drank wine, and argued over the relative merits of LA versus New York City. Conversation was bubbling along casually when suddenly, out of the blue, Bridget dropped the question.

"So, Evie, you gonna tell 'em about the man of your dreams?" Katie and Jasmine turned to look at Evelyn, who blushed.

"Ooh, I like this," said Katie. "We gonna meet him?"

"No, no, sorry to disappoint. Bridget's just messin' with ya." She paused. They sat, all eyes trained on her, waiting. Her mom put down her knitting and sat forward.

"I dream . . . a lot," said Evelyn, "about a man."

Her sister let out a hoot of laughter. "O-kay. We all dream. What's different here?"

"I've dreamed about this guy dozens of times, but it seems like more than a dream. I, er . . . It's like I know him. I know, I know, it's crazy. Bridge, you shouldn't have—"

"No, we're enjoying this," said Katie. "Describe him."

"Well, he's British."

"Ooh, I like British," said Jasmine. "Did you see him on Masterpiece Theatre?"

"No, I didn't. Now stop it. I've never even met him. I don't know what's happening to my brain. It's just spooling the tape round and round, like it's stuck." She paused. "Okay. He's tall and broad and he lives in London. I think. We've gone hiking and sailing and mountain biking, and I don't know what to say, I wake up with the smell of his cologne on my pillow. I know. It's crazy."

She looked down at her lap.

"No, it's romantic," said her sister, smiling.

"Oh, stop it. Stop it, all of you."

"Man, you got it bad," said Katie, who was promptly hit in the face by a napkin.

They all descended into fits of laughter.

As they sat in the living room later that evening, Evelyn looked at the faces surrounding her. Her sister was feet away, but she already missed her desperately. Her visits were always far too short. Next to her sat Bridget, who was laughing at one of Katie's bad jokes. Her friend was as dear to her as a blood relative. She didn't know what she'd do if she ever lost her.

Looking across at Jasmine, the tug on her heart was fierce. Conflicting emotions wrestled inside her. She ached for the years she'd missed, for the memories that had never been made. Those years could never be recovered. And yet the gap yawning between them was in the process of being repaired. Not only that, the child chatting to Bridget was now unmistakably a burgeoning young adult. The metamorphosis was almost complete. Gone the awkward teenager, Jasmine was currently employed as an admin assistant by an advertising company on the West Side. Humble beginnings, of course, but a job was a job. Things could have turned out so much worse.

As she reflected on why her daughter had returned, she realized she hadn't asked. Nor did she feel any desire to do so. It would reap only discord and pain. It mattered only that Jasmine was sitting opposite, that her laughter echoed around the room, that her smile filled her with joy once again.

Gazing around at them all, Evelyn found herself unexpectedly grateful for small mercies. Her mom used to tell her to thank God for moments in time that shone with grace. Her mom's words sounded from across the years, from a kitchen table, from beside her bed. Evelyn didn't hold to her mother's beliefs, but she couldn't avoid a surge of gratitude welling up in her heart. Her daughter had returned. Her sister and best friend were sitting right there in her home. This was surely one of those moments of grace. That was it. Moments of grace. Søren jumped up on the couch. She stroked his head as he buried his nose under her legs.

The evening ended abruptly. As they left, Evelyn felt a hollowness inside, as though she was losing them and they would never return. She hugged her sister, struggling to hold back the tears.

Katie held her tightly. "I'll call you," she said as she left. "Come on, Mom. Let's hope those old folks you live with haven't trashed the place. They're so rowdy." She smiled as she took her mom's arm and left.

Evelyn closed the front door and slumped onto the couch, a half-empty glass of wine in her hand. Rubbing her eyes, she was about to head for bed when something red caught her attention on the mantel. She rose and went to investigate. A small parcel, covered in scarlet wrapping paper, was set discreetly behind a photo frame. She opened it. Her mother's locket and *Titanic* whistle fell into her open hands, along with a note.

Dearest Evelyn,

After your dad left, I put these in a drawer and, with all the chaos, I just forgot about them. You both deserved better from us. I'm very sorry. You were so angry back then, but recently I've seen a change in you. You seem more settled. So I want you to have them now. To remind you of those precious times at the Thanksgiving table.

I never look at them without giving thanks.
I hope one day you will do the same.
With love,
Mom

Later that night, as Evelyn lay on her bed, she started scratching the back of her leg. The lichen planus was getting worse. She was using a new cream, but it wasn't doing much. The spots were spreading all the way up the back of her right leg, and some had started on her left leg too. She rubbed on the ointment and grabbed the remote, hoping a movie might take her mind off the itching. As the opening credits rolled, she fell asleep.

The following day when Evelyn came home from work, she felt a lot better. She was looking forward to cooking with Jasmine, who was due to come over at seven. She intended to use the new Chinese cookbook her mom had given her for Christmas. Once inside, Søren greeted her in his customary manner, his tail a blur of quivering white fluff. Within minutes, bowls and spices littered every possible surface. Spills and seasoning went everywhere. Evelyn turned up the music and danced her way through bean sprouts and meat preparation.

As soon as Jasmine arrived, she started talking and barely drew breath all evening. Two years was a lot to catch up on. They ate fried rice, Szechuan stir-fry, a couple of seafood dishes from northern China, all accompanied by piles of prawn crackers and generous quantities of sweet sauce.

Jasmine had just launched into yet another story about her new boss, when the doorbell rang. Evelyn was buried in the couch at the time and took her time getting up. She put her wineglass down and ambled over to the door, unsure who would be calling late in the evening. When she opened the door, there was no one there. She went out and looked up and down the street. Nothing. As she turned to go back indoors, she spotted it.

Standing to the right of the door was a piece of cardboard. She groaned inwardly and picked it up. *YOUR TURN.*

"Mom?" Jasmine called out.

Evelyn was already calling the police, her eyes fixed on Duncan's house. He was standing under a porch light, his face clearly visible.

He winked, and blew a kiss in her direction. She looked down at the cardboard.

Attached to it was a dog's lead.

~ 24 ~

THE TRUTH WILL SET YOU FREE

Truth is tough. It will not break like a bubble . . . you may kick it about all day like a football, and it will be round and full at evening.
~ Oliver Wendell Holmes Sr.

March 7, 2005

The law is a strange beast, unmoved by common morality. A barrister fights for the client like a warrior, suppressing suspicions of guilt, as long as the story is consistent. Hearty congratulations following an acquittal verdict tend to soothe any lingering doubts over the defendant's innocence. Later that day, the same barrister can often be found writing to *The Times*, expressing outrage at the rise in crime on the streets of Britain. And no one bats an eyelid. Truth, it seems, is a casualty of the system, too weak to put up its own defense.

Aidan had lived and breathed the law for decades, accepting its internal contradictions. But then a case like Dragan's came along. As he sat opposite his client in the interview room, Aidan found himself discomfited by the truth. It was demanding attention.

It pummeled his temples.

It sought a hearing.

He was alone with the big man this time, Fenwick surplus to requirements. The Serbian looked like a man whose demons tormented him from dawn till dusk and then picked up steam through the night. He pleaded "not guilty," but the forensic evidence, in particular, pointed directly to him. Emails. Text messages. He was constantly communicating with other traffickers. And yet at one of the exchanges, he was the driver. It simply didn't add up.

Aidan felt compelled to dig deeper. He knew he should concentrate on casting doubt on the forensics, and highlight the duplicity of one of the main witnesses for the prosecution, Tatiana. But suddenly the truth mattered. And he thought he might be able to discover it if he trod carefully.

He was about to launch in when Dragan blurted out, "Guilty. I want to change to guilty. You are my lawyer. I change to guilty." His face was flushed; he folded his arms and hunched his shoulders.

"Guil—" began Aidan.

"*Guilty! Kriv!*" Dragan interrupted loudly, jabbing his forefinger at the man in front of him.

Aidan absorbed the shock wave of angry words. He was worn out. He loosened his tie and leaned back. Tilting his head up, he stared at the ceiling. So much for finding the truth. His client clearly wasn't in the mood to open up. He could hear him shifting in his seat. Aidan stood up and walked to the door. Four steps. Eight more and he'd crossed the room.

"This room's a bit small, isn't it, Dragan?" He paused. The Serbian twisted awkwardly, trying to follow Aidan, who'd now moved behind him. "Not much bigger than the room you slept in." He leaned in and spoke softly in Dragan's ear. "They claim *you* were the one in charge. I find that hard to believe."

Aidan walked round the table and sat down. He felt claustrophobic and deflated. The case seemed hopeless. The opposition had forensics, emails, and a defendant who was permanently angry—a man who was trapped in his own lies, digging a hole so deep he didn't have a hope of ever getting out.

It was laughable really, the futility of it all.

As he rubbed his eyes, his brain slowly connected the dots, until the truth appeared before his mind's eye. Starkly and undeniably. Of course. How could he have missed it? Dragan wasn't the only one digging. Of course he wasn't. Deep down he'd known this for a while, but somehow he'd managed to avoid the obvious parallels. He'd become accustomed to the mental gymnastics. In fact, he'd been doing it for such a long time, it was like a leopard's spots—just part of him. A way to protect himself.

What a pair of mugs they were.

That's when the laughter started. Looking back, Aidan had no explanation. He supposed it could have been the tiredness, or a desire to ease the tension. Or maybe it was the disquieting reflection of his condition sitting opposite him, which could no longer be denied. Whatever it was, it was extremely funny. He chuckled away to himself for several minutes until he was spent. Wiping tears from his eyes, he eventually looked up, feeling not an ounce of embarrassment. Losing all hope really felt quite relaxing, and he was pleasantly surprised by the Serbian's reaction. His expression had changed; now he looked mildly amused.

Aidan hesitated. "I like a . . . flutter," he said. He waved his hands about in a rather absurd fashion. "In William Hill, Ladbrokes, paper betting slips, they float, they flutter . . . to the ground." Another wave of laughter broke over him. "Sorry, Dragan, I don't know what to say. It's been a long day." He paused. "I bet on the horses, and I used to be quite good at it." His voice grated as he spoke. "Thing is, I don't win any more."

Dragan stared at his barrister, his large face gradually softening into an expression Aidan had never seen before. He grinned. "I like bet. National Lottery. Everyone's winner. Is not true. Not everyone." He smiled broadly.

"No, not everyone." Aidan smiled back, and leaned forward.

He pulled a photo out of his inside pocket and placed it on the table in front of him. He turned it round. It showed a couple holding a small child in their arms. Dragan's smile disappeared. "That's you, isn't it? With your parents." A ripple of discomfort crossed the Serbian's face, but he said nothing. His shoulders drooped.

Aidan then showed him the photo of the soldiers. Twelve men stood looking into the camera; half were smiling. Dragan wasn't. Instead, he held his weapon proudly in front of him, a determined look on his face.

Aidan waited.

It was getting late, so he reached out to pick up the photograph. He was too slow. Dragan grabbed it and leaned forward. "This one." He indicated the young man standing next to him in the photo. "This boy. Guilty. *Kriv!* He murder children."

He slammed the photo down on the table.

Aidan pulled a bottle of Gatorade out of his briefcase, and placed it in front of his client. Dragan twisted off the cap and sucked back half the contents. His hands were shaking.

"Who else is *kriv*, Dragan?" said Aidan. "Who else is guilty?" The Serbian was breathing heavily, his eyes darting around the room. "Who's Zora?" Aidan reached out and picked up the photo of Dragan's parents. He slid it slowly across the table toward his client. "Tell me about Zora." He held his breath, waiting for a response, hoping against hope that a few cracks would develop.

He got a lot more than that.

Almost inaudibly, Dragan began unburdening a lifetime of suffering. Aidan had to ask him to speak up. He knew he should have been taking notes, but he just sat, mesmerized by what he was hearing. The story was so appalling, so dreadful, that at first, he could barely believe his ears. Dragan spoke for half an hour, and when he was finished, he sat back and bowed his head. When he looked up, his expression was vacant, drained of all hope. "If she find me now, she kill me," he said.

"Not if we find her first."

It was a long shot and sure enough, they scoffed. The look on Molsberry's face was particularly irksome. After outlining Dragan's account briefly, Aidan asked the prosecution team to accept a guilty plea for the imprisonment and the pimping in return for dropping the human trafficking and rape charges. His opponent looked at him as though he'd lost his mind. Well, it was worth a try.

Back in court, the public gallery began to fill up. Both sets of barristers watched as people began shuffling in sideways to take their seats. A man with a thin mustache entered and made his way to the corner of the back row. He looked at Aidan and nodded imperceptibly. Fiona, her antennae buzzing, leaned across. "Who's that man?"

"Plainclothes."

"To what end?"

"Recently, I've discovered the Bible can come in handy, Fiona. Proverbs 26, verse 11." She scribbled the reference on a pad in front of her. He continued, "Every big fish needs bait."

"Well, well," he said, watching Tatiana take her place two seats down from Thin Mustache. "A tickle is better than nothing."

"A dog returning to its vomit." Fiona closed a court Bible and put it down.

"Yup. And with any luck, our dog will want to do exactly that."

She didn't understand a word he'd just said, but she smiled nevertheless. Aidan rose to his feet. "The defense calls Dragan Bakic," he announced loudly. Repressed whispers from the public gallery rippled round the court. He suspected the assembled company had been watching too much courtroom drama on TV. Putting a defendant in the witness box was considered a risky strategy by TV scriptwriters, a chance to ratchet up the tension. In reality, it was common practice and, in fact, a refusal to answer the prosecutor's questions was likely to damage the defense. He approached Dragan, trying to make eye contact, trying to put him at ease. His first few questions focused on the aunt. Aunt Zora.

When Aidan had finished, he stared at the jury. Half were appalled. The other half looked skeptical. All the prosecution had to do was undermine the sandcastle he'd built. Then knock it over. So with a few unanswerable questions, Molsberry did just that.

It was a pity, thought Aidan.

But at least his client had told the truth. He could ask no more.

~ 25 ~

WORSHIP

Thou hast made us for thyself, O Lord, and our heart is restless until it finds its rest in thee.
~ Saint Augustine

March 9, 2005

Gamaliel spooned some seafood salad onto his plate and went to sit down at the head of the table. "I recommend the crab," he said. "Nathan does something to it to accentuate the flavor. A little lucidus magic." Aidan and Evelyn surveyed the spread on the sideboards, and when they'd heaped their plates with food, they sat down next to each other. Evelyn's hunger was unusually intense and she was soon tucking into a plate of shrimp that was exceedingly good, especially when dipped in a sweet sauce that temporarily overwhelmed the taste buds. Next to her, Aidan took a large bite of the crab. Gamaliel was right. It was absolutely delicious.

"Spider-Man!" said the tall lucidus out of the blue.

"Gotta love the suit." Aidan smiled, pleased with himself for his brisk retort.

"No, no. The suit's a veneer. I want you to focus on the central quote from the movie. With great power . . ." He paused.

". . . comes great responsibility. Uncle Ben," said Evelyn.

"The use of the will is a dangerous thing, is it not?" said Korazin. The humans were silent, neither of them sure where the conversation was heading. The lucidus continued. "The will, of course, is essential to growth, as we mentioned last time. Unfortunately, you want to have your cake and eat it. You want your freedom, without the inevitable responsibility it entails. In fact, sometimes you talk about yourselves as though you're referring to pets. You believe the Father owes you a warm bed, a tickle on the tummy, good food, regular exercise, and all the benefits of a loving home. You're *owed* this. How dare he deprive you of such things? But the analogy is mistaken. You are not pets. You are children, and as such, you are created specifically for soul-making. Perfection."

"I don't get that," said Evelyn. "What has perfection got to do with soul-making?"

"Oh, they're effectively the same thing. I know the word 'perfection' is often related to ethical purity, but in fact, its real meaning has to do with growth and development."

Gamaliel stood up and began pacing. "Growth is only possible for creatures who are able to determine their futures. Self-determination is a great gift, but a huge liability. The Father knew what he was doing when he set the world in motion, because he cherishes greatly the creation of the fully mature human being. And why is that?" He paused. "Love. It's always about love, isn't it?"

Evelyn felt confused. "How is this about love?"

Gamaliel smiled at her. "Love is the most powerful thing in the entire universe, as I've said more than once. It is rich, dynamic, and enduring. Indeed, it has such a high value, the Father chose to permit the existence of horrendous evil in order to create an environment in which it can flourish. A seed within a decaying compost. Love is freely given and freely received. It is never coerced, never produced through manipulation and undue pressure. Not even the Father can force someone to love him. And he certainly can't force you to love each other.

"Love is the fullest and most glorious expression of freedom a soul can experience. It nourishes and revives a flagging spirit, it heals and soothes a wounded heart, it transforms all it touches, and brings light into the darkest of places. Ask any prisoner in any prison what happens when they are the recipient of a selfless act, an act of love. Transformation. Regeneration. Renewal. And the evocation of new possibilities."

"And love freely offered to the Father leads to worship," said Korazin. "The ultimate destination toward which human beings are headed."

Worship. The word rang around the room. And inside Aidan's

head. To him, it sounded alien. He hadn't used it for many years. It reminded him of the period when he attended church with Naomi. He'd attended for her sake, constantly going through the motions, though the facade was hard to maintain. A believer in his teens, he'd lost his faith at university, while finding a bride whose love transformed his life. When she became his wife, he didn't have the heart to abandon church altogether. Naomi had been a marvelous hostess, and visitors to the house after Sunday services used to be frequent. He felt he had done his best to make them feel welcome. His connection with the church community was brittle, however, and when Naomi died, the tie was severed.

"Worship's rather out-of-date in a country like the UK," he said.

Korazin adopted an expression of mock confusion, raising one eyebrow, and tilting his head to the side. "You're kidding, right?"

Aidan found himself wrong-footed. "What?"

"Sports . . . Aidan. The gathering of the faithful . . . arms aloft . . . communal singing . . . salvation figures . . . the outpouring of devotion. Modern-day worship. But when it comes to sports, we prefer to play than watch. When you've worshipped the real thing, anything else is . . . disappointing. Having said that, who can forget Michael Owen's late winner to snatch victory in the 2001 F.A. Cup Final? Was *that* not a moment to savor?"

"Unforgettable." Aidan's face lit up.

Korazin turned to Gamaliel, a grin spreading across his face. "You got your shorts back from the wash?"

"Hey," said the tall lucidus, getting up. "Just don't wear that Chelsea kit again. You know what I think about Mourinho."

"Love him or loathe him, he's a great manager." Korazin started heading for the door. Evelyn watched the two lucidi in bewilderment. Her knowledge of the English Premier League was meager at best. Manchester United she'd heard of. And Chelsea. The names of the managers, however, were beyond her.

Korazin stopped at the door. "The pitch is down the path to the left once you come out the front door." He winked at Aidan who smiled back broadly. The two lucidi disappeared through a back door, leaving both humans staring at their retreating backs.

"Pitch," said Evelyn. "That's the field, right?"

They walked through the hallway and out the front door. From the front drive, they followed the lucidus' directions and found their way down to a wrought iron gate. Once through, Aidan immediately stopped. "Oh my gosh, just look at that!" He shook his head in disbelief at the vision before him. Over twenty lucidi, their faces glowing gently, were kicking balls around a full-sized football pitch. Half of them were wearing yellow, while the other half were decked out in red.

"Arsenal and Liverpool. I don't believe it." He felt like a kid in a candy store. Korazin walked over. "Your kit," said the lucidus, pointing to a pair of black shorts and a black T-shirt.

Aidan picked up a whistle lying next to the kit. "I'm the ref?" The lucidus was grinning from ear to ear. "But I've never—"

Korazin wasn't listening. He'd already started juggling a football.

Evelyn was enthralled. "This should be good," she said.

Once he'd changed, Aidan ran out onto the pitch, feeling a little nervous. Twenty-two players with wings. How hard could it be to enforce the rules? After all, he was English. The game was supposed to be part of his heritage. Both teams gathered round with serious looks on their glowing faces.

Aidan gulped. "Okay, so no wings. Don't tell me you don't have any, because that cat is out of the bag. So the rule is, no flying. Do I make myself clear?" One of them cracked a small smile but he decided to ignore it.

Toward half-time, Arsenal came forward with a flowing move. The ball was swung out to the wing, where it was trapped by a player who was the spitting image of Cristiano Ronaldo. No matter he's a Manchester United player, thought Aidan, watching him use some fancy footwork to beat a defender. The lucidus reached the byeline and cut inside. One step-over, followed by another, and "Ronaldo" buried the ball in the top corner.

Both teams went wild.

That's when Aidan lost control of the game. All twenty-two lucidi took off. Their wings burst out of their backs and they swamped the goalscorer, who wriggled free and flew up into the air to begin some sort of samba dance at two hundred feet.

Aidan blew his whistle frantically, while Evelyn hooted with laughter. "Whatchu gonna do now, Mr. Referee?" she shouted. "Book 'em all?"

"Yellow cards for everyone!" he announced as he looked up, half in wonder, half in frustration. He was promptly mobbed by the lucidi, who lifted him up on their shoulders and carried him around the pitch as if he was Eric Liddell in *Chariots of Fire*.

"Impress me," said Korazin, once they'd put him down.

The game resumed with Aidan playing as a holding midfielder for the red team. He was supposed to play deep, but one of the Arsenal team slipped and he took his opportunity. Reaching the edge of the box, he let fly with the crispest, sweetest shot he'd ever struck. He was eighteen again, with a strength, balance, and agility reminiscent of his younger days. The ball looped up and over the two players in front of him, swerved to the left and pinged off the inside of the right post, landing in the back of the net.

His delight was spontaneous and uninhibited. He ran to the corner flag and sank to his knees, his arms held high. Evelyn faced him, jumping up and down as she pumped her fists in the air. Seconds later, the lucidi picked him up and put him on their shoulders again.

"Feel it, Aidan. Feel it," said one. He couldn't work out whose voice it was but it didn't matter. He was lost in the ecstasy of the moment. They were about twenty feet up before he realized what was happening. The speed of their flight was starting to make his eyes water. When he looked down, the ground was worryingly far away.

He became anxious.

"Trust us," said a voice nearby. He'd been sitting on the shoulders of two lucidi, but when he was about fifty feet up, two strong arms transferred him onto the back of one whose wings were spread wide, beating vigorously to gain height. Moments later, Evelyn appeared at his side on the back of a lucidus who was rising effortlessly on the warm air current.

Aidan gripped the neck of his ride, as they climbed to about three hundred feet, where they hovered, bobbing up and down gently to the rhythm of the lucidus' powerful wings. He could see right along the coast and far out over the ocean. The water sparkled like diamonds spread out on a vast blue-green canvas. He turned round. Mountains covered in sequoias and redwoods stretched out as far as he could see. A buzzard flew past and disappeared into the wood nearby.

"Worship," said the lucidus. "It generates an intoxicating liberty of the soul, without equal and without limit. For to be loved and return that love with overflowing joy is the very definition of freedom. That's why we were made. It's why you were made too."

The lucidi moved gracefully, weightlessly, lighting up their surroundings with beaming faces and radiant joy. Their laughter filled the air, possessing a beauty all of its own. Aidan had heard the lucidi laugh before, but never so many at the same time. The music of their voices penetrated his ears and worked its way into his body.

Into his soul.

Deep down, Aidan felt a grating contrast between his present experience among the lucidi and the world he'd left behind in London. That world now seemed repugnant. Haughty sophistication, satire, and cynicism—hallmarks of his culture—clung to him like dirty rags. He winced at the thought of the skepticism that so often triggered his responses. Seated on a lucidus whose laughter swirled around and through him, he couldn't escape the shame washing through his soul.

He felt sullied.

He longed to be clean. He wanted to believe again.

Aidan looked around at the lucidi who were now fooling around, flying upside down, and doing loop-the-loops. The sight filled him with wonder, but most of all, it filled him with an intense desire to give thanks. If this was a gift, then he ached to find the giver.

For the first time in many years, his soul longed for its Maker.

The lucidi carrying Aidan and Evelyn circled the house twice, wafted along by the breezes blowing in off the ocean. They landed on some scrubland just above the cliffs. The humans climbed off their backs and collapsed onto the ground, their chests heaving. They were both out of breath from the exertion of holding on. Not to mention the rush of adrenaline that had been coursing through their bodies.

"Woo-hoo!" shouted Evelyn. They exchanged high fives.

Aidan returned to the changing rooms and showered, joining Evelyn for the walk back up to the house. They took a circuitous route, enjoying the late afternoon sun, the wind caressing their faces. Holding hands, they savored their physical closeness.

Gamaliel met them an hour later as they walked through the front door. "Aidan," said the lucidus. "I believe you're stirring. Time to take that pill." He indicated the door behind him. Together, they walked into the Descartes Room, where they found a couple of armchairs. Water and pills were laid out on a side table nearby.

Aidan sat down. Evelyn knelt in front of him and held his hands.

"Okay," she said. "So I've been thinking. We need to work on getting my name and address into your head. So maybe concentrating on those details just before we leave—who knows—perhaps that will help. What do you think?"

"Can't hurt, can it?"

"Now look at me and visualize my name and address. Evelyn Machin. 437 Dell Avenue, Venice Beach, Los Angeles. Evelyn Machin . . ." She repeated her name and address a couple more times. "Now close your eyes and see my face." She watched him close his eyes. "I love you," she whispered. "You hear? Evelyn Machin. 437 Dell Avenue. I love you. Now take that pill." He popped one into his mouth and took a gulp of water. He kissed her, and collapsed back into his chair.

As soon as he was gone, Evelyn felt a huge weight of sadness. Reaching out, she lifted up Aidan's hand and squeezed it. It was still warm. She kissed him on the cheek and went back out into the hall, where she stood looking up at Michelangelo's masterpiece until her neck was aching. She rubbed it as she sat down in a chair opposite *The Last Supper*.

Gamaliel entered the hall and joined her.

"Glass of juice?" he said.

"Mmm. Thank you."

He returned with a tall glass of fresh mango juice. The first sip revived her. She turned toward the lucidus. "I'm scared, Gamaliel. My neighbor. He, er—"

"We know." His voice was soothing, reassuring. "Have you thought about moving?"

"All the time, but I . . . I love my house."

They sat in silence for a while.

Evelyn scuffed her shoe against the chair leg. "You may not believe this, but I've prayed." She paused. "Thought you'd approve." He smiled and was about to reply when she continued. "But I've got a question. I just don't understand why this father of yours is so distant from us. So much of the time. If he loves us—if he loves us as much as you make out—then why don't we perceive him, feel him more than we do? Especially when we suffer. We cry out desperately and we're met with a ringing silence."

"It hurts, doesn't it?"

"Yes. Yes, it does."

"So there must be some kind of explanation."

"I would hope so."

"Okay. Well, this might not completely satisfy you, but here's a start. Consider the primary goal of the Father: to produce loving relationships with his creatures. Contrast that with the aching desire within most humans—to know. You're like kids at a magic show. You want to know how the trick is done. But mere knowledge is not enough, and even if you *were* given answers, it wouldn't lead to growth and it wouldn't lead to relationship."

"But what's wrong with wanting to know why you're suffering? It's completely natural. If he revealed himself . . ." She stopped.

"Right," said Gamaliel. "If he suddenly shone some lights in the sky, with his name and a cute response, what would be the result? The same anger. The same raising of fists. Would it produce faith? Or love?"

"Fair enough," said Evelyn, cutting in. "But the setup he's given us produces the same thing. We're still angry and we *still* raise our fists."

Gamaliel was quiet; deep in thought. "You're quite right, my dear. Either way, the human heart remains in darkness." He paused. "The truth of the matter is, human beings don't want to submit. In your condition, it feels like humiliation. Your rebellion, I'm afraid, goes very deep. So instead of coddling you with information, he withdraws in order to give you an opportunity." He paused.

"An opportunity?"

"Yes, an opportunity to exercise faith. Obscurity invites you to bow the knee and surrender. It brings you face to face with your wretchedness. And without that, you will never reach out. It turns out true knowledge is gained by acknowledging your limitations and your need."

Evelyn stared at the floor, thoughts racing around her head. It was a lot to take in. She knew, in her heart of hearts, that Gamaliel spoke the truth, but she didn't want to admit it.

"Just one more observation," said the lucidus, sitting forward, "and then, I believe, you must return home." He fixed her with a gaze full of compassion. "Discovering why humans suffer will never solve your deepest problem."

"And that is?"

"Separation, my dear. You are separated from your Creator, and as you well know, it hurts very much to be separated from someone you love. In the end, answers alone do not lead to healing and growth. What you truly need is the Father himself, who loves you more than you know."

His eyes shone as he smiled at her.

She felt he was looking right into the depths of her soul.

Yet she felt safe. And loved.

~ 26 ~

SKELETONS ON TV

Nothing is more wretched than the mind of a man conscious of guilt.
~ Plautus

March 11, 2005

As he walked into Evelyn's office, Miloš had his eyes down. He wasn't paying attention, so when he looked up after sitting down, the sight before him came as quite a shock. A human skeleton stood in the corner of the office, supported by a metal pole and wires that kept the bones in place.

"Like my new friend?" Evelyn jiggled the skeleton's right arm. "I'm thinking of calling him Jack. After the character in *The Nightmare Before Christmas*. Ever seen that movie?"

The young man started to hyperventilate. He tried to push his chair back, but it was already pressed against the wall. His knuckles whitened as his grip tightened on the armrests.

"Miloš?" said Evelyn. "What's wrong, Miloš?"

He'd seen the pictures on TV a couple of years after the conflict. He'd been sitting on the couch with his uncle and two of his cousins. They'd managed to get CNN a week before. The satellite was stuck proudly to the side of their small house in Tuzla, dwarfing the one belonging to their neighbors. Miloš could speak some English, unlike his cousins whose vocabulary only stretched to Big Mac and Game Over.

When the item came on, they all watched in silence.

The camera panned across row upon row of skulls, as the commentator described the atrocities of July, 1995. At the end of one row, the reporter had squatted down near some skeletons to speak to the camera. He waved his arm across the cavity in the earth filled with bones, their whiteness contrasting with the dull brown earth. Miloš watched for about thirty seconds until he couldn't stand it any longer. He got up and changed the channel.

His uncle looked at him but said nothing. He respected the code of silence that operated in countless homes across Bosnia after the war. No one wanted to know. Pandora's box was best left sitting unopened in the hearts of the former soldiers who now worked, drank *rakija*, and played football with their kids. It was left in a dusty corner of their souls, festering, kept far away from their families. Skeletons in the closet shouldn't appear on TV. So he'd changed the channel.

Three months later, Miloš and his family left for the United States.

A new life. A new beginning.

A place to bury the memories.

On Friday, July 14, 1995, he was with Bojan and a dozen soldiers from his unit, assigned to a group of men forced to sit out the night in a warehouse in Kravica, a village to the northwest of Srebrenica. Many of the men were stripped to the waist. The smell of human sweat and filth was unbearable.

A couple of young soldiers started it. They tossed a couple of grenades inside. No one ordered them to do it. They just pulled them from their belts, signaled to each other, and threw them in. The explosion was deafening, even for Miloš who stood some distance away. Inside, the effect was horrific. Instinctively, the other men on guard started shooting at the prisoners inside. Pieces of flesh flew everywhere and stuck to the walls. Blood sprayed out all over the place, screams of terror filling the cavernous building.

Miloš walked round the back of the warehouse with Bojan at his side. He glanced across at him. The man looked shell-shocked. "They're pigs, remember," he growled. As they reached the far end of the building, they caught sight of some men running up the hill opposite. They gave chase immediately. There were three in all, he was sure of it. But when they came over the hill, all they could see was a boy standing next to a tree with his back to them.

"This one's yours," said Miloš. His partner approached and raised his gun. He ordered the child to turn around. The boy who stood before them was no more than eight years old. He stared back, wide-eyed, barely able to breathe, his whole body shaking. Urine was starting to dampen his jeans; he had no shoes. Very slowly, he brought his palms together in the universally recognized position denoting prayer and supplication.

Without saying a word, the child begged for his life.

For a moment, all three of them stood there, unmoving, unblinking. Miloš stared at his compatriot. Bojan's pale face was even whiter than normal. His gun shook. Abruptly, the man's demeanor shifted. He lowered his weapon. "No," he said emphatically. "I won't. He's just a boy." He turned away and began striding up the hill.

Miloš's next act remained with him for the rest of his life. He lifted his gun, pointed it at the boy's forehead, and pulled the trigger. The back of the child's head exploded, his body thrown back by the blast. He fell to the ground just like dozens of others, but this time, a cord wrapped itself around Miloš's heart. Since that day, he had never managed to love or care for any living creature. He was bound within a cage of his own making, half dead, suffocating from the horror of what he'd done.

As he looked at the skeleton in the corner, his chest began to tighten. The guilt from ten years ago was crushing the life out of him. He found himself enveloped in panic, barely able to breathe.

Evelyn rolled her chair up to him and took hold of his hands. "Miloš," she said. "Look at me. Look at me. Breathe. Come on. Breathe with me. In . . . and out. In . . . and out. Come on. Follow me." He began to breathe normally, but the terror remained on his face. The blood had drained from his skin completely, leaving it pasty and sallow.

"You wanna tell me what that was all about?" she said.

"I can't. I can't," he stammered.

"It's okay, Miloš, I'm a doctor. Nothing leaves this room. You tell me what that was about and I'll find someone for you to see."

The young man bent double. He began sobbing, his broad shoulders rising and falling for what seemed like an age. Evelyn looked at her watch. She needed to press on. Instead, she picked up the phone and told the front desk to postpone her next appointment.

"I'm very bad man," said Miloš, using a Kleenex to wipe his eyes and face. "I'm from Tuzla," he continued. "In Bosnia. My family, we come to America seven years ago. No. Eight years ago." His accent thickened and his English regressed. "I fight in Bosnian war. I fight in Bosnian army."

Evelyn had read about the Bosnian conflict, but her knowledge of the details was scant. She remembered the news bulletins from the nineties too. Reporters, their voices dripping with gravitas, recounted tales of atrocities, pointing to holes in the ground, and wandering among wailing women in headscarves. She felt sick. She didn't want to know any more. It was none of her business, and if she continued the conversation, another patient would lose their slot.

"War is a terrible thing, Miloš," she said. "I'm sure you saw terrible things. Am I right?"

"I didn't just see." He began to hyperventilate again and took a minute or so to calm down. "I . . . I . . . I do." He got up and stumbled out the door.

Evelyn stared at the wall, thoughts crashing around her head. She looked at her watch. She was miles behind. No time even to think. She pushed a button on her phone.

"Candy. Send in the next one, please."

The following day, a Saturday, she went shopping with Jasmine. Her daughter was planning a surprise party for one of her coworkers. Evelyn was still treading carefully, trying not to pry too much, and slowly the barriers were starting to come down. Once the jokes started, it felt almost like old times. "Is there food in this packet?" Evelyn stifled a laugh as she held up a box of Fruit Loops. "Because I'm not sure. I don't think I've seen a color like that in the natural world."

"But they taste so great. I prefer this one though. Marshmallows *and* chocolate pieces."

They wandered down another aisle.

Evelyn was on a roll. "Mood music. A lack of easily available exits. No windows. It's like IKEA. You can't get out. Once they got you, you're stuck. Plus, do you see any Ralphs employees with those badges saying 'Fifteen years of service'? You gotta wonder about those guys. Is that a cause for pride or a plea for help?" Jasmine couldn't help sniggering. "I mean, just look at that guy." They passed a man pushing a cart containing four bags of Cheetos and five bottles of Coke. Evelyn whispered loudly, "He was probably sent here by his wife to buy some eggs. Just get me six eggs. You know what his wife is gonna do to him when he gets home? Because it won't be pretty."

"Stop it!" Jasmine giggled, digging her mom in the ribs. "Now help me find the baking aisle. I'm making a chocolate cake for dessert."

Evelyn watched her daughter fill her cart. She had changed beyond recognition. A couple of years in the world had altered the way she held herself. Independence suited her, but it didn't affect a mother's inbuilt antenna. On arrival back at the apartment, they bumped into the roommate, who was wearing just a towel. Though Jasmine insisted she and Brian were just good friends, his semi-nudity was met with a look of maternal disapproval that was impossible to hide.

"Don't!" said Jasmine, anticipating a lecture.

It didn't take much to ignite the spark. As Evelyn came out of the bathroom, she spotted them down the hall. It was just a quick glimpse, but it was enough. Brian put his arm on Jasmine's back, kissed her on the cheek and went to his room. Evelyn knew she shouldn't say anything but she couldn't help it. Walking into the kitchen, she blurted out, "Jasmine—"

"Don't!" There was an edge to her voice.

Evelyn squirted dish soap into the sink and began vigorously scrubbing a large pan. She winced with regret, knowing full well she'd blown it. As she got into her car later, she made a mental note not to open her big mouth again.

Driving home, she considered swinging by the care home but decided against it. Her mom normally slept during the afternoons; mornings were the best times to visit. Traffic ground to a halt on the freeway. She looked to the left at the cars inching forward in the opposite direction.

And stopped breathing.

The man she saw in her dreams was in a big red SUV about twenty feet away. It was definitely him. No question. She stared at him, her mouth open, and was about to open her window when the traffic started moving. The whole encounter took no more than ten seconds. There was no point in turning the car round. He'd be long gone. Oh, for goodness' sake, what was she thinking? Of course he wouldn't be long gone. He was just an illusion, a figment of her imagination.

She gripped the wheel a little harder to stop her hands shaking.

Work on Monday was routine—a couple of gunshot wounds and an accident involving battery acid. Sadly, Patrick was off climbing a rock face in Yosemite. She missed his wisecracks. After work, she stopped by to see her mom, arriving home just as the sun was descending behind the horizon.

As soon as she walked in, Evelyn's average day disintegrated.

She dropped her bag and started to scream.

Her beloved West Highland terrier, Søren, hung suspended above the kitchen sink, blood soaking his shaggy white hair. Piano wire had been used. It encircled his neck and was attached to the curtain rail at each end. He looked dead. She felt like passing out, stumbling forward and grabbing the counter to steady herself. She looked up again. No, hold on. The dog was twitching. Please, God, please. She climbed up onto the sink and unwrapped the wire from the wall mountings. As carefully as she could, she lowered her precious dog, sobs shaking her body.

Her screams had summoned a passerby, and it wasn't long before others arrived, drawn by the commotion. Her house rapidly filled with people—a vet, four police officers, and sundry neighbors, all chattering away. Once she'd calmed down a bit, Evelyn gave her statement as coherently as she could, while the vet tended to Søren's wounds. She told them about Duncan, convinced he was the guilty party. A police officer assured her they would investigate.

It turned out the dog had been lucky. In his haste, the assailant had wrapped part of the wire across the collar, reducing the pressure on the animal's neck. The vet, a balding man in his sixties, assured Evelyn that her dog could only have been hanging for a short time. He had an air of authority and a soothing manner that helped settle her. Before Søren was taken away for overnight observation, she knelt down next to him. Picking him up, she held him against her chest, burying her face in his fur. Soaking him with her tears, she rocked back and forth, unable to think, capable only of feeling.

As everyone left, the hubbub in her house subsided. The last neighbor expressed her regret and closed the front door, leaving Evelyn sitting alone in the living room. She glanced at Søren's empty basket and buried her head in her hands. She was still shaking.

In the fading light, Evelyn found herself going over and over the past hour. She'd declined the offers of help from neighbors and ignored the advice from the police. Now she was alone with a dangerous man quite possibly just yards away. No wonder she was scared. Although his house was clearly empty, it made no difference. It certainly didn't make her feel any safer. Evelyn rubbed her eyes. Looking up, she caught sight of the locket on the mantel. It seemed like a welcome distraction, something to take her mind to calmer places.

She went and picked it up.

It was over twenty years since she'd really studied the photograph inside, decades since she and Katie had peered at it after Thanksgiving dinners. She brushed off some dust and inspected it more closely. The woman in the photograph stared up at her, but Evelyn's attention was caught by the casing on the opposite side. It had a small white cover sheet, and tucked behind it, she noticed a thin piece of paper protruding ever so slightly. It was tiny and easily missed. She found some tweezers in the bathroom and used them to tug on the paper. Bit by bit, a second photograph emerged and lay in her hands.

A smartly dressed man in a pin-striped suit was standing proudly next to some potted plants. He was an imposing, barrel-chested figure, who possessed an air of self-confidence. She looked more closely. His eyes, even in sepia, exuded warmth. Without thinking, Evelyn whispered "Thank you," believing, irrationally perhaps, that her great-grandfather could only have been saved by a truly good man, one who deserved her gratitude.

For she was quite certain whose photograph she held.

After inserting the photograph back behind the glass, she stared down at both faces, and was immediately struck by their contrasting demeanors. Growing up, she'd never once noticed just how desperately unhappy the woman looked. Her mouth indicated a smile, yet it had failed to reach her eyes, which remained vacant, almost lifeless. Her pose was regal, statuesque, her beauty indisputable—high cheekbones, aquiline nose—and yet her palpable sadness dulled her appeal. Even across the many decades, Evelyn sensed a deep, abiding melancholy that seemed to seep out from the image, her weak attempt at levity utterly failing to prevent the leakage.

Evelyn put the locket down and picked up the whistle, returning to the couch, where she collapsed, exhausted. She turned it over in her hands. It had become to her an irreplaceable gift, and she was determined to treat it as such. She pressed it against her cheek. The brass was cold to the touch but its weight felt reassuring.

A Bible was lying on the side table. Her mom must have put it there. Hesitating briefly, Evelyn picked it up. Its weight was also reassuring. She opened it. *I know that you can do all things; no purpose of yours can be thwarted.* Her mother's words came to mind: *You gotta hold on to hope. Because without hope, there's nothing.* What could she lose?

She bowed her head and prayed.

~ 27 ~

MARKETING

*The power of man has grown in every sphere,
except over himself.*
~ Winston Churchill

March 17, 2005

As he entered William Hill, Aidan knew there was no excuse. But he thought he'd just take a look at the odds. Just a quick look. They all knew him in there and he was affable, so he took time to shake several proffered hands. From executives to men on the dole—they were all men—they spanned the demographic spectrum. He was about to leave when one of the regulars told him the running was soft at Cheltenham. He'd won on Tiramisu last month after a heavy rainfall. The horse was running again.

Aidan looked at his watch. "Rod, mate, you're killing me," he said.

In the end, it was the accumulator that sank him. Ten pounds really could turn into a thousand, if you were lucky enough. If you had five wins in a row. The problem was he started off picking winners. And there was a delay between races. He couldn't take his eyes off the screen, so when he should have been arriving in court, he was immersed in the 2 p.m. at Chepstow. He was shouting at a TV when he should have been beside Fiona as she rose to her feet to do the closing speech.

Days ago, he'd decided to give her the closing, not only to encourage her, but for strategic reasons. He'd watched the way the jury had responded to her during the trial. They had warmed to her. If he'd been there, he would have witnessed a remarkable performance.

If he'd been there. But he wasn't.

In court, Fiona looked at her watch. Where was he? Fenwick arrived looking sharp in a double-breasted suit. "Where's Aidan?" he whispered as he slid in.

"No idea," replied Fiona, without looking up. She glanced sideways at the solicitor, her expression blank, giving nothing away. The show had to go on. It was in her hands now. Quentin Molsberry completed his closing statement first, managing to make Milošević sound like a saint compared to the man in the dock.

The QC took his seat with a flourish.

Now it was her turn.

Fiona stood up and took a deep breath. "Ladies and gentlemen," she said, surveying the jury with as much confidence as she could muster. "What is the purpose of our justice system? Is it about justice . . . or winning . . . or truth? In many law schools, if you mention the word 'justice,' people nod and wink a lot. We've become a cynical lot, haven't we? Everybody knows, of course, that justice is an enigma. It's unattainable in its purest form, and in its place we're simply left with . . . marketing. Marketing, ladies and gentlemen. We try to persuade you our version of the case looks more shiny, has more bells and whistles, is more *believable* than the other side's. Forget the truth. Forget justice. It's *all* about appearances."

Fenwick looked up at Fiona. Before, she'd seemed almost invisible. Not anymore. She was—well—she was nothing short of magnificent. It was a risky strategy, of course, to imply that the jury had been listening to nothing but spin for the past four weeks, but he was confident she knew what she was doing.

Fiona looked straight at the jury, enjoying the moment. "Well, I'm afraid that's just not good enough. Justice demands we seek the truth. We have a responsibility to submit to its demands, come what may. You might accuse me at this point of . . . what? Marketing?" Several jurors smiled at each other. "Well, you might have a case were it not for the fact that the defense has conceded to *two* of the charges. Mr. Bakic has pleaded guilty to those charges that are true, because *truth matters*. It matters to the defendant that he was able to tell his side of the story, which you heard so eloquently and painfully the other day. And it matters to his defense team that he did so. But in pleading to those charges, we reject the two most serious offenses: human trafficking and rape. Those are *not* true, as I shall make clear."

She proceeded to highlight the weaknesses in the prosecution's case. Battling valiantly, she made the most of the prosecution's missteps and focused especially on the characters named Goran and Jakov. They emerged as vindictive, barbaric, entirely without compassion. Her major problem, however, was the forensic evidence that pointed straight to Dragan. The only hope was to pin the blame on the mysterious figure behind it all: Aunt Zora.

When it was over, she sat down, exhausted.

Fenwick looked across and smiled. "Wonderful," he said. "You're a superstar, Fiona. Well done."

She let out a sigh of relief and thanked him. Glancing at the jurors, she could hardly bear to speculate on what was going on in their heads. One of them, a youth in a black hoodie, seemed bored. Another, a heavily made-up woman whose hairdo was wilting, was busily writing on her notepad. Now they'd heard two diametrically opposed descriptions of the same man, but there was no way of knowing which way they'd land.

Their blank faces told her nothing.

By the time Aidan arrived at court, Fenwick had already left. Fiona was sitting alone, tapping at her phone. She looked up as he approached. He'd thought about lying, but gave up the idea when he saw the look of disappointment on his junior's face. He could have coped with anger, but disappointment, that was the worst. There was nowhere to hide.

"At least tell me you won *something*," she said, trying to lighten the mood.

"Fell at the last," he admitted softly. "I'm really sorry." He sat down next to her, head bowed. Neither spoke.

After a while, Fiona broke the silence. "What is it . . . twelve steps?"

"So they tell me."

He felt as though he was trapped at the bottom of a deep pit, straining to see some daylight above. Instead of enjoying the relief that often came when a trial drew to a close, he was suffocating. And when Fiona began recounting the events in court, the shame just intensified.

He should have been there. But he wasn't. He was about to apologize again but she saw it coming, so she spoke first. "Don't, Aidan. Just . . . you know . . . get some help."

Wind was whipping round the headstones when Aidan arrived at the cemetery. Leaves scampered about the path and between the graves like unruly children. Overhead, whispering tree branches swayed back and forth; their susurration swept through the churchyard, drowning out the sounds of the city. Aidan stooped a little, pulling up his collar and hooking his thumbs into the lapels of his overcoat.

He was early, so he found a bench and sat down.

Opposite his brother's resting place.

Bruce's gravestone still looked relatively new, the inscription in gold lettering remarkably bright and unweathered. As with any headstone on which dates were engraved, it was hard not to read it without calculating the person's age. Nearby was a grave in which a child of twelve had been buried. *Taken too soon*, followed by pleas for God's mercy, were enough to soften the hardest of hearts, evoking sympathy for the unknown Emily, clearly treasured by her family.

A story lay behind every name, every date, every epitaph.

Aidan stared unseeing at the green grass growing in front of Bruce's headstone. Grief was no respecter of time-bound humans; ten years rendered void by the pain of loss still buried deep. To lose brother and wife on the same day was a memory still too jarring to walk through, so Aidan cast his mind over the court case, hoping that distraction might deaden the ache inside.

He was jumping from thought to thought, unable to tread a straight path, when he became aware of his father who was approaching, hands in pockets, head held erect. They murmured their greetings, but the conversation died before it began. What was there to say? The annual ritual of visiting Bruce's grave together was almost unbearable for Aidan. He wasn't even sure why they perpetuated the custom.

His father sat down next to him, staring straight ahead. The chasm between them was as wide as ever, the vast universe of things unexpressed an ever-present reality to which they had become accustomed. They spent so little time together nowadays that they found themselves woefully ill-equipped for such a meeting. Especially since their grief was not shared, but rather wordlessly acknowledged. In the aftermath of the accident, Aidan's father had folded in on himself, unwilling or unable to give or receive solace in time of need.

He was, to Aidan, a withered soul.

And so, when his father spoke, his words seemed unreal, almost otherworldly. "I miss him," he said, his voice monotone.

It wasn't much, but it was something. The distance between them was still cavernous and yet there was a slight change in the atmosphere. As though his father was calling to him from a point far removed. He remembered all the times when Bruce had invited his father to his matches, to his triumphs, and occasional embarrassing failures, only to be turned down. Aidan himself had stopped asking long before Bruce, but then his brother was made of sterner stuff. As he thought back, those beaming smiles were surely a little forced at times. Enthusiasm could hold off a tide of pain, but it could never hide it entirely. And of course as Bruce entered adulthood, he too had become cut off from his father. It was inevitable, a preordained path from which there was no escape.

How Aidan missed his brother. He couldn't get used to the loss—didn't want to. But what right did the man by his side have to share in such emotions? Aidan's softening was momentarily swamped by a subdued hostility, bitter as bile. *You are not worthy to miss him. You lost that privilege before he even passed away.*

"Still gambling?" said his father.

The words sliced his son in the deepest part of his soul. Aidan bit his tongue, blood unexpectedly seeping into his mouth. It tasted metallic. He'd become familiar with his father's jibes, but to be goaded on their annual visit to the cemetery, that was especially hurtful. They were so very far apart.

The truth was, they both grieved, but they did not grieve together. At most, they walked along parallel paths, like train tracks disappearing into the distance that only appear to merge, but instead remain separated forever. It would take more than an annual visit to a cemetery to improve their relationship. If you could call it that.

"I have a meeting," said the older man as he rose.

Aidan looked up at his father, but he had already turned away. The wind tugged at the older man's coat and ruffled his hair. He hesitated, as though he might finally express something of significance before departing. Instead, he started walking briskly toward the exit.

The following day found Aidan sitting in his home surrounded by boxes. He'd discovered that it didn't take long once the official receiver was involved. His name was Kenneth and he'd written out a list of items that his client was allowed to keep. Sadly, the flat wasn't included. It had been put on the market while he found a one-room bedsit in Kentish Town from a local rag. There would be no more Sky TV. Or cleaners like Carmen.

The movers drove in two directions. The larger truck went to a storage facility; the smaller one followed him to Kentish Town. When they arrived, they had trouble getting the sofa up the stairs. The side ripped on a nail, but the man responsible didn't say a thing. Aidan just watched gloomily. He wasn't in the mood for confrontation.

His cell phone buzzed.

"Simon?"

"Dad. You must come over for dinner tonight. Beth's cooking up a storm." His son's reconciliation with his wife still warmed him inside. It was something his demise couldn't dampen. "That's very kind, Simon," he said, "but I'm . . . I'm kind of busy over here."

"Oh, that's right. Today was moving day, wasn't it?"

He didn't know how to respond. He felt defensive as well as embarrassed. That's why he hadn't asked for his son's help. His heavy oak desk was sitting in the middle of the room where the movers had left it. He was going to need help. He just didn't want to accept it yet.

"Listen," said Aidan. "I'll see you next weekend."

He hung up.

When Simon came over later that night, he found the door unlocked and his dad curled up on the couch. A half-eaten Waitrose lasagna lay on the floor next to him. The heating was off and it was getting cold. He put some coins in the gas meter. The lights were all off, and the only light was coming from a laptop lying next to his father. Roulettewinbig.com was blinking its offers in bright colors, illuminating Aidan's face intermittently in red and blue.

Simon sat down by his father's side and closed the laptop. There was no need for conversation; they just sat there in the dark. A long time passed before either of them stirred. It was a camaraderie of sorts, though not one they would have chosen. Simon hated seeing his father like this. He respected him too much, loved him too much to enjoy sitting with him in the dark.

"Make us some coffee, will you?" Aidan sat up, rubbing his eyes.

Simon rose from the couch, turned on the light, and negotiated his way past several piles of boxes through to the tiny kitchen. The idiom "not enough room to swing a cat" came to mind. He thought he might bring a cat poster over when his dad was in a better mood. After digging around in one of the boxes, he found a kettle and some coffee. A half-empty tin of cookies sat on the counter. He picked up a couple of the chocolate-covered ones and, once the coffee was made, walked back to the main room with a tray.

"Thanks." Aidan sipped his coffee.

"Fulham struggling in the league, I see."

"Yup. Tommy's down in the dumps—he's a big Fulham fan. Mind you, they still have Papa Bouba Diop."

"A name you can't say without smiling, right?"

"A player who brings joy to us all!"

They both laughed.

"Dad?"

Aidan sensed a shift in the atmosphere. He looked away.

The silence between them felt dense and suffocating. A pause before the inevitable breaking to come, it lingered briefly, then shattered. As Simon ruptured the quiet with a soft but insistent voice, he had no idea of the relief that flooded through his father's soul. "I can't watch . . . 'this' . . . any longer, Dad. I talked to Harry at your chambers. Or rather, he contacted me. We're in cahoots. Good word, that. Cahoots. Once I found out where you were moving, he and I found a meeting for you. It's literally just down the road." He stopped, waiting for the usual tirade. Normally, his father started with seniority—*What gives you the right to lecture your dad?*, moved onto privacy—*It's got nothing to do with you*, and finished with rejection—*Leave me alone.*

But this time, there was nothing.

Only silence.

"Okay," said Aidan finally. "You got me. You *and* Harry. I'll have words with him later." He paused. "Fine. I'm stuck." Simon was about to speak when his father continued. "As stuck as a tube of superglue in a pot of honey . . . in a bog . . . full of superglue. That's how stuck I am."

When he looked at his son, they both burst out laughing.

Simon put his arm around his father's shoulders.

He kissed him on the forehead.

"I love you, Dad," he said. "You old sod."

~ 28 ~

THE PROBLEM OF GOODNESS

The savant does not study nature because it is useful; he studies it because he takes delight in it, and he takes delight in it because it is beautiful. If nature was not beautiful, it would not be worth knowing and life would not be worth living.
~ Henri Poincaré

March 18, 2005

Aidan awoke on an upright chair in the hall. He rubbed his eyes and looked around. When he turned to his left, he noticed a large wooden door he hadn't seen before. Had it always been there? Or was it new? He trawled his memory but couldn't come up with anything useful. Must have missed it. Rising from his seat, he went over and peered at the plaque on the door. It was silver with gold lettering on it. *Living Room*. He looked more closely. The word *Living* was glowing gently, like the lucidi's faces.

He opened the door and walked in. Well, it certainly felt like a living room. A coffee table sat in the middle, and floor-to-ceiling bookshelves lined the walls on either side of a roaring fire. Beneath a long window, flanked by thick red curtains, was a broad, sumptuous sofa, with an armchair on each side. Rain was spattering the windowpanes. Lamps sitting on various occasional tables bathed the room in a soft, yellow light. Aidan glanced at the painting above the mantel. Then he took another look.

The Return of the Prodigal Son by Rembrandt.

The Dutch masterpiece was capable of penetrating the most resistant of souls. Aidan went and stood in front of it, casting his eyes over the detail, the different expressions on each face. The tall man to the right seemed cold—angry even. His hands were clasped together in front of him; he looked down his nose with barely disguised irritation. The cloak around his shoulders resembled the one his father wore, yet his heart was withdrawn, devoid of mercy or grace toward the one who knelt. Behind the father, two figures looked on, one with an enigmatic expression, the other with warmth in his eyes. Way back in the far left corner stood a figure almost too faint to see. Perhaps a maid of some kind? He didn't know and didn't spend time ruminating on the question.

He found his eyes drawn inexorably toward the pair in the center left. The emotional focus of the action was also the most brightly lit. The two figures, in subdued lighting, compelled one's gaze. Aidan found he could barely look at the son without a lump developing in his throat. The man was so exhausted, so completely spent, that he slumped forward into his father's arms. One of his shoes was shredded and had come off, a sign his journey had utterly depleted his resources. He himself did not reach out and embrace his father. His contrite heart and shame would not allow it. Instead, he was in a position of meek acceptance, kneeling, while gratefully enjoying the gentle caress of his father's hands.

Aidan gazed at the central figure in awe. The father's hands rested gently on his son's back. Unlike the wild displays of affection that were now commonplace, the father's embrace was muted yet entirely sufficient to communicate his love, his forgiveness. The emotional impact of the encounter, it seemed to Aidan, lay in the details. The slight tilt of the father's head, his eyes that looked down fondly at his child, the son's disheveled clothing, and the manner in which his head leaned in toward his father's clothing.

The son's eyes were not visible but Aidan felt certain they were closed. Well, that was only appropriate. In receiving grace, surely it was only natural to savor the moment. These few exquisite seconds in his father's arms would remain with him forever. They would doubtless define the rest of his days. And that's exactly how it should be.

Aidan felt the truth deeply within him.
Some truths didn't require explanation.
They just were. Discovered. Revealed. Unveiled.
He turned away.

Out in the hall, he walked over to the bifold doors overlooking the balcony. The rain had died away and the clouds were beginning to disperse. A shaft of sunlight pierced the canopy, illuminating a patch of ocean swell. The water danced with light, glinting like sapphires strewn across undulating velvet. He could hear seabirds calling from their nests on the cliff face.

Aidan walked into the Descartes Room. "Gamaliel?"

He stopped short. Evelyn was sitting quietly near the window.

She looked up, tears in her eyes.

On arrival, she hadn't wanted to cry. She didn't want to associate her time in the Espacio with tears alone. As soon as she saw Aidan, however, she found she couldn't protect herself, couldn't hide. Evelyn wiped her eyes with a Kleenex and attempted a smile. Aidan didn't pry. He just tucked himself into the armchair, took her in his arms and waited. In time, the story came out. Evelyn described the events of the past week, leaving out none of the details. "Søren's a fighter, Aidan. And he already hates his stitches."

"Is he in one of those plastic cones, to stop him scratching?"

"Yup. Managed to get it off twice yesterday. He would have made Houdini proud." She smiled weakly. "Oh, and just so you don't worry 'n' all, I've been staying with Jasmine for a few days. According to the police, my neighbor's under surveillance."

She looked out along the coast. A rainbow soared over the white cliffs off to the right. The house faced west. That was her decision. Even if technically there might not be a west, she didn't care. She decided she was looking west. A very American sentiment.

"Have you seen anyone?" said Aidan. "Man, I'm starving."

"I arrived just before you, I think. Haven't seen anyone." Evelyn got up and went to the French doors. "I was thinking of exploring the hills further round behind those vineyards. Wanna come?"

Aidan hesitated. "What is it you guys say? Something about testing the weather? I just need to find something to eat."

"A rain check, Aidan," said Evelyn, laughing. "And it's fine. I won't be long."

She went into the hall and out of the front door. Leaning against a wall was a bicycle with a helmet on the saddle. She walked over and picked up a note jammed between the brake wires. *E, wanna chat? G.* She got on the bike, headed up the drive, and began making her way into the foothills behind the house.

Physical activity produced the same restorative effect as it did at home. With every turn of the pedal and every stretching sinew, she felt the pain diminish. She emptied her mind of its worries and focused her attention on the sensation of physical effort. Tuning in to the rhythm of her movement, she became lost in the joy of exertion, a joy heightened not lessened by the straining of her muscles and the rapid increase of her heart rate.

As she ascended, the vegetation began to thin. Scrub grasses were replaced by rocks and slate. Her ears popped as she continued to climb, arriving at last at a wide plateau edged by a huge drop. She got off her bike and laid it down. The view was magnificent. Dense greenery below stretched into a haze on the horizon many hundreds of miles away. She walked toward the edge of the cliff and peered down into the valley.

Far below, large birds were circling—possibly condors—the expanse of their wings visible against a gray mist above the forest floor.

One of them separated itself from the others and headed in her direction. She watched it rise toward her. Long before it arrived, however, she knew it wasn't a bird at all. The lucidus circled at her eye level for a minute, rising high in the sky before swooping down and landing a few feet away. His face shone and his eyes sparkled, as though the effort of flying had heightened his senses. When he folded in his wings, they seemed to disappear into his back.

"Evelyn," said Gamaliel. "I'm so very pleased to see you up here. It's one of my favorite haunts." They sat down next to each other on a large rock. The lucidus continued, "I cannot take away your pain, I'm afraid. However, there are some benefits to be derived from a visit to the Espacio." He shuffled closer and picked up her hands, closing his eyes as he did so. A soothing warmth filled her body, helping her relax.

She closed her eyes and sighed.

"Father," he prayed. "Your glory fills the heavens, the Espacio, the earth, and every dimension of reality you have created. I worship you, for you are glorious beyond human imagination, even beyond the capacity of your lucidi to conceive." He paused. "You know all . . . cherish all . . . sustain all . . . love all. You have given me your child, Evelyn, to care for. And for that I am grateful. She has become dear to me, yet her value to you is far, far greater." He breathed deeply. "She is in need of your presence, gracious Father. Protect her from fear, for perfect love drives out fear. We thank you that you are never far from those who seek you, who call upon you. And for that we are grateful. Amen."

Evelyn opened her eyes. "Thank you," she said, surrendering herself to the spirit of the prayer and wishing for it to continue. She squinted, shading her eyes as she became accustomed to the sunlight. In the distance, she made out some snowcapped mountain peaks. From below the cliff, the call of a hawk on the wing rose to meet them. The vegetation far below looked tropical. It coated the lowlands right up to the base of the escarpments running along each side of the valley. Down the center, a broad river meandered slowly, serpentine and without rapids to disturb its sluggish progress toward the ocean. She looked up into the sky. The sun was becoming shaded by a thickening cloud bank. The air felt cooler.

"It's beautiful here," said Evelyn.

"No more beautiful than the earth, in fact." Gamaliel closed his eyes and tipped his head back.

"Maybe what takes place here gives it its beauty."

"Hmm. That's an interesting point. I hadn't thought of that, my dear." He paused. "Well—"

"Mind you, beauty is in the eye of the beholder."

The tall lucidus instantly sat forward. "Ha ha!" he said. "That old chestnut." He grinned broadly.

She looked at him quizzically. "What? You disagree?"

"I do indeed."

"How so?"

"Well, it's a common error, sparked by a failure to distinguish between perception and source. What is in the eye of the beholder is the *pleasure derived* from viewing something beautiful. Given that humans are varied, they are bound to respond variously to what they see. However, it does not follow that beauty *itself* is subjective.

"When you see the Eiffel Tower, your response might be awe or, if you're standing under it, you might be impressed by its size and grandeur. Now, does it not seem as though there are beautiful things, crafted either by human hands or within creation, that are more deserving of your admiration than others? Is it not appropriate and right to admire the Eiffel Tower, the Grand Canyon, or the wing of a bird? And if a person said to you, 'My finger painting is just as admirable as the *Mona Lisa*,' wouldn't you wish to correct such a misconception?"

She tossed Gamaliel's words around in her head. "The *Mona Lisa* is a great work of art and a finger painting . . . even by my daughter, is not nearly as . . . ," she struggled to find the words.

"Likely to sell for millions?" The lucidus let out a guffaw; Evelyn giggled along with him. "Sorry," he said. "Couldn't resist."

"A finger painting," she said, "it just . . . doesn't possess the same quality. It, er . . . I can't find the right words to explain it."

"Perhaps I can help. What you're reaching for, Evelyn, is the sense that the *Mona Lisa*, or any work of art found in a famous art gallery for that matter, is intrinsically worthy of admiration. Beauty is not so much 'in you and your response' as 'out there.' It's not subjective, it's objective, something therefore to be discovered by the sense perceiver.

"This is why when you're in the presence of great beauty, you will sometimes feel drawn toward it. Beauty is not a means to an end but an end in itself. A rose should be admired for no other reason than that it's beautiful in itself. At the same time, and this might seem paradoxical, beauty is deeply embedded in the truth it communicates to the viewer. Often this truth has a moral or functional element. A great cathedral is beautiful not only because it is designed for the glory of God—a moral good—but also because its design, reflected in the upward trajectory of its columns and ornate high ceilings, exhibits a functional beauty. Well-designed engines, clothes, towns, even weapons can possess functional beauty."

"Can we be mistaken, then, about what's beautiful? If we draw conclusions from what we see, presumably, being human, it's possible to be wrong . . . but that just doesn't seem right."

"Well, your subjective experience isn't technically wrong, it just is what it is. However, your evaluation of 'what's beautiful and what's not' may well be wrong. The fifteen-year-old who says that Bach's music is awful is categorically wrong. He doesn't yet possess the ability to appreciate the music of a great composer. So yes, it's possible to be wrong. Most humans don't like to hear that, but it happens to be true.

"Beauty is like a nymph, beckoning you to go deeper into the wood. It touches a chord within you because you long for ultimate beauty. The tension between your subjective response and the objective reality of beauty creates a yearning for resolution. Whether the human heart acknowledges it or not, it seeks true beauty. In short, it seeks a standard, a means by which to measure and evaluate subjective judgments. Now clearly, this standard cannot exist in the physical world. It must be independent of finite, limited human minds. No, this standard must be both non-physical and infinite, a perfect representation of beauty in a non-physical, spiritual realm."

He paused. "Do you understand now why beauty draws you and taps into your deepest longing, yet at the same time, seems incapable of truly satisfying your desire? It is because your desires can only be satisfied by ultimate beauty, a beauty so magnificent that it utterly eclipses the impoverished versions in your world." He paused. "You know who I'm referring to, Evelyn. We lucidi have been worshipping him for as long as I can remember."

They sat quietly for a while.

Evelyn breathed deeply and gazed at the clouds in the distance. They were thinning, allowing shafts of light to illuminate the tops of the mountains. It was exquisite, as was all that lay before her. She looked across at the lucidus who sat with eyes closed, enjoying the wind on his face.

Then it struck her. He was beautiful. So very, very beautiful. No wonder his face glowed. He was a living reflection of his Maker, speaking truth with patience, love, and grace. A sense of shame rose to swamp her. The contrast between her condition and his nobility drew invidious comparisons, and she couldn't help feeling her own brokenness inside.

"Am I—?" she began.

The lucidus interrupted. "Beautiful?"

She nodded.

"Oh, Evelyn, my dear child. You are far more beautiful than you can imagine, for you bear the image of the one who made you, and since he *is* Beauty, it's not surprising you look partly like your Father."

"But—"

"No buts, Evelyn." He took her hands in his. "Believe me when I say you're gorgeous . . . truly lovely. And you are loved by a loving Father. Nothing can change that. He invites you to love him back, because only in so doing can you find true fulfillment and joy. I do hope that on your return, these words will remain hidden in the deep places of your soul."

She found it hard to accept Gamaliel's words. She scuffed the ground with her feet and was grateful when she looked up, to see him walking to the cliff edge. His wings burst from his back.

"Wanna ride?" he said, his face glowing brightly.

Evelyn climbed on and held tight. He seemed to grow beneath her, his muscles tightening and relaxing in the constant rhythm of flight that quickly lifted them far out over the valley. Eyes wide open, she was too entranced by the experience to worry about the tears washing down the sides of her face. "This is better than skydiving," she whispered. Occasionally, they dropped several hundred feet, sending her stomach up to her mouth and causing her to hang on for dear life. It was utterly exhilarating and when she noticed they were coming in to land, she couldn't help mourning the brevity of their time together. Her joy blended with disappointment as they touched down. Leaving her, the lucidus left an emptiness in the atmosphere, a residue of sadness within Evelyn that ached.

The flight was over. Gone forever.

Life seemed so fleeting, its precious moments draining through her hands like sand. And yet it also felt like one long series of opportunities, a continual invitation to grasp the good. A chance to wrap herself in beauty. It dawned on her just how extraordinary her life was in the Espacio, and what potential remained back home. She felt loved and cherished, and her inability to explain what was happening to her mattered not at all.

As she walked back into the house, her serenity vanished. A deep, mournful wailing resounded through the building. It grew louder, intensifying. It would have touched the hardest of hearts. She entered the Living Room and discovered Korazin standing in front of the large windows overlooking the balcony. The ocean blinked in the distance.

The lucidus was weeping.

Grief filled the room, a heaviness permeating the air, deadening the spirit. Although the day was warm, Evelyn found herself shivering. She watched as Korazin's shoulders shook, his weeping gradually petering out until he collapsed, spent, into an armchair.

"These bodies they give us," he said, looking up at her. "Now that I have a physical body with which to express myself, I find I share the human inability to control certain aspects of my behavior. Who would have thought it?"

"Feelings need bodies?"

"No. We lucidi can feel, but inside a body, my emotions display themselves in, er, unpredictable ways. I suppose it's a bit like driving a car. I'm behind the wheel, but the car has a mind of its own sometimes." He was silent, sitting with his eyes closed.

"Why the tears?" said Evelyn. "If you don't mind my asking."

"A visit to a hospital in Thailand, my dear." The lucidus rose and went to stand by the fireside.

Just then, Aidan walked in and sat down quietly. Korazin continued. "In Bangkok lies a two-year-old dying of leukemia. Tamarine. A beautiful child, who is incredibly brave. As are her parents, who sit by her bedside."

"So why hasn't he intervened?" said Evelyn. "Coz he could, couldn't he?"

"Yes," said the lucidus. "Yes, he could. We all know the Father is capable of softening the harsh edges of a broken world. No lucidus believes that free will justifies the suffering of children. Yes, the Fall of Man has contaminated the earth, releasing horrors, but alone, it can't possibly explain the pitiful wailing of a child dying in pain." His voice faded away.

Evelyn looked at Korazin with new eyes. The idea of a lucidus questioning the Creator was something she hadn't ever anticipated. She went to a sideboard and served them all drinks. "I'm guessing you have a response, though, right?"

"Indeed we do," said a deep voice from the doorway. Gamaliel walked in and stood near the window. "My friend here is actually no different to many lucidi. Especially those who have spent time with humans. The complicated matter of unlocking the problem of evil is just that. It's complicated, requiring multiple related replies. And even when you've put them together, you've hardly started." He paused, gazing out of the window. "By the way, have you explored further down the coast yet? It's really quite lovely." He flashed them a smile. "Meet in the hall in ten?"

Aidan changed into shorts and a T-shirt, while Evelyn descended the stairs looking gorgeous in a pale blue summer dress. Leaving through the back door, they found a route round the back of the herb garden and began navigating a path bordered by wildflowers. The rain had left droplets sparkling on the greenery that lined the trail they followed down toward the beach.

Once there, they left the lucidi, wandering off together toward some distant rock pools. On their stroll back, they found the two lucidi leaning against some marram grass in the sand dunes. Their faces were a picture of contentment. Korazin was whittling a stick with a hunting knife, whistling as he worked. They sat and chatted for a while about Jasmine, the conversation helping to calm some of Evelyn's fears. After a while, they turned to the subject of Dragan's trial. Aidan recounted the events of the past few days, ending with a description of Aunt Zora that made Evelyn gasp.

"The human capacity for cruelty," said Korazin. "At times, it appears limitless."

"But this woman sounds evil."

"Indeed. And if there is evil, there must be good."

She bristled. "But those girls in the brothel didn't need a lecture on good and evil, they needed rescuing. Where was this father of yours when they cried out to him?"

Neither lucidus replied. They allowed stillness to settle, sylphlike, on the spirits of their guests. The steady rhythm of the surf, and the wind rustling the dry grasses on the dunes, blended with the quiet of their companionship. The humans both waited for the lucidi to respond but it was a while before one of them spoke.

When Gamaliel finally broke the silence, he chose his words carefully. "You're quite right, Evelyn, they didn't need a lecture. Suffering doesn't trigger the intellect, it primarily stokes the emotions. I didn't hear much argument while you stood on that clifftop. However, the emotions don't function in a vacuum. They are connected within the soul to both the mind and the heart or will. And the heart seeks an answer to perhaps the deepest question of them all: What does it mean to call the Father good?"

He paused, allowing his guests to consider the question.

"Well, if he *is* good," said Aidan, "we often struggle to see it."

Gamaliel leaned forward. "That is quite understandable. However, I'm afraid the struggle is largely one of your own making. As humanity has elevated itself, it has at the same time lowered its evaluation of the Father. To many, he has become closer to an abstract idea than the person we lucidi enjoy each day. The further removed he seems, the more callous he appears.

"In addition, the universe does not deliver a justice system in which the evil suffer and the virtuous are blessed. In reality, the wicked prosper and the innocent suffer . . . or vice versa. It is the randomness that offends. Humans would like to find order where there is none. And yet . . ."

Korazin leaped in. "Humans *still* believe in the idea of justice, and yearn for it. Zora should be punished, right?" Both humans nodded their assent. "Yet, if there is justice, there is a standard, a means by which to measure 'the just.' That standard is also the foundation of 'the good.'"

"You're saying God is that standard?" said Aidan. "Really? He may claim to be good . . . but what are the grounds? Because he says so? Sounds a bit arbitrary."

The Problem Of Goodness

"Ah, well, now we come to the heart of the matter," said Gamaliel. "First, may I assure you the Father's goodness is neither a function of his power, as though by asserting it, he makes it true, nor a separate standard to which he must adhere. I refer you to Plato's Euthyphro dilemma, a fascinating read for another day."

"So what's the solution?" asked Evelyn.

The tall lucidus stood up, his expression serious. After a deep breath, he began.

When Good by Man is contemplated
Each act with care is measured, rated
Yet virtues revered by their age, venerated
Do wane over time, by degrees, deprecated.

The Good made good by heav'n's decree
'Tis but a mask, disguise for potency
What good is Good when forged by Will alone?
Its grasp o'erreached, 'tis then by Love disowned.

Forgotten gauge from ancient times, plumb line
'Gainst which today are judged e'en acts divine
Human hearts, however lost, desire a measure
Creator bent before the norms they treasure.

The Good defined by pow'r and norm, denied
It lives in God where Love and Judge collide
His nature formed in essential perfection
His measureless beauty our worship's reflection.

The lucidus sat down.

The poem echoed in their hearts, and meandered through their minds, their ruminations accompanied by the rumble of the surf. Soon, however, Gamaliel broke the silence. "That last stanza," he said, "is sufficiently important that it's worth reiterating some of its ideas." He paused for a moment. "You see, the Father is good by nature. He is intrinsically and essentially good. Goodness is therefore an intrinsic character trait. His nature itself defines what is good, because he is good by nature. Not only that, he is an entirely different category of being to a human. Humans are derivative. All that they are comes from their Creator. This is why, in the book of Job, the Father reminds his servant of his vast power and the unfathomable depth of his knowledge. The human being must come to the Creator on the Creator's terms, or not at all. That is only right.

"Dear Evelyn and dear Aidan, the one who made you is *not* distant and he is *not* callous. He is close to the brokenhearted and he is profoundly good. Just consider all he has done for you. He has made you and surrounded you with beauty in the natural world. He has given you freedom to enjoy relationship with others and with your Maker, if you turn to him. He has permitted a fallen world, yes, but he is not himself the architect of your fallenness. Indeed, we lucidi celebrate his goodness and generosity every day, reveling before his beauty without ever tiring of our praises." Gamaliel bowed his head.

Korazin said, "There is one final question, and it is perhaps the most urgent. Where is he when the world is dark and it feels like hope has died? The cancer victim, the abused, the person who has lost his home and family to a tsunami, they all cry out. The depressed would like to do the same but they can barely raise themselves from their beds. Where is he, indeed? We lucidi long to bridge the gap but we cannot. Only he can do that. Yet suffering accomplishes something that is impossible during times of plenty. It exposes the human heart.

"The most important question turns out to be this one: Will you turn to him when all seems lost? Will you trust that he is good when the evidence appears to speak to the contrary? Do you believe, Aidan, that he can set you free? Will you call on him, Evelyn, believing that he's able to heal the brokenhearted? For he is glorious and good; furthermore, his love is everlasting."

The sun was setting on the horizon, casting its beams across the water. Peace had descended on the group, cloaking them all and binding them together invisibly. Korazin picked up a stick and wrote a word in the sand in large capital letters.

STORY.

Aidan read the word aloud.

The lucidus said, "For those who are separated from the Father, it is helpful to enter the one story that gives light to all the stories ever told. However, I believe you are stirring, Evelyn. You will both have to wait until next time."

~ 29 ~

A LITTLE CLOAK AND DAGGER

Though justice be thy plea, consider this that in the course of justice, none of us should see salvation: we do pray for mercy.
~ William Shakespeare, *The Merchant of Venice*

March 21, 2005

Aidan looked across at the public gallery, tapping his pen on the pad in front of him.

"All rise!" pronounced the clerk of the court.

The judge entered.

Dragan stood up, fear creating lines on his face. The guilty verdict from the morning's session was weighing heavily on him. The jury had decided he was a trafficker, but not one who raped. Dorina's testimony had destroyed that particular charge. The rest, however, had stuck, much to the chagrin of his legal team, who felt they'd done enough to quash the idea that he moved human beings around like zoo animals. The verdict on that charge had especially hurt Fiona. She couldn't understand why the jury hadn't believed their client. To her, he'd seemed convincing, but apparently the jury hadn't agreed. She couldn't help going over her performance, trying to work out if she was responsible.

"It's not your fault," said Aidan, reading her thoughts. "And it's not mine. But if we manage to pull off a little something today, maybe the appeal will be sooner rather than later."

"The 'little something' doesn't have anything to do with that man sitting in the back row of the public gallery, does it?"

He smiled at her. "You missed your calling, Fiona."

In spite of his behavior on the day of the closing, she still held Aidan in high esteem. He knew he didn't deserve it, knew he'd let her down badly, but she'd never wavered in her support. His debt to her was larger than any he'd owed a bookie.

A woman in her sixties entered, her head covered by a red and blue scarf. She sat down in the back row. She had jet-black hair and wore large gold hoop earrings. A younger woman came in shortly afterward, edged past two others, and sat down next to her. Tatiana looked up at Dragan, her face giving nothing away. When the wearer of the scarf looked up, Aidan let out a sigh and closed his eyes.

"Mr. Manning," said the judge. "Do you have anything to say in mitigation?"

Aidan composed himself and looked the judge squarely in the face. Highlighting the defendant's willingness to plead guilty to two of the charges, he reminded the court of the open and honest remorse his client had demonstrated. As for the human trafficking charge, he staunchly asserted the defendant's innocence, declaring his hope that, in time, he would be able to prove it. Unsurprisingly, the prosecution called on the judge to hand down the longest possible sentence.

As he rose for a short adjournment, Judge Prendergast frowned. When he returned half an hour later, his mood hadn't improved. Aidan could sense what was coming.

Dragan was ordered to rise.

"Mr. Bakic," said the judge. "You have been found guilty of trafficking persons into the United Kingdom for sexual exploitation, contrary to Section 57 of the Sexual Offences Act 2003. You have also been found guilty of false imprisonment and controlling prostitution for gain. You operated an establishment that forced girls to submit regularly to physical and sexual abuse of the worst kind. You are guilty not merely of treating human beings as chattels, but of profiting from their suffering. Words cannot do justice to the revulsion this court feels toward your behavior. The jury was quite right to find you guilty.

"As I was preparing to sentence you just now in my chambers, my eyes settled on a Bible. Consequently, I was reminded of the ancient Hebrew law, 'an eye for an eye and a tooth for a tooth.' When I have completed my summing up, it is *your* freedom that will be withdrawn. The removal of freedom—locking you up—is as far as our society will go in punishing criminals. We do this not merely to protect law-abiding citizens from those who would do them harm, we do this to punish wrongdoers."

He spat out the last two words. "Punish . . . wrongdoers. That's a phrase I quote regularly in this court and it's taken from an inscription on the Old Bailey, our most famous criminal court. Human trafficking is wrong. Robbing a person of their freedom robs them of their humanity." He paused. Aidan looked from the jury to the public gallery. The entire courtroom was still, mesmerized. The judge continued. "How appropriate, then, that the very thing that you counted of such little value to your victims, you will now lose."

He sentenced Dragan to a total of twenty years in prison, which to his lawyers seemed steep. The big man looked shell-shocked. Glancing across at the woman in the headscarf, Aidan took note of her bearing. It was muted but readable. She grinned at Tatiana, who looked back at her with an expression that made perfect sense. She was frightened.

Aidan and his team filed out of the courtroom and stood to one side. Tatiana exited with the woman wearing the red and blue scarf. They were followed by a plainclothes detective, who winked at Aidan as he walked past. Two policemen strode up and spoke to the woman, who kept on walking. When they grabbed her by the arm, she began shrieking and beat her fists on the chest of one of the officers. It was almost comical. Seconds later, she was cuffed and led away, leaving Tatiana in her wake.

"A dog and its vomit," said Fiona. "Enlighten me, although I think I can guess. How on earth did you manage to get her to come to court?"

"As you say, a dog and its vomit. Must have thought she was in the clear. Never suspected a thing. The police gave Tatiana a deal based on getting her in. Who would have thought she would come up trumps like that? Mind you, even if Zora hadn't come to court, I think with Tatiana onside, they had the whole thing sewn up."

"Aunt Zora," said Fiona. "Actual relative?"

"Absolutely. She used Dragan from the day he arrived. Put him in a tiny room at the back of the Camden Town brothel, fed him drugs like a puppy, and when it all went south, she fed him to the lions."

Aidan walked out of the court building and stood on the steps. He watched a policeman put a hand on the woman's head as she got into the back of the car. The wind blew her scarf off her head, revealing her curly jet-black hair. Looking up, she caught his eye, a look of unmitigated fury on her face. He looked back at her impassively, giving nothing away. He wasn't in the habit of second-guessing an appeal, but watching her twist and turn as she was forced into the back of the car, he liked his chances.

He left a message on his father's voicemail letting him know the trial was over. The ritual was a habit remaining from happier days when he'd finished his first case many years before.

Head bowed, he headed for the Tube.

Dragan climbed sluggishly into the police van. Although glad to be at the end of the back-and-forth from Brixton to court, the prospect of prison life was bleak in the extreme. As he hauled his substantial frame into the back of the vehicle, the verdict simmered away in his soul. Guilty on all counts bar rape, he was looking at fifteen years minimum, even with good behavior. The van was soon swaying from side to side, weaving its way through London, while Dragan strained to look through the iron grille. Enclosed in a metal box with barely enough room to sit down, claustrophobia began to set in.

On arrival at Her Majesty's Prison Brixton, the prisoner was escorted to his cell in B Wing. The door clunked shut behind him. It was early afternoon, and many of the prisoners were still at their workshops. He shared the cell with Dean, an irritating youth who constantly protested his innocence; but that afternoon he wasn't there. Maybe he was with the chaplain. He'd probably found religion. A lot of them did. Prison was like that.

It brought a man to his knees.

Dragan sat down on the bed and stared at the stone floor, his head in his hands. Casting his mind back to his childhood, he couldn't avoid the inevitable inward reflection arising from a guilty verdict. Looking forward was so empty, so desolate, that the mind retreated from it. Its only recourse was to go back, to seek in the past some explanation, some solace to soften the despair. But going back was worse than hovering in the present. He knew he should have just picked up the paper and lost himself in the sports pages, but instead he descended into self-recrimination, brought on by shame and self-loathing.

Brought on by his past.

Brought on by looking down at his knees.

When the news arrived, he felt its impact even before hearing it. There was something about his aunt's face, a blankness of expression telling him something was terribly wrong. Instantly, he feared the worst, his stomach tightening and his eyes welling up with tears. He listened from underneath layers of lace and dense cotton, the words "crash" and "parents" muffled, but perfectly distinct.

For a long time, he stiffened and hit out, then grabbed and held fast. The to-and-fro between pushing away and holding on was accompanied by sobbing, his aunt's arms enveloping his constantly moving body. His nose ran until it seemed there was nothing left inside him to pour out. Time passed through them and over them, bypassing them, giving a little boy the space to grieve without forcing him to rejoin the flow of human events of which he was a part. As the turmoil of emotions slowly subsided, his body relented.

Numbed by pain, he let go and ran indoors.

He'd just turned six and was now an orphan.

Except he wasn't really an orphan. He lived with his Aunt Zora, who cooked him delicious *ćevapi* and *ćufte* at the weekends; Bosnian foods that filled his stomach and comforted his heart. She taught him to tell the time, tie his shoelaces, and even make a yo-yo rise and fall without getting all twisted up. And he played with his cousins, Goran, who was just a year older, and the eldest two, Jakov and Janko, who played football with him in the street. His Uncle Josif, a quiet, diffident man in his early fifties, was also kind to him, though somewhat withdrawn. He preferred to play dominoes with his friends down at the local *kafana*. However, a few months after Dragan turned eight, everything changed.

Aunt Zora's drinking escalated.

Dragan saw the bottles of *rakija* accumulating in the pantry, but he was too young to join the dots. He simply watched and suffered the consequences. The beatings were infrequent at first, and only occurred when his misdemeanors happened to coincide with a bout of drinking. Gradually, however, she took out her rage indiscriminately. He remembered the foul stench of her breath when she leaned in close, spitting out expletives.

Her behavior was impossible to predict. Often she withheld punishment to see what effect it would have on him. That was how he spent the next few years. Many were the occasions when Aunt Zora would yell at him, but just as he recoiled, ready for a slap, she would draw him to her bosom, kissing him on the forehead. The confusion gave him stomachaches.

Worse followed when she started with the rice. One night, while he was asleep in bed, he felt a sudden yank on his vest. His aunt dragged him downstairs to the kitchen. She sprinkled rice on the floor, and snapped "Kneel!" Dragan looked down and did as he was told. At first, the rice was uncomfortable but manageable. Within a few minutes, however, the pain began to increase. Even a slight movement caused the rice to dig into his flesh until he began to bleed copiously. The blood seeped out onto the floor, making it slippery. Whenever his knees slid about, his aunt would slap him on the back of his legs.

When she repeated the punishment the following day, he was certain he was living in hell. She forced him to kneel on the rice every night for a week until his knees developed calluses. Later, after giving him a couple of weeks off for them to smooth over, she started again. The calluses had faded and his knees were pink and fleshy. As soon as he knelt down, the bleeding started almost immediately. So with hands clasped tightly together, he begged. The agony reduced him to pleading. There was no further down for him to go.

He remembered Aunt Zora crouching down in front of him. Her disgusting gray stockings and the way she swayed from side to side were forever imprinted on his memory. "Are you praying?" she asked softly. Grabbing his hair, she pulled his head up until their faces were inches apart. "Because no one is going to hear you. You're nothing,

Dragan. Without me, you're nothing. Now get to bed." The next time he begged for leniency, she struck him hard across the face.

Over time, the abuse subsided. As he grew, his size became a defense. Instead, Goran became the toxic one. He pushed his cousin around, smacking him across the back of the head just on a whim. It was hard to take. Jakov and Janko couldn't help him, they lived in their own worlds, spending most of the time out of the house, while Uncle Josif spent more time in the *kafana* than anywhere else.

On his twelfth birthday, Aunt Zora called Dragan into the kitchen. An oversized chocolate cake was sitting on the table. In silence, she cut a huge slice, pushed it forward, but just as he stepped forward, she pulled it back, a small smile flickering across her face. "When you get back," she said, handing him a package. His instructions were to cycle to the next village and meet a man behind the bar opposite the bus stop. "Hand it over and bring back the one he gives you." The following weekend, she asked him to deliver another package. He knew better than to ask what was in it, but he wasn't stupid. He knew what was going on, and willingly consented. Besides, the chocolate cake tasted delicious.

When he was fifteen, the family moved to Sarajevo. His aunt's connections to organized crime provided plenty of opportunities for him to develop his talents. During his teens, he learned to pick a lock, break a nose, and hide a suspicious parcel. He took pride in his work. Smuggling was his bread and butter, but he was a quick learner, adept at pickpocketing, breaking and entering, and, in his later teens, extortion. His status improved. It felt good. His spirits lifted.

But of course it hadn't lasted. He was still locked up, still trapped by his family. Goran was still a bully, and his aunt knew his every movement. It seemed she had a bent cop in every police station, or whatever passed for law enforcement in those days. He was eighteen and desperate to escape when he spotted an advert in the paper.

Without telling his aunt, he ran off to join the Bosnian army. He even gave a false name in an attempt to hide from his family. At first, he'd loved his unit, the camaraderie, the dirty jokes. Military life was a good fit for him. But the anger never really went away, so he got into fights. When he took on his commander one too many times, it was over. He was dismissed for insubordination, returning to Sarajevo with no prospects and a pile of debt, owed mostly to former soldiers with a disturbing lack of patience.

Aunt Zora was especially pleased to see him back. She slapped him on his right ear, and told him to take out the trash. For days, he hid in his room, cursing anyone who came near. But he couldn't cut himself off forever. One night, Goran and Jakov invited him to snort some coke. They sat at the kitchen table with huge grins on their faces, the powder carefully arranged in four neat lines. It proved to be his undoing. When he looked up, Aunt Zora was standing in the corner, smirking. The memory still made him shudder.

His relatives' decision to move to England without him felt like a godsend. He couldn't believe his good fortune. He found a job at a garage and managed to keep his head down for a while. He also started dating local girls, and even had enough to rent a small apartment. However, Goran possessed very long arms. A fat little man named Kuzman started delivering a parcel every Saturday morning, along with some choice expletives for good measure. Normally he mentioned something about tips, ownership, and crushing intimate body parts, though Dragan wasn't really listening. He was too interested in the white powder to take notice, never mind think about the implications.

A couple of months later, he was served his sentence.

An airline ticket arrived with his name on it. The packet also contained a hairband he recognized. It belonged to Ajna, a girl he liked. A note fell out. *Kuzman will pick you up. In one piece or many. Your choice.* Dragan remembered how Goran had once threatened a dealer. Casually talking about the cracking sound legs make when they're snapped in two, his cousin had caressed the man's hair, then grabbed his earlobe. The following weekend, Dragan had spotted the man walking down the street with bandages over one ear. They were leaking blood.

Looking back, he recalled a moment's hesitation, but it didn't last long. His cousins met him at Heathrow Terminal 1 on a wet and windy November morning. As soon as he walked into the Camden Town brothel, he experienced a sinking feeling in his stomach. He followed

Aunt Zora down a dark passageway to his room. When he saw it, he stared in disbelief, fuming inside yet too fearful to complain. It was smaller than the one he'd occupied as a boy.

Later, as he sat in the kitchen trying to come to terms with his new circumstances, Goran and Jakov came in and began blowing coke. They laughed at their own jokes, slapping each other on the back and knocking back shots of *rakija*.

"Come on, Dragan. It helps with the libido!" His cousins both howled with laughter.

Dragan pulled out the two photos his barrister had given him before the end of the trial. He stared down at the one of his parents holding him in their arms. He guessed he was about three at the time. They were all beaming at the camera, filled with life and love for each other. It was a photo taken to recall warmth and happiness, but it did nothing of the kind. It produced a powerful, relentless feeling, one that never left him—abandonment, grief, and anger, all mixed into one overriding sense of despair. The day he lost his parents was the worst day of his life and he would never forget it. Dragan was certain life wasn't fair. There was no purpose and no meaning. But especially there was no justice. So what did it matter if he lost control when he was angry?

Kriv. He knew it referred to him.

On a cold evening in December, he went up to investigate the sound of a girl crying in one of the rooms at the back of the house. As he made his way along the dimly lit corridor, he tried to work out where the noise was coming from. Stopping outside the last room on the left, he recognized the voice. It was the one he liked, the pretty one from Romania. A scrawny man with tobacco-stained teeth exited the room and pushed past him, doing up his fly as he left. Instinctively, Dragan grabbed him by the collar and pushed him into the room opposite Dorina's. The shove sent him crashing into a Jimi Hendrix poster on the wall. Falling back, the man aimed a kick at his assailant, connecting with his groin. It hurt. Dragan grimaced, fingering a hunting knife that he kept on his belt for protection.

And then it happened.

All the fury coiled up inside him exploded.

All the frustration, all the hatred, all the years of humiliation, it was all directed at the babbling wretch in front of him, the man now staggering to his feet. Dragan pulled out his knife and lashed out, burying the blade in the man's neck right up to the hilt. He pierced the carotid artery so that when he pulled out the knife, blood went everywhere. It sprayed out all over the room, drenching the pink bed sheets and smoke-stained carpet. Spurting out in large droplets, a red shower soaked the man's clothing as he collapsed onto the bed, coughing and gurgling. Dragan just stood and watched, briefly fascinated by what he'd done. The man's convulsions, his head banging against the bedstead, finally jolted him out of his shock. His victim pressed his hands against his neck to stem the blood flow but it was useless. He was dying, his body jerking back and forth in ever decreasing spasms. The process was quick but seemed to take forever. When the man eventually stopped moving, Dragan stood in silence, just staring. Collapsing onto the bed, he pulled out his cell phone.

He called his aunt.

When she walked in later, she found him sitting on the bed, the lifeless body face down on the floor at his feet. Moving it and cleaning up the room took over half an hour. First, all the clients were asked to leave, then the girls were corralled in the front room and locked in under the watchful eye of Jakov. No explanations were given. Zora wrapped the man up in a large bed sheet and scoured the room with various cleaning products. Picking the man up by the arms and legs, Dragan and Goran carried him downstairs to the garden.

He remembered digging the hole. The physical exercise took his mind off what he'd done. When they'd dug down to about five feet, they heaved the cadaver over the edge. One of the arms cracked as the body landed, and the sheet ripped, revealing the man's face, eyes still open. His death stare still appeared occasionally in Dragan's dreams. An hour after the murder, it almost looked like nothing had happened. The flowerbed against the garden wall was home to the remains of a slowly decaying corpse, and nobody knew except Goran, Jakov, and Dragan.

And Aunt Zora, of course.

Kriv.

Dragan caressed the silver cross he wore round his neck, turning it over in his hand. He took it off and placed it in his right hand, squeezing it hard so that it broke the skin. Blood seeped out the bottom of his fist, dripped onto his shoe, and rolled down onto the cement floor. Alternately squeezing and relaxing his fist, he moved the small silver piece of jewelry around in his hand so that he could vary its bite into his flesh. Finally, he wiped his left forefinger across his palm, coating it with blood. Inserting the finger into his mouth, he sucked. It carried the bitter, ferrous taste of his own mortality. He wiped it across his palm again, moistening it with more blood.

This he used to make the sign of the cross on his forehead.

The sign of the cross.

A ritual the priest had performed on him as a boy.

A ritual he himself had performed his entire life.

~ 30 ~

POSTMAN NAT

Listen to your life. See it for the fathomless mystery that it is.
~ Frederick Buechner

March 24, 2005

Aidan sat in a waiting room, flicking through a magazine. The room was stark and featureless with cold, plastic furniture and abstract prints on the walls. A part of him had expected crystal balls and lots of velvet but of course, that was ridiculous. He wasn't visiting Madame LeBoeuf or some charlatan with a caravan and a pack of tarot cards. He was visiting a trained hypnotherapist with letters after his name; one who should know what he was doing. He put down the magazine and picked up a business card from the table by his side. Okay, what *she* was doing. *She* should know what *she* was doing. He expected her to be a professional.

His cell phone buzzed in his pocket. It made him jump.

He looked at the screen. "Simon?"

"Hey, Dad! Just a quick reminder about the event at church this weekend. That bloke from TV is coming, remember?" His son's enthusiasm burst through the ether. Aidan was about to reply when Simon continued, "Anyway, think about it," he said. "Saturday, 7 p.m. Text me or something."

As he put his phone away, Aidan glanced over at a door marked Private. He hesitated, recalling a talk from way back highlighting the dangers of hypnotism. He couldn't exactly remember the reasons, but that hardly mattered. He began to feel nervous. And pressured. He needed more time to think. That was it. He needed a little more time. He got up and went over to the reception. "Excuse me?" The receptionist looked up. "Er, would it be possible to postpone my appointment?"

"There's a cancellation fee, I'm afraid."

"That's fine. No problem." He paid and left.

Wandering down the road, he soon found himself outside Abney Park Cemetery. It looked peaceful in there and he needed somewhere to gather his thoughts. As he entered, he looked around. The whole place had a disheveled appearance. The paths were muddy and unkempt, and the chapel in the center was derelict. Ivy sprawled over many of the graves. Its one redeeming feature was its relative quiet. There was just a distant buzz from the traffic. He strolled along looking at the names on the headstones until he found a bench where he sat down. He closed his eyes and let out a deep breath.

He began to pray. Unexpectedly.

The words were immaterial; he was barely aware of them. Warmth flooded his entire being, his body, his soul. Deep within, rebirth took hold, conveying him from a place of isolation to the calm shores of divine intimacy. In the simple act of reaching out, he discovered security, he encountered love. And yet, when he opened his eyes, the world didn't look any different. The trees were still budding, the graves were overgrown, and it was starting to rain. Nevertheless, the new world he'd entered was one filled with hope. It was a world in which he was sheltered, held, and loved. He'd been given another chance. Just like a son whose shoe has come off and who feels the warm embrace of a loving father.

He looked to his right. A hundred yards away, a postman was pushing his bike along. The man's profession was easy to identify. His bike had large red panniers on the back, bulging with letters, and he wore a red jacket with the Royal Mail insignia on the front pocket. As he approached, Aidan noticed the tire looked flat. When he reached the bench, the postman leaned the bike against a tree and sat down, letting out a sigh. Aidan shot him a glance. He was medium build and looked about fifty, with swarthy skin and rough hands. On his head was a blue baseball cap with a large red letter *A* embossed on the front. The *A* had a halo around its peak. On his lapel was a badge showing two ladders in the shape of a cross. That seemed a bit unusual.

The man pulled out his lunchbox and opened it. "Crab sandwich?"

he said, offering the box. Aidan was assailed by a strong feeling of déjà vu. He opened his mouth to speak but nothing came out. "Don't like crab?" continued the postman. "Well, not everyone does." He leaned back and took a huge bite.

"No, no. I love crab," stammered Aidan. For some reason he didn't expect a postman to eat a crab sandwich. And why would that be? You could get crab in specialty stores all over London. In fact, Waitrose probably stocked it. What possible reason could there be for a postman not to eat crab? It was a delicious kind of seafood, healthy, nutritious.

The postie interrupted his thoughts. "Say, do you have a spare moment?" His voice was deep and gravelly, his gaze steady. Déjà vu swamped Aidan once more. He was about to say something when the man spoke again. "I've got a flat tire. Any chance of some help?"

"Sure. No worries."

They worked in silence together, removing the inner tube, finding the hole, and patching it up. After they'd finished, the postman sat down on the bench, stretching his arms over the back. "Well, thanks for your help with this. I appreciate it." He paused. "So, er, what brings you to a cemetery on a cold day?"

Looking back, Aidan couldn't even remember hesitating. He simply opened his mouth and his story poured out without any thought of the consequences. The man by his side listened, a calm look of concentration on his face. When Aidan came to the part about hallucinating, he didn't look shocked or surprised. In fact, it was almost as if he heard stories like this every day of the week.

The postman waited for a lull. When it came, he said, "She sounds nice, this woman you meet in your dreams . . . and in court." They smiled at each other. "Listen, Aidan, I don't know what you think of divine providence, or even if you believe in God, but let me just say this. The Father never coerces, he waits patiently for those who seek him. And he is not so far from any of us. So listen to your life, for he is always speaking."

As the man mounted his bike, Aidan stared at him, unable to speak, unable to move. "Oh, and one other thing. It's okay to take a risk now and then." He was about to start pedaling, when Aidan found his voice. "What's your name?"

"Nathaniel Lucas. I work out of the Stoke Newington depot." He flashed a smile with sparkling green eyes, turned and cycled away.

Aidan looked after him in a daze. He took a deep breath and began walking along the path, his mind racing. The late afternoon sun was coming out from behind the clouds. Glistening drops of water hung from every branch and leaf, reflecting the sun and sending out flashes of light in all directions. When he reached the end of the path, he stopped. In front of him stood three stone statues mounted on marble plinths. Each one depicted an angel. Two of them had their arms draped over a cross, looking down forlornly. He approached one of the graves, the final resting place of a man named Philip Edward Griggs, who "fell asleep after a painful illness" in 1895, aged forty-two. Below his inscription was a passage in verse.

We shall come with joy and gladness
We shall gather round the throne
Face to face with those who love us
We shall know as we are known
And the song of our redemption
Shall resound through endless day
When the shadows have departed
And the mists have rolled away.

He looked up at the statues and stared from one angel to the next. Angels. An American accent floated through his mind, indistinct but recognizable. As he turned to go, he stopped and looked up one final time. Angels. The City of Angels? Was this listening to your life? Could you do that when your heart was thumping away in your ear?

He ran out of the cemetery and found a bus stop. Jumping on the 393 to Chalk Farm, he went and sat near the back, drumming his fingers nervously on the seat back in front of him, beads of sweat forming on his forehead. The bus pulled off down Stoke Newington High Street and turned a corner. With the swaying of the vehicle and the passing of time, Aidan gradually began to calm down.

When the bus turned into Fortress Road, a woman with shiny

auburn hair turned and spotted him sitting on the bus. He didn't notice her at all. He was looking down, tapping at his phone. If he'd glanced up, he'd have seen her gesticulating wildly as the bus pulled away.

But he didn't.

That night, he slept sporadically. After rising and consuming a meager breakfast, he sat on the bed with his laptop on his knees. All he needed to do was call in and tell them he'd be unavailable for the next few days. Harry liked to be kept informed. Google flashed its inviting search field up at him. He typed in "cheap flights" and hit return. A flight at the absurdly low price of £285 round-trip popped up. It departed the next day, giving him four days in Los Angeles between Friday and Tuesday. Well why not? What could he lose? He punched in his debit card number and was about to click "Buy Now" when the doorbell rang.

Donning a white shirt and a pair of shorts, he ran along the landing and down the stairs. The communal hall was littered with leaflets for pizza parlors and Chinese restaurants. When he opened the door, a slew of paper on the floor obstructed its movement. He reached down to clear a path. Looking up, he blinked into the sunlight.

A woman was standing on the doorstep.

She had auburn hair and bright eyes.

~ 31 ~

BRIEF ENCOUNTER

March 25, 2005

There was no parting of the clouds; nor were there any shining lights or trumpet voluntaries. Sweet sounds from choirboys backed by a full orchestra, along with sudden bursts of recognition, followed by hugs and kisses—these were also entirely absent.

Instead, they stood and stared at each other.

For a full seven seconds.

Evelyn had spent three days in London and all but given up the search. Discouraged and feeling a little foolish, she was due to take a flight back to Los Angeles in two days' time. The previous afternoon, she'd found herself just north of Camden Town, a name she remembered from one of her dreams, when she'd spotted Aidan sitting on a bus. The shock of seeing him right there with her own two eyes almost disabled her. However, when the bus pulled away, she gave chase, and although she couldn't catch up, she noted the number.

Quickly flicking through her London guide, she worked out the route, and jogged along in pursuit. If the bus had had a clear road, she probably would have lost it, but as it happened, there were several sections with temporary lights, which allowed her to catch up. After about a mile, she watched him get off the bus. His face seemed so familiar from her dreams. She followed him discreetly until he turned up a short path toward a red door with a big brass number on it.

As she stood staring at him, he dropped a couple of leaflets onto the floor. "My name is Evelyn Machin," she said. Her voice woke him up, transported him back to reality.

"Yes," he mumbled. "Evelyn Machin. Right. And I'm Aidan

Manning. What a pleasure to meet you. Do come in."

Her mind flooded with relief at finally hearing a name. Aidan. She liked the sound of it. Before she'd left LA, all she'd had was a name beginning with A and an address in West Kensington that had turned out to be wrong. As Evelyn walked in, he mumbled apologies for the smell of deep-fried chapatis, apparently courtesy of Mr. Singh who lived on the ground floor. She followed him up to his bedsit feeling a little nervous. He hadn't said a word since inviting her in. She'd imagined him as a white collar professional, but judging by the surroundings, she felt obliged to lower her expectations.

Aidan offered tea. Evelyn accepted. Neither said anything during the teamaking process. The only sounds were the clinking of teacups, the murmur of the kettle and the rustle of fabric as Evelyn shifted in her seat. She looked at the boxes of books piled up in the corner of the room, noticing one of the titles. *Pompeii* by Robert Harris. She felt the author's name was significant, but for the life of her, she couldn't remember why. So he owned lots of books. That was a good sign.

Watching him pour the tea, she was overwhelmed by a feeling of familiarity, a dim sense that they had a past. How did she know he didn't take sugar? It was all so confusing. She knew less about him than her hairdresser. That he was real was enough of a shock. That she was drawn to him left her feeling completely out of control.

Aidan had been struggling for a while. The woman from his dreams was now sitting on an upturned box in his living room and he was serving her tea. How appropriately British of him. He looked at her more closely. So she was real. And beautiful. Not a bad start.

He handed her a cup of tea on a china saucer. "How did you find me?" he said, squeezing onto a bucket chair full of clothes. "No, sorry. That's not the first question. *Why* did you come looking for me?"

As soon as the words were out of his mouth, he regretted them. Instead of engaging in polite conversation, he sounded inquisitorial. A strange mix of emotions flooded through him: attraction and curiosity, mingled with confusion and anxiety. His entire frame of reference felt under threat, as though the kettle might start rising up from the counter. The woman he encountered frequently in his dreams had turned out to be real, and with that revelation, he found his brain was turning to mush.

"You like mountain biking, don't you?" he blurted out.

Evelyn stared at him, a look of mild suspicion on her face. "Y-es."

"Sorry. It's just that in my dreams . . . you've told me things."

"What things?"

This wasn't going well at all. He felt like a phony TV medium who rifles through the audience's personal data and then masquerades as a mind reader. "Just . . . I don't know . . . stuff." Evelyn blushed and stood up.

His heart sank.

"Aidan, I think we need to do this again. Start again. We're in the middle of something extremely weird. I'm just as uncomfortable as you are, so, I dunno," the question popped into her head, "why don't you ask me out on a date?"

Aidan hesitated. "A date. Right. Of course. Sorry." They both laughed, desperate for a reset. He stood up. "Evelyn," he continued. "Will you come out to dinner with me tonight?"

"I would love to. You can pick me up at seven." She handed him a brochure from her hotel. Slightly taken aback by her suggestion of the time, he said, "Right, seven. I'll book a table. Any particular food preferences?"

"Surprise me. I like crab and, if I'm not mistaken, I think you do too."

After she'd left, Aidan collapsed onto the bed, adrenaline coursing through his body. The rest of the day flew by. He considered calling Edward but decided against it. He was in his own metaphysical bubble with a woman who'd traveled over five thousand miles to find him. He didn't want to share it with anyone else. Not yet anyway.

When he picked her up, he thought he'd never seen a woman looking lovelier, his late wife notwithstanding. She wore a short blue and white dress with a sash around the middle that drew attention to her slim waist. Her auburn hair, thick and wavy, was only held back by the slimmest of headbands, allowing it to fall down over her tanned shoulders. Her eyes, deep and brown, shone with life. Above all, however, was the person who resided in the body before him. She had lost the nervousness from their previous meeting. Now she looked energized and happy.

He took her to a seafood restaurant on Jermyn Street in central London. Ignoring his official receiver, he ordered lobster. Evelyn ordered the crab. The difference between the morning and evening was night and day. Aidan found his form in no time, entertaining his audience with tales from the law courts, while she shocked him with several accounts of near-death operations. After telling her a little about his family background, he even confessed to the reason for his humble abode. She took it well, exchanging details about her daughter that she'd only shared with her sister and Bridget. Doing so surprised even her. They both relaxed.

Sadly, the evening disappeared with a rapidity that crept up on Aidan, catching him unawares. When the waiter started placing the chairs upside down on the tables, he realized their time was almost up. To say the evening had flown by was an understatement. The urge to hit pause was intense—anything that would permit him to organize his thoughts and feelings into coherent sentences. Instead, time gobbled him up. She was stepping forward. She was kissing him on the cheek.

She was saying goodbye.

"Let me take you to the airport tomorrow," he stammered.

"Sure. I'd like that."

She turned and was gone.

The following day, Aidan took a cab and went to pick Evelyn up. The weight of things unsaid was so heavy the conversation died within seconds. He stared out of the window on the way to Heathrow, and when they arrived, he thought he would burst with the agony of it. He tried telling himself that now he'd met her, he could visit. But that did nothing to dampen the sensation that she was slipping away. The pressure to do something, say something, was unbearable.

It was all happening too fast.

They arrived at Terminal 3.

Aidan couldn't keep up with the thoughts cantering through his mind. Trying to pin them down was like nailing Jell-O to the wall. He stared dumbly at the check-in clerk. Every comment he made from then on was superfluous, covering up a jumble of emotions. When they arrived at immigration—accessible only to ticketholders—he turned to Evelyn. "I would love to visit one day. If, er, you'll have me, of course." His mind was blank, befuddled by the speed at which the end was approaching. For a moment, she looked like she might cry.

"Yeah," she said, looking at her feet. "You can come visit. That'd be nice." Her voice cracked on the last word. She kissed him on the cheek, and walked away without a backward glance.

~ 32 ~

THE MOST WRETCHED OF DEATHS

Only the sacrifice of an innocent god could justify the endless and universal torture of innocence. Only the most abject suffering by God could assuage man's agony.
~ Albert Camus

In all their affliction, He was afflicted.
~ Isaiah

March 27, 2005

Evelyn arrived frustrated.

She walked into the Living Room to discover Aidan sitting casually in an armchair by the fire, a magazine open on his lap. When he saw her, he looked up, a blank expression on his face. She perceived this as nonchalance, which didn't improve her mood. "So . . . what happened down there?" She perched on the edge of the couch.

"We had dinner, and then, I don't know. I—"

"Whaddya mean you don't know?"

"Evelyn, we'd only just met," he said, sitting forward. "What did you expect? I'm not the same person down there as I am up here."

"But you didn't do anything! Where's your initiative?"

"Initiative? Hmm, okay, so let's get something straight here. I spent most of the time trying to figure out what was going on. I thought I was doing pretty well just inviting you in. That takes initiative."

"Really? Well, I'll tell you what takes initiative—getting on a plane based on a bunch of vague impressions from my dreams. I thought at *least* you'd work out how much I'd risked to come and find you." She paused. "You know what? Once you've worked out how you're gonna fix this, just—" Words failed her.

She got up and walked out into the hall. There was nobody about.

Leaving through the front door, she made her way round to the back of the house and took the path down to the clifftop. The air was clear and fresh, like a spring day when the beauty of the season assaults the senses from every bush, flower, and tree. For the first time, she noticed the wildflowers clinging to the side of the path. Reds, yellows, and purples seemed to rise from the ground and spread out into the distance, as though the colors had been hiding but were now emerging to display their loveliness.

She sat down on a boulder and did what she always did in that spot. She tipped her head back and felt the cool breeze blowing up from below. She sighed. Perhaps she should cut him some slack. After all, meeting someone from your dreams was pretty wild. And she'd only been with him a few hours. Poor guy, he'd probably spent half the time wondering if he was going insane.

Looking up, she saw Aidan standing nearby.

She suddenly felt a little guilty.

"I'm sorry, Evelyn," he said, sitting down next to her. "I'd have been disappointed too. I don't think I told you, but, er, you arrived the exact same day I was booking a flight to LA. All I had to go on was your city, Dell Avenue, your face, and a foreign name associated with a dog."

"Really?" She brushed hair out of her face. Loose strands stuck to her cheeks. "You never mentioned that."

"No. No, I didn't. What with all that blood rushing to my head, it must have slipped my mind." He was silent for a while. "You're drop-dead gorgeous when you get mad, did you know that?"

She looked across at him, a small smile crinkling the corners of her mouth. Aidan moved closer and gathered her into his arms. She did not resist. Instead, she pressed her face against his chest. "I guess I got used to the existential craziness quicker than you did."

"Are you saying I'm slow?"

"Well, let's just say the jury's out, Mr. Barrister."

They laughed. Aidan took off his sweater and laid it across Evelyn's lap against the cold. As he pulled her closer, a cough nearby disturbed their intimacy. They both looked up to see Korazin approaching through the heather. He wore a somber look on his face.

"It hurts to be separated from the one you love, doesn't it?" said the lucidus. Neither replied. "Come. It is time."

Aidan's vision cleared quickly. They were standing on a hill overlooking an ancient city. The sun was setting, bathing the scene before them in a golden glow. Evelyn was by his side. She reached out and took his hand. Korazin stood nearby, quietly contemplating the view over Jerusalem. The city walls surrounded narrow streets and densely packed houses. Browns, ochers, and creams blended together beneath a darkening sky. The temple was easy to spot. Its high walls dominated the eastern portion of the city. As the light receded, the rich evening colors turned pale. Stars started to pierce the night sky.

The lucidus led the way down the hill along a stony path lined with pomegranate trees. By the time they arrived at the garden, it was almost completely dark. Aidan felt a light breeze blowing through the olive trees, stirring the leaves. The music of cicadas singing in the branches filled the air as they made their way further down. At the end of the path, they were met by Gamaliel and Aliza.

"Welcome to the Garden of Gethsemane." Gamaliel bowed slightly, and distributed torches among the group. He led the party along a narrow path down toward a denser part of the garden. After passing some wild mustard plants, they approached a group of men who were hunched against a mature olive tree with a broad trunk. Aidan and Evelyn knew what they were seeing, but the immediacy of the moment, the fact that it was taking place right in front of them, made them uneasy. They didn't know quite what to expect.

Each of the men wore the customary clothing of the era. Tunics, belts, and sandals were worn by all of them; a couple also wore cloaks. One wore a scarf on his head. The snoring coming from at least four of them would, in normal circumstances, have been amusing. But these weren't normal circumstances. The significance of what they were about to see began to play on their minds. They braced themselves.

Gamaliel led the way along a further path to a clearing with two large boulders in the center. Next to one, a man was kneeling, his head bowed, hands clasped together. He did not need to be identified. When Evelyn saw him, she was taken aback. She hadn't expected him to be so . . . small, so vulnerable. In fact, he was a Jewish man of medium height and build, dressed like the men they'd just left. Perhaps the boulder nearby made him look small. Or maybe she was having trouble taking in what she was seeing. And hearing.

The man was in distress.

His upper body rocked gently back and forth, while from deep inside, he emitted a mournful groaning sound. Evelyn felt oddly detached, uncomfortable with her position as a voyeur. It was only when he looked up toward the sky that she entered in. His eyes and cheeks—lit up by the moon—ran with tears, but when he brushed them away, his sleeve caught some mucus, which smeared across his beard. It was a most human act, reminding her that she was indeed in the presence of another human being. She looked across at Aidan who was watching, transfixed.

The man's groaning finally stopped, followed by muttering in a foreign tongue:

ܐܒܐ ܐܢ ܨܒܐ ܐܢܬ ܐܥܒܪ ܡܢܝ ܟܣܐ ܗܢܐ

Gamaliel whispered, "He speaks in Aramaic, pleading with his father to remove the cup. You may remember the passage."

The man slumped against the boulder. Great beads of sweat dribbled down his cheeks and into his beard. The moonlight reflected off his forehead, the sheen catching the light so that his whole face stood out against the dark rock behind him. As he looked skyward, a subtle shift occurred. The sweat changed color, becoming a crimson tide that flowed down his face and splashed onto the ground. Evelyn had read of the condition during her training but had never seen it. The mixture was diluted, so it flowed more like water than blood. The man raised clasped hands above his head for a moment, all the while mumbling prayers of deep anguish until he crumpled to the ground.

Through the trees, a figure in white clothing approached, carrying a bowl of water. Gamaliel whispered, "You are privileged, today, to witness the lucidi. You are our most honored guests."

The lucidus arrived at the man's side and offered him the bowl. He drank. Filling his hands with water, the lucidus doused the man's face. The washing was as sacramental an act as the humans had ever seen. With his face tilted upward, he received streams of water poured slowly onto his forehead. The intimacy between the two figures was palpable, yet impossible to put into words. After the washing, the lucidus unfolded his wings and cradled the man in his arms. His wings wrapped themselves around both bodies until all that could be seen was a bank of cream feathers glimmering in the moonlight.

"We call it a velum, a covering," said Korazin. "When a lucidus confers the grace and power of the Father to a person in need. It is used very rarely." The lucidus placed the man carefully down on the ground, kissed him on the forehead, and walked silently out of the garden. When the man stood up, he seemed to have regained his strength. He walked with purpose toward the group of sleeping men.

The atmosphere shifted, as did the mezcla.

Aidan and Evelyn found themselves a few paces away from the group who earlier had been sleeping. Now the men stood around, wide-eyed and terrified at what they were hearing. They chattered nervously among themselves. Dots of light from lanterns and torches could be seen coming down from the direction of the city. The sound of blades slashing at branches was clearly audible through the trees. Soon after, weapons were visible too.

When they arrived, Evelyn was surprised at how many there were. Ten soldiers, heavily armed with swords and daggers on their belts, were accompanied by five men in fine tunics and ornate headscarves. Yet none of them led the party. Instead, it was led by a man wearing the apparel of an ordinary man.

They all knew his name.

He approached his master and kissed him on the cheek, receiving a curt reply. Neither Aidan nor Evelyn understood the language, but they knew the story. What they hadn't anticipated was the look of distress on the Master's face. Even though he had surely known what was to happen, he had yet to live it, and living it was what counted. It was in the hearing of his betrayer's voice and the fake affection communicated by his kiss that the dagger was driven deep. His face displayed his pain. It was impossible for him to hide, for he wore a human body and possessed a human heart.

There was no time to linger on the moment, however. The pathos was shattered, replaced by movement and violence. A large man pushed his friends aside and stepped forward, brandishing a dagger. He blundered as he came, neither aiming nor thinking, his action borne of pure emotion. A flash of iron, a scream, and a young servant fell to the ground, clutching his ear. In an instant, soldiers were pulling the large man back, though restraint wasn't needed. He was paralyzed by shock.

They watched the servant writhing on the ground. Blood was pouring from the wound. His cries of pain echoed around the small clearing. Aidan was horrified by how little attention was paid to the man after he went down. None of the soldiers or temple officials came to his aid. His bleeding meant nothing to them. Each side stood glaring at the other, waiting for the other to act. The moment crystallized into a snapshot of hostility, each face depicting the darkness within.

Only one man stood apart.

"Ἐᾶτε ἕως τούτου," he barked—"Stop! No more of this!" His words were brusque and authoritative, chiding his disciple, and excoriating his adversaries simultaneously. He walked forward and knelt down next to the wounded servant. Placing his hand on his ear, he whispered some words; the bleeding stopped immediately.

At first, the youth couldn't believe it. He patted his ear, tugging on it, unable to take in what had happened. The ear was perfectly restored. He wanted to thank his healer but the man was already standing. He was addressing the large man, who stood trembling, the knife still in his hand. "Ἀπόστρεψον τὴν μάχαιράν σου εἰς τὸν τόπον αὐτῆς, πάντες γὰρ οἱ λαβόντες μάχαιραν ἐν μαχαίρῃ."

Gamaliel translated. "All who draw the sword will die by the sword. Never a truer word. Notice the emphasis on non-violence, a hallmark of the coming kingdom. And look at the young servant," he went on. "A healing by Yeshua is a life-changing experience. I must tell you the story of Malchus another time."

As the lucidus was speaking, two soldiers stepped forward, holding coarsely made ropes. Though their quarry was unarmed, they grabbed his arms and yanked them behind his back, tying them up tightly. Simon Peter stood looking at his Lord, unable to process what was taking place. His bravado was gone. Inside, the reprimand still stung his soul. He winced at the pain of his master's words, so harshly delivered. The world they had constructed and the kingdom they had hoped for was dissolving faster than a morning mist on the Sea of Galilee. Yet the disappointment was swamped by fear for his life. So while the soldiers were taking turns to beat the prisoner, he and the other disciples fled.

Within a few yards, many were sobbing.

The mezcla shifted.

Aidan and Evelyn opened their eyes to find themselves standing to the side of a courtyard. Torches were affixed to the walls every few feet, though the light they shed was dim. The first thing they noticed was the smell. Pungent body odor quickly had them both covering their noses with their hands. Gamaliel led the way past the crowd toward some stone steps leading from the courtyard to another further down, a smaller one. From there, they were able to watch the proceedings and gain a view of some servants who had gathered around a fire, warming themselves against the cold night air.

A loud voice resonated around the upper courtyard. All eyes were on the speaker, the high priest. "Ἐξορκίζω σε κατὰ τοῦ θεοῦ τοῦ ζῶντος ἵνα ἡμῖν εἴπῃς εἰ σὺ εἶ ὁ χριστὸς ὁ υἱὸς τοῦ θεοῦ."

Korazin said, "They ask him if he is the Messiah, God's Anointed."

They all moved a little closer to get a better look. The bound man stood in front of the Jewish governing body, the Sanhedrin, who sat on large wooden chairs wearing expensive clothing. The accuser—the high priest—wore his ceremonial robes, a turban on his head, a girdle, an ephod adorned with elaborate embroidery, and a breastplate covered in precious jewels. He looked magnificent. He was also angry, his face contorted with indignation and affront. The man on trial had not yet spoken and already he'd insulted the judge and jury. Around the edges of the courtyard, the crowd looked on. The kerfuffle as the soldiers dragged in their captive had drawn out the curious and the gossips. From rich to poor, they gathered in clusters to watch the illegal proceedings.

The accused looked up at his accuser. One of his eyes was already closed over with a dark swelling. His hair was matted with dirt and his face was bruised and bloody. In spite of the ropes that bound him, he stood as erect as he could.

He said in reply, "πλὴν λέγω ὑμῖν, ἀπ' ἄρτι ὄψεσθε τὸν υἱὸν τοῦ ἀνθρώπου καθήμενον ἐκ δεξιῶν τῆς δυνάμεως καὶ ἐρχόμενον ἐπὶ τῶν νεφελῶν τοῦ οὐρανοῦ."

"He quotes from the book of Daniel, chapter seven," said Korazin. "You will see the Son of Man sitting at the right hand of the Mighty One and coming on the clouds of heaven."

The words caused an immediate rumpus. Every member of the Sanhedrin began talking loudly to his neighbor. The prisoner, however, paid them no attention. He had his eyes fixed on the group gathered around the fire in the lower courtyard. Aidan followed his gaze. It wasn't hard to spot Simon Peter. He was remonstrating with a bunch of servants, wagging his finger while his forehead poured with sweat.

When Aidan looked back at Jesus, a soldier was tying a dirty piece of linen over his eyes. He'd barely tied the knot before another soldier stepped forward and struck his victim on the back of the head. The thunk of the stick on his skull caused Evelyn to wince. She turned away, unable to watch.

"*Prophetiza nobis Christe quis est qui te percussit!*" shouted the guard, slapping the accused on the side of the face. Next, a servant walked forward, spitting insults in Aramaic. He tipped his head back and hawked up a huge yellow dollop of spit and mucus. It hit his target in the face and splattered across his nose and left cheek. Seconds later, a soldier punched the prisoner hard on the chin, pushing his jaw upwards. Teeth cracked and blood dripped to the ground.

Korazin's voice interrupted the humans' troubled thoughts. "I offered my back to those who beat me, my cheeks to those who pulled out my beard; I did not hide my face from mocking and spitting."

The abuse continued while the Sanhedrin looked on. Most nodded approvingly, their debasement laid bare. Some, however, disliked the raw violence and walked out into the night; among them, a tall man in a long flowing robe who walked down into the lower courtyard. He passed Simon Peter, who was backing away from his interlocutors, his voice raised in anger.

It was hard to make out the words but the tone was unmistakable. Simon Peter was terrified. The moment Aidan looked back, his entire world stopped. For he caught the look upon the Savior's face. Blindfold ripped off, Jesus stood staring at his friend, the fisherman with whom he had shared his life, the one he loved like a brother.

His eyes betrayed the anguish in his soul.

In the distance, a rooster crowed.

Korazin put his hand on Aidan's shoulder and whispered in his ear, "Surely he hath borne our griefs and carried our sorrows." He made ready to catch him.

Aidan began to float, emerging from a mist to gaze up at his mother, his limbs streaked with blood. Her face was distorted by pain and anger, causing cramping in his stomach. Inside, he longed for her, and when she handed him roughly to another woman, he felt a rupture inside, as though he was splintering into small pieces. Looking up at the midwife, the image began to change.

He closed his eyes and opened them to discover the face of the man from the courtyard, who smiled down at him, pulling him to his chest. "You are my beloved," said the man. The words entered his soul, and began piecing him together.

A mist covered his sight.

When it cleared, he was fully grown in front of a mirror. He walked into the reflection and saw a crowd of people in their early twenties gathering outside a church. He approached them nervously. Jack Stonehouse was standing with his back to him, but as soon as the curate turned round, he began to recede into the background. By the time Aidan reached the group, he was merely a speck disappearing into the distance. A man who'd been talking off to the side came forward, holding out his hands. His Lord, face glowing with pleasure, started introducing him to the others. He whispered in his ear, "Never forget, son. You are included. And greatly loved." The words strengthened him and he was about to express his gratitude, when he suddenly found himself walking into the hall at home.

He was ten years old again, recently returned from school. His father came out of his study and walked straight past, without even glancing at him. Aidan felt himself crumble, breaking into fragments. He fell back, reaching vainly for his father. When his head hit the hard wooden floor, he passed out, though not for long. On regaining consciousness, the first thing he saw was the blood-soaked face of the man from the courtyard. His Master. His beloved Savior who in turn called him beloved.

The hole inside closed a little.

It was still there but it was smaller.

And that made all the difference.

On one side, Gamaliel held him up and on the other, Korazin whispered in his ear, "Surely he hath borne *your* griefs and carried *your* sorrows, Aidan." He paused. "He suffers alone so that you will never be alone. He takes rejection to put an end to yours."

The mezcla shifted.

It was no longer nighttime. The sun was about to rise and the air was crisp; the sky was a pristine pale blue. As she gradually became aware of her surroundings, Evelyn stiffened. She grabbed Aidan's hand. He too seemed nervous, alive to what was coming.

Aliza, who had not yet interacted with either of them, felt their fear. Evelyn was her prime concern, so she walked over and stood next to her. She looked calmly at the soldiers as they arranged their weapons on a wooden block nearby. Then she put her arm around Evelyn's shoulder. "He takes the punishment for your sake, my dear. We know how distressing this will be, but few have the chance to view the ultimate sacrifice. It is painful, we know that, but it is also a gift."

What came next was appalling by any standard. Worse than either of them could have imagined. They knew a Roman scourging was horrific, but to witness one yards away was almost more than they could take. Their twenty-first-century sensibilities could barely cope with it.

The Roman soldiers first tied their victim to a block of wood. Passing a rope through an iron manacle, they threaded it back through two iron "bracelets" on the prisoner's wrists, already chafed red raw. The equipment was laid out on a table nearby. Thin rods lay next to several flagella—short whips with wooden handles to which two or three oxhide thongs were attached. The thongs themselves were knotted and embedded with pieces of zinc and iron.

They began with the rods, whipping Jesus on the backs of his arms and legs, before moving onto his torso. No part of him escaped the beating, which seemed to go on forever. Angry welts and contusions sprang up all over his body in response to the blows administered by two large Roman guards. He cried out, screaming in agony, his nerve endings receptive like any other man's. He was spared nothing.

A lull descended as the guards selected some new implements.

Evelyn turned and grabbed Gamaliel's arm. "Why so much?" she demanded.

"That is a good question, my dear. Why so much? Why do they go on and on? It is a question asked by countless people every day around the globe. Perhaps some suffering might be expected to refine a soul, but many are dumbfounded by the excess, the sheer quantity of human agony. Often without apparent redemption or meaning to it." The lucidus looked with compassion into Evelyn's upturned, tear-streaked face. "I believe we have addressed these points during earlier conversations, Evelyn, but there is nothing so persuasive as a man who takes upon himself the excess of which he is accused. Never let it be said that he has not considered the question. Nor given a response to it with every cry of pain and every drop of spilled blood."

The men started to lose control, whipped into a frenzy by their bloodlust. They had to be restrained by a centurion who pulled them back, bawling them out with expletives delivered in Latin.

Korazin added his own thoughts, quoting from the prophet Isaiah. "See, my servant will prosper; he will be highly exalted. But many were amazed when they saw him. His face was so disfigured he seemed hardly human, and from his appearance, one would scarcely know he was a man."

Two more soldiers stepped forward, each carrying a flagellum. The cords clinked together as they approached the bloodied man, who was standing, trembling with anticipation. One blow and Evelyn was in tears. Aidan held her tightly, forcing himself to witness the atrocity as he clasped her to him. Every now and then, Evelyn managed a quick glance, doing her best to remind herself of Aliza's words.

The brutality was staggering to all who watched. The first few blows of the flagellum sliced the prisoner's back diagonally, producing deep lacerations from which blood immediately began to flow. The blood burst from his capillaries and his veins, sprinkling the arms and faces of his tormentors, and spraying out in a wide arc. It saturated the piece of linen he wore around his waist, and trickled in rivulets down his side and legs. Catching the sunlight in bright red droplets, the blood spurted out. It oozed and poured, streaming down his body and splashing off the flagstones at his feet. Pools collected on the ground making the surface slippery. He slipped and slid about, further chafing his wrists against their bonds. In time, he fell silent. He simply collapsed to his knees, grunting and rocking to the blows as they drove him down onto the ground.

Evelyn, who'd buried her head under Aidan's shoulder, suddenly turned on Gamaliel. She grabbed his robes and brought her face up to his. "There had better be a reason for this," she hissed. "And it better make sense to everyone. You hear me? *To everyone!*" She crumpled into a heap, weeping uncontrollably. Aidan knelt down and wrapped his arms around her. By the time she had recovered, the scourging was complete. Through her tears, Evelyn watched the crowd shuffle away. The only sound came from the soldiers who were joking with each other, callous and hardened to the end.

The mezcla shifted.

Aidan opened his eyes, instinctively knowing what followed. They stood on a hill, looking up at two criminals who hung on their crosses, one of them wailing pitifully. When they turned round, they saw a large crowd coming up a path. Roman soldiers led the way, followed by two men, one with a crossbar across his shoulders, the other naked and bloody. Behind them, donkeys carried the high priest and other temple officials who rode with fixed stares.

When the procession reached the top of the hill, the guards grabbed hold of the crossbar and laid it down on another longer piece of wood, nailing the two together. Dragging their victim by the arms and legs, they maneuvered him onto the cross. They stretched out his arms, strapping them to the crossbar. With hammers, they banged six-inch nails through his wrists. The pounding caused many of the women to wince and turn away, but one nearby who wore a hood kept looking. She refused to take her eyes off the man before her. Her face was streaked with tears, but still she looked. As she did so, she gripped the hands of the women who wept softly by her side.

Gamaliel's voice interrupted the banging and the cries of pain. For a moment, the sounds of execution faded into the background. "Evelyn," he said. "You ask if the punishment makes sense to all." He paused. "The answer is no, it does not. For millions have shut up their hearts and do not wish to comprehend. Do you have eyes but fail to see, and ears but fail to hear? The suffering of the servant is only understood by those who are willing to open their eyes and ears to receive the gift."

"And what gift is that?" she said, gazing up at the cross as it was lifted up.

"Oh, I think you already know." He paused. "Mary of Magdala, she certainly knew." From the moment Evelyn turned toward the hooded woman, she was captivated, unable to take her eyes off her. She knew her name, but little else. One look at her face, however, and she felt a connection.

With a woman who'd suffered.

With a woman of strength.

She watched as Mary walked over to stand in front of the cross. Evelyn moved closer, eager to see what she would do. Mary lifted her hands and face, and quite unexpectedly, she smiled. Sorrow and joy embraced, blending on her upturned face. As she smiled up at her Savior, tears flowed down her cheeks and dripped onto her clothing. His gaze was fixed on the woman and he too was smiling, albeit faintly.

With a burst of recognition, Evelyn understood what should have been obvious from the first.

He was hanging there for love. Of course he was. He bled for love. And there never was a sacrifice more complete and right than this one.

The righteous for the unrighteous.
The lovely for the unlovely.
The good man for the sinner.
Jesus smiled at his beloved and his beloved smiled back.

Evelyn bowed her head and gave thanks for eyes to see and ears to hear.

Aliza came and stood next to her, placing her hand on her shoulder. Seconds later, Evelyn was in her living room, ten years old, padding after a man who held the hand of her sister. Katie opened the basement door and went down first, followed by the man. When they all reached the bottom of the stairs, Evelyn looked up at the man, terrified. She was about to scream but stopped herself. It wasn't Mr. Henderson at all. It was the man who hung on the cross. His face was not bloody but clean. His body was not broken but strong and healthy. He knelt down and looked up into her ten-year-old face; from behind his back, he pulled out a book.

"Story?" he said, grinning.

"Yes, please."

They sat on the couch next to each other, a wave of joy washing over her, so that when the story was over, she was sure that if he kept reading until all the books in the world were read, he could read them all over again and she would never become bored. All his attention was on her and her delight could barely be contained. When she interrupted and jumped up and down, all he did was laugh. She thought she might burst for the ecstasy welling up in her heart. When he'd finished reading, he picked her up and carried her to her bedroom, where he laid her on the bed. He tucked her in, leaned over her, and grasped her hands in his. "I have my eyes on you, young lady. Always. I have given you a healthy body to enjoy this earth and all its treasures." He placed his hand on her forehead. "Be healed now. Be well. You are loved. And protected. You are redeemed." He paused and leaned in closer; he whispered in her ear, "You are beauty."

He kissed her on the forehead, and was gone.

Evelyn rubbed her eyes and thanked Aliza for holding her up. She looked across at Aidan who gave her a look of encouragement.

Their peace, however, was short-lived. A yell went up from the band of soldiers nearby. One of them was laughing uproariously. He threw some dice onto a makeshift wooden table, and bellowed something in Latin. The others were laughing too hard to see him cheat by turning the dice onto high numbers. When they regained their composure, he was sitting with his arms crossed, a wry grin on his face. He proceeded to hold up a purple piece of linen admiringly, boasting that his fortune had now doubled. The whole scene lasted no more than a few seconds.

For Aidan, however, it lasted much longer.

They were gambling for the Master's clothing.

His shame burned inside like a fire. He tried to hide it from Korazin but the lucidus knew him too well. "It is not merely your sin he carries, but your shame and much more besides," he said. "He carries your shame, Aidan, so that you can let it go."

The lucidus led the party a little farther off, away from the crowd. They found some boulders to sit on and when they were comfortable, he continued. "What you see before you has been called many names—atonement, propitiation, expiation—each revealing a nuance of a many-splendored truth, that a life of purity and perfection must be crushed to death to give life to the dead. A woman in labor endures agony for her hour has come, but when the child arrives, her suffering is forgotten, so great is the joy of new birth." He closed his eyes.

Gamaliel took over. "And that's how it is with love. It is forever welded to the pain of this world. For you were made out of love and for love. Little wonder then, that in suffering, the Savior gives expression to what he truly loves. Bleeding may hurt—the lashes and nails cut deep—but when the sacrifice is born of love, it is done willingly, a surrender for a greater good. Your good. To rescue you. To repair you. To reconcile you to your heavenly Father." He paused, his face glowing with enthusiasm. "The beauty of your Creator is far beyond the capacity of even the lucidi to conceive. For though we are ageless, we are still paddling on the shore of a vast ocean stretching out before us."

The tall lucidus stood up. "Come," he said. "Let us draw near."

They walked back and stood in front of the three crosses. "Go on, Aidan, take a look at him! Look up, Evelyn! Gaze upon the man who takes upon himself not simply your sin, but also the task of defeating evil. For on that tree all injustice and every manner of sickness and decay are vanquished. Every drop of blood announces the triumph of good over evil. He hangs there in your place, but he accomplishes so much more. His self-sacrifice makes a declaration about the true heart of your Creator. It is his supreme act of self-revelation."

Aidan did as he was told. He looked up. So did Evelyn. Their souls soared. So it was a jolt when Gamaliel interrupted their thoughts. Without warning, the lucidus made a loud announcement in Spanish and the heavens burst open. Both humans immediately stepped back and reached for each other. What they saw overwhelmed their senses. The lucidi had to hold them up.

Above the crosses, several enormous ladders, twenty yards wide, stretched up until they disappeared into a gray mist. Up and down them teemed a great multitude of lucidi, some surging heavenward, others descending, in a vast flurry of feathers. They beat their powerful wings, their movement fluid and in balance. The humans couldn't count them. There were too many. Each lucidus knew instinctively when another wished to pass by, moving aside gracefully so that the whole display was dance-like, seemingly choreographed. At first, Aidan thought he would be overjoyed by what he saw, but unexpectedly, he felt depleted and sad.

The source of his melancholy was not hard to discern. His spirit tuned into the music filling his ears and entering his heart. Lucidi hovering above the cross played on instruments the humans had never seen, and the music they played was in a minor key. So haunting and mournful was it that both humans began to weep. It touched the very depths of their souls. Each minor strain blended together with the next until both Aidan and Evelyn were clinging to each other.

The lament of the lucidi drained them of all emotion.

Aidan fixed his eyes on the face of a lucidus who had flown down and was seated nearby. The lucidus sang as he looked up at the figure on the cross. The sight before him evoked profound grief, his agony reaching out and filling both humans. They were powerless to resist. Yet moments later, without warning, the tone changed. The entire musical performance shifted. From despair to hope. From minor to major. The change was intoxicating, catching both of them by surprise. Aidan looked at Korazin and Gamaliel, searching for answers, but discovered the answer within, as did Evelyn.

Agony and ecstasy.

The music encapsulated the very heart of the Father.

Pure joy and abject sorrow.

With a rush of divine revelation, their souls gained insight into the connection between the Three-in-One and his creation. His transcendence, that part of him that is beyond, independent, and "other," is only one description of his being. He is also immanent and, being thus, he is woven through the entire fabric of his creation. Every moment, he delights in countless acts of kindness performed by his image-bearers. The rapture in the heart of the Father in viewing virtue displayed by his creatures is a deep well of ecstasy. And this is just the beginning. He also loves oceans and caterpillars and duck-billed platypuses. Wildebeest, Rocky Road ice cream, deserts, black holes, waterfalls, rainbows, icicles, movies, cream-colored ponies, crisp apple strudels, electrons, and hippos are also among his favorites, because the entire creation is his favored thing. Its light and waves, its balance and flux, are all a wonder to him and fill him up with joy. He is truly enchanted by what he has made, for though it has suffered a calamity, it still mirrors his goodness and speaks out his praise.

With never-ending intensity, he experiences within himself the joy that causes the child to squeal with delight as she receives a red balloon because red is her favorite color. Every sensation of satisfaction and contentment, all pleasure and happiness flowing through the human heart flow also through his. Every mother who holds her newborn, every father watching his son kick a football, play a violin, perform in a play, all the souls who cherish their loved ones, they are all essential to the Father's joy. The bond he shares with his creation runs deep, far deeper than a human can comprehend.

He truly is in a constant state of ecstasy.

The major key lies right at the heart of his experience as the loving Creator.

Yet so too does the minor key. There is no denying it.

For while he experiences the joy of the child who holds a red balloon, he also aches when clammy fingers let it go so that it drifts up into a cloudless sky. He is fused to his image-bearers in a way they can neither perceive nor understand.

No wonder his beloved Son hung just a few feet away.

For God so loved the world. It was such a simple statement.

For if he loves his creation, he does so with every infinite fiber of his being. He does not merely observe the mistreatment of slaves, he experiences their desolation and despair. He feels their wounds and the shock to the system that comes with every whipping. He is in agony along with the physically and sexually abused. He cries out at the injustice of robbery and corruption. He hungers and thirsts, feels the heat and humidity of summer, and the bitter cold in winter. He feels the isolation of rejection and the slow drip of despondency within the depressed. He screams in horror at the gruesome acts of Manson, Mengele, and Stalin. And he laments the pitiful sight of babies who lie in their own filth in Romanian orphanages. He winces in the tiny wooden shoes of Chinese women, imposed by brutal men. He feels loss along with the bereaved, whether they seek him or not.

Aidan and Evelyn looked up at the man on the cross.

And with a surge, the final revelation came to them.

They were in the presence of unimaginable beauty.

The ugliness of the human heart was all around. From the sneers of the onlookers to the brutality of the soldiers; from the taunting of the religious to the insults still coming from one of the criminals. The entire scene was ugly in every possible way.

And yet it was beautiful.

It hardly seemed possible when at first they became aware of this truth. Ugliness kicked and screamed and demanded the final word, but its efforts were futile. Darkness was shunted aside by the raw power of symmetry. For everything was in its place. Just like Gamaliel's cathedral, thought Evelyn. Like the astonishing structure of the cell, leaf, and crustacean, every part was in perfect balance.

The Most Wretched Of Deaths

The beauty they beheld could not be denied. Fulfillment, that very Christian word, was never clearer than in that moment, when a bloodied man hung on a tree before his executioners. It was from the paradox that the beauty emerged. For what seemed like defeat and disgrace was actually victory and exaltation. What seemed ugly was in fact beautiful, because it precisely reflected the will of the Father, Son, and Spirit. Both humans were in awe as they gazed up at this vision of Trinitarian glory, shining through the blood, pain, and tears.

What appeared ugly was in fact beautiful, because God made it so. He declared it so. They bowed their heads and thanked God for eyes to see and ears to hear.

The mezcla shifted and when they looked up again, they saw their Savior look up to the sky. He cried out in a loud voice, Τετέλεσται—it is finished. His head slumped forward.

A centurion standing nearby declared, "*Vere homo hic Filius Dei erat.*"

"Yes, indeed," said Gamaliel. "He certainly is the Son of God."

~ 33 ~

FROM THE EMBERS

Love is our true destiny.
We do not find the meaning of life by ourselves alone
—we find it with another.
~ Thomas Merton

April 8, 2005

Aidan looked up blearily at the flight attendant. He rubbed his eyes. She was holding a carton of orange juice and wore an expression somewhere between fed up and "If I hear one more complaint about the legroom, I'll hit someone." His whole body felt shattered, as though he'd just finished a marathon, in combination with a severe sugar low.

"Orange juice would be great. Thanks," he said, taking the proffered plastic cup from the attendant's hands. The liquid revived him instantly, seemingly flooding through his veins to the parched places of his body. It was getting dark outside. The man in the window seat hadn't closed his blind, so the gift of a prolonged sunset, which a plane chasing west gave its passengers, was still visible on the horizon. The red, yellow, and pink reflections on the clouds were receding, but the colors lasted all evening, fading only gradually.

Aidan looked at his watch.

They'd be arriving at LAX in the next few hours.

An hour after touching down, he was checking in at the Crowne Plaza in Redondo Beach. Airline food, well, it was . . . airline food—so with a rumbling stomach, he crossed the street and entered Ruby's Diner. The hamburger chain, decked out in 1950s regalia, served large portions to large people. After wolfing down something called a Cobb Premium Burger, Aidan finished off his banana malt and sat back.

He pulled out a photograph of Evelyn and stared down at it.

He'd taken the photo at the restaurant. Catching her off guard, he'd captured a coquettish "keep away" expression, sparkling with life. He smiled to himself. The recklessness of what he was doing seemed suddenly rather amusing. He hadn't called, too fearful she would tell him to stay away after the awkwardness of her departure. So the romantic impulse had kicked in. He'd just jumped on a plane. Simon wasn't overly impressed, but Tommy thought it was a hoot, declaring loudly, "Sweep 'er off 'er feet, sir!" The blur of adrenaline-induced euphoria as he took the Tube to Heathrow was still there, though it was fading fast. He yawned. Jetlag was kicking in; he was too tired to drive over that evening.

The following day, he slept until noon, awaking from his lengthy slumber with a light headache and a hearty appetite. He threw on some shorts and a T-shirt and went to find some lunch.

The afternoon slipped by quickly.

It was just past 5 p.m. when Aidan climbed into his hire car and joined the 405. Using his GPS, he was soon merging onto the 90. He turned onto Lincoln Boulevard and hung a left onto Washington Boulevard, where the traffic immediately turned to gridlock. He peered into the sky. A dark haze was rising from somewhere near the beach. Smoke? A fire engine whistled past him, followed shortly after by another. The traffic stuttered along, then ground to a halt.

He lost patience and turned into a side street where he parked. Using the map he'd picked up at the hotel, he began walking in the direction of Evelyn's house. As he approached, the haze grew thicker. It was definitely smoke, wisps of it floating up into the sky. He reached Dell Avenue and increased his pace. Several hundred yards down, a crowd was gathering. When he caught sight of a police cruiser, he began to jog. The crowd was thickening, but he pushed past people, desperate to find out what was happening. Passing a police officer who was holding back a West Highland terrier straining against his leash, he paused for a moment. Was that Evelyn's dog? He remembered a photo she'd shown him in the restaurant—but if so, where was *she*? Reaching a stretch of yellow and black tape, he ducked underneath.

Then he stopped and stared.

Firemen were spraying water over an area where a house had once stood. Half the structure was gone; the other half was blackened, the contents a charred mass of indistinguishable items. Various police officers were milling around, one of them barking orders into a walkie-talkie. Water was flowing down the driveway, over the curb, and along the street toward the drains, carrying with it ash and debris.

A pall of smoke hovered above a pile of ashes, while on the far side of the property—well to the side of the original floor plan—a woman was sitting dazed and unseeing. Staring straight ahead, she scraped the back of her right leg with a broken teacup, apparently unaware of her strength. She scratched hard, breaking the skin. Blood seeped out, rolling down her calf and dripping onto the ground.

Aidan moved forward, ignoring a policewoman to his right who started shouting at him shrilly. Nothing would have stopped him reaching his beloved. His whole being was set on a course toward Evelyn, to hold her and comfort her. When he was ten yards away, she looked up and noticed him, her expression blank and listless. In a simple act of supplication, she reached out to him, both arms held forward. He took her in his arms and sat cradling her for a long time, saying nothing.

Evelyn did not cry, she just sat there, numb with shock. After a while, however, a gathering swell of emotions sought expression. They were so strong and so contradictory, she feared her capacity to contain them. The agony of her loss bore down on her, weighing upon her with a force that was crushing. Her beautiful home, packed with treasured memories and priceless mementos, was gone. The few photos left over after the burglary had been destroyed. So had numerous items of clothing from Katie, Bridget, and her mother, each one soaked with kindness and love.

Yet it was just a house. And houses could be rebuilt.

It was people who counted, not objects. Deep down, she knew this truth, but it collided with the harsh reality of the ashen wasteland surrounding her. Her kitchen, her living room, the places where she had shared so many good times with friends and family, were all flowing down the drain, coating faces or drifting up into the sky. The cruel juxtaposition of losing her home while retaining its happy memories throbbed inside, dully.

At the same time, her sorrow blended with the joy of seeing Aidan, of holding and being held by him. She closed her eyes and clung to him, breathing in his scent and pressing her head into the crook of his neck. In response, he wrapped his arms around her and enjoyed the warmth of her affection. After a while, Aidan broke off his embrace and looked into her eyes, pushing a strand of hair to the side of her face. He kissed her.

When their lips met, a shock of familiarity ran through them both. The lips they kissed were not new. The intimacy they shared did not feel like friends becoming lovers, but lovers finding each other after a long absence. It felt mysterious and unfathomable, a meeting of their bodies that deepened the merging of their souls.

Aidan pulled back. "Strong déjà vu."

"Hmm, me too. And I smell of smoke and ash. No wonder you find me so attractive."

When they looked into each other's eyes, Evelyn was the first to crack. Her laughter, however, was short-lived, and when he kissed her again, she began to weep. The shock of seeing Aidan and losing her home was a vast dam breached only by the absurdity of their opening exchange. So she wept—in lament over her dearly loved home, for joy at the embrace of her lover. And to her relief, only one response lingered. She was soon luxuriating in the first glow of requited love, a sensation that dulled the pain of her loss. Wiping away tears, she couldn't help laughing again, though she did so with an embarrassed look on her face.

"I feel like I'm sweet sixteen."

"Sweet, yes, but no longer sixteen. And frankly, if you were sixteen, they'd arrest me." He smiled down at her, and started wiping ash out of her hair. "I'm so sorry about what happened in London. I still don't really understand how we know each other. I just know I'm in love with you." He paused. "Have been for months."

He looked deep into her eyes. Caressing the side of her face with his fingers, he moved his lips gently over her forehead and down her nose to her mouth. He kissed her lightly and picked up her hands. "We should make a move," he said.

They wandered down the road and were met by Bill, a neighbor two doors down, who'd always been kind to Evelyn. He invited them in but needed to leave for work, so left them sitting on the front porch drinking sodas.

"Have you called anyone yet?" said Aidan.

Evelyn shook her head, then borrowed his phone to call Bridget and Jasmine. He held her as he listened to two tearful conversations, both of which included frequent uses of the phrase, "I'll be all right."

A fireman walked up. "Ms. Machin? I believe these belong to you." He handed over a whistle with the engraving "Titanic" on the side, along with a gold-plated locket, complete with gold chain.

~ 34 ~

BRATWURST AND CORN DOGS

April 9, 2005

The rest of the week flew by in a blur. They stayed at Jasmine's—Aidan on the couch and Evelyn in the spare room conveniently vacated by Brian the weekend before. The distress of dealing with insurers, policemen and fire officers was assuaged by the presence of the curious newcomer who drank gallons of tea and wondered why Americans couldn't pronounce "herbs" correctly. Evelyn felt as though her senses were assaulted by extremes. The dull rhythms of daily life were gone. Instead, she was either distraught when dealing with her loss or acting like a kid in a candy store just looking at her new prize, an Englishman who listened to the BBC on shortwave radio and quickly developed a keen interest in *Judge Judy*.

"This is just a show, right?" he said.

"Nope. It's called American justice. You'll soon work it out, Aidan. If something can entertain in America, it will eventually wind up on TV. Even justice."

The hospital authorities gave Evelyn two weeks off after they received news of the fire. She was fortunate they had hired a new surgeon the week before. As for Aidan, he called Harry with a departure date that almost gave the poor man a rash. He promised his senior clerk he'd do extra bail applications on his return, and even gave an assurance that he'd help Gordon with his murder case.

The week turned into one long series of introductions. Aidan smiled internally at the American propensity to assume he knew the Queen. Every other person wondered if he'd had tea with the reigning monarch of the United Kingdom. Regarding geography, he promised he would behave himself when encountering people who didn't know which parts of the map actually comprised the UK.

But it was hard.

"You're from Britain I hear," said one of Evelyn's coworkers during a visit to the hospital.

"Yup."

"My family's from England."

"Great. You still have relatives who live there?"

"No. My great-great-great-grandfather, I think, was from a village in Cornwall. Am I saying that right? Corn-wall?"

It took some getting used to, the American practice of claiming European heritage based on distant relatives. "I'm German" generally meant that, way up the family tree, Helmut—or Ingrid perhaps—had traveled from Germany back in the nineteenth century and you were talking to the great-great-grandson. Or maybe his grandson. Aidan prided himself on smiling politely and finding something encouraging to say. Sometimes he came across as a little patronizing, though that wasn't his intention. "I hear the bratwurst is fantastic in Germany"—a comment he made to an administrative assistant—brought a look of complete confusion. It didn't help matters much when he explained that he was talking about sausage, since American sausages were food items to be avoided, while the German variety was a delicacy and absolutely delicious.

"Bratwurst, Aidan?" said Evelyn as they left the hospital. "What were you thinking?" He just laughed.

The second week was a runaway train, powering forward with no likelihood of slowing down. They visited the Norton Simon Museum and the Griffith Observatory, and spent one full day biking up in Big Bear. On Thursday, they met up with Bridget and Reggie to go skydiving. Evelyn drove her Explorer with Bridget next to her, sunroof open, voices raised.

Aidan was in the back with the tall African American. "So the bald pate, Reggie . . . An homage to Michael?" Sharp intakes of breath came from the front seats, neither of the women quite sure how Reggie would react. He sat stern-faced, toying with the silence, then tipped his head back and roared with laughter. "David Beckham here thinks he knows his basketball!"

Evelyn breathed a sigh of relief.

"Kareem, then? Charles Barclay? Ray Allen?" said Aidan.

Reggie was stunned by how much Aidan knew about the NBA. They both lamented Shaq's departure from the Lakers, and wondered how a white guy named Steve Nash was managing to take over the league.

"Mind you," said Aidan. "John Stockton was a white guy."

"Yeah, but he was a nobody without the Mailman!"

They both laughed.

Arriving at Lake Elsinore, they piled out of the car. Evelyn and Aidan both had experience, while for Bridget and Reggie it was their first time; they each went tandem with an instructor.

As the Twin Otter reached just above twelve thousand feet, Bridget's nerves caused her mouth to run riot. She gave her opinions on a new video-sharing service she'd read about, called YouTube—it'll never catch on—and the new pope—too old, too German.

"Bridget!" exclaimed Evelyn.

"So how did you know where to find Aidan?"

"I didn't," shouted Evelyn, hurling herself out of the plane. Falling to earth generated the same joy as usual, the same endorphins. The hormones flooded through them all, especially through Reggie, increasing the volume of his voice by several decibels. Once they'd landed, he let the people in the next valley know he was more than satisfied with the service at Skydive Elsinore.

During dinner later that night, Bridget quizzed them on their dreams. They remembered *The Last Supper* and the *Pietà*, but the content of their discussions was vague.

"You have a temper," said Aidan, grinning.

"And you can't dive."

"I saw you in court."

"I saw you on the freeway. And—"

"And my mother saw you both on TV," said Bridget, interrupting. "Now stop it! Evie, how did you know where to look?"

Evelyn looked deep into Aidan's eyes. "An address in West Kensington and the kind of recklessness that makes a person jump out of a perfectly good plane!"

On Friday, two days before he was due to leave, they went to Disneyland where Aidan regressed into a playful child who insisted on going on the Teacups too many times. Evelyn felt like a teenager with a crush. She was happy just to be near Aidan and feel his arm around her. She knew the honeymoon period was destined to be short-lived, but she didn't care. Decisions about the future could wait.

She stopped. "Last one to Space Mountain eats a corn dog."

"One of those disgusting things on a stick?"

"Yup. Covered in mustard." She took off through the crowds, certain that Aidan had the legs to catch up. Ten minutes later, he was eating processed meat on a skewer.

Back home in the evening, Aidan started retrieving clothing from various rooms in the apartment. Two days left; time was nearly up. They finished off some leftovers; Aidan made some tea. "I'm on a plane in two days. And you're back to work." He was sullen, unable to lift himself for the conversation.

"I have more vacation time next month," she said. "I'll visit."

"No. I'll be back. I won't take any big cases."

"Can you afford it?" He gave her a look.

The day before, he'd confessed to his gambling problem and though grateful for her gracious response, he couldn't avoid the shame that still lay in the lower reaches of his soul. He smiled sheepishly, worried that attending GA meetings wouldn't be enough. "Knights in shining armor can afford whatever they want to afford."

Once she'd said goodbye at the airport on Sunday afternoon, Evelyn returned to the apartment and became embroiled in an argument with her daughter over a message from the insurance company that Jasmine hadn't passed on. They rowed and Jasmine stormed out, slamming the door.

After consuming half a packet of *Chips Ahoy!*, Evelyn went to her bedroom and lay down. The back of her leg was itching; she scratched at it vigorously. The lichen planus, which had been improving, was starting to flare up again. She rubbed on some ointment. Aidan had been gone four hours but the visit to Disneyland already felt like it had taken place in another lifetime, on another planet.

The following morning, however, brought an entirely new sensation. She awoke from her slumber filled with overwhelming joy, her whole body tingling. Her recollections of her last dream were vague—something about a wolf, a large stage and . . . a cauldron maybe? Yet, as always, it was not the details of the dream that mattered. Instead, she luxuriated in the feeling it left inside her.

She was elated. Ecstatic.

~ 35 ~

THE BIG STORY

I had always felt life first as a story:
and if there is a story there is a storyteller.
~ G.K. Chesterton

April 24, 2005

Aidan awoke on a damp patch of earth. His head rested on a large, flat boulder, his side wedged against an anthill. He sprang up and started brushing stray ants off his clothes. Looking around, he wondered what was going on.

The Viatici House was nowhere in sight.

Instead, he was in the middle of a clearing surrounded by thick forest, below a darkening sky. A star-studded canopy was becoming visible above him, the light dimmed by a rising moon still hidden by the tops of the trees. He stood up and looked down at his clothes. He was wearing worn leather trousers tied up with long laces just above his ankles. On his upper body, he wore a white linen shirt underneath a black leather waistcoat. His shoes were made of leather, the fastenings reminding him of some he'd once seen at a play in Shakespeare's Globe Theater in London. They were unusually comfortable. Looking down at his waist, he saw a dagger tucked inside a sheath.

He walked round behind the boulder, and discovered a sword lying under a bush. On the crest of the hilt was a circle of burnished bronze with a Celtic cross inside. The hilt itself was awash with engravings of mythical creatures and encrusted with precious jewels.

Words ran around the base, raised and clearly legible:

Nor shall my Sword sleep in my hand.

Surprisingly, it wasn't as heavy as he'd expected. Gripping the handle tightly with both hands, he planted his feet apart and began

The Big Story

swinging it to and fro over his shoulders. The blade was soon swishing through the air, making figures of eight. It was while wielding the sword that he first became aware of his arms. And his shoulders.

"Wow," he whispered under his breath. He lifted up his right arm and felt his bicep. "What have they done to me since my last visit? Given me to Thor?"

He picked up a scabbard lying a few feet beyond the bush and attached it to the belt around his waist; he thrust the sword inside. Looking about for some indication of what he was supposed to do, he investigated the surrounding area. At the far end of the clearing was a small pond, and beyond it, at the base of a pine tree, a quiver of arrows with a bow nearby. He picked up the quiver and placed the strap over his head; the arrows sat snugly against his side. Okay, Robin, where's the lovely Maid Marian? He found he was gaining confidence.

Through the forest, Aidan spotted a flickering light. It seemed as good a direction as any other. When he reached the bank of trees, he discovered a narrow, rocky path lined with dense undergrowth. The route took him along the side of a bog, soaking his shoes, which weren't designed to withstand water. In time, however, the trail became wider and drier; he was relieved when he came out the other side of the wood.

Dense heathland stretched far out toward the horizon. The moon was now lifted up in the sky, full and bright, bathing the undulating hills in a pale silver light. A light breeze rustled the grasses; behind him, pine trees cast shadows that danced around him. He stopped and peered into the distance. A torch was affixed to a post about a hundred yards away. When he reached it, he found an envelope held in place by a rusty nail. Opening it, a piece of parchment fell out.

> *A maiden in peril, her enemy circling*
> *A valiant knight, his belovèd protecting*
> *The heart of a warrior*
> *The strength of his will*
> *Forsaking his body*
> *His blood he did spill.*

Yet on that clear night, his enemy dead
The victory won and his cloak steeped in red
A new knight lies prone
A phoenix we're told
For a new man is born
From the scars of the old.

Aidan thought the words "spill" and "his blood" were positioned uncomfortably close together. Not to mention the line about a "cloak steeped in red." He folded the paper and thrust it inside his waistcoat.

"Well," he whispered. "Got the clothes, got the sword. Need the maiden. Where the heck is Evelyn?" He was about to leave when he noticed a small paper bag nailed to the far side of the post. He pulled it off and peeked inside. The pills he normally took to return home lay at the bottom. He stared down at them; after a moment's hesitation, he shoved them into his pocket.

When he looked up, he saw glimmers of light several miles away, and since there was no sign of what he was supposed to do, he decided to make for them. The night air was bracing, but Aidan's pace rapidly warmed him until a light sweat broke out on his forehead. The path, which was descending rapidly, veered sharply to the right, taking him down toward another wood. He was bordered on each side by thick vegetation, so he had no option but to keep going.

Entering the woodland, he had to slow down. The moonlight scarcely punctured the canopy, making it oppressively dim. Taking care not to trip, he picked his way through a section with small rocks and fallen trees. As he rounded some large oaks, he came upon a creek no more than a few feet across. He knelt down and drank deeply.

A wolf howled in the distance.

Aidan stiffened; he fingered his sword nervously.

It howled again. This time closer.

He began to run; a slow, loping run along the edge of the creek where it was soft and grassy. In time, his eyes adjusted to the gloomy surroundings. Spotting movement to his right, he glanced across and caught a glimpse of yellow eyes alarmingly close. His pace quickened. When he looked again, some kind of large wolf was clearly visible, its muscles rolling up and down along its back as it stalked him. The animal's tongue lolled out of its mouth; its teeth were bared and sharp.

Aidan's heart rate went through the roof.

He was tempted to call out for help but thought better of it.

He came to a halt, his breath rasping in his throat. Pulling out his sword, he faced the beast, which stared at him from under fifty paces. Without thinking, he yelled with all his might, swinging his sword over his head and sticking his tongue out like a savage. "Yaaaaah!" He did it again, planting his feet apart. When nothing happened, he stepped forward, pointing his sword aggressively at the animal. The beast stared back, unblinking; it grunted at him and sloped back into the forest behind.

Relief flooded Aidan's body.

He tried to insert the sword back in its scabbard with one hand but found it was shaking too much. Taking some deep breaths to calm himself down, he collapsed onto a grassy tussock. He wiped his forehead, glancing around warily, afraid the beast might still be nearby.

He heard nothing.

Eventually, feeling a lot calmer, Aidan sheathed his sword and continued along the path, aiming for the lights he could see blinking through the greenery. The trees thinned and he emerged on the far side of the wood. Before continuing, however, he scanned ahead, searching for any signs of danger—but there were none.

Two torches lit the path before him.

Down at the bottom of the hill, he could see a long, thin lake. The moon's reflection quivered on its surface. Near the shoreline, he spotted a wide, flat area surrounded by torches mounted on tall posts. In the center, a flag was flying from a flagpole, flapping in the breeze. He strained his eyes to see better. Was there something or someone tied to the flagpole? It was impossible to tell from such a distance. To reach it, he was faced with a steep descent down a rocky incline. He stumbled as he scrambled down, grazing his hands on the rocks.

Once down, he started running.

"Aidan!" The wind carried Evelyn's frightened voice up the slope. In his peripheral vision, he caught a movement—the same yellow eyes, the same gray fur. He ran as fast as he could. Dodging fallen tree branches and leaping over rocks on the path, he became a man possessed, terrified of arriving too late. When he reached the outer edge of the clearing, he powered over a large boulder and sprinted toward the flagpole. As he ran, he glanced behind him. The beast was a couple of hundred yards away but gaining fast. Reaching Evelyn, he discovered she was tied to a post. He pulled out his dagger and started cutting her bonds.

"Large wolf or dog or something," he mumbled, slashing through the ropes around her wrists.

"What are they playing at?" she muttered.

"Don't know, don't care," he said breathlessly. He was about to give his bow and quiver to her but it was too late. The beast, a massive wolf covered in black-spotted gray fur, ran straight at Evelyn, its jaws open. Aidan's reactions were swift and instinctive. He threw himself at her, knocking her to the ground; the animal snapped at the air just inches above them. Its claws caught the side of his body, ripping his clothes and drawing blood. At the same time, a trail of saliva spewed out of the animal's mouth and coated them both; the stink of it made them retch. Seconds later, Aidan was on his feet, wiping the drool from his hair and facing his enemy. Fortunately, the animal didn't turn and attack immediately but instead walked away, licking its lips.

"Are you okay? You're wounded," said Evelyn.

"Stand behind me!" he ordered.

"Give me something to fight with."

"Shut up and get behind me!"

There was no time to argue; she did as she was told.

The beast began circling, walking round them calmly, never once taking its eyes off its prey. It pawed the ground. The fur on its back was raised, and every now and then, a low growl rose from its throat. Aidan stared back at the wolf, carefully pulling out his dagger and handing it to Evelyn. His sword he grasped with both hands. They both stood on the balls of their feet, their muscles twitching with anticipation. This went on for several minutes until Aidan could bear it no longer. He laid the sword down on the ground, took the bow off his shoulder and pulled out an arrow. After taking careful aim, he took his shot but sent it harmlessly past. The wolf ducked the second one, its reactions lightning quick. Aidan threw the bow and quiver to the side.

"Oh, come on, you stupid, pathetic excuse for an animal. *Come on!*" He picked up the sword and waved it out in front of him, trying to goad the beast into action.

"I like it. Perhaps we can curse it to death." Evelyn's joke made them both laugh, though their laughter was primarily a release of nervous energy. The wolf, however, sensed weakness and charged. Its powerful legs took it the short distance in about three seconds, but Aidan was ready. He stepped aside at the last moment and slashed at the beast, opening up a deep wound on its side. Blood sprayed out over him as it passed.

It turned immediately and pounced. He was slower this time, and the animal managed to claw his shoulder, tearing open the waistcoat and slicing through skin and muscle. Blood began flowing down his side, staining his shirt. He cried out and rolled over, a claw narrowly missing the top of his head. Evelyn crouched behind him, shaking with fear. The dagger looked utterly feeble in her hand. The wolf, meanwhile, was licking its wound. It paced up and down, snarling and baring its teeth.

Aidan gathered his strength, ready for the next assault. When it came, he was perfectly balanced. The wolf charged, leaping straight for his throat, but as it pounced, he stepped to the side and swung the sword down as hard as he could on the beast's neck. The blade carved through the hide and cut the animal open. In one fluid motion, he swung again with all his might, driving the point of the blade through the animal's heart.

"Aaaaah!" A war cry erupted from deep inside him. The beast arched its back and let out a high-pitched squeal. Its body shuddering, it breathed its last, slumping to the ground dead.

Aidan sank to his knees.

"Okay. Now it's starting to hurt," he said, breathing heavily.

Evelyn ran over. First, she ripped off the clothing around his wounds, then she lowered the flag and tore it into strips that she soaked in the lake. She washed the wounds as best she could, and bound them tightly.

"You'll fix right up."

"I think you were my maiden in peril," he said, pulling out the note. By the time she was gathering him into her arms, he'd passed out. She checked he was still breathing, and retrieved the poem from his grasp. His head cradled in her lap, she cast her eyes over the words, smiling, her emotions thoroughly confused.

She was furious with the lucidi, but she was also exhilarated to be sitting with her lover on a moonlit night after he had killed a huge beast. She felt like a princess in a fairy tale, though her modern mindset resisted the stereotypes they had ended up playing. But, oh, wasn't he brave? She couldn't help swooning a little inside. She felt him stir. Aidan came round, wincing as he tried to sit up.

"Hold your horses, Legolas," said Evelyn. "You need to rest."

He grimaced as he examined his shoulder. They both looked up toward the hills, Aidan squinting in the half-light. "Why does the heath look like it's moving?" he said.

Dozens of lucidi started arriving, each carrying pieces of an oak table, chairs, and food. They assembled the oak sections into a long table, similar to the one in the Descartes Room. Others approached with lanterns and an assortment of dishes. A sizable buffet appeared before them: chicken, beef, salads, vegetables, and the usual selection of lucidi-inspired desserts. Small fires were lit; over them, wrought iron cauldrons of soup and stew were suspended. Delicious odors wafted toward them.

They stood up and went to sit at the table.

As the meal was being prepared, more lucidi appeared, carrying large pieces of wood. These they used to construct a wide stage. Fifty feet across and twenty feet deep, it had stairs leading up to it on each side. Lanterns were placed at all four corners, and when the task was completed, each lucidus approached the table and bowed. The last one to leave was tall and regal; he wore a long, dark robe and his face shone brightly. Aidan guessed he was probably a seraph.

"Welcome, Aidan." He bowed. "And dear Evelyn." He bowed again. "Welcome to the big story."

Huge wings erupted from his back and thighs. Rising into the air, he hovered for a moment before flying off, silhouetted against the moon.

"Look," said Aidan, pointing. From the other direction, three figures flew toward them; it wasn't hard to guess who they were. They arrived in a flurry of beating wings and stray feathers. Evelyn remembered she was supposed to be angry. She crossed her arms, her expression stern.

"Welcome," said Gamaliel grandly. She scowled. "Come now, Evelyn. A short conversation should help resolve your feelings of resentment." He walked over to one of the cauldrons, picked up two bowls, and filled them with soup.

"Eat. The soup will revive you," said the tall lucidus, placing his hand on Aidan's shoulder and closing his eyes. He whispered a prayer in Spanish, then went to fill his own bowl with soup. Aidan pulled off the strips of cloth and inspected his shoulder and side. The wounds were healed, leaving a slight scar in both places.

"Better?" Gamaliel took his place at the head of the table.

"Much better. Thank you."

They all filled their plates and began to eat. The food was even more delicious than usual. The soup in particular, a lucidus concoction containing herbs, caused them both to stop everything and just taste. Evelyn's anger started to abate. In spite of her best efforts, holding onto it was becoming increasingly difficult.

"Evelyn, you—"

"Aidan could have been killed," she interrupted. "We both could." Her tone was aggressive.

Gamaliel put down his spoon. "You could have taken the easy option." He turned to Aidan. "And yet you didn't." Aidan pulled out the pills and placed them on the table. The lucidus continued, "Even when facing extreme danger, you chose to fight not flee." He paused. "Excellent, excellent! The question is why." He took a sip from his glass, allowing the question to hang between them. "Do you want to live a life that shirks danger, avoids risk, requires nothing of you?

No, of course not. Do you want to be given an iPod, a big-screen TV, and a salt and sugar hookup so you can stop living and speed up the process of dying? Because we have had some of those here. One howl from the wolf and those pills are gone."

Neither replied.

"You, Aidan, are a brave man. You possess a profound desire for your life to mean something, and you understand that acts of valor rate highly in that regard." Aidan smiled and looked down, a little embarrassed. "Besides," said Gamaliel, eyes shining, "we tampered with some of your brain chemistry and pumped up those muscles. How did the sword feel?"

"Like a toothpick." Aidan smiled.

Aliza, who hadn't yet joined the conversation, could contain herself no longer. She held up her glass. "I declare," she said, "a brief intermission. More wine or juice?" Filling their glasses, she turned to Evelyn, eyes bright. "I hear congratulations are in order." Her voice was playful, teasing. Evelyn blushed. "Come on. I want to hear every detail."

The conversation was full of life and joy. Aidan corrected Evelyn at various places, drawing some firm "shushes." The lucidi plied them with food and drink, laughing in the right places and asking pointed questions. Evelyn did most of the talking. Aidan was happy just to watch and listen. She spoke with such fervor and with such effervescence that he forgot the story was real. She liked to embellish her recollections . . . utter despair after leaving London . . . raging inferno . . . covered in ash from head to toe . . . He didn't recognize every part, but it didn't matter. It was enough to bask in the knowledge that the gorgeous woman waving her hands about, occasionally wiping tears from her eyes, was in love with him.

"Coffee?" said Korazin, interrupting Aliza, who'd launched into an in-depth discussion with Evelyn on mother-daughter relationships. After half an hour, however, he decided to draw their attention to weightier matters. "So who likes a good story?"

Evelyn looked suspicious; her brow furrowed. "Why do I always get the sense your questions are loaded?"

"Because you're smart, Evelyn," said the lucidus, grinning. "But

The Big Story

seriously, TV shows, soaps, books, movies, everywhere you look, you're surrounded by stories. What's that all about?"

"It's our way of making sense of the world. Must be," she said. "But where are you going with this?"

Gamaliel joined in. "Well, for stories to work, there are certain essential elements. That's why all seven of the basic story types contain common themes."

"So to work, they have to be formulaic? I've always thought the best ones bend the rules, if not break them."

Gamaliel's face lit up. "You never fail to brighten my day, Evelyn. Yes . . . hmm . . . well, I suppose the best stories are . . . predictably unpredictable." The lucidus smoothed back his hair and leaned forward. "Stories are like oceans. They work best when they rise, fall, and rise again. The essential ingredients of conflict, obstacles, and enemies generate a story's flow, its movement. Which often spurs growth. Without that beast, Aidan, all you had was a walk on a moonlit night, which doesn't make much of a story. But the point here is that stories draw on a deeply felt human intuition—that the world *isn't the way it's supposed to be*. They help you make sense of a world that you feel instinctively *has gone wrong*. They're the means you employ to put Humpty Dumpty back together again, to create order out of chaos."

Korazin rejoined the conversation. "It should go without saying," he said, "that the best stories tap into human longings." He paused, waiting for a reaction.

Evelyn responded. "Longings . . . for what?"

"Well, what are your hopes and dreams, your longings?"

She thought for a second. "Love, of course. And happiness."

"Indeed. Those two seem obvious, don't they? And you want peace too, don't you?" They both nodded.

Gamaliel jumped back in. This was his favorite part. "And this brings us to what we call the big story. Think about your short story just now, Aidan. You gave expression to valor, fortitude, and love. Yet these ideas, these concepts don't just float about, they are crying out to be justified, grounded by a larger story. Only big stories, universal ones, make sense of your desires, the things you truly value." He paused. "So it should come as no surprise that the story we're about to tell satisfies the heart's deepest longing. The narrative is driven by love . . . leads ultimately to peace . . . and though it entails great suffering, it does lead to happiness. Even joy. It puts right what's gone wrong, for it involves the ultimate triumph of good over evil. Right. Finally. Aliza!"

The lucidus rose to her feet and went to stand on the stage. Her dark hair was adorned with small white flowers and she wore a long, dark green cloak, embroidered along the edge with biblical scenes that Evelyn recognized from Sunday school. The burning bush, Jacob's ladder, and the sacrifice of Isaac were there. So was Samson, who lay beneath a pile of white rocks.

Without warning, the back of the stage suddenly burst into life. Two enormous ladders started rising on either side, with a colossal white screen stretched between them. The entire structure was a hundred feet across and fifty feet tall. With a flash, the screen abruptly lit up brilliant white, dazzling everyone so that they all, including the lucidi, covered their eyes.

As their eyes adjusted to the light, they all gazed up, straining to see the screen that now displayed what looked like a galaxy revolving in circles. Seconds later, a garden appeared, rich with tropical greenery; animals prowled around, and in the center stood two human beings, completely naked. As Aliza spoke, her voice echoing around the clearing, her words were interpreted on the screen.

The Word outspoken, from nought to all
Matter unfolding in widespread call
Density, immensity in cosmic expansion
Till spiraling planets, celestial blue ball.

Animals roam in splendid array
In verdant surroundings their colors display
Dust to dust stands, tolling names by the score
A world made for wonder, His name to adore.

A cry from the depths of a soul, tormented
The image divine is forever fragmented
We lucidi wept, watched the earth spoil and crack
Accursed and bound tight upon destiny's rack.

Flood then tower, judged then scattered
Nations formed, prospered, shattered
Ever turning, never changing
Hope of future . . . never mattered.

Aliza bowed her head. Once she'd finished speaking, her last words lingered, weighing heavily on their spirits. Aidan looked across at Korazin, his eyes searching for a response.

"The pagan world," declared the lucidus. "Trapped in a hopeless circle! First, the inhabitants of this world look down . . . and then they look up. Down below, they observe the growth of edible plants and the animals they kill to clothe and sustain their families. The food upon which they depend is reliant upon forces above them: the rain that falls, the sun that shines, and what appear to be spirits who control their destinies."

"Look up with me! The heavenly bodies!" announced Aliza from the stage, taking over; the images on the screen matched her words. "Surely they are the key to human destiny—and how regular are their movements, and oh, how circular. Gaze up at the moon! Every thirty days, it waxes and wanes, just like the cycle of a woman's body. And just look at the plants. The earth gives birth to them, they grow, die, but each year they are born again. All of nature appears to be both circular and dependent on these forces beyond human control. They must be placated to gain control of what seems like a very uncertain world.

"Behold the birth of the first gods in Mesopotamia, the world's first civilization. Human beings offer them assuaging sacrifices, yet the gods are not kind. They are often in conflict; they are demanding. There is no harmony, only the desperate fear within humans that their sacrifices are insufficient. Nanna-Suen, the moon god of these early peoples, is male, so his priestesses engage in an orgy of sex and blood sacrifice. The young give themselves willingly, for human life has no dignity and one's fate is written in the stars. It cannot be changed." Her tone was shot through with melancholy, as though the recollection of such depravity and waste still pained her.

She took a moment to compose herself. "It is the circularity that holds the ancients in bondage—depicted on their monuments with the spiral, an image of eternity." A vast waterwheel appeared on the screen, revolving slowly. "For them, the universe is eternal and all that takes place has already occurred. They are bound upon a wheel of fire with no prospect of finding alteration—"

"Until!" announced Gamaliel loudly, "ah, yes, until that night!"

Aliza's face shone as she spoke.

One night in the silence, a man knelt and prayed
To his gods, heard a voice bid him pack
Leave his home, risk his life
Bearing nephew, wealth, and wife
Promised land far afield
Promised life from his loins
Firm of faith, blessed, dispatched
With no chance of turning back.

"The answer," said Gamaliel, "to the fall of humankind, is not the cross—at least not at first—it is the call of Abram."

Evelyn sat forward. "The Old Testament, right? But doesn't it all end in failure?"

"An excellent question," said the tall lucidus, picking up a pitcher of water and filling each glass.

"The story can be read that way," said Aidan.

The lucidus hesitated. "Well . . . sadly, it has been read that way. But let me make this absolutely clear. The Father never fails at anything. Ever. There is another way to read it. A much better way."

He gestured toward Aliza.

She stepped forward and swept her cloak over her shoulder.

The Big Story

The story begins with a king bold and bright
On a throne set up high, in a realm set apart
Power and perfection, full of truth, full of grace
Surrounded by knights
Each one loyal, each one right
All hail to the Crown
Boundless beauty laced with light.

Explosion of matter turns chaos to order
A temple of concord for Creator and likeness
A kingdom to marvel and leave us all breathless
Until in the darkness, a ripping and rending
So heartless the heart of rebellion that births
A dominion of death, and a reign of decay
For stalking the earth from thence forth till today
Walk two princes of pride we call Satan and Self.

Creation of nation in Abraham's seed
Jacob and sons flee to Egypt in need
Crossing the Sea pulling carts stacked with plunder
Lightning and smoke, mountain quaking like thunder
A people at last in the Land of the Promise
With God as their king and a law for their hearts
Yet the blood of the bulls and the goats merely spoke
Of the need of a Savior and new life for the broke.

A nation corrupted, the Father undaunted
The prophets foretell a Messiah, anointed
Apostasy, crime of a people devoted
To Baal and Asherah, in places high mounted
Israel in shame is exported, transported
To a land far away,
Drenched with tears, bruised and battered.

House of Souls

Returning exiles from great loss to rebuilding
A nation remaking, reworking, rekindling
The hope of a king who would heal, lead, and bind
Yet the same old bad habits poach their peace, leave them blind
So they flinch from their prophets
Who weep, judge, and curse
A stiff-necked assembly with faith poor or worse.

Centuries pass till a night full of wonder
When a baby in rags is laid in a manger
Line of David and Judah
Up from Egypt and danger
A man of compassion, a kingdom reborn
In the hearts of the poor, the down, and the needy
With nought for the rich, for the priests and the greedy.

The kingdom is led by a king bold and bright
With rough, calloused hands, bent for others, upright
Serves the weak, heals the sick
Casts out demons aplenty
With ear for the outcast, the lonely, the filthy
A war waged in love, a fight for the people
The battle, a struggle between good and evil.

A son of man, Messiah, the king claims his throne
After taking a thrashing right down to the bone
Power of love to the loveless
Gift of life to the lifeless
In his pain, toil, and grief, he gives hope to the hopeless
For there on the tree, with his blood flowing down
His body all broken, his head thorny-crowned
In crimson 'tis written: the dragon's defeated
With a cry, he declares, it is finished, completed.

The Big Story

The temple replaced, from the grave, resurrected
The heavenly kingdom is launched, germinated
No more bulls, no more goats
Curtain torn, dead reborn
The Savior lives on in the hearts of the brave
In their suffering united in vast joint endeavor
Called to walk with the lost and the blind and the beggar
In a world filled with pain, with a cross as their sign
They remember their king in the bread and the wine.

They sat quietly, allowing the words to work their way down into their souls. As they did, the poem created in them a deep well of questions—too many to process.

Evelyn said softly, "May we hear that again?"

After a second hearing, they retreated into their own minds, uncertain what to say, lost in their thoughts.

At last Gamaliel broke the silence. "In their suffering united in vast joint endeavor, called to walk with the lost and the blind and the beggar. And much more besides, dear Evelyn, dear Aidan. The suffering of those who follow Yeshua binds them mystically to their Savior. To suffer for the sake of the Kingdom, that is most admirable of all. However, Aliza's poem is incomplete, as she will readily admit; she has left us wanting more."

Aidan looked at the lucidus quizzically.

"The resurrection of the body," said Gamaliel. "A hope beyond all others." He placed two pills on the table.

The lucidi got up and bade their farewells. They walked down to the edge of the lake and stepped apart. Their wings burst from their backs and thighs, lifting them effortlessly into the air. Hovering, they turned, and flew off toward the horizon, watched by the humans who never tired of the sight of a lucidus in flight.

Aidan picked up the pills. He fingered them thoughtfully but set them back down. Rising from his seat, he went and sat down next to Evelyn, a small smile spreading across his face.

She was immediately curious. "What?" she said. "Don't tell me you're an axe murderer or something."

"Well, I do like Mike Myers but no, no axes in my closet. I do, however, have something that Korazin has kindly lent me for the occasion."

He went down on one knee.

Before he'd even opened the box, she let out a scream.

Aidan's little speech, so carefully prepared, was soon lost in a jubilant, verbal torrent.

~ 36 ~

TIERRA-7

*One short sleep past, we wake eternally
And death shall be no more; Death, thou shalt die.*
~ John Donne

April 25, 2005

Aidan arrived back in England on a crisp spring day. The weather was a welcome surprise. The air was fresh, the cherry blossom abundant, and the budding greenery in London's parks and front gardens gave the impression that the city was once again breathing after a long, dark winter. As the taxi joined the North Circular, he couldn't help looking out of the window toward West Kensington, wishing he was heading back to his old home. But that prospect lay many months ahead. In the meantime, he felt sanguine, with an inner determination to rid himself of his gambling addiction. With Evelyn in his life, he now inhabited a world of new possibilities; no challenge seemed too great.

On arrival back in chambers, Aidan was met by half a dozen curious faces, and a senior clerk attempting to bar his way to his office. Fending off the inevitable interrogation, he slalomed past, closing the door behind him. Gordon was away, his desk left impeccably neat and tidy. As Aidan walked past, he noticed a small photo tucked into the corner of Gordon's monitor. He was still holding it when the door swung open and Fiona walked in, her face reddening the moment she caught sight of the smiling faces.

"The puffy shirt is a great look," he said.

She flushed. "I told him not to do that." Stepping forward, she quickly removed the offending item from Aidan's hand and hid it in a drawer. "Please, Aidan. Don't tell anyone. I'm not ready for the backchat yet."

He put his index finger on his lips. "Mum's the word. Between you and me, though, I'm thrilled. Absolutely thrilled." She gave him a coy smile, eyes sparkling behind her thick glasses. He'd never seen her so happy. Or attractive, for that matter. If she ever decided to come out from behind those glasses, and wore a color other than gray, he had no doubt she would draw admiring glances.

Gordon should count himself lucky.

Later that day, the meeting with Mr. Blenkinsopp, the Head of Chambers, was an awkward one. Aidan's intention to take yet more time off did nothing to endear him to a man who liked a chambers that worked with calm efficiency. Aidan was not a QC, but his work was regular, and solicitors' firms didn't like it when their favorite barrister was unavailable. He was popular and they often requested him specifically. Another visit to California was essential, but it would have to be a short one.

Over dinner that evening, Aidan turned down Simon and Beth's offer of a loan. Several times. Beth was made of strong stuff, however, and wouldn't let the subject go. So, for the sake of a quiet life, he ended up surrendering to their goodwill and generosity. For most people, that would have been the end of the matter. But not for Aidan. Such was his competitive spirit that he managed to cajole his son into the promise of a game of tennis every other Saturday for the foreseeable future.

A week after touching down on British soil, Aidan was back at Heathrow Terminal 3. A few hours later, he sank into his seat. A quick rummage in the seat pocket in front of him, and he managed to find a polyester sleep mask.

Thirty seconds later, he arrived in the Espacio.

He woke up on a lounger on the patio outside the Descartes Room. The light pink on the horizon and the nip in the air suggested it was still early. He jumped up and went indoors to be greeted by a spread worthy of a UN gathering. Laid out in long lines were tamales, dim sum, spaghetti, enchiladas, pad thai, kongguksu, and Spanish omelet. The aroma in the room was sufficient to cause instant salivation; his stomach growled.

Korazin entered with a huge smile, his face glowing softly. "Aidan! How very good to see you." The lucidus was about to continue speaking when Evelyn ran past him and threw herself into Aidan's arms. They kissed, and when they looked up, the lucidus was gone.

"I've missed you too," said Aidan, looking toward the door. "I think we frightened him away."

They folded themselves into an armchair, and Evelyn began jabbing Aidan's chest with her forefinger. "Am I supposed to get married up here, and sit around on my own down there? What's the plan, Mr. Wolf?"

"Ah. Yes, well, hmm, let me see. First, I don't think it's 'down there' any more. More like 'out there.'"

"Don't get smart with me—"

"But don't you think," he said, interrupting. He wriggled so that she was forced to let him get up. He walked to the table and grabbed a piece of bread. "Don't you think part of the excitement and flavor comes from the relish?" He paused as he spooned on some chutney. She missed his knowing smile. "Specifically relishing what's to come?"

"You just want the waiting to be over, Evelyn." A voice boomed from the doorway. "Quite understandable." Gamaliel stood there, his arms outstretched. He was dressed in a double-breasted suit with a neatly folded handkerchief in the top pocket. His beard was newly shorn and, as he walked forward, there was a spring in his step. "Delayed gratification," he continued. "Aidan is quite right. Anticipation is what makes the consummation so satisfying. And not just yours, Evelyn—I suspect he may pop the question on his next visit—but the consummation of all stories. Especially the big one. Please. Do serve yourselves. You must be starving."

Korazin entered with a tray of drinks and started handing round glasses. The buffet provided tantalizing choice, so it was a while before they were all sitting down at the table.

They chatted about the past week, including Simon's willingness to provide a loan. The lucidi assured Aidan there was nothing to be ashamed of, while Evelyn thought the offer was kind of sweet. When the conversation drifted round to her life, Aidan was relieved to hear it couldn't have been Duncan, the neighbor, who had burned down the house. Apparently, he was in police custody on the morning of the fire. The cops had let slip that he was up on a charge of sexual harassment.

They all sat back feeling extremely bloated. When Korazin noticed Aidan covering his mouth to release a surreptitious burp, he took it as a cue. "Eating is wonderful," he said, "but you can't just do it forever. To truly enjoy food, I've discovered, it helps to be hungry."

"Is this greater goods again?" said Aidan, unsure where the conversation was heading.

"Perhaps in a different guise," said Gamaliel, running his fingers through his hair. "There is no question that humans struggle with the concept of delay, yet it's one of the major themes in *The Books*. Abraham had to wait twenty-five years for Isaac. The Hebrews waited for hundreds of years before the arrival of Moses, who himself spent decades in the desert. The Israelites, as I'm sure you know, spent forty years in the wilderness. I could go on."

Korazin continued the theme. "Delayed gratification is an absolute requirement in all good stories. Along with conflict. And yet your modern society is precisely designed to avoid delay. Microwaves, cell phones, the internet—the faster the better, which makes it hard for you to accept that genuine happiness requires delay. Getting what you want, when you want it, might satisfy your physical desires, but it can never lead to lasting joy. And that's a deep desire, whether you're aware of it or not."

"Shalom," said Gamaliel, offering them both more juice. "Peace. When things are *the way they're supposed to be*. But we have another word to describe this state of affairs. We call it heaven."

Evelyn's face darkened. "Is heaven the justification for the suffering on earth?"

Neither lucidus replied.

"Not a justification, my dear." Aliza stood in the doorway. When she spoke, they all looked up. Evelyn's face lit up. The bond she had formed with the lucidus was strong and made stronger with every new encounter. "Heaven places suffering in its proper context. It gives meaning to suffering by holding out the promise that, one day, justice will be delivered, evil will be destroyed, and death defeated. The knowledge of this we call hope." She paused. "And from where does it spring?"

She walked over to the French doors. Spinning round with her arms open wide, she announced loudly, "Resurrection! The event that cut history in two. The Resurrection of Yeshua changed everything. *Everything.* Not only did he conquer death, he presented the world with a foretaste. In the resurrected Savior, the first believers saw a prototype of what bodies will look like in the new creation." The lucidus went to the table and sat down.

Aidan looked down at himself. "So we'll have bodies like his? Is that what you're saying?" Aliza nodded.

"So is that heaven, then?" said Evelyn. "But what about now?" She paused. "And don't you guys normally live there?"

"Excellent questions." Gamaliel smiled broadly. "Yes, to all of them! Heaven is a space beyond, where the Father is worshipped by the lucidi."

"A space . . . beyond?" said Aidan. "Not like this one, surely."

Gamaliel laughed. "I can see your mind is straying toward harps and clouds. Those images have a lot to answer for, I must say. Human language, limited as it is, cannot hope to capture the ineffable, especially since heaven isn't what most people expect. You see, it's *primarily* the effective will of the Father, made visible in the life of Yeshua." He looked straight at Aidan, fixing him with a steady gaze. "And it's made visible in your lives too. In the lives of all who follow in the Master's footsteps. It turns out, Aidan, that the answer to the problem of evil . . . is you."

He turned to Evelyn. "You, Evelyn, are the Father's answer to the problem of evil. Not you alone, of course, but you and many like you who live in communion with their Creator. It turns out the one force in the universe that we all hope and dream will triumph . . . really will. Love wins in the end. Of that you can be sure."

"Okay," said Aidan. "So evil is defeated, peace reigns, but . . . what actually happens to us?"

"Tierra-7," replied Gamaliel abruptly. "One day, you see, both heaven and earth will merge into one. The most beautiful picture given in *The Books* is that of Jerusalem, the holy city, being lowered to earth. It's an image of a joyful union. You long not for engagement, Evelyn, but for marriage, and rightly so, for your heart desires not anticipation but consummation."

Aliza rose and went to stand near the patio door; she looked out over the ocean. The morning light was playing on the whitecaps; a pod of pelicans passed by, diving down below the cliff edge. She turned and faced her guests. "It's never been about the answers, has it?" she said, her eyes searching theirs. They both looked away, saying nothing. "You just want the pain to stop." Her voice rippled out as a whisper.

There was stillness, her words settling gently on all their hearts. Evelyn looked up and stared into Aliza's eyes.

"How about we finish that story?" said the lucidus.

She took a deep breath and began.

The dragon, beast, and seer
On misty pyre cast down
No more to plague, the deathly mark
No more the heart of earth made dark.

For here at last appears
A lamb once slain, now crowned
Bejeweled cube, heav'n earth full blended
The curse of God on Man rescinded.

Behold the faithful few
The book of life there named
On earth reborn, renewed, restored
Blows Spirit, Sun by all adored.

Where grief made shrouds, now joy
Where death fed tombs, now life
Creation recast, resplendent, alight
New story begins, all things set aright.

By the end, Aliza's face was glowing intensely. "And to get it all started, there is a wedding. And a banquet with food and dancing and joy and life and laughter. It's going to be one heck of a party. Woo-hoo! Aidan, it's time for action. Let's get this show on the road!"

The lucidi rose from their seats and left the room. Aliza could be heard humming Bach's *Jesu, Joy of Man's Desiring* as she departed.

"First anthem I sang as a choirboy," said Aidan wistfully.

"Really?" said Evelyn. "I would *love* to hear you sing it again."

"Don't! Don't mock me."

"I'm not. I promise." She burst out laughing.

Seconds later, he was chasing her around the room.

Aidan's flight touched down in Los Angeles in the late afternoon. He was so preoccupied with his thoughts during the drive home that when Evelyn turned off toward Hermosa Beach, he didn't even notice. He looked out the window as she chatted about work, friends, and insurance companies. She decided to omit the most relevant detail, waiting for his reaction as they pulled up.

"I'm sorry," he said. "I'm miles away, still back on that plane. I am *so* sorry. What a dream. And . . . and where are we?"

"Rental. Finally. Ta-da!"

After dinner, they went for a stroll on the boardwalk, holding hands, Søren scampering on ahead. His stitches had been removed a couple of days before and he seemed like his old self. On their way back, they wandered down to the shoreline. Aidan took off his shoes and started kicking water at Evelyn, who returned in kind. Soaked and a little out of breath, they collapsed onto the sand; when they kissed, their lips tasted of salt. Aidan buried his head in Evelyn's hair, breathing in deeply. Unruly at the best of times, it fanned out on the sand, and though saturated, carried her unmistakable scent.

They sat up and took in the view. A couple of swimmers were beating their way through the waves near the pier, while barefoot joggers loped past, followed by a gaggle of teenagers who threw themselves into the shallows. Wisps of cirrus cloud, high in the sky, were flecked with pink by the dying rays of the sun. They seemed familiar to Aidan, though he couldn't explain why. No more could

Evelyn, whose soul carried the memory too deep for conscious recollection.

"Right!" said Aidan, as Søren began digging a hole nearby. He stood up, his heart racing with the anticipation. Getting down on one knee, he looked into Evelyn's eyes and was swamped once more by déjà vu. He had barely managed to pull the little box from his pocket, before it was clear he'd have to forego his speech yet again. Evelyn sprang forward, knocking him back onto the sand. Her salty kisses made any kind of speech impossible.

The joy in the Viatici House was unrestrained. Korazin ran around the Descartes Room, shrieking with delight. Aliza just sat with tears streaming down her face. As for Gamaliel, he lost all his inhibitions and proceeded to perform a jig on the patio. He couldn't stop smiling for days afterward.

~ 37 ~

GRACE

By the life we live through the grace of Christ, the character is formed.
~ Ellen G. White

May 3, 2005

Evelyn didn't want to wait. Nor did Aidan. Events and decisions came thick and fast. Apart from planning a wedding due to take place in just over a month, they were faced with the biggest decision of all: where to live. The idea of delving into an entirely new legal system in his mid-forties wasn't something Aidan relished, but he was prepared to take it on. However, after much debate and not a little disagreement, they decided the adjustment for Evelyn was likely to be far less severe. Medicine was the same the world over and they discovered that a well-qualified American surgeon should have no trouble finding work in England once the papers were sorted out.

The wedding date was set for June 11.

They booked a hotel down near the marina in Redondo Beach, called The Portofino. A gazebo on a patch of grass wasn't quite how either of them had envisioned the occasion, but time was short and the venue was available. Evelyn liked its proximity to the water and Aidan pretended not to know the price. By the time the day arrived, she had given up worrying about the details. She didn't really care that her bouquet was wilting a little, or that her makeup was seeking new forms of expression. None of it mattered because, from where she stood, the future looked dazzling.

As the pianist attempted a rendition of Einaudi's *I Giorni*, Evelyn began her slow walk down the aisle, Søren trotting on ahead, two shiny rings attached to his collar. His tail had never wagged quite so enthusiastically. Looking back toward her, Aidan stood waiting, a small smile of contentment on his face. He was flanked by Simon, Edward, and Sean, with Katie, Bridget, and Jasmine standing opposite.

Evelyn walked alone, but she didn't feel alone.

She felt as though the whole host of heaven was by her side.

And she was partly right.

The ceremony was officiated by a beaming African American pastor, whose enormous personality put everyone at ease. His wit made the Americans laugh, and his voice made the English feel as though they were listening to Morgan Freeman. He spoke joyfully of love and commitment, his smooth baritone voice deftly evoking both laughter and tears from a congregation held securely in his palm.

Yet the minister was eclipsed by the divine.

For it was a wedding dripping with grace.

During the reception, in particular, grace emerged as the preeminent guest among guests. The unmerited favor of the Creator toward his creatures poured through the room, trickling down the walls and flowing through the chairs. It ran up and over the tables, through the food, and into the hearts of all who ate and talked and laughed. It tasted good. It streamed down the curtains and swirled around the room, filling everyone up and carrying them along, as though conveyed by a relentless force that kindled in them not only joy, but goodness, kindness, and love. Grace buried itself inside each and every heart, and saturated the most trivial of conversations. In fact, such was its intensity, the bride and groom felt as though, whatever it was, it must be running through their veins. Every peal of laughter, every word spoken, and every show of affection was powered by it.

Everywhere they looked, they detected its presence. It didn't just bring healing to those with pained hearts, it achieved a great deal more. It gave them hope that the world was a place where love would ultimately triumph over loneliness and disappointment, over adversity and loss. Aidan and Evelyn were the focus of everyone's attention, yet it was copious quantities of grace, washing through every heart, that transformed the room, bringing light into the darkest of souls. For though the married couple's joy touched all who were present, it was no match for grace. This silent, extravagant guest permeating every word, smile, and kiss was the gift that truly satisfied the yearning of the human heart.

Down the table, they could hear Katie telling jokes to Harry, who tipped his head back and howled with laughter. He poured himself another glass of wine, filling up Katie's without asking her. Next to them was Tommy who was enjoying the shrimp, leaving a large pile of discarded shells on the side of his plate. Further down, Beth looked radiant in a light blue off-the-shoulder dress that she wore with confidence and panache. She sat with her hand on Simon's, but her back was to him; she was deep in conversation with Bridget on the other side, who kept wiping her eyes. Simon himself spent most of his time listening to a cousin of Bridget's tell whoppers about his surfing antics. He didn't believe the half of it but, ever the diplomat, he kept plying the Californian with questions about half-pipes and cutbacks.

Evelyn looked across the room at Reggie. He was sitting with the pastor, Dorrice, and his wife, Daloris. The rest of their table was so different, she felt like she was inside someone else's bizarre dream. How had she managed to manufacture a conversation involving three African Americans and an English barrister in his early seventies? Mr. Blenkinsopp stood up to mime a bowling action used in the game of cricket, the Americans watching with bemusement. When Reggie stood up to have a go, the elderly barrister grabbed his elbow and started lecturing him on the need to keep his arm straight. Dorrice and Daloris couldn't hold out. They were soon shaking their heads and wiping tears from their eyes.

Over in the corner, Aidan's father was holding forth on the British criminal justice system to Patrick, Evelyn's favorite paramedic from work. It looked like a very one-sided conversation. Aidan was grateful to Patrick for his patience, hoping the discussion wouldn't stray into politics. His father tended to call Americans "Yanks" and had already complained about the size of Los Angeles and its notorious gridlock. It was little wonder he was booked on the first available flight home following the reception.

"Gooood evening!" The DJ, attired in a sequined jacket and adorned with a bouffant hairstyle, stepped forward with the microphone. At his request, the bride and groom rose to loud applause, and made their way to the center of the dance floor. Everyone watched as they shuffled about in circles, Aidan doing his best not to step on Evelyn's dress.

They separated and Aidan grabbed the mike. "Thank you, everyone, for coming," he said. "But no, we won't be doing the salsa. Not even for your amusement, Simon. Be quiet. As you can tell, dance is not my calling, but we're honored tonight to be in the presence of a couple who can not only dance, but also make it look good." He signaled to his coworkers.

The look on Gordon's face was nothing short of priceless. He appeared to take the invitation with great seriousness, while Fiona merely reddened with embarrassment. However, once they'd started, they put on a show worthy of *Dancing with the Stars* in the final dance-off. Gordon's tango gave the distinct impression that he was aiming for a score of forty from an actual panel of judges, such was the vigor and sincerity of his performance. By contrast, Fiona could only take so much attention. To her partner's clear disappointment, she broke away and beckoned everyone to join them, until the usual wedding dance floor scrum began to take shape.

Both Aidan and Evelyn made the rounds, dancing with no less than five different people each. Afterward, they collapsed into their seats, rather out of breath, and drained their glasses. Jasmine walked past with her new beau, Carter. They watched them go up to Tommy and drag him onto the dance floor. To their surprise, Aidan's clerk had moves; he began doing an Elvis impersonation, with several guests dancing round him in a large circle. Evelyn's eyes wandered over the dance floor and scanned the rest of the tables.

That's when she spotted him. He must have arrived late.

Near the door sat Miloš.

He wasn't alone. Katie was chatting with him, oblivious of his past, which was certainly for the best. Evelyn had agonized long and hard over inviting him. She wanted to be sure she wasn't doing it out of pity. It seemed such a small thing to invite a person to a wedding, yet somehow as she sat watching him nod and listen to her sister, it felt like the conversation between the two of them was the most important one taking place in the room. It felt as though grace, if it meant anything at all, had to include compassion for people whose actions had caused great harm.

She wasn't naïve. She knew perfectly well it was not her place to offer him forgiveness, that only his Creator could give him absolution, whatever he might have done. She knew he didn't deserve his seat, or the food, or the kindness of her sister. He probably deserved to be in prison or worse. But there he was, chatting to a beautiful woman who was offering him friendship, when all he deserved was punishment.

It made no sense to Evelyn. But then the good news wasn't like a math problem. It was vast and unfathomable, held together by a being who preferred to reveal his heart than explain his motives. Grace and its cousin, love, were far too mysterious to submit to human calculation. If she'd learned one thing in the past few months, it was the simple truth that in receiving grace, she was called on to extend it to others, even when doing so might seem a step too far to some. This wasn't just a new life she'd begun, but a new way of living, and she wanted to start on the right foot.

"You okay, honey?" Aidan's words jogged her from her thoughts.

"Yup. I'm, er . . . I'm good, thanks."

Aidan left the ballroom and went to the reception to ask about a taxi for his father. The receptionist looked up, recognizing him as the groom. "Congratulations, sir," she said, smiling. He was about to thank her, when she continued, "Someone left you a gift." She handed over a small rectangular box in bright red wrapping. Aidan opened it and stared down at the contents nestled in scarlet velvet.

At first, he thought he was looking at a symbol he saw almost every day: Lady Justice holding scales in one hand and a sword in the other. However, as he peered more closely, he noticed she wasn't holding a sword at all. Instead, she held a pole encircled by serpents, with wings fanning out at the top—the caduceus. The two symbols of justice and medicine, fashioned in solid gold. The piece of jewelry was attached to a chain. It had a short rigid section with the appearance of a ladder.

Aidan pulled out a note. There was no name, just a couple of questions.

How's that car we fixed for you? Morris Minor, wasn't it?

He smiled.

The honeymoon was short, a week down in Mexico lolling on a beach, with a couple of trips to see some pyramids. Aidan wished they could have gone traveling, but time was short. Evelyn was needed back at work and the goal of moving to the UK threw up mountains of paperwork. It turned out she might need additional training before applying for jobs in the National Health Service.

Aidan left for the UK toward the end of June, both to work and to arrange for Evelyn's arrival. They talked almost every night on the phone, but it was hard. They missed each other, ached for each other during the evenings, and the spoken word was no substitute for the physical touch they craved.

The lucidi invited them to the Espacio frequently, not to discuss deep questions, but so they could be together. They went mountain biking and sailing, and sat for hours in the Living Room, reading and talking. On various occasions, they woke up together in the same bed and made love. Aidan resisted at first, a little unnerved to be using a borrowed body for such purposes. Evelyn just laughed. She didn't care in the slightest.

On a dull morning early in July, Aidan was returning to chambers from a meeting, but decided to stop off in the West End to do some shopping. He strolled down Oxford Street, pausing to admire the shoe display in Russell & Bromley, and was about to go in when his phone buzzed in his pocket. Simon wanted to meet up for coffee. "I'm at King's Cross, Dad. I'm off to Cambridge, but I've got some news. Wanted to tell you in person."

"Can't you just tell me over the phone?"

"No, Dad. It has to be done face-to-face. I want to see your reaction."

He looked at his watch and told him he'd meet him in an hour.

Setting off, Aidan spotted a Betfred down a side street, and decided to pop in. But as he stood there looking at the horse races on the TV screens, he felt something break inside him. The urge to place a bet, though still there, was waning; the grip on his heart and mind appeared to be loosening. As he walked out without placing a bet, he cherished the hope that a new life might actually be possible. He felt a lift in his spirit. Freedom was within his grasp.

At Marble Arch, he found a bus stop. He preferred the bus to the Tube if he had time. It was generally slower, but he preferred it to jam-packed carriages, body odor, and tight spaces underground. He hopped on the number 30, and found a seat on the upper deck at the back.

Pulling out his paper, he started reading an article on London's successful bid to host the 2012 Olympic Games. He glanced across the aisle and spotted a shameless headline on the back of a tabloid. It read *Eiffailed*, a reference to France's losing bid, which made him smile. The woman holding the paper spotted his reaction and, within seconds, they were chatting. It turned out she was a primary school teacher. Another woman entered the conversation, a nurse. Both women were delightful, nattering away about their lives and quizzing him on his circumstances.

When they found out about his recent marriage, they offered their congratulations with great enthusiasm. Their laughter filled the back of the bus and, unbeknownst to them, settled on the hearts of all who sat nearby. Though their exchange was short-lived, it was rich and deep, seasoned with kindness and affection.

The teacher got off at the next stop. Aidan smiled at her just as his phone lit up. It was his father calling for the second time in as many days—an unusual occurrence. He was most complimentary about Evelyn. The afterglow from the wedding had left a residue of goodwill in his soul and Aidan found himself the beneficiary of his father's good mood. Normally Aidan would have found an excuse to hang up, but instead he found himself softening toward his father. As he listened, he slowly became aware of a completely new sensation. Pity. It filled his heart and flooded his soul and, rather than fight it, he embraced it.

A man sat down a couple of seats ahead carrying a backpack that he placed under his seat. Aidan paid no attention to him. The nurse answered her phone, her expression becoming serious as she listened. She looked up. "Some kind of disturbance at King's Cross," she said. "That was my brother. Apparently loads of people are coming out of the Tube there."

The bus left Euston station and was met by police who directed it along Upper Woburn Place. Aidan quickly realized they were being diverted and decided to get off at the next stop and walk. He said his farewells and walked down the aisle toward the stairs.

The bus arrived in Tavistock Square. At 9:47 a.m. on July 7, 2005, the man with the backpack detonated a bomb, killing himself and thirteen other people. Aidan was thrown back by the blast.

When his head struck a seat, he lost consciousness.

~ 38 ~

HOLDING ON

Suffering produces perseverance; perseverance, character; and character, hope.
~ Romans 5:3b–4

July 7, 2005

The bedsheets were crisp and clean. Aidan grabbed them, awaking in a mild state of shock, initially unable to process what was happening. He remembered a loud explosion and extreme pain.

Then nothing.

He was surprisingly calm as he sat up and swung his legs over the side of the bed. The thought that he might be dead should have induced panic, certainly fear, but instead, the calmness in the house settled his nerves. He could hear music playing downstairs. Trying to connect the serenity of his present location with the horror of the bomb blast was too difficult. The disconnect was too great.

His thoughts turned to Evelyn. She'd be worried sick.

He walked over to the window and looked out toward the cliffs in the distance. Opening the window, he smelled salt in the air. A light breeze rustled the hedges bordering the garden below. The sun was behind the house, casting a shadow over the grounds. He got dressed and made his way downstairs.

In the Living Room, he found Korazin reading a book by the fire. Taking a deep breath and trembling slightly, Aidan went and sat down in an armchair. "You're in the hospital," said Korazin, sitting forward and putting his book down. He exuded warmth and concern. "In the Royal London, to be exact. In the care of a physician who knows what he's doing."

"What happened to me?"

The lucidus explained the details of the bus bombing and went on to describe the attacks in some detail. Fifty-two people, along with four terrorists, died after four bombs—three on the London Underground and one on the bus—were detonated on the morning of July 7. Thirteen were killed on the bus alone.

"Will I, er . . . will I regain consciousness?"

"Too early to say."

Aidan was struggling to take it all in. His fear was oddly distant, which surprised him. The joy of the previous month made things easier, not harder. His mind wandered over the hour before the bombing. He recalled the pleasure of talking to the women on the bus, how happy he'd felt sharing his life with strangers. He remembered speaking with his father on the phone.

Korazin said, "I believe you're stirring, Aidan. It's time to rejoin your family."

He handed him a pill and a glass of water.

Aidan felt himself rise from the depths of an ocean, bubbling up to the surface. Light rippled above; he tried to swim upwards but soon felt a current tugging him down. Falling back, he receded into the darkness, and began to lose all feeling. All he could see was dappled light high above, which was fast fading to black. With the loss of light went the loss of hope. He couldn't breathe. At the moment of surrender, his energy all but spent, a powerful arm propelled him up. He burst through the darkness into the day.

Starched hospital sheets caressed his arms and legs; they were cool against his body. He took several long breaths. His right arm felt heavy as he lifted it up and touched his face. Its warmth was comforting. In time, light began to filter in past his fluttering eyelids. He blinked repeatedly as he adjusted to the increasing light stimulus.

He turned his head to the side.

His wife was seated in a chair, rubbing her eyes. After rushing over from LA, she had spent the past hour recovering from jet lag.

"How long have I been out?" He smiled weakly at her.

She glanced at her watch. "Eighteen hours." She leaned forward and kissed him, interrupted by a white-coated man, who introduced himself as Dr. Bristow. He promptly outlined Aidan's condition and the risks associated with surgery. On discovering that Evelyn was a surgeon, their conversation became technical, but the reality was sobering. Aidan had a splenic rupture and they wanted to manage it conservatively. "If the bleeding increases, we'll need to operate; but for now, we'll keep an eye on the vital signs. The usual."

The doctor left.

Evelyn sat down next to the bed and looked at her husband with a surgeon's eye. He was in a critical condition, and though he'd recovered consciousness, it was misleading to take this as a sign that he was improving. She knew perfectly well that, with bomb blasts, the majority of the damage was internal, hidden from the naked eye.

Aidan's eyelids were drooping.

He soon fell asleep.

When he awoke several hours later, the first thing Aidan saw was his grandfather. The elderly man was reading a newspaper in the corner of the ward.

"Your wife went to find the doctor," said Sidney, folding up the paper and sliding it under his chair. Aidan tried to sit up.

"Now, now, you just lie back, my boy." It took some effort but the old man managed to drag his chair toward the bed. "Looking at you there, I must say I'm reminded of the war. Did I ever tell you about the drop?" Sidney embarked on the most detailed description of his war years Aidan had ever heard. In the past, he'd always clammed up when questioned, but now he held forth as though he were planning the D-Day landings. Aidan knew he had taken part in the events of June 6, 1944, but until now, he'd never heard the details. After a while, he began to float on the ebb and flow of his grandfather's soothing tones. As he listened, he was filled with regret. For things not done. For visits not paid. For care not expressed. He desperately wanted to apologize and make things right, but he found himself at the mercy of the medicine he'd taken earlier. His grandfather's voice became muffled, as though the old man were retreating into another room.

He closed his eyes.

Sidney leaned forward and held his grandson's hand. "We kept fighting, my boy. Now you do the same," he whispered. "It's bad enough for a son to lose a father. But for a father to lose a son . . . well, that's just not right."

Aidan didn't hear; he was already asleep.

~ 39 ~

SALVATION

And how can man die better than facing fearful odds, for the ashes of his fathers, and the temples of his gods?
~ Thomas Babington Macaulay

July 9, 2005

"But why now?" demanded Evelyn, her face flushing.

"I believe we've been over this, my dear," said Gamaliel. "This is primarily for Aidan's benefit."

"Well, I still don't get why we have to do this now. He's fighting for his life down there!"

"More than you know." The lucidus spoke softly to soothe her.

Aidan appeared suddenly in the doorway. He felt fantastic in his body. After hours of discomfort, the free movement of walking down a flight of stairs made his heart surge with optimism. He knew it didn't make any sense, but the feeling was inescapable. He felt hopeful, even though he knew his own body was struggling for survival in a London hospital bed. Evelyn ran to him and threw her arms around his neck, struggling to maintain her composure.

The lucidi left the room to allow them a few moments of intimacy. As soon as they'd gone, she vented her frustration. "I don't know what they're thinking. They're planning one of those trips again. I—"

"Hey, stop, stop." He took hold of her shoulders. "They've never done anything to hurt us, have they? I think they know what they're doing. They always have." He pulled her close.

When the lucidi returned later, they brought with them heavy overcoats and life jackets. "We have something to show you," said Gamaliel. "Please put these on."

Evelyn glowered at the lucidi as she pulled on her coat.

Aidan laced a safety cord round his waist. He wanted to know more about his prospects, but knew it was pointless asking. They'd warned him against enquiring about the future. "So what's with the life jackets? The Pacific Ocean again, to see what I missed?"

"North Atlantic," said Korazin, handing them each a glass of water.

The transition assaulted their bodies. From the warmth of the Viatici House, they were pitched into a rowing boat in sub-zero temperatures. The water was flat, the air freezing. Aidan untangled himself from some ropes at the bottom of the boat, and hurried to Evelyn's aid. They were glad of the warm coats they wore, and upon discovering some gloves in their pockets, they put them on and sat down.

The lucidi had already started rowing by the time they found their seats. They were about half a mile from the *Titanic*, the ship's lights blazing out over the murky surface of the ocean. Over the lap of the waves created by the lucidi as they pulled on the oars, they tuned in to the sounds echoing across the water. A hubbub of voices punctuated by frequent shouting and screaming drifted toward them. Evelyn caught Aidan's attention. "Can you hear that?"

The unmistakable sound of chamber music was clearly distinguishable, becoming louder as they drew closer.

Nearer, my God, to Thee, nearer to Thee!
E'en though it be a cross that raiseth me;
Still all my song shall be nearer, my God, to Thee,
Nearer, my God, to Thee, nearer to Thee!

The ensemble played the tune again and the lucidi began to sing, their voices plaintive and mournful, weighed down with melancholy so that the humans could barely listen without weeping.

Aidan glanced behind him and noticed a dim glow on the horizon. He sheltered his eyes, peering into the distance.

"*The Californian*, Aidan," said Korazin, pulling rhythmically on his oars. "Its crew saw white rockets but when they reported this to Captain Lord, he thought they might be 'company rockets,' used by ships to identify themselves to liners of the same company. *The*

Californian used Morse lamps to try and contact the *Titanic*, but without success. So Stanley Lord, captain of a ship no more than five miles away, failed to investigate. Many considered him negligent; he certainly lived in ignominy for the rest of his life, shunned by most of society. As did Bruce Ismay, the chairman of the White Star Line, who managed to find himself a seat on a lifeboat among the women and children. Come on, take these oars."

Aidan swapped seats with the lucidus and struggled to keep up with Gamaliel, whose gray hair belied his considerable strength. Evelyn also took her turn, and within about half an hour, they were approaching the vast mass of the *Titanic*. The sight before them was heartrending, intensified by the knowledge that they could do nothing to save those drowning not more than a few yards away.

As they watched, two men pushed what looked like a large piece of furniture into the water and jumped on. "Aidan, that's your great-grandfather, Henry," said Gamaliel, pointing. "He's the one in the dark overcoat. The man next to him is John Ware, a carpenter who helped him build a raft from two wardrobes."

On the deck of the liner, a young man barged his way through the crowd, ran full tilt, and hurled himself into the air. He landed with a thud on the wardrobes. There was a glint of metal, which they all saw clearly. A crowd cheered and shouted insults, bloodlust rising in them as though they were betting on dogfights in a London cellar. Henry grabbed the man's wrist to defend himself and they fell, wrestling, on the raft's slippery surface. A knife went clattering away into the darkness. The fight didn't last long. Henry was far too strong. He twisted the man's arms behind his back and held him down with a knee on his back.

"'E knifed me!" shouted the youth, his face pressed against the wardrobe. "'E's a common criminal!"

Henry released him; the lad immediately dived into the icy water and swam back to the ship. He clambered on board and ran back up the deck, passing a well-dressed gentleman, who was writing feverishly in a notepad. Henry, his chest heaving, stood up and announced to the crowd, "The next man who tries that, well, he'd better watch out!"

Evelyn couldn't tear her eyes off the action.

Nor could Aidan. "So he acted in self-defense."

Korazin nodded. "But the papers never let the truth get in the way of a good story, do they?"

Henry and his companion began to drive two pieces of wood into the water, using them as paddles. The rowing boat followed close behind, but after a minute or so, its occupants all stopped to look back. The ship hadn't even sunk yet, but already people were dying. Some had ended up in the water after a fight. Others had fallen in, and were now trying to reach half-empty lifeboats. Still others were on their knees weeping and wailing, while a few with heads bowed, mouthed silent prayers. They watched the last lifeboat being lowered into the water. An officer, still wearing his standard-issue cap and greatcoat, pointed a gun at a man trying to climb in, and shot him.

He announced in a loud voice, "Gentlemen, each one for himself. Goodbye." He placed the barrel against his temple and pulled the trigger. They all flinched, including the lucidi.

The mezcla shifted.

When the *Titanic* was at roughly a sixty-degree angle, the weight of the stern became too much. With a terrible growling, wrenching sound, the ship shuddered and cracked, the back end collapsing into the water, crushing the unfortunates floating beneath. Screaming filled the air. The bow had sunk below the surface and was now pulling the entire ship down. People were falling down the deck like rag dolls, tumbling headlong into each other and bouncing off every hard object on their way down. Many had died by the time they hit the ocean. Hundreds were in the water by this time, desperately calling out for lost relatives.

The stern, having risen high into the sky, stopped motionless for several minutes, before the end came. Creaking, and spitting steam and water, the great ship slid down almost languidly, its enormous hull disappearing into the depths. The largest vessel of its era vanished from sight, sucking down those who had the misfortune to be caught in the eddies and swirling water it left behind. Everywhere they looked, people were screaming and moaning, thrashing around in their search for loved ones.

The mezcla shifted.

They instantly became aware how quiet it was. The cries for help had stopped completely. Floating nearby were people with frost forming on their hair and beards. They were already dead. Looking across at the raft, they could see small waves lapping at its sides. There were now three men on it, soaking wet. None of them stirred.

"What happened?" asked Evelyn. "Hold on, who's the other man?"

Gamaliel pulled in his oars. "That, Evelyn, is your great-grandfather, Fearghas, rescued just now by Henry." Aidan gripped the side of the boat; he sat gawping at the raft with its bedraggled cargo, barely able to register what he'd just heard. Evelyn stared at the lucidus, who was gazing across at the men who lay prone on the wardrobes, unmoving.

"My . . . my great-grandfather?" she said. "You're not serious." She looked across at her distant relative, who was now trying to raise himself onto his elbows. They could see Henry stirring. He rolled over and reached into his pocket, pulling out two items. There was a glint from a gold chain and a thunk as something solid landed on the hard, wooden raft.

When Henry picked it up, Evelyn gave a small gasp. She watched him hand a brass whistle to the Irishman, straining to hear their conversation. The men were clearly speaking, but from the rowing boat, all they could hear was a low hubbub of voices.

"Why didn't you tell us before?" said Evelyn.

Gamaliel's eyes glistened.

They all stared at the raft bobbing up and down on the light swell. The men had stopped talking. Silence enveloped the area, interrupted only by faint weeping and muted shouts from the lifeboats. Aidan found it almost unbearable to see his great-grandfather. He wished Aunt Grace could have been there to see him vindicated.

"He's dying of exposure, isn't he?"

Neither lucidus replied. Korazin placed his hand on Aidan's shoulder and squeezed. As they all sat quietly, trickles of blood seeped from the eyes of the lucidi. Neither human noticed. Their attention was fully focused on their relatives lying, immobile, on a couple of wardrobes. Gazing across at them, their thoughts were running wild through a landscape of heartbreak and implications.

Aidan's settled on his grandpa, trudging toward a big car, dragging an iron bird along the ground. The little boy had needed his father—as do all boys. Moreover, to observe the death of his great-grandfather at such close quarters was especially painful. The man's absence had inflicted a wound passed on to each succeeding generation. Aidan felt it still, even as he stared, mesmerized, at the heroic Henry, lying prone upon the raft.

"He was a good man," he said quietly.

Korazin handed round some bottles of water.

Together, they all drank.

On arrival, they found themselves sitting on a wooden bench opposite a railway line. The sun was streaming through the beech trees in front of them, falling in shards of light across the tracks. The air was damp, the dew still fresh on the ground. On the waiting room walls hung advertisements for Rowntree's chocolates, Mackintosh's toffee, and Pears soap. Down the platform, a man dressed in a tweed suit was sitting, fiddling with a button on his collar. Beside him sat a small boy, tugging on his sleeve. A few other passengers were scattered along the platform, occasionally glancing at their watches.

"Come," said Korazin.

They walked over and sat nearby. Although it had all taken place long ago, they initially felt slightly uncomfortable in the role of voyeur. Curiosity, however, quickly got the better of them. Aidan and Evelyn both moved closer, eager to hear every word.

Henry rose to his feet and squatted down in front of his son. Sidney had just turned five; he wore gray flannel shorts, a mud-stained striped green shirt and a flat cap. His father took out his handkerchief and wiped some crumbs from the corner of his son's mouth.

"You look after yer mam, you hear?" The little boy sniffled, fighting back the tears.

A steam train pulled into the station, clanking and whistling for all it was worth. A tall woman, dressed in an austere dark blue dress with a cream shawl draped over her shoulders, came round from behind the waiting room. She gave her husband a perfunctory peck on the cheek. The distance between Henry and his wife was palpable. He crouched down and pulled his son close.

The boy's voice piped up. "I want to go with you, Daddy. I want to go on the big ship." He started to cry.

"There, there," said his father, pulling out his hankie. "Come now. A few days, and Bob's your uncle, I'll be home again. Maybe then we can both take a ride on the unsinkable ship." Sidney tried to smile through his tears, while his dad patted his cheeks with the handkerchief. Henry ruffled his son's hair, picked up his suitcase, and climbed aboard the train.

He did not look back.

As the train shrank from view, they looked across the tracks at the opposite platform. Inside a small waiting room, they caught sight of a tall, striking woman in a large, wide-brimmed hat. It partially hid her face. She stood staring, unseeing, into the distance. Her petticoats ballooning around her, she left the waiting room and sauntered onto the platform. She gazed down the tracks toward the puffs of white smoke that were billowing vigorously, yet diminishing with each passing moment.

Evelyn looked across at the lucidi, who were clearly entranced by the woman's every move. "Oh my gosh, I know her."

"So you should," said Gamaliel softly. "Her portrait is sitting on your mantel even now."

"Aunt Grace's mother?" said Aidan. "Mildred?"

The tall lucidus didn't reply. He was lost in thought. Silence shrouded the group briefly, as the tall woman turned and swept across the platform toward the exit. Her skirts flowed down the wooden stairs like water through shallow rapids. A piece of fabric caught on a nail, so she turned to unhook it. Looking up, she stared right through the assembled company on the far side.

Her face shimmered in the morning light.

She turned and left.

"Better to have loved and lost," began Gamaliel.

"Than never to have loved at all." Korazin lowered his gaze.

Aidan looked across at the lucidi, whose sadness seemed to

permeate the very air around them.

Gamaliel sighed and began to speak. "Henry was a good man, Aidan." He paused. "But choices have consequences. As you both observed just now, Edna was a wretchedly unhappy woman. Miserable for most of her life. As a young woman, she resented her younger sister, Mildred, whose beauty stole the limelight whenever there was some going. It seemed the gods had smiled on Mildred, but on Edna they had smirked and looked away."

"Until the day she met Henry." Korazin took up the story, turning to address Aidan. "Do you know much about your great-grandfather?"

"Very little, I'm afraid."

"Well, your Aunt Grace may have mentioned that her uncle was the son of a local landowner and, given the mores of the time, rather above Edna's and Mildred's social position. At a local dance, however, Edna fell in love with the dashing curate from Chudleigh, a few miles down the road. Within a week, Henry had asked her to various social events in his village—a dance, a fete, and a month later, a visit to the theater.

"Mildred was sixteen when Edna began stepping out with Henry, yet she herself didn't set eyes on him for many months. The only knowledge she gained of him came from her sister's excited lips. The first time they met was the day when Henry came to the house to ask for Edna's hand in marriage. Mildred, I'm afraid, blushed whenever he looked at her, which was too frequently for a man intent on marrying her sister. Henry was a good man, but he was also confused."

Gamaliel stood up. "Perhaps you think the story should have taken a different turn right there. Henry should have, could have, slowed things down with Edna, but it was not to be. Edna's parents harbored expectations, and Henry's parents were keen on the match. So, Aidan, the marriage of your great-grandfather to Edna took place on April 2, 1906. Mildred wrote in her diary, many years later, that she was lost from the moment she set eyes on her sister's fiancé." He hesitated. "We lucidi have never experienced romantic love, but we see its effects everywhere. It appears to be a stallion in full flight—exhilarating, immensely powerful, yet utterly out of control."

Korazin continued the story. "When the newlyweds returned from honeymoon, they came to live in the vicarage in Bovey Tracey, just round the corner from Mildred's home. Henry was appointed as the new vicar in the local parish church. On Sunday mornings, Mildred used to sit in the front pew staring up at the man in the fine black cassock, her thoughts miles away from the Bible. She was eighteen and full of life—an unexploded bomb seated dangerously close to the couple entering their first year of holy matrimony. Edna was twenty-two, radiant, and oblivious, her thoughts also untroubled by the Bible. However, in her case, she spent the first few weeks of married life wondering whether they might be able to afford a new Singer sewing machine.

"Back then, social norms required church attendance, so Henry and Mildred's paths began to cross regularly. There were coy looks, along with surreptitious physical contact at social occasions, which did nothing but stoke the fires. So Mildred took action. She married a young man from the town—Neville. They had Grace in 1911. Neville, I'm afraid, was killed at the Battle of the Somme five years later, leaving Mildred both a single mother *and* a widow who never remarried. She died in 1958, the saddest day of your Aunt Grace's life.

"Henry's story you know better. And now you have seen first-hand how he died. He understood that his love for Mildred would destroy them both. So he left for America to seek a new life, with the intention that Edna would join him later." He paused.

"Did they ever—?" asked Evelyn, unable to finish the question.

"Not even a kiss, my dear."

Aidan got up and walked down onto the railway. About a mile away, the tracks disappeared into a tunnel. He stared down the line bracketed by rickety billboards. He'd often looked at the sepia photographs of his great-grandfather, wondering about his innocence. Now he wondered how much Aunt Grace had known, growing up. A few months ago, she'd defended Henry vigorously, and she'd always been fiercely protective of her mother. No doubt the Henry she'd heard described at home was upright and noble. No story in the paper had been able to change that. But more importantly, she had remained unerringly firm in her belief that one day all things would be resolved. Somehow.

Aidan was in no doubt. His aunt was a woman of great faith.

Korazin came and handed him a bottle of water.

He felt no need to ask the lucidus where they were going.

He trusted him.

~ 40 ~

THE GAP

Every sin is an attempt to fly from emptiness.
~ Simone Weil

July 9, 2005

After one sip, they were sitting on a bench overlooking the front lawn at Marston Hall. Far off in the distance, a game of football was taking place. A referee's whistle could be heard, carried on the wind.

"I'm sure this isn't an easy place to visit," said Korazin.

Aidan stared at the ground. He was trembling.

Why had the lucidus insisted on bringing him here?

Rather than ruminating on Carpenter-Isaacs and inedible school meals, his mind searched for comfort.

He found himself entering a twelfth-century church near Walkhampton, the scene of some of his most precious memories. They were all wrapped up in the musty smell of a hilltop church, with candlelit interior and a congregation packed in like proverbial sardines. His long, red cassock and starched, white surplice came instantly to mind. The carol concert of '71 was about to begin. He remembered how his eyes darted constantly over the many hat-covered heads, seeking his parents. To no avail. They were nowhere in sight.

The lights overhead went out.

As the choir processed down the nave, he continued to scan the congregation. The hats, a resplendent array of color, fanned out across the church, making it impossible to see the faces beneath. He was still squinting during the headmaster's welcome speech, when suddenly the whole choir rose to its feet. He grabbed his folder and looked over to his right. Mr. Fielding the choirmaster, his robes flowing behind him like Gandalf, floated across the ancient flagstones. He reached the front and beamed at them, his eyes shining with excitement. Rehearsals were over. This was the moment. The organ gave the introduction.

Joy began.

They sang six anthems in all, most traditional, but with a couple of African American spirituals thrown in, much to the chagrin of the more starched and staid parents. Aidan loved them all. Each time they finished one, a touch of sadness settled on him. All those hours of practice for one burst of exhilaration, like a firework exploding in the night sky before dying away into dust.

As they recessed down the aisle, Aidan looked from side to side, wondering where on earth his parents could be. The church disgorged its contents into the cemetery, where parents began frantically seeking their offspring. Mothers found their sons and enveloped them in lung-sapping embraces, planting lipstick all over their cheeks. The seniors reddened at being called "darling" and "sweetie"; the younger ones simply clung on for dear life, soaking up the maternal tenderness they'd missed. But there was no time to chat. Teachers barked out orders, organizing the boys into two long lines for the descent into the village.

Once down the hill, the PE teacher, Mr. Stebbings, approached Aidan. "Give you a lift, son? Your parents are probably avoiding the crush." On arrival back at the school, a steady stream of wooden chests was wending its way out to the cars. Aidan sat on the stairs, watching. His parents were never late; his dad was a stickler for punctuality. A sinking feeling started to grip his insides.

As Mr. Cutteridge approached, Aidan felt like he was falling. Something was wrong. The tall, hook-nosed headmaster normally fixed boys with an intense gaze that caused his pupils to wilt, but not this time. As he came up, he seemed completely different, almost embarrassed. The man refused to make eye contact.

"Manning, we received this letter from your parents this morning. They notified the school last week." Aidan took the letter, struggling to hold back the tears. The writing was his mother's.

The Gap

Dear Aidan,
Things have come up. We can't collect you today. You'll stay at the school until Christmas Eve. Mr. Cutteridge tells us the matrons will look after you.
Don't break anything.

Mum
P.S. Oma died last week.

He read the letter but couldn't take it in. He cast his eyes down it again, his head beginning to throb. A matron came up and took him by the arm. "Come on," she said. "Time for a nice hot bath. The TV's on down in the staff room. You can watch whatever you want."

Aidan kept reading the letter as he walked toward the stairs. *Things have come up.* What things? He thought if he carried on reading, its meaning would become clear. Whatever *Things* had come up, they were bigger and more important than him. That much was clear. Well, his father certainly dealt with *Important Things*. That must be why he closed the door to his study in the evenings. He knew *Things* could interrupt almost anything. Things like a burst water main or meetings. There were always a lot of meetings to attend, apparently.

Mother had *Things* too. Bridge tournaments. He knew his mother was one of the country's leading bridge players. Being a Leading Bridge Player was an Important Thing. Maybe she had a tournament that had taken her away from home. And his dad had probably travelled up north again. His work took him there sometimes. Perhaps that was it. But why couldn't he stay with Oma, his beloved grandma?

Because she was dead.

No, that must be a mistake. He'd seen her just a few weeks ago. Mum must have written that by mistake. She was often distracted. Especially when she was on the phone. She probably scribbled that at the bottom while she was talking to Penelope from the Association. Yes, that was it. Or maybe the cat had died. Or the goldfish.

He ran up the stairs, jumped onto his bed and pulled out a game with tiny racing cars stuttering around a green plastic box. It involved banging a button as fast as possible. Aidan hit the button repeatedly. It got stuck, so he banged it again. When it stopped working, he threw it at the door and shoved his head under the pillow. He pulled his legs up and curled into a ball. His fingers picked at a scab on his knee. He worked it loose, rubbing blood up and down his leg.

After making swirls on the white sheets, he picked up a badge from his bedside table and jabbed the pin into the wound. Pain shot up his leg. He kept digging the pin into his knee, pulling on the flesh until he'd created a small hole. Pushing in his finger, he pressed hard; blood began to seep out and drip down onto the sheets. He kept pressing until the pain was too much.

Exhaustion sent him off to sleep.

Rain was bouncing off the roof of Marston Hall. The tall, drab building blended in with the dark clouds barreling along behind it. Korazin handed Aidan an umbrella that he opened, tilting it against the southwesterly blowing in off the moor. The lucidus turned and led him out across the front lawn toward the sports fields.

Aidan wasn't surprised at the sight that greeted them once they arrived at the football pitch. He almost felt it coming. His sporting exploits were recorded on various wooden boards running up the main stairs of the school. He was a big fish in a small pond at Marston Hall, excelling at almost every sport.

Along the touchlines stood a thin line of bedraggled parents, hunched against the weather. When the ball approached the opposition goal, the cheers rose in volume, each parent unconsciously hoping their support might magically induce sufficient skill in the team to conjure up a goal. Aidan ignored them; he strained his neck, desperately searching for himself. When the Marston Hall number 10 ran past, he broke into a smile. The boy weaved past a couple of players and passed to a diminutive teammate with blond hair, who immediately lost the ball.

"Piers was useless at football." He spoke without taking his eyes off the action. They watched the game to the end. Marston Hall lost 6-1. The number 10 scored the only goal, which he celebrated with a fist pump and a huge grin on his face. Aidan wanted to run out and congratulate himself. After the final whistle, the captains led three cheers, and traipsed off with their teams toward the school.

He was watching himself walk off, when he spotted his father. The man was standing on his own, without an umbrella, his hair completely soaked; he was blinking water out of his eyes. Aidan watched the number 10 walk past him without even the faintest sign of acknowledgment. The look that flashed across his father's face was there for less than a second, yet it pierced his heart. He had seen a similar look on the bleeding man in the courtyard.

"Again!" he demanded, holding up his hand.

"Sorry?" said Korazin.

He faced the lucidus. "I want to see that again. Please. Please let me see that again."

Korazin snapped his fingers and the mezcla shifted back two minutes. Aidan approached his father to get a closer look. He watched the twelve-year-old schoolboy walk across the pitch toward his father. Yet instead of waving to him, he had kicked a piece of mud along the ground, eyes down. Yes, there it was. The boy looked down to the side just as he was passing. Aidan watched the expression on his father's face again and gasped. "I did that many times, didn't I?" he whispered.

"It's not—"

"I know," he interrupted. "It wasn't my fault. I was just a boy." He stood trembling, hardly bearing to watch his father, who wandered away, head bowed. "The shame of it," he whispered. "Please make it go away."

Korazin placed his hand on Aidan's shoulder. The power of the lucidus flooded through him, soothing his soul and easing the pain inside. A couple of teachers started taking the nets down from the goals. The rain had stopped and the sun was setting just above the horizon, bathing the moor and school in a thin pale light.

"That's Mr. Jenkins, isn't it?" said Aidan, indicating a man wearing a tattered tweed jacket.

The lucidus took a deep breath, and began speaking in a carefully modulated voice. "Alfred P. Jenkins. Born March 4, 1921. Poisoned his father September 14, 1938 with arsenic. Percival Humphrey

Jenkins, a decorated veteran of the Great War, survived on account of a coughing fit during which he spilled half his nightly tonic. Containing said poison. Jenkins Senior went on to serve in the War Office during the Second World War, at the end of which he was knighted, becoming Sir Percival. Alfred, however, had always called his father "sir," and the deference never left him.

"His father passed away on October 24, 1959, and although he hadn't seen him much during his latter years, Alfred wept bitterly on hearing the news; he was inconsolable. He insisted that all the men in uniform wear full military regalia at the funeral. And from his meager teacher's salary, he spent lavishly on flowers, headstone, and newspaper notices. Above his bed a large black-and-white photograph of his father still hangs. The man stands erect, shoulders back, expression blank. His mother's photograph, rather smaller, even now sits on his desk. He has never mentioned the poisoning to any living being. It is known only to his Creator, various lucidi, and his conscience. Furthermore, there is no creature on earth or in heaven who can possibly understand the damage inflicted by his father's harsh, belittling words."

Aidan remembered his geography classes. Unsurprisingly, there were no clues that Jenkins had an attempted murder in his past. If anything, the teacher, routinely dressed in brown, had just seemed bland. He watched him fold up the nets. The man looked worn out.

"So why the grief?" asked Aidan.

"Ah, how to explain the deep currents that drive human behavior? Hmm, well, in short, the Gap. We call it *El Hueco*. You see, every boy longs for his father, though exactly what he longs for, he does not know. For inside all boys there exists a gap, a space inside, tender to the touch, undiminished by time." The face of the lucidus grew haggard, as though he carried Jenkins' agony in his very body. His shoulders slumped. "A gap that, to some, feels more like a chasm— one capable of destroying a young man's sense of self. It is a chasm between what a boy craves—love—and what he so often receives— criticism, indifference, and abandonment."

The lucidus was silent, waiting; his words left Aidan feeling numb. The mezcla shifted.

The Gap

They blinked to find themselves standing in a sparsely furnished room with a wooden dresser against one wall and a threadbare chair on wheels nearby. In a corner stood a sink with a cracked mirror above it. There was no carpet, just an old thin rug covering well-worn floorboards. Above a single bed hung a picture of a tall ship in full sail. The room contained three people. A woman lay on the bed, her legs apart, face contorted. A midwife was wiping the woman's forehead with care, yet at the same time she seemed fearful. A man sat in a corner, smoking, tapping his keys against his chair. Aidan looked around the room; it took a while for him to take stock of his surroundings. The woman tried to sit up, puffing and panting with the effort. She cursed the midwife and started demanding more pillows.

"I don't recognize this room at all," said Aidan. Something didn't seem right. The man in the corner got up and started pacing up and down. He opened a window and blew a cloud of smoke out into the cold.

"Your fault!" shouted the woman. "This is your fault!" He ignored her. A woman in her late sixties entered the room and walked over to the woman in labor. She was met with expletives but didn't blanch. Instead, she turned and whispered in the ear of the man who was now biting his fingernails.

"Yes, Ma," he said, looking down.

Aidan examined the man closely but couldn't work out who it was. The lucidus looked away, unwilling to open up.

The climax came quickly. The top of the baby's head appeared, covered with dark brown hair, matted and seemingly stuck to his head with too much papier-mâché. The woman's face tightened for the last few pushes, then flooded with relief. The baby was out. The midwife picked up a surgical knife, and cut the umbilical cord. She scooped up the child and washed him in the sink; his lungs announced him to the world with screams that filled the room. When the midwife had bundled him up in blankets, she brought him back to the bed.

"Take it away!" shrieked the woman.

The effect on Aidan was immediate. He clung to Korazin and stared wide-eyed at the scene before him. The woman's words cut him open like a butcher's knife through tender meat. He was sure that only the power of the lucidus held him together.

The midwife looked enquiringly at the man, unsure what to do. He stared back with a dumb look on his face, and when Aidan saw the vacant uncertainty it expressed, his mind burst with recognition. He began to relax a little. Of course. He was looking at his grandfather, Sidney. The slightly awkward way in which he carried himself was clearly on display. He wondered how he'd missed it before. He was biting his bottom lip, a nervous habit that still persisted. And he wore a corduroy jacket with patches on the elbows, a practice he continued into his nineties.

"What?" snapped the woman in the bed. "Stop looking at me!"

Sidney shuffled about, averting his gaze to examine the floorboards. Aidan felt weak. Korazin led him into an adjoining room where they found some chairs by an open fire. The lucidus poured him a glass of water from a jug resting on a side table.

"My father's birth?" It was taking time for the truth to sink in. They sat in silence for a while. "My grandpa sporting the latest corduroy fashion, I see." He attempted a smile. Harsh, angry words drifted in from the room next door, causing Aidan to grimace. He continued, "It's all a long time ago now. You move on, don't you?"

"Is that right?" said Korazin. The pendulum in a grandfather clock nearby swung back and forth, the gentle rhythm appearing to slow down time as they sat together. The lucidus waited patiently, his face glowing softly in the half-light.

"I'm sure you got me all figured out, haven't you?" said Aidan.

Korazin ignored the comment. He just waited.

Aidan turned away.

He was in a world of his own, high up in the mountains, surrounded by skiers and snow flickering brilliant white. He'd tripped up, falling flat on his eight-year-old face. His skin was freezing but he burned with humiliation.

And yet from the ashes arose the unexpected.

From out of nowhere, his father reached down, offering an outstretched hand and a look of encouragement on his face. He remembered grabbing the hand as though it were a lifebelt on a storm-ravaged sea. The strength of his father's arm, dragging him up the slope, lasted no more than a few seconds.

But those seconds had never moved time forward.

He was still there over thirty-five years later.

His father had held his hand. A gloved hand, but his hand nevertheless. This from a man who never, ever touched his boys. Ever. He never slapped him on the back, nor ruffled his hair. He never wrestled with him, never put him on his shoulders, never tickled him, or carried him over puddles. And after that one brief encounter, Aidan couldn't remember his father ever having held his hand again.

Not once. With or without gloves.

"Will my dad ever—?" Something caught at the back of his throat.

"Probably not," said Korazin, blood beginning to seep from the corners of his eyes. The lucidus paused. He knew what was coming. He was imbued with all the wisdom and strength of a lucidus who has breathed in the grace and mercy of Almighty God for millions of years.

The fragmented pieces of Aidan's soul began to split apart, carried on a wave of agony he could contain no longer. As the man beside him broke apart, the lucidus cried out to the Father for the strength to comfort a soul in torment. He prayed fervently for him.

When the tears came, Aidan did not cry for pity.

Nor did he cry for shame.

He wept before the image of a newborn child, thrust away impatiently by a bitter, heartless mother. He wept for a lost childhood. His own at first. Followed by his father's. He wept for a past that could never be recaptured, for a loss too great to contemplate.

Comforted by the lucidus, whose arms enveloped him in divine love, the tears abated. And in the silence, he reached out to his heavenly father for healing.

He made his first few tentative steps toward a Roman cross.

~ 41 ~

THE BLEEDING

This is my blood of the covenant, which is poured out for many.
~ Jesus

July 10, 2005

The first thing Aidan saw when he woke up was his father asleep in a chair next to his bed. He closed his eyes, recalling a time when he was ill in the sick bay at school. He'd had chicken pox but was on the mend. As soon as his dad had entered the room, he'd closed his eyes, pretending to be asleep. He could have sat up, should have sat up, but he hadn't. He'd hidden behind his eyelids until, after a couple of hours, his dad had creased his paper into neat folds and stowed it on the rack on the wall. His father never spoke to him, never said a thing. He just walked out. The anguish of the memory was still with him, blending with the pain of his injuries.

He opened his eyes and blinked just as a nurse walked in. She approached the end of the bed and picked up his chart. "Ah, Mr. Manning." She checked his pulse and blood pressure. "Now you're awake, I'll call the doctor." She was about to leave when she turned back and whispered in his ear. "By the way, he's been here all night. We couldn't get him to leave."

Aidan's father woke up. When he saw his son awake, he leaned forward.

"How are you feeling?"

"Not great."

For a moment, it was as though they both stood before a whole new region of unexplored territory. Aidan desperately wanted to communicate his gratitude for his father's care, but was too slow and too weak to speak. In any case, his father vacillated, deciding instead to retreat down well-worn paths, engaging with his son as he always had. He began to vocalize his opinions on politicians, the police, and religious zealots, all of whom he deemed to be the cause of the bombings.

Aidan was exhausted by the end of his father's jeremiad. "Thanks for coming," he mumbled. His father harrumphed and fussed with his tie. Rising from his seat, he walked over to the bed, and ruffled Aidan's hair affectionately. He was about to leave, when he turned. Leaning over the bed, he placed his lips on his son's forehead and kissed him. "I'll be back this evening," he whispered.

He put on his coat and left.

The ache in Aidan's heart was so fierce, it was overpowering. A burning sensation was mixing with the pain from his injuries. At first, he wondered if it might be regret. The thought flashed across his mind that his distress arose directly from their fractured past. But as he lay there, recalling the tenderness of his father's kiss, he abandoned that idea. Instead, the burning inside created warmth in his spirit that seemed to lift him; it turned gradually into a kind of anesthesia that flooded his entire body. For a time, he basked in the pleasure generated by his father's touch—just feeling, not thinking. His father's kiss, so brief, began to stitch him together.

So when he tuned back in, the conclusion was inescapable.

He understood that, instead of regret, he was filled with joy.

Pure joy.

The following day, Aidan felt much improved. He was sitting up in bed when Evelyn arrived bearing gifts just after 10 a.m. He was soon opening card after card, and laughing at the awkward expressions of concern from his work colleagues. Tommy had written *Come on, sir. Got a hot tip for the dogs. Prancer. Like the reindeer!*

At around midday, Aidan was able to take a light meal of noodle soup. His surge of energy, however, did not last. By 1 p.m., he lay back down and closed his eyes. Evelyn sought out Dr. Bristow only to be told that her husband's condition hadn't really changed. The encouragement from the morning disappeared rapidly, leaving her with a sickening throb in the pit of her stomach.

During the afternoon, visitors came and went. Beth sat holding

Aidan's hand for a long time, not saying very much, just trying not to cry; while Simon found it too distressing to do anything but work on *The Times* crossword. Just after three, Edward walked in, carrying a huge bowl of fruit, half of which he immediately began consuming himself, while venting his anger at "evil men" who deserved to have painful things done to their private parts.

"They were suicide bombers, Ed," said Aidan. "They're gone."

Feeling the awkwardness, his friend turned the conversation toward innocuous subjects such as delays on the Bakerloo Line and Sean's latest exhibition, all the while interjecting his customary good humor. Bonhomie, it seemed, was integral to his makeup, as much a part of him as a dalmatian's spots. As he talked, he dodged any expression of affection. It was simply too painful to speak about his fears for Aidan's life. The banter served to keep the worry at bay, and quite successfully at that. Raised to believe that emotions were like children at the opera—preferably silent, or better yet, absent— he possessed neither the ability nor the desire to break convention. So telling jokes about judges was about all he could manage. "Sean wanted to be here, you know." He avoided Aidan's eyes. "He sends his regards." He stood up and shuffled about uncomfortably. "Hang in there, old boy."

He drew back the curtain and walked out.

It was evening when, at long last, Evelyn had Aidan all to herself. She had given his relatives and friends some space, but was relieved when they had all disappeared. Slumped in the seat next to his bed, she looked up every so often to see if he was awake.

He opened his eyes and smiled at her. "Hey, beautiful." The smile was an effort and died quickly. "How you doing?" His voice sounded strained.

"Trying not to worry, my love." She reached out and picked up his hand, caressing it against her cheek.

Aidan turned away. "Took the wrong bus."

"Stop it." Evelyn got up and moved some of the tubes aside. Her desire to be close to him was acute, and if that meant breaking a few rules, then so be it. Perched on the edge of the bed, she slowly lay down beside Aidan, bringing her head down until it lay on the pillow, inches from his face. He turned toward her.

Looking into his eyes, she was assailed by a dawning realization that rose to consume her. She knew as certainly as she knew herself that her love penetrated her entire being. The desire to take on her beloved's pain was so strong, she found it overwhelming, swamping her spirit and drawing from her soul words buried deep, far deeper than she was aware of in that cold, sterile room.

"Love is the most powerful thing in the universe, Aidan."

Her voice ignited a tingling sensation that crept up his spine and flowed through his whole body. The pain of his injuries abated, deadened by his beating heart and the thrill of his soul rising in response to her voice. "It is a seed within a decaying compost," he murmured, smiling at her.

Evelyn's reply was eager yet soft. "And love is freely given and freely received. It is never coerced . . . never evoked by manipulation and undue pressure." She paused, feeling the words surge up inside her, unbidden but received joyfully, thankfully. "Love is the fullest and most glorious expression of freedom a soul can experience. It nourishes and revives a flagging spirit, it heals and soothes a wounded heart, it transforms all it touches, and brings light into the darkest of places."

"Love is noble," he whispered. "It is brave, bold, and resilient. Many waters cannot quench it; neither can rivers sweep it away. It is offered freely or not at all."

They stared into each other's eyes and there was stillness, the words binding their souls together in a shared communion that went further and deeper than they knew.

Aidan's eyes danced with joy as he gazed into the eyes of his wife. "I love you, Evelyn," he said. "More than I can say."

The effort of the conversation had worn him out. She felt him recede, borne away, and could do nothing to slow his progress. She stroked his cheek with her hand and fought back tears, clinging to as much hope as she could muster. She had so much more to say but it would have to wait.

He'd started to snore.

It was late when Evelyn arrived back at Simon and Beth's house. She inserted the key into the lock and let herself in. As quietly as she could, she crept upstairs to the spare room. The room was furnished with Beth's impeccable taste, but she hardly noticed.

She knelt down next to the bed and bowed her head. "Lord of love, of mercy, and of all good things that come from thee, have compassion, I pray. Have mercy, I pray . . ."

She began to weep.

Moments later, she was upstairs in a bedroom. Rising from the bed, she walked over to the window. The sun was going down on the horizon, a golden disk of liquid light melting into the water, with its outer layer streaming out and dancing on the mottled surface of the ocean. A couple of fishing boats were returning to port. She spotted a lucidus near the stern pouring fish into a large container.

The house was silent.

She opened the door and went downstairs.

Finding the Descartes Room empty, she crossed the hall to the Living Room. Gamaliel and Korazin both stood at the far end, with Aliza off to the side, sitting near an open window. They appeared to be expecting her; there was a tranquility about them that permeated the room. They did not need to speak. The looks on their faces were enough, especially Korazin's, whose eyes brimmed with tears. He was incapable of hiding the grief inside. And though they soon held her, their touch could not possibly dull the anguish. Their care was incapable of holding back the agony that overcame her soul.

She wept, of course. Sobs flowed through her like an ocean swell, rising and falling, swept along by the currents beneath. She did not fight them. Instead, she clung to Aliza, squeezing whatever small matter of comfort she could from a lucidus who had only ever shown her kindness and love. Shock and pain blended into one, a suffocating concoction that engulfed the heart and defied any effort to control or direct it.

When the initial impact weakened, Evelyn's response was unexpected, even to her. Perhaps because she stood in the Espacio, or maybe because she had already screamed at her Creator, she

The Bleeding

was not tempted to jump off a cliff. She did not seek explanation or justification. Nor did she bargain or flee. Instead, in her grief, she sought only solace and healing. She turned not away from her Father, but toward him, for she knew instinctively that this was the path of least resistance.

Once the initial trauma had passed, Evelyn walked the shoreline for hours, enjoying a cool breeze that stirred the grasses on the dunes. Looking out across the water, the wind dried her tearstained cheeks, the pain assuaged by the beauty of where she stood.

On her return to the house, Evelyn discovered Aliza sitting alone. More tears flowed. They could not be stopped. After sitting down beside the lucidus, she felt strong arms around her; quiet settled on them both. After a while, however, Aliza began to speak, her voice soft and kind.

Grief, your name is tempest, pit, and thief
A distant shore on which the soul finds no relief
Seared, shorn of hope for bright tomorrows
Alone, weighed down by darkened sorrows.

No age grown dim from life full sated
No joys of home, their future blighted
No cord of three, bound ever tighter
The vacant space, a wound, a fissure.

Cast aside the mask of stoic firmness
A fixèd face to block the graceless
Receive, instead, cool draft of time-borne soothing
A balm for darkened dreams and woeful weeping.

Unbeknownst to grieving soul once found, now lost
Veiled from heart too hurt to feel aught but cost
The pit will flatten, thief imprison, storm be dead
Nailed hands reach out, whose palms have bled.

> *And though the soul now burns, it rages long*
> *We bid you sit, remember arms widespread and strong*
> *They hold you as you faint and fall*
> *Their strength unseen, the might of All-in-all.*

They sat for a long time in the stillness.

When at last Evelyn asked how her beloved Aidan had died, she felt the reply before it was given. "Bleeding, Evelyn," said Aliza, her voice cracking. "He died from the bleeding. I'm so sorry."

Of course he did. He died from the bleeding as we all do. We cut and tear each other to pieces, driven by uncontrollable, sinful urges from corrupted hearts. And we often injure those we love the most. We do not all kill and maim like terrorists, but we inflict damage with our words, wound people by neglect, and give expression to our pain by hurting others. We are all bleeding and will one day bleed to death. We bleed bodily from our veins and capillaries, we bleed in our souls from our sin, and only the man who bled copiously before his executioners can staunch the flow. Only the man from the courtyard, the lonely figure on the cross, is capable of healing a broken heart and comforting a soul in torment.

So she went to him and poured out her pain and her anguish.

Again and again.

He did not remove the pain. Nor did he bring Aidan back from the dead. The agony of loss persisted for many hours, many days even, throbbing inside her body and soul until she thought it would never diminish. Yet it did. Slowly and surely. And in unseen ways, her Master *did* hold and sustain her, *did* comfort and love her.

And this brought healing, as he led her tenderly along a path toward recovery.

~ 42 ~

BLUE JEANS, PURPLE T-SHIRT

The Word became flesh . . . and we beheld his glory.
~ The Apostle John

July 18, 2005

A week later, Evelyn awoke to an unexpected but welcome surprise. As soon as she opened her eyes, she was swamped by both grief and exhilaration. Aidan was standing near the fire, smiling at her. As she recalled later, hugging a deceased person was undoubtedly the most surreal experience of her life. It was also one of the most significant, for as he held her, his touch left a residue deep within, for consolation in the days to come. She retained the memory of his embrace in her soul, a reminder of how much he had loved her.

The lucidi had agonized over bringing Aidan to the Espacio, worried that his presence might prolong Evelyn's grief. In the end, however, it was decided that a few visits would give her the opportunity to say goodbye. As it turned out, they saw each other every day for over two weeks.

There were no more philosophical discussions, no more inquiries into the rationale behind human suffering, just the calm saturation of two souls into one; in short, the opportunity to be married for a while. Aidan enjoyed chasing Evelyn through the hills on a mountain bike, though he was barely able to keep up with her. And they took the boat out one last time. In the afternoons, they helped the lucidi dig the foundations for the new extension, enjoying the sun on their backs and the sweat on their brows. They mixed cement, listened to Asaph describe the wonders of heaven, and sunbathed next to the pool. Basking in the golden glow of the sunset, they sat on the patio reading in quiet communion and listening to music.

Later, they retired to bed where they made love, their bodies arching in shared ecstasy even as their souls clung to each other, desperate to love and be loved as intensely as possible in the short span of time they had left.

Early one morning, Aidan ventured into the hall to find a man removing the poem near the bifold doors. His straw hat was shedding stalks, his boots were dusty, and his overalls were stained and dirty. With rough, steady hands, he hung a new work on the wall. Standing back, he put his hands on his hips and admired it.
"New poem?" said Aidan, approaching him.
The man turned slightly, a small smile spreading across his face. He stroked his beard. "Needs a title." His demeanor seemed open and inviting, so Aidan stepped forward to read.

Who measures life? Whose love bears the waiting?
By word given form, dust breathed into being
The humerus, thorax and hip, spinal cord
The tibia, fibula firm, standing awed?

Who measures life? Whose love bears the shame?
Earthy clods called to rule the earth whence they came
Who jaundice their justice with judgments absurd
Do behemoth, leviathan lie down at their word?

Who measures life, strength of Atlas surpasses,
Carried high on the wind, is it you, fading grasses?
Or tested and true, One who opens the seals
Whose body once bloody and broken reveals
The Wisdom, the Fool who feels every fissure
Whose face bathed in red illuminates treasure?

Who measures life? Whose scales do the weighing?
Who made the sea creatures, twice helix conveying?
Brace yourself like a man, your questions consume
The orbs set in space are birthed from whose womb?

Who measures life? Whose book tells the story?
One who left tow'ring heights, out of love shed his glory
Only he, wrapped in three, the fulcrum found worthy
The song of the heavens, the Son who is holy.

"Are you the poet?" asked Aidan.

"I made the frame." The man stared up at the writing on the wall as silence lay down gently between the two men. "I like making things." Aidan felt his gaze, though the man's eyes never left the poem.

"I'm not sure it needs a title," said Aidan finally.

The man smiled, continuing to stroke his beard. "You've come a long way, son." He patted Aidan's shoulder affectionately, then without another word, turned and walked out the front door.

When Aidan looked back at the poem, a title had appeared above the text, in gold lettering: "From the Whirlwind." However, as he left the hall, it was not the poem he carried with him, but the memory of a hand on his shoulder. He did not know why or how, but the man's touch had left an indelible mark on his soul.

Evelyn had imagined that the final hours would be agony, but instead she faced the prospect of separation with remarkable fortitude and good grace. She wept, of course, now and then, as they sat watching the sun go down, but she was never tempted to resist the inevitable. She accepted it, using the time to give thanks for small mercies, acutely aware that few were given such a gift. With as much effort as she could manage, she forced herself to focus on the present, drinking in the pleasure of sitting with her husband, who wrapped his arms around her and held her tight. Looking out over the shimmering surface of the ocean, the beauty of the Espacio flooded through her; it brought her relentlessly to a place of gratitude, to a place of worship.

On the last Sunday in July, Evelyn awoke in the hall, instantly conscious of the significance of her visit. The day of Aidan's departure had arrived. Anticipating the separation to come, she became fearful, unable to trust the mountainous sea of emotions she knew would soon engulf her. However, Aliza had prepared her on various occasions by praying with her and calming her fears.

Aidan's embrace, when it came, felt like a lifebelt in a gale. It felt reassuring, even though it was incapable of staving off the worst of the storm to come. She clung to him for a moment, mild desperation briefly taking hold. It passed quickly. As the doors behind them swung open, they both prepared themselves.

Aliza stood in the doorway. "It's time," she said.

The Descartes Room was lit softly with candles on the table and in sconces on the walls. On the table, there was nothing but a loaf of bread, a jug of wine, and five glasses. Gamaliel sat at the head of the table, with Korazin on his right. Aidan and Evelyn took their places and waited. Aliza closed the doors and joined them.

The ceremony was simple. Gamaliel took the loaf and tore it apart. "His body, broken for you." He handed a piece of bread to each person seated around the table. They ate in silence and gave thanks.

The lucidus allowed the moment to linger. He rose slowly to his feet, his face faintly glowing. "The celebration of Holy Communion is a sacred tradition inaugurated by Yeshua and handed down by the Father's faithful people through the centuries. It reminds us of the one true sacrifice that gives hope. It brings before our minds the most wondrous of truths, that the Creator has not forgotten his creation, but has begun a campaign to rescue those whom he loves. To do so, he sent his beloved son to die for the lost and the broken.

"Communion commemorates the spilling of blood for sins and holds out the prospect of new life to all who would draw near. It is an invitation to live a new kind of life; one that confronts evil with every act of compassion and every offer of help to the helpless and needy. It announces the defeat of Death and the celebration of Life. For it is new life that endures and, while today we mourn the passing of Aidan, we look forward to his resurrection and the coming of Yeshua in the new creation, when all tears will be wiped dry and all pain will cease. Come. Let us drink." The lucidus poured wine into the glasses and handed them round. "In memory of the one who bled for you."

They gave thanks. They drank. They bowed their heads.

When they were finished, Korazin led them through the hall and down a passageway that was unfamiliar to them. As they walked

Blue Jeans, Purple T-shirt

along, Evelyn noticed several wooden boards hanging on the wall. They were covered with thousands of names in gold lettering, each one painted on with a careful hand.

She stopped. "Who are these people listed here?"

"Ah," said Korazin, walking back to her. "Well, the celebrated names in your world are not always the ones deserving of recognition." She looked at him, nonplussed. "These are the people who have displayed two of the most important features of a rich life. We honor them here." He turned to go.

"And those features are—?"

"Obedience and faithfulness, my dear," said the lucidus over his shoulder. "Obedience and faithfulness. *¡Vámonos!*"

Aidan looked up at the list. It was just a quick glance but he didn't recognize a single name. Not one. He hurried after the group. "I've been meaning to ask. Why the Spanish?"

"Well," said Korazin, smiling broadly. "What do you expect, señor? *Es el idioma del cielo*—the language of heaven!"

They came out through a side entrance and started up a stony track, one they hadn't taken before. It took them up into the hills. Coming over a rise, they spotted a lone olive tree atop the next incline, about a hundred yards away. A man appeared, walking toward it; he wore blue jeans, a purple T-shirt, leather jacket, and hiking boots. When he reached the shade of the tree, he stopped and waved.

Aidan recognized him instantly. He waved back.

The lucidi gathered round. Their voices blended so that they spoke as one, their eyes seeping reddened tears. They were three, yet they were one. So while the blessing came from all three, he heard just one voice. It filled him, strengthened and carried him.

Turning to Evelyn, he felt no shame in his tears. They flowed freely. She saw no need for words. She spoke eloquently with her touch, holding him tightly. After kissing him, she stepped back.

"Love you," she mouthed, smiling weakly.

Aidan Manning, believer, husband, father, friend, and beloved child of his heavenly father, turned and walked down the short incline and up the other side. Evelyn watched him go, her grief momentarily dampened by her curiosity. She saw the two men meet. The man in the purple T-shirt embraced Aidan, and they stood talking together briefly. Suddenly, laughter broke through the air. Aidan turned and waved. Evelyn waved back, smiling, thinking her heart would break. Whether for joy or sorrow, she did not know. His face was aglow with happiness, his eyes shining with contentment.

Aliza began to speak, her voice soft and melodious.

> The sound and the fury, the rage and the spite
> Released by the soul whose tears flood the night
> The shadow, the candle that burns darkly bright
> Glimpsed dimly in dreams, a prince and a knight
> Neither petty nor senseless, nay, hallowed the pace
> Comes the hour
> Darkness falls
> The end of the race.
>
> Seconds build a day
> And days grow up to years
> Do not hunger, do not thirst
> For more than you are given
> For one day Death will die
> And Life will be reborn
> A time of great rejoicing
> When the Sun becomes the dawn.
>
> See him go, let him go
> See his sorrow soaked with joy
> Our agony, his ecstasy
> Here precious Lord and King
> See, look, they meet, embrace
> In His hands He holds his face
> Do not pity, do not cling
> To a man with Everything.

The two men turned and walked away, deep in conversation.

"I am continually with you," murmured Gamaliel. "You hold me by my right hand . . . you will guide me with your counsel . . . and afterward receive me to glory."

The last rays of the sun were fading; twilight had descended. The last image Evelyn remembered of her husband was his silhouette against a cloudless sky. As he talked, his Lord listened and nodded, with an arm draped over his child's shoulder.

Aidan did not look back again.

Evelyn faced Gamaliel. "Where will they go?"

"To paradise, my dear. To paradise. To enjoy the presence of the Father until the culmination of all things, when he will be given a new body to live in the Father's new creation. When earth and heaven meet, and knowledge of the Lord's glory fills the earth as the waters cover the sea."

Once back at the Viatici House, Evelyn stumbled into the Living Room, and collapsed on the couch. Then it all came spilling out. She could contain herself no longer. The crushing reality of Aidan's death rose to consume her. She fell into Aliza's arms and wept for a long time, a pile of used handkerchiefs slowly beginning to accumulate nearby. As the tears flowed, the lucidus prayed silently, waiting for her to recover.

When Evelyn finally sat up and composed herself, she noticed Gamaliel and Korazin sitting in the armchairs. They moved over to join her on the couch.

Gamaliel said, "I know your thoughts are with Aidan, my dear." He paused. "However, it is Henry who comes to mind. He was a remarkable man in many ways. The decks of the *Titanic* were filled with men who accepted their fate, but Henry was not one of them. He clung to life with a ferocity and fervor that marked him out as exceptional. That's why he built the raft. It's why he dived into the ocean to save your great-grandfather."

Aliza leaned forward and picked up Evelyn's hands. "It is in giving up your life that you declare to the heavens how valuable it is."

"Your life is not over, dear Evelyn," said Gamaliel. "It is simply entering a new phase. Make cakes. Go surfing. Be kind and patient, slow to judge, and quick to forgive."

"Listen well, climb mountains, and floss." Korazin grinned.

Aliza said, "Trust your Father and remember that you are loved. So very loved. Bounce your baby."

There was silence.

Evelyn stared at the lucidus next to her. "What?"

"Oh, I wasn't supposed to tell you. I'm sorry. Ah!"

"I'm pregnant?"

As she began to laugh, held by the lucidi, who embraced her and spoke out their congratulations, tears rolled down her cheeks. Laughter became weeping and back again, in a swell of emotion beyond her control. Her grief and her joy blended into one and, in a burst of revelation, the agony and ecstasy of her heavenly father were revealed to her one final time.

She understood how deep and how wide is the love that binds him forever to the created order, to its pain and its delight. She gave thanks for the Son who bled for her and whose love knows no bounds. And she gave herself up to the Spirit, who flooded her being. As she departed, she did so boldly, for she trusted her Father to heal her broken heart and reap a harvest of goodness from the grief within her soul. But the last thing on her mind was not her grief.

It was baby names.

"*L'chaim!*" she said, popping a pill into her mouth. "To life!"

~ 43 ~

A NEW WAY OF LIVING

Summer 2011

Evelyn draws back the curtains and looks up at the sky. Dawn is breaking, and when she opens the window, the wind blowing in off the ocean caresses her skin. She closes her eyes and enjoys the feel of it on her face. She still lives in Venice Beach, though not on Dell Avenue. After the fire, she purchased a three-bedroom house a little further north. She also moved hospitals. Now she works at Little Company of Mary in Torrance as a surgical oncologist. She prefers the hours to Harbor-UCLA's, though they are still long.

It is still early, but Evelyn likes to rise before the others. She toasts a bagel, brews some coffee, and sits down at the kitchen table. Opening her Bible, she reads a passage from Ecclesiastes, followed by one from the New Testament. As she eats, she prays, mulling over some words from John's gospel. A short time later, the serenity of the morning is broken by the scampering of busy feet. A little girl runs in from the back of the house and launches herself at her mom.

"Morning, Lucy," says Evelyn, picking up her daughter and placing her on her lap. "Sleep well? Cereal?"

Lucy is five years old with dark brown hair that betrays auburn flecks in the sunshine. Her cheeks are dotted with freckles and her eyes are a deep emerald green. Every day, Evelyn takes delight in her, yet every time she looks in her eyes, she sees Lucy's father. After five years, her grief and her joy are so entwined she cannot separate them. Lucy is a constant reminder of the one she has lost and a daily cause for thanksgiving. She also has her father's smile.

"*I* can find it," announces the little girl, with heavy emphasis on the "I." She wriggles off her mother's lap and starts digging around in a cupboard. Like many five-year-olds, she possesses an independent streak that induces both pride and despair in her mother. Evelyn gets up and lays the table for five, setting out bagels, cereals, fruit, and a selection of pastries.

Another child comes in, bouncing. Her name is Hope; she is Simon and Beth's daughter, visiting from England. A week younger than Lucy but an inch taller, she mimics Tigger all the way to the kitchen. The two girls are firm friends. They pull out some dolls. Lucy also likes dumper trucks, so after a minute, Barbie is digging for gold among some stray Legos.

Simon and Beth walk in from the spare room, wiping sleep from their eyes. Beth kisses Evelyn on the cheek and pulls out a couple of plates from a kitchen cabinet. Simon pours coffee and picks up the paper. "Hope, darling," says Beth. "Time for breakfast. Come on."

Simon and Beth have visited California every other year since Aidan's death. Evelyn has made regular trips to London to maintain contact with her son-in-law and his wife. Their mutual affection has not lessened over time; it has grown stronger, their relationship deepened by the births of their daughters who play together like twins. During this visit, Hope's skin has turned golden brown from long hours spent down at the beach. Beth loves the weather and Simon has taken up volleyball. He's formed a bond with Reggie and some of his church friends, who tease him by talking in silly accents.

After breakfast, they all pack bags for the beach. Evelyn brushes her teeth while rummaging through a cabinet under the sink looking for sunscreen. Her hand knocks over an empty bottle of calamine lotion. She looks at the label and throws it into the trash can. Her lichen planus cleared up just after Aidan's death and has not returned. Her legs are now tanned and smooth, unblemished by the rash that afflicted her back in 2005.

Coming into the bedroom, she reminds herself to pull out her suitcases when she has a spare moment. In two days—after the relatives have left—she will travel with Lucy to Nicaragua. Since 2006, she has spent two weeks each year with a team of medical missionaries, providing emergency surgeries to local people in the capital, Managua. It's funded by a charity she supports.

Half an hour later, Evelyn finds a parking spot not far from the boardwalk. Soon they're transporting enough gear to supply a small army. Parasols, chairs, bags, and coolers are all hauled out the back of the Explorer, and ferried across the sand to a sparsely populated area near the end of the beach. Once settled, the moms start covering their daughters' skin with sunscreen.

"What's this I hear about Dan?" asks Beth, squeezing lotion onto her palm. "Bridget dropped a name the other day."

"She didn't!"

"Afraid so. Come on. Spill the beans. What's he like?"

Evelyn describes a handsome doctor who has shown some interest recently. For the first three years after her husband's death, she was unable to look at another man. Only after the pain of loss had diminished to a dull ache was she able to open up. The first few dates were a disaster. Dan, however, seemed nice. She met him last month at a medical conference in Portland and he's been calling. A widower for the past six years since his wife died of cancer, he has two grown children and is well past the need to project an image of undamaged goods. To Evelyn, he feels solid, and that's a good start.

A scream interrupts the conversation. Hope runs to her mom and says breathlessly, "Lucy's bleeding! She's bleeding!" Evelyn jumps up and rushes down to the shoreline, where her daughter is lying on the sand, holding her foot. As the little girl wails, blood seeps through her fingers. Evelyn examines the site of the injury and offers comfort, the role of parent and doctor combining seamlessly.

"What is it?" asks Beth.

"Something metallic, I think. Thankfully, she's had her shots."

"It hurts, Mommy. Make it stop." The wound isn't deep. Evelyn removes a small piece of metal, rinses the cut with water, and applies some antiseptic. The foot she then wraps in a bandage. "It's still hurting, Mommy," whimpers Lucy. "Make it stop."

"I can't, honey," says her mom, kissing her daughter on the cheek. "The pain will go away, I promise. It will go away eventually."

After lunch, the girls play on the dry sand, while Beth reads and Simon snoozes. Evelyn picks up her bag and tells them she's going to stretch her legs. When she reaches the end of the beach, she climbs up on some rocks and sits down. Pulling her Bible out of her bag, she opens it to the third chapter of John's gospel, the one she was reading earlier in the day. *The wind blows wherever it pleases. You hear its sound, but you cannot tell where it comes from or where it is going. So it is with everyone born of the Spirit.*

She fingers the locket that rests close to her heart. Its original portraits now sit on the mantel in small silver frames. Opening the tiny door, she peers down at their replacements. Aidan faces left, and appears to be smiling directly at his daughter, Lucy, who is reaching out toward him from the image opposite. Though they have never met, their mutual affection is irrepressible. It evokes intense sorrow in Evelyn and yet, at the same time, her sadness is riven with inexplicable joy.

She looks out over the ocean, her thoughts taking her to far-off places. A sailboat a few hundred yards away catches her eye. It rocks from side to side, its white sails billowing in the breeze. The man at the helm is bringing the boat into wind. By his side, a woman is frantically turning a winch handle. They're going about. The sails fill and the boat keels over. A flock of pelicans glides past, the birds touching their bellies on the water. They fly up over the cliff in the distance. She watches them and gives thanks . . .

For the chance to be born and the chance to pass on
For the barley and rye and wheat ripe for plucking
For the soldier with heart full of courage undimmed
And the nurse with a smile for the man in Bed 3
For the wrecking ball's swing
And the builders and brickies
For the tears and the laughter, the grief and the jig
For the rocks in a pile and the souls turned to mercy
For the kiss, the embrace, and the time spent alone
For the winning and keeping and giving, releasing
For the ripping and tearing and mending, repairing
For the hush before dawn and the babble of voices
For a wartime of struggle and the peace frail and brittle
For the pleasure and pain and the sunshine and rain
For travail and the wonder of a world set in place
By a God filled with mercy, bent by love, rich in grace.

Evelyn closes her eyes and enjoys the sensation of the wind brushing her face. It rustles the pages of her Bible.

Seconds later, she is flying.

High up above the ocean—a vast glassy sheet of blues and greens—she flies. From the corners of her eyes, water trickles. The speed is exhilarating, filling her with inexpressible joy. When she looks down, she sees the face of a lucidus, pure and beautiful. It transports her to a place of wonder, where joy and sorrow kiss and find peace.

The lucidus dives down toward a large house overlooking a clifftop. Together they fly over a sports field and a swimming pool, skimming the ocean, and soaring up over the hills. After circling a couple of times, they glide down toward the entrance of the house. As they draw closer, Evelyn catches sight of three figures staring up into the sky.

The lucidus who carries her swoops low, so she can make out their faces more clearly. Two are dressed in fine linen suits; the other is wearing an elegant dark green dress, her hair blowing in the breeze. One has long, silver-gray hair and kind eyes; another is grinning broadly. They are all waving. Their emerald eyes shine like stars, as wings burst from their backs.

Within seconds, they are flying up to meet her in the air.

~ EPILOGUE ~

A lucidus unhooks a carabiner, lets out rope, and begins to climb. He slips and beats his wings to maintain his balance. The lucidus below bellows up, "No cheating!" Korazin just laughs and hauls himself up, his climbing shoes barely able to find the holes he needs to make progress. Covering his hands in chalk, he continues up the rock face.

An hour later, both lucidi are lying on the summit, their chests rising and falling from the exertion. They sit up and look out over a mountain range stretching hundreds of miles into the distance. It caresses the sky and wraps them in joy.

They give thanks for another day in the Espacio.

Gamaliel hands his friend a water bottle. "I was impressed by your Romanian last week."

"A little rusty in places, I must confess."

The tall lucidus smiles at his companion. "We must send you to Eastern Europe a little more often."

"As you wish, my friend."

They stow their climbing gear in a locker behind a small shed. A path takes them along a clifftop toward a house perched on the edge of a precipice. Several thousand feet below, condors are circling.

The lucidi walk in through the large front door and stop to worship. The art, sculpture, and panorama before them speak of heaven, the beauty entering them with a force that fills and draws them.

Gamaliel says, "Our guest struggled last week."

Korazin nods. "His anger lingers."

"So I've invited someone from his past. Should be here soon."

Korazin looks surprised. "Oh yes?"

"Iron sharpens iron. Especially when reconciliation is required. The heat may hurt, but after comes peace."

They enter the Mandela Room; the name is inscribed on the door. A bull of a man dressed in jeans and a leather jacket is sitting at the far end of a long rectangular table. His shoulders are massive. He glances up when they enter, a terrified look on his face.

"Молим те Драгане! Please, Dragan!" says Korazin. "Немаш чега да се плашиш—there is nothing to fear."

~ ACKNOWLEDGMENTS ~

Writing can be a lonely business. It helps to have friends. It helps even more to have talented friends, whose knowledge and skills add immeasurably to the quality of your work. One has been indispensable—Jonathan Pountney, my agent, without whom there would be no book. My gratitude to you is unending. As for my copy-editor and friend, Heléna Nowak-Smith, she is a rare gem—patient, kind, the consummate professional. The manuscript thanks you. To Bruce Petersen (cover and logo design), Chris Gonzales-Aden (web image design), Alec Burns (web design), Anna Danese (proofreader), Dr. Alan Hultberg (Koine Greek) and Slavko Hadzic (Serbo-Croat), I wish to express my heartfelt thanks. I've been surrounded by people with exceptional gifts. It's been a joy to work with you all.

Thank you also to my friends, Christy Tharenos and James Gilbert, two fine doctors whose medical knowledge (from both sides of the Atlantic) has been invaluable. With regard to all things chambers-related and legal, I am indebted to Tom Cleeve, a London barrister with years of experience in the law. Thank you, Tom. I'd also like to thank Craig Hazen and all the professors at Biola University who poured their knowledge and wisdom into me during my Masters in Christian Apologetics. Without their teaching, there would be no *House of Souls*.

The names listed next belong to those who have answered my myriad questions and encouraged me. Gary Lindblad, Leah Homer, Ian Castro, Andrew Paxman, Paul Allcock, Tamsin Gilbert, Jim & Holly Favino, Fiona Hudd, Jeannette Barlow, Jon Roberts, Catherine Jones, Jeenie Gordon, Tom Clark, Theo Brun, Helen Overmyer, Beth Peterson, and Lou and Marissa Delgado, thank you all for being a part of my story. As you can imagine, I have left out many others, including those who read the very first version of the book. Though you are unnamed here, you are not forgotten. I am grateful to you all.

Writing this book has been costly—for me, certainly, but also for my family. At times, it has been a burden, one you didn't ask for, and yet you have been there to help me carry it. Often without knowing. I pray that the "greater good" spoken of by the lucidi will become ever clearer to you as the years pass. You nourish and revive my flagging spirit, heal and soothe my wounded heart, and bring light into my dark places. Os quiero mucho.

Media enquiries: houseofsoulsbook@gmail.com
Book clubs: A study guide can be found at www.stardust-books.com

And I heard a loud voice from the throne saying, "Behold, the dwelling place of God is with man. He will dwell with them, and they will be his people, and God himself will be with them as their God. He will wipe away every tear from their eyes, and death shall be no more, neither shall there be mourning, nor crying, nor pain anymore, for the former things have passed away."
~ Revelation 21